PENGUIN BOOKS
THE QUIET OF THE BIRDS

Nisha da Cunha was born in 1934. She went to school in Simla and Delhi. She studied English literature at Miranda House, New Delhi before going on to Cambridge, U.K. for postgraduate studies. She taught English literature at Miranda House for five years and then for twenty-five years pursued an extremely successful career at St. Xavier's College, Mumbai, from where she resigned as head of the department in 1985. Nisha da Cunha has directed several plays, including Carson McCuller's *Member of the Wedding* and Ibsen's *Wild Duck*. She has published four collections of stories: *Old Cypress: Stories* (1991), *The Permanence of Grief* (1993), *Set My Heart in Aspic* (1997) and *No Black, No White: Short Stories* (2001).

Nisha da Cunha is married with one son and lives in Mumbai.

Praise for Nisha da Cunha

'There is a sadness which is quite unsentimental and is linked up with some of the great tragic themes of western literature' —David Daiches

'Whatever she writes is strongly individual and deeply felt . . . The dialogue is skilfully crafted, capturing each nuance of feeling' —*Sunday Observer*

'da Cunha weaves her magical spell through short sentences, deceptively simple and yet bristling with impact' —*Hindustan Times*

'Original and amazingly sensitive . . . The stories flow with a natural grace and instinctive rhythm' —*Tribune*

'There is a finely-crafted feel to all the long passages that suggests thoughtful consideration rather than a hysterical spontaneity' —*Independent*

'da Cunha's descriptions are often powerful and compelling' —*Indian Express*

The Quiet of the Birds

Collected Stories
Volume One

NISHA DA CUNHA

PENGUIN BOOKS

An imprint of Penguin Random House

PENGUIN BOOKS

USA | Canada | UK | Ireland | Australia
New Zealand | India | South Africa | China | Singapore

Penguin Books is part of the Penguin Random House group of companies
whose addresses can be found at global.penguinrandomhouse.com

Published by Penguin Random House India Pvt. Ltd
4th Floor, Capital Tower 1, MG Road,
Gurugram 122 002, Haryana, India

Penguin
Random House
India

First published by Penguin Books India 2005

'Three Lives', 'Partly Living' and 'Because It Is My Nature' were first published in
Imprint; 'Pigeon' in P.E.N.; 'A Grief Ago' in *Bombay* magazine; and 'End Cottage'
in *Man's World*.

10 9 8 7 6 5 4 3 2

ISBN 9780144000012

Typeset by R. Ajith Kumar, New Delhi

Printed at Repro India Limited

www.penguin.co.in

MIX
Paper from
responsible sources
FSC® C047271

To Dom

Contents

Old Cypress

The Visit

It was the garden really that decided everything, or most things. And we said, yes this is it. And again, oh yes no question, no question at all. Mark said, 'Don't you want to think about it a bit more, I mean you do have at least till tomorrow to decide—why not sleep on it, don't you think?' I liked that. I mean, I realized that he ended most sentences with, 'don't you think?' I liked it because it helped my own feeling of indecision, or panic, at such a big step. Also, it wasn't really indecision so much as helping one to work out things rhetorically, a help in every sense.

Except for nodding from time to time and gazing at the view my husband hadn't actually said very much. But then that is very much his way, I mean, he wasn't really going to turn cartwheels on the old lawn out of sheer happiness—he wasn't that sort of man and I should know. But the old tennis-court at the back of the bungalow, I think, really swung things for him. I do tend to dither. Especially if it's very important. Also, if the decision is not just for me. My husband said, 'Perhaps we could come back in the evening, if that's convenient? We do have to leave tomorrow—early.' That was the perfect solution. In every way. I realized that, because apart from everything else we would look at things in the evening light, see if it was a kindly light as the morning had been friendly. There's a lot to light, I thought, yes that's what we must do—if the light is friendly, we will know, because we will see what happens to the garden in the evening. So we will know. And the house? Oh, but the garden dominates this house, so if the light is friendly in the evening then the house had to be perfect. The garden is the house. Mark and my husband had strolled on and I realized I was talking to myself. I'm glad because anyway, after a certain point, nobody listens to anybody else—as long as they listen to bits and pieces it's a lot to be grateful for. There was a bit of an old wall. I sat on it and dangled my legs. I could look at the house from here. I realized I hadn't been quite fair, I don't think I could have meant that the garden dominated the house, no. As I sit here I see the house from the garden and I feel both garden and house—and I know that that is what I felt when we were inside the house, that the garden came right in. That's it. It's a real unit—it's not separate at all. So really they complement each other not dominate—also it's odd even though we have looked at so many houses, and quite liked one or two, this one is quite different. This one feels quite other. As if I knew what it might feel like when one was actually living in it. Something about it, even now as I sit on this old wall, I feel as though I've done it before. A sun-warmed old wall—as though I have looked at the house from here before, and then been called out to, then jumped down from the wall and crossed this bit of lawn with long shadows on it, and gone straight through the side veranda and into the study. But it's odd. How can I know when I have never done that before? It shouldn't feel familiar, surely? It must be a good sign, a friendly sign. This is the house that will look after us on our new journey far from everything we have known before—at an age when we are not old certainly, but not young any more. That's behind us. Being young—whatever we may feel inside of us. Now I must find the others and tell them this is our house, our home. I've had a sign. My husband is a cautious man, so he said, 'Yes, well, but we'll come back in the evening anyway,' and Mark said, 'Yes, that would be best,' and I said, 'Please don't let anyone else look at it before we come back,' and Mark said, 'You must be joking! Anyone else look at this house before you come back this evening. Dear lady, nobody has shown the least bit of interest in Old Cypress except you—and I've been here for the last fifteen years. I think word's got round about the cypress.' I said, 'Cypress, you mean the cypress near the old tennis-court? But it's magnificent! I've never seen such a cypress before in a private garden, it must be at least a hundred years old.

I mean thereabouts,' and Mark said, 'Well, not quite a hundred but certainly very old, but it's a bit gloomy certain times of the day or season, and of course it spreads.' I said, 'How do you mean, spreads? You mean the tree, but, it has to,' and Mark said, 'No well, not quite, I mean that too, its roots are spreading and causing problems to some of the paving stones near the old tennis-court but that's to be expected, also its branches, but they can always be pruned, but no, what I really meant was that word about the cypress spreads, that it's rather gloomy and dark and the sun never goes near it so it has a kind of reputation that hasn't been exactly kind— oh you know the kind of thing—so of course the house has been neglected too.' Good, I thought, I'm glad, I thought, nobody will come near it, and that's why we will live in it because other people haven't loved it the minute they saw it, like we did. Old Cypress is part of the house and garden, they all go together, the person who built the house planted the tree, laid out the garden and that old wall I sat on, and the tennis-court, everything. It's one whole and it's all evolved together.

'We'll come back this evening.' And that was that. A mist came curving in from somewhere as we walked the same road that evening. I wonder if it's much thicker in the winter. It will soon enclose us all. I'm glad we are all close together. It's strange. It's thick. I can hardly see two feet in front of me. I'm glad Mark is with us. He'll know where the gates of the house are. Where they ought to be. The ground feels gravelly, quite suddenly. So we must have turned into the gates. Rain, that must be why there is this mist. It's raining somewhere. Soon it will rain here; we don't need rain just now—it's our evening for deciding and I can't see a thing. Perhaps I said some of these things out aloud without realizing because Mark said reassuringly, 'It won't rain, it's not going to. Wrong season, you'll soon get used to this mist, it goes as it comes, I should have explained it, of course it does give one a bit of a shock creeping up like that but not to worry, no rain. Just put it down to these hills. Perhaps, it's good for the tea. The sun will come back for you, to your bungalow, Ma'am, don't worry.' Dear Mark I must say if I hadn't taken to him already I did right then for saying not 'the bungalow' or 'it', but specifically 'your bungalow'. Also his calling me 'Ma'am' made me realize how much I missed that. There had been a long time in my life when it was the most familiar sound—'But surely Ma'am, Yeats couldn't have meant that!' or 'Do you think Ma'am that we could have a free lecture?'—yes, that was a time. And Mark had just called me Ma'am. 'Of course some people,' he was saying, 'don't get used to it too easily. Young Anand hasn't, it still depresses him on a lovely clear sunny late afternoon to see the mist suddenly appear from nowhere, but then he hasn't really been here all that long, it's bound to pass, don't you think? I mean his depression. Anand is my young assistant, lives in a bungalow further down this road. He'd be your closest neighbour. We might go and see him after we've finished here.'

By now we had reached the end of the long driveway and we could just begin to pick out the bungalow—the sloping roof, a bit of wall, a pillar, steps from the garden, 'See what I meant about the mist? It goes as it came.'

And it was true. He was quite right—the light brought the shape of the bungalow back first and then gradually all the details, the marvellous windows, the deep bow window almost touching the lawn, and the wooden pillars of the veranda, and the quaint covered bit leading off to the store rooms and the servant's room, the stone flagging, a chimney, bits of creeper—indiscriminate details shone through the mist.

Colour returned.

I think at this point a word or two of explanation might be in order. Why we were here in the first place. Also, how Old Cypress happened at all. Mark and so on. To start at the start, a dear gay friend of ours, mine really, had said, 'When you're there among those hills why not try those tea-estates—sometimes an old cottage or an old bungalow left over, you know the sort of thing? Not quite dilapidated, but well on the way, sort of left over, you know darling—weedy now but once wonderful: planned-garden, bird-bath-in-corner, low wall, creepers, low sloping roof, old trees, an old aga in the kitchen, a bit of parquet flooring—I know I'm getting a bit carried away, darling, but I think your search might well be over this time—you can thank me later if you find it—but somehow

The Quiet of the Birds

this time I feel, yes, try the old tea places—after all they knew how to build exactly what they wanted, and I know what you want. Everything romantically gone to seed, you know the kind of thing? You might just find something to suit your rather outdated tastes (darling, I do mean this absolutely affectionately) and there's sure to be a spare room and I might come and stay—for a bit—once you're all organized.'

'Good idea,' I said and thought—just what we need, lots of good ideas—even inspired ones, and we would accept because time, I felt, was running out. This business of time running out was very real but also needs some explaining because it's part of early retirement and takes every individual rather differently. There is a kind of urgency about it for some because it's not merely a question of a decision but it's also a kind of psychological landmark and to mix metaphors, it's a kind of plunge, a high dive the first time you try, scared as hell even though it's water down below. And if you wait too long looking down from that great height it stops being water, it stops being friendly. It's just fear, it's just panic then. And so it is with early retirement—you have to move fast once you decide or the faint-heart part of one takes over. Now to move fast you have to have a roof over your head and a prospect. Not just dreams. And this is where the real problem lies. It can't just be any old roof, nor can it be any old prospect. Because as my other good friend said, 'This time it's for keeps, baby! Who needs it? You do—I can see that—so if you're sure you're sure then there's no need to get your knickers in a twist now, is there?' Sweet reasonableness is the hallmark of that friend—as you can see. I suppose he's right anyway; if you can begin to extricate yourself from his rather vivid speech. I mean, once you move and you put everything you have into that move there'll be no more changing of minds—it's the last move and you have got to be one hundred and nine per cent sure. So it's tricky, to say the least. Mind you, at fifty plus you do feel certain of what you like and what you dislike— also of what you love and what you absolutely loathe. But the problems don't get less for being certain, they seem to multiply. Then I suppose my colourful friend would say, 'No sweat, baby! Just chicken out. No crime. Go back on the whole idea. Early retirement! Why not just go on as before, everybody you know is going on as before. Why not live as if life goes on and on? So why? For what?' Now this is the real danger zone. This is when you have to get that roof over your head and the prospect that pleases and then you're fine, home and dry. More or less.

Really that friend who mentioned tea-estates and leftover bungalows did us more than a good turn, actually perhaps helped us find it. Old Cypress—I like what it's called, the bungalow whose gates we have turned into, with the mist cleared and the place feeling like home already and Mark saying, 'Just down these steps and to the tennis-court and one last look at the old tree and then you can be quite sure.' And so we did that. The steps were old, bits of flagging broken at the top and a garden urn and then a kind of graveyard darkness because of the tree. There it was, very dark and looming over the uneven, weed-covered, tennis-court. People in white had actually flashed about calling out, 'Beautiful shot! My serve, I think.'

'What do you think?' said Mark.

'I think that this is going to be our home.'

'Good, that's decided then,' my husband said.

A sudden strangeness in the stomach.

'Now,' said Mark, 'let us pay a visit. Your closest neighbour, Anand. I mentioned him earlier, remember? My new assistant and his feeling about the mist? He'll feel reassured, I mean, you can tell him how the mist disappeared so quickly and that's how you decided about your new home, don't you think?' 'Yes,' I said, 'that's a nice idea, but won't he mind us just barging in like that?' 'Nonsense, rubbish, it will jolly him up no end, and we'll take him back for tea. Velu will be really pleased, he usually makes more scones than I can eat and I hate to disappoint him.' 'Velu and scones?' I said and Mark said, 'Velu is my chap, I inherited him from the manager here before me. I think he goes with the territory, he really does make the most incredible scones, they are his best thing after his soups—crumpets too, but not quite.' But that was in another land. By now we were walking down a winding lane and I thought, Mark really is full of surprises, there seems no end to the surprises of Mark, tea-gardens and scones and sudden mist,

The Quiet of the Birds

an old cypress, what more. Truly my cup runneth over.

Later that night, undressing for bed, I said, 'I love that bungalow.'

'I know.'

'Is that all?'

'That's a great deal—good, I'm glad.'

'Really? Are you really glad? Not just for me?'

'Look if it's all right with you, Radha, I'm tired, really bushed. I must sleep—we have a very long day tomorrow. All that travelling. Start so early.'

'I wish we could talk for a while about today, there's so much, I'm so excited—'

'I know there's so much, but no, we can't talk about it tonight, please I need to sleep. Try and sleep. Goodnight, Radha.'

I tried and tried to sleep and became more and more awake.

I saw the gate and the garden and the old wall and the creepers and the sloping roof and the veranda and the wooden pillars and the urn and then the broken steps down to the tennis-court and then the great tree spreading dark, almost black, spreading and— it's useless. 'Why don't you take something? A Calmpose—and don't try so hard.'

She thought, I wish two people could want to talk about things at the same time, I wish excitement for two people could mean the same thing, I wish sleep could come to two people at the same time, I wish that he didn't feel so bad about leaving Bombay, he loves Bombay he's always loved it, no matter what has happened to Bombay he still loves it. If trees are cut down, if garbage heaps get higher and higher, if neighbours are rude, if neighbours chuck sanitary towels out of windows, he still loves Bombay. If taxi drivers are rude he thinks it's me—he meets nice polite ones! I suppose while he's working he doesn't think about it all as I do, but when he's not working any more he'll see how terrible Bombay has become. Bombay is unfriendly when you're growing old. It's different and that difference is sad. We have a choice, we're lucky, so many people don't have a choice.

She had watched the streets with no pavements left and huge trenches left uncovered and the pushing and shoving and she'd watched how the old were treated. Old people in Bombay. Nobody had time for them. She had watched living in flats for old people— the staircases, the lifts, the crossing of roads for old people, how they cowered and pretended to be brave, how they were pushed aside, brushed aside, how they could never get into buses any more and had to pretend they preferred to walk. She'd watched the crowds—old people shopping, old people in queues, the rudeness of people when you were old. No city for old people. And soon we will be old. Oh, we've been through all this before. That's why we are here. But he loves Bombay. He hates leaving and all that it implies. It's a watershed. Well! What about me? I love Bombay, in my fashion. It's what we've known together for thirty years. I hate leaving. It's every bit as difficult for me as it is for him. So he could try. Perhaps it's different for him. Perhaps. He's lucky though, he can sleep. She saw old people staring out of upper balconies at kites. At nothing.

Packing

She hugged her delight in the place—it helped her in all the weeks of packing and wrapping and chucking out of stuff and mostly keeping stuff that she knew ought to be thrown out—especially old letters and postcards that went back years and years—surely she'd need to look at them! Going away didn't mean throwing away one's past, and the letters and postcards were like all the old photographs and all the books—they were one's life, proof of everything or most things that had happened in one's life—so she looked at them all and read them all and then pushed them all back into a spare suitcase and felt she'd need them always. Punting on the river Cam—David—Ruth—Suzanne—Joan—Christopher— Kim—Lizabeth—Colina—impossible to throw anything away, anyway it was all very neat and she felt extra tired that day and when Rohan asked her that evening she said, 'Oh, today I've been dealing with huge sections of my life and yours, so I'm very exhausted.' 'What can you mean, what have you packed, specially?' She said, 'Letters, postcards, bibs and bobs.'

Rohan said, 'Oh God, Radha, are you carting all that around? I'd hoped at last you'd chuck it all out, just collects dust, has done all these years, don't tell me you're taking all those old half-used bottles of turp and linseed oil and filthy, squeezed-up tubes of Flake White?' 'Of course,' she said, 'we might feel like painting again, and we'll have the time, anyway all that's done already. Today's packing was quite different, it made me curiously sad—shall we have a drink?—it all somehow made me realize how something would never happen again, never be young again, never sit on an elephant in Jaipur with my mother and father again, do you know what I mean?'

'I'll get us a drink and, yes, of course I know what you mean. I wish you wouldn't go on packing day after day—you're very tired. I told you we could get the packers in—for everything—'

'Not for most things, they can't deal with one's past—packers, I mean.'

'They wouldn't be here to deal with your past, your blessed, aching youth and happy-sad-times, they'd just pack impersonally and finish a jolly sight faster than you and without being on the verge of another nervous breakdown.'

'Surely that was a bit unnecessary, cruel. Have you had a very bad day again at your work?'

'No, nothing unusual. But I'm fed up of coming home evening after evening to all this muck all over the place and you looking a mess.'

'What on earth can you mean? Muck and mess? Where do you expect all the packing to be done—it's not muck, it's our life. As for my looking a mess, this isn't a movie where people look nice even when they're cooking a four-course meal.'

'I'm sorry, really I am. Let's have a drink. Let's talk about something else. All right, Radha, I said I was sorry. Okay and speaking of a "four-course meal", I hope there's something reasonable to eat—?'

'Of course, bits and pieces, leftovers, when have you ever had a square meal in this house? Let's get sloshed and not think any more.'

'Good idea, probably means anyway that you hadn't thought about what we'd eat, right?'

'Naturally. Rohan, do you think about Old Cypress a lot? I mean do you keep remembering things about it, I mean quite suddenly?'

'No, I don't as it happens. I've got far too much on my plate at the moment. I suppose you do. Do you?'

'Yes, I do, it helps me to get through all this business of winding up here. You know, I think of that garden and the old wall and how the sun will warm it and then I think of that front room with the deep bow windows almost touching the grass. We'll have long, old-fashioned breakfasts and . . .'

'We might start by getting a toaster, we both love toast but for thirty years we've never had a toaster.'

'Right, we'll get a toaster. Tomorrow I'll go and buy one. Oh, I think we are going to be very happy, I feel that. Do you?'

'I fell very hungry—let's eat.'

'Oh you are so, so somehow without excitement. I thought you might begin to feel, when are you going to say anything about Old Cypress, I mean, I think about it so much of the time and I want to talk about it to you—the old tennis-court we saw together, we are going to live there together quite soon, isn't there anything about it that you feel?'

'No. If you must know I feel nothing at all. There. You made me say that. I wasn't going to say anything—I just hoped you'd realize on your own—you always want things said. Always. Now let's eat and not talk. I'm tired.'

'You are so awful. I do hate you so often, I don't understand why we have lasted so long. Do you?'

'There you go again, and since you ask me I'd say no, really I don't know how we have lasted so long, as you put it. Perhaps we haven't lasted at all!'

'You always try to spoil everything. Why do you have to say such things? You are a hurting man. But I won't listen to you. I'll pretend you never said it. That you never meant it.'

'But I did mean it. You live in a world of your own—you have for a long while. You don't see anything that's really happening. Oh, just let's leave it.'

'There you've done it again, you say dreadful things and then

The Quiet of the Birds

retreat, how can you say the things you say and then say "leave it"? I can't leave it. So tell me.'

'No, I said no. Not now. Soon. Some other time. Not now. I'm going out for a bit, I'll get a bite to eat. You carry on, don't wait up.'

'Don't go. Please don't go, not now, not just now.'

'I must. I'll not be long. But I must.'

One evening he'd come back from work to find her an island in a sea of open tea-chests and mountains of old newspaper; she was tired but dogged—Judas 2 lying in an exhausted, drugged heap near her. She said cheerfully, 'Another few days and I'll be done, I think. Just the breakables—like this!' And held out a bowl, a white bowl with blue flowers at the rim. It was seeing that in her outstretched hand that made him say, 'I can't go with you, I mean I'm not coming with you.' She said, not understanding, 'You mean I'm to go ahead, before you, you'll follow after, is that what you mean? Is something up at work?'

'No,' he said, 'nothing's up at work. I'm not leaving here. I'm not going to Old Cypress.'

'You mean not just now, or never?'

'Never.'

She said, 'But it's ours, our new home, Old Cypress belongs to us now. It's all arranged, what can you mean? Are you feeling all right? I mean, are you ill? Are you joking? Because if you are I don't feel much like joking, I feel tired like death, I feel like a jolly old drink. What's the matter? Why are you looking like that— looking like this—at me?'

'I'm not coming to Old Cypress. It's like a full-stop, that old bungalow. Here I'll keep going. With you and Old Cypress I'll grow older quicker, it's like the last stop with nothing further. Death the next stop. It's too quiet there. And that mist every evening! No, I'm not leaving here—here it's noisy, it's dirty, it's crowds and it's traffic but I'll always be with people.'

'Oh, you've just got cold feet, I get like that sometimes thinking about it. Sometimes it feels so final, so unfamiliar. But it won't be like that once we're there. Soon you'll love it. You're tired. You're anxious and worried. Don't be. Please. You didn't really mean those awful things you said—I hope. Not all of them, anyway.'

'I do mean them. And worse. I hate that place. Miles and miles of forest and then miles and miles of tea-bushes and shade trees and absolute quiet. A graveyard would be more lively. And then that old tree—as I said a graveyard's the proper place for that tree. It looms and glooms over that old house—no wonder nobody wants to live there.'

'But I didn't do all this on my own, in fact if you hadn't thought about retiring early none of this would even have started happening, don't you remember? And about Old Cypress, we saw the sale notice about it together at the club and we both followed it up and then we met Mark who took us there—Good God man! Have you forgotten everything? And you said you liked it—we both liked it. We saw it twice—all morning and it was sunny, and then we went back in the evening—you never once said you didn't like it, in fact, you didn't say anything about graveyards or anything distressing about the place, why else did we follow it up? Why else did we buy it? Why else am I packing and packing as if my life depended on it? You said that Mark had told you early autumn would be a good time to aim for so that we could be settled, more or less, before winter set in—'

'Oh hang Mark and anything he said, I'm not going. And about liking it, well—you loved it so immediately and I thought I might get to like it—given time. But, I don't have the time. And I'm not coming with you. I'm staying here. I'm not stopping you. You must go.'

'Do you mean it's to be a holiday place—closed most of the year and then opened up for a month every year? Have you gone quite mad? That wasn't the idea at all—we are going to live there always. You're retiring in less than a month and we're leaving. It's here that we might visit from time to time. Oh, what is the matter? Please tell me?'

'No, I mean, I'm not coming at all. I'm involved with someone—it's become very important to me—so I—'

'What are you talking about—who are you involved with? What has become so important to you—what?'

'I'm, well, very close to a woman, and I'm not leaving her. That's about it.'

The Quiet of the Birds

'What's about it? You're not that kind of person! You mean you love some woman? I mean, someone has become that important to you and you've never told me? Never given me so much as a hint? It's not possible. It's the one thing that just is not possible. It's not you. I'm not listening.'

Early next morning she woke him up with, 'How old is she—tell me? Did last night happen? Did you say those things?'

'What's the time?—are you mad—I have to sleep.'

'You can sleep later, dammit—how old is she? You must know. I want to know. You've slept quite a lot anyway—how can you sleep?'

'Must you know? Must we go on and on—'

'Yes, and I don't remember going on and on—'

'Half the night—'

'I don't remember, anyway yes, I want to know. How old is she?'

'She has a name—just in case you plan long conversations about her.'

'How old is she?'

'She's younger, younger than—'

'You mean younger than I am or much younger than you are?'

'Younger than both of us. Actually she's—'

'Why can't you get on with it, why can't you just say it? If it was all right carrying on with her for so long, why do you find it difficult to tell me how old she is? Has the enormity of it all just struck you? She's not a minor, is she? She can vote, can't she? Why is it worse for you to name it?'

'She's twenty-six.'

'Bravo! There now that's said. I'm sure you feel a lot better. Lucky you. I can't say I feel a whole lot better, but then that's not why I asked you, is it? To use an old, hackneyed phrase of attack—or abuse—isn't it cradle-snatching? Our son is—rather will be—twenty-seven this year. I suppose that's neither here nor there?'

'Yes, well, you did ask.'

'Yes, I did ask, as you put it. Asking for trouble, I am. Is that what you mean? With all my questions. As to your sensitive observation about her having a name, do you and she talk of me using my name? Do you—I mean it is quite simple really—why do I find it difficult?'

'We don't talk about you—I mean it's possible. We just don't.'

'Yes, I can see that. Anyway she and you have a head-start— I've been in the dark. What did you tell her every time we went looking for a place to live in? Surely she's a wee bit curious sometimes? How did you pretend so well, how could you disguise so well, how could you make me believe—or rather her believe, and me just assume or imagine—all was well? Or do you mean I should have guessed? Say something, anything. What about trust, loyalty, fidelity? What about friendship?'

'I don't know, I wasn't sure—I—'

'Bastard!' she said, 'you weren't sure—you mean it was always either, or? And me not to know, me get the raw end of the deal either way—be left or bereft, if you came, or if you didn't? We weren't a unit any more anyway, for you to worry about? I was not to know—and, oh horrors—I would never know if things hadn't worked out for you. How could you?'

At last he said, 'Look, I didn't mean to hurt you—you have to believe that. Let's leave it at that, no need to try and—'

'Try and what? Try and understand? No need, you say? Every need, there is every need. I need to know. I have to. So that I never ever again—oh hell, is it men? Is it true, then, that men are so different? What has so often been said but that I thought couldn't be really true. Have you and I been so different all these years. Us. Perhaps, you are right, there is no need to try and understand because there is nothing to be gained. Nothing. I suppose deception, betrayal happen stealthily, not brazenly, openly. But. Not you, not you. Not us. Because you are my friend. And I thought that I was yours.'

'But you are, you are—I really have no other friend like you— nor will I ever. But there was something I needed—'

'Yes, so it would seem. But, as you say friend, what can you mean not telling me, not warning me, lying to me, being untrue to me? Think if it had been me? Can you think of that—and there were times—I did feel a great deal for someone else—I really did. We were, you and I, having what was more than a bad patch. I was very lonely, work was going badly, I was not all that well and yes, there really was someone who cared a great deal for me—really cared and made me feel loved and desired and special. But there was always you. God knows why I worried so much—why I didn't allow anything to happen. I wish I had. It's no use now. I wish women were more like men; I suppose some are. Anyway, so you have a "chick"? What do you feel when you are with her? Remember how you and I used to joke about a chick on the side?'

'I feel younger, she makes me feel younger.'

'Younger? Yes well—'

'Yes younger, altogether, I mean as though, well, like I used to feel . . .'

(God, she thought, I asked for this, this I really did ask for.)

'Look,' he said, 'I know this hurts you, is hurtful, but I didn't want to hurt you, didn't mean—didn't ever mean—'

'Oh shut up, how dare you talk of didn't want to hurt, you don't begin to understand what you have done—undone—over twenty-nine years together. More than that really. Something built over more years than most people alive. And what about the years before, before the twenty-nine years? All those years?'

'I thought it would pass, I mean, I thought it might not last,' he said. 'I didn't realize how much it meant to me,' he said.

She hated him so much that she could scarcely breathe. And she thought, the other times I've hated him, wanted to leave him, get away, go away from him, from my life with him—and never done it—never done it because there was something good we had at solid rock bottom. She thought, what I felt was true must be so for both of us. Apparently not. More fool she. Me. Me miserable which way I fly—myself am—

Another day she said, 'Then why did you come to the hills, why did you plan with me, why did we do all that, why did you go ahead with all that? I mean, if all the time . . . if all that time . . .' she said.

He said, 'I wasn't certain it would work out.'

She said, 'Work out? You weren't certain it would work out with me or with her? Can't you be more precise, even now? What is it with you, anyway? Who is she? I really do need to know. Also I want to know.'

Old Cypress   15

'Why, why must you?'

'Why must I? At best, why not? At worst, curiosity—I mean apart from being young, other things. I she tall, is she small, is she thin or is she fat, does she laugh a lot or not at all, does she read, has she a dimple? I'd like to know the kind of person you fell for to put it in crude or youthful terms.'

'Stop it! Just stop it.'

'No, no, I'll not stop it. How can it possibly upset you? And you're surely not worried about upsetting me, are you? I mean, having done the worst, and having told me the worst, this is all small cheese. So. What is she like? What does she look like? Who is she?'

'Well if you must—'

'Yes, I must.'

'Well it's Aditi . . .'

'You mean the Aditi in your office? That one? Not possible.'

'Yes, that one. And yes, more than possible. You asked—remember that.'

'Yes, I did ask. And I do remember that. The one I had taught. The one who'd joined you soon after her first child was born. Good lord we went to her home for a ceremony for the child—I didn't know where to hide my *peda* and you said wrap it up in your handkerchief, no one would notice. But then—oh, it's not possible, it just doesn't bear thinking about.'

'Then don't. Just leave it. Leave it alone. It's bad enough.'

'Bad enough, is it? What do you mean? Bad enough for you, or her? Or me? Or just the whole thing? And I won't leave it, I just can't believe it. Give me time. After all, you've had a great deal of time, a real head-start! But how can you stand her? When she's not gushing, she's coy—when she's not coy, she's embarrassing.'

'You don't know her; you don't know her at all. You haven't the right to discuss her.'

'Of course I do, I have every right. We've often discussed her, you and I. I have every right. My husband is about to marry someone. Are you? My husband has had a long and fruitful affair with someone he is going to marry, my husband is throwing up—giving up—a long relationship contained in a marriage that has

The Quiet of the Birds

lasted twenty-nine years and seven months. I have every right to discuss her—to talk about her, to tell you what I think about her, and to tell you what I think about you and her. I've never fancied myself. It's you that fancied me. Remember? And now. Oh well, I must say I'm disappointed in you. I thought it would be someone spectacular. In every sense. After all, you are giving up quite a lot. You are, you know. And I don't mean me. I mean our life, our ways together. Our quarrels, our journeys, our illnesses, our child. Our child when he was little, and now when he is not. My God, does she know you snore? Oops sorry, of course she does, it hasn't been all platonic has it, for so long? How on earth did you manage? I mean her husband, your wife, her child, your child? How did you juggle it all, keep all the balls in the air and not drop any one of them? How? And when? And the secrecy, the hypocrisy, the others in the office, and me at home? And tennis right through it all! I do wish—I wish—that I had known or guessed. It all seems such a waste. That I worked quite hard at it all because it mattered so much to me. A waste. All, all of it a waste and all the beastly, unbearable hurt to other people because you mattered. I can't bear it. I don't think I can bear it. How did you? How can you bear it? Do you, did you, just stop thinking? Or didn't you think at all? Or is it really that different being a man? And guilt, was there none of that either? No sleepless nights, days, anxiety, off your food–drink? Good lord we went cottage hunting together. Friends. You and I. Friendship. You and I. Always you and I. What a fool I've been. I assumed, I took for granted, our life. You pretended so well. I didn't think you loved me. But I felt you liked me more than anyone else. Just as I do, did. That's so much after so many years. You and I have talked about that too—rather often—about how lucky we were, are. We compared ourselves to other people, we—oh let's stop this anyway. I want to finish the packing. The crates will have to leave quite soon. You didn't help much, did you? I mean, in the way of packing. I suppose I'll have to unpack some of the stuff. I mean, it's all been packed as though we were both going. I take it you will want some of it. Not just clothes, some of our shared things.'

'No, not to worry.'

'What does that mean—not to worry? We'll have to separate our things, specifically—books, paintings, furniture, oh for God's sake almost everything. How are we going to do it? When are we going to do it? Why didn't you make up your selfish, beastly mind sooner—before I'd started packing? You're a coward, you knew all the time. And it wasn't kindness to me, it was weakness. You didn't know how you'd put it—say it—or some such finicky detail. Having done the worst damage you could ever do, you suddenly found it difficult to tell me. Coward, worse than coward. There is no word for what you are, for what you have done. I still can't somehow believe all this has happened, is happening. Is it true? Did you less than an hour ago tell me that you were leaving me? Did you tell me that you were leaving me for someone you'd love for a long while and now were planning to marry? Were these things said—done? Have they happened? Somewhere between wrapping blue and white bowls bought in Batot in a little tea shop—it was so cold and twelve white bowls with blue flowers on the rim lay on a dusty shelf and we bought them for a rupee each. We both liked them very much, they were the first things, almost, that we bought. I wanted eight and you said six would be fine. We used them for soup, one broke when I fell down the stairs in our first home, one when the child was two—that left four. That's when they became bowls for nuts. Judas knocked two of them off a low table with his great tail. Now there are just the two, semi-wrapped in newspaper. You take one. I'll pack the other.'

'I don't want it. Please take them both, please don't cry, don't cry.'

'Don't touch me, leave me alone. And what do you mean, you don't want it? You don't want a white bowl with blue flowers on the rim? Why not? How can you not? Don't you want it to remember, don't you want it to forget? We'll divide everything up. A division of the spoils! That's it! We'll divide it all up—whatever we can. Till we come to Judas 2 and the child! That way it will be fair. That way you'll feel pain, begin to feel some of this. Why should you be spared? Even bastards feel pain, don't they? Don't come near me—I'm not a child, I'm not a pet, don't come near me with your warm familiar ways of bringing comfort to me. All the times—when my mother died, all the things I couldn't bear, thinking I'd die of grieving—you brought me back. But not this time. This time you've brought death, betrayal, everything, so don't dare come near me—cold comfort, dissembling, pretending. And now you take one of these white bowls with blue on it and think back on a very cold morning high in the mountains, you think of us two young people. Two graves with white and purple iris. A tea shop. Very hot, sweet, too sweet tea but so welcome and opposite a dusty counter and twelve white bowls of thick ceramic with a blue pattern on them. Can you see them? And I said, "Why don't we buy those bowls," and you said, "By all means," and I thought we'll buy all twelve or at least eight so if any of them broke we'd still have plenty and you said, "Six will be plenty." Mean, but sensible. And the man at the counter smiled and said they were Chinese and that's why they would cost a rupee each and wrapped them up in old newspaper and there were six small rings of dust on that counter. Can you forget? It was only twenty-eight years ago! Too long? You always did say, "Travel light, travel light," that's why I suppose you can be up and off like the young these days, everything they need stuffed into a small rucksack, and a "peach on the pillion". I'm very tired. I'm going to bed. I wish I had my own room. I've always wanted a room of my own. You'll put out the lights. Come on Judas2. I wonder if he's guessed—he usually knows when something is up.'

At the Station

'Thank you for coming to the station, you dislike . . .'

'Don't be silly, you must know . . .'

'It's a Saturday, where will you go from here? Have a good read at the Will? Ignore me, I wish the train would leave now . . .'

'You're lucky to get this coupé—I mean, what with Judas 2—'

'Yes. I hope he's good at stations—I mean performing—he'll miss you a lot—'

Judas 2 straining at the leash, trying to get to Rohan and yet frightened and sitting very close to her.

'We never took him on a journey before—to get used to this sort of thing . . .'

'No, we didn't.'

'But, finally, Rohan why? Why has all this happened?'

'I can't answer that, I wish I could. Okay then, take care . . .'

'Yes, you too.'

Dog straining, now seriously worried. 'Stop it.'

'I think it's time.'

'Yes.' I can't believe it's me, I can't believe it's him.

As the train started pulling out she said, 'I'll miss you—us—you know?'

'Yes,' he said. 'We always had a lot of fun . . .'

'Yes'—I wish he'd say some more—'What? I can't hear you—what?'

'I said not just a lot of fun—I mean a lot of things—together—also I really do love you . . .'

'Yes, but you love her more.'

'No, it's not like that, it's more complicated.'

'No, it's as horribly simple as that. Leave it now.'

'Look if you need anything, I mean . . .'

'Need what? Like what? It's done now. You must know I wouldn't ask you or . . . look, let's just leave it.'

She sat down and pulled Judas 2 very close, turned her back to the window; this time the train really did leave. She was glad they were alone. Now she could cry—that's what stations were for. That's what trains were for.

The Bad Times

One life to live—lead. Enjoy—say the young rather quaintly, and quite right too!

In the middle distance—two horses cropping non-existent grass. Tails flicking flies. One very dark black-brown and the other white with a large brown patch. Lovely and lonely in the sun those two.

Also in the shade. A bell tinkles as they move. You can't really be thinking about death on a day like this—with one almost painted green bird poised at the very end of a twig deciding—shall I or shall I not? There was a rhyming game when they were all young— girls played it when they were skipping. Not boys. It was sissy, they said, to skip.

Two little dicky birds sat upon a wall—
One named Peter, the other named Paul.
Fly away Peter, fly way Paul—
Come back Peter, come back Paul.

Silly when you said it just like that but it was nice if you skipped well—sometimes you skipped together with a special friend, facing her—oh yes it was fun—such a long-ago time that. When?

I contain that time in me. Now. Both then and now.

Always went backwards—I mean I did—and I still do. Long ago and then again not so long ago. Rohan would say, 'If only you could try and not let your mind dwell on the past—let it go—just let it go—'and Radha would say, 'How—how? It's with us all the time—except sometimes more than at other times—surely, surely— the pastness of the past—the past is not chronological—it isn't, you can grieve today for that flower that died, very now, and twenty years ago a death—you can feel the sharp pain, and then the dull, on-and-on pain, a death twenty years ago it doesn't leave you, it's like today—Rohan you know exactly what I mean though I've put it so badly. The pain doesn't pass—it's there all the time—in every way. In sounds, in smell, in touch. The smell of a sari worn by someone. The smell of mogra in the hair—the long-ago person is there. Is here.

'The feel of the person, the sound, and it's not memory, and it's not just nostalgia. It's the here and the now. It's real in the present. Longing to hold, hug, talk, walk. The "thereness" of a person doesn't go merely because it was a long-ago time. Present, past, it's the same thing, it's just been made convenient to separate it. The past lives securely in the present because it's the same thing.

When people say—"Forget it, put it aside, put it away, don't relive it, don't think of it, blot it out, think of something else, don't dwell on it"—that's it. That's the point. There is no way you can do those things. It's unnatural. But I suppose there would be no way to carry on living. So. We try to force ourselves to do something that is unnatural. Or we pretend.'

And Rohan with great patience, 'But try—that's all I said. Try. Or Radha you'll always be grieving for everything that goes—let it go, naturally, like the leaves on a tree—'

The now Radha wanted to say, 'Have you done it—do you remember, Rohan? Nothing, anything of our days and ways?' She wanted to say, she wanted to shout, wanted to cry out, 'Look—remember that time—cats in Venice—the Dali retrospective, wine and cheese and olive sharp on the tongue as if this minute shared—how can you forget, how can you say, laugh it off, forget, the past is done, it's over?'

How are you managing, I wonder—I suppose, very well. But damn you, damn him. I miss him. I miss. I miss him and that's why I can't—don't—get on with this unpacking and living each day as I should. Try. Start now. Start. I will tomorrow. Yes, I really will tomorrow. Just now I'll go to bed. I don't want to try and sleep. I want to sleep easily each night, as head touches pillow. Not think and think about—betrayal. I am so burdened with sorrow. I don't need it, I don't want it. Tomorrow. Come on Judas 2. I wonder what your thoughts are? Do you think of Rohan? Do you miss him? Do you have long thoughts—as you lie there—about betrayal? Judas 2—if he came up the path just now, would you recognize his footsteps, his smell, his touch? Would your tail wag and wag till it nearly fell off? Would you love him as though nothing had happened? Wouldn't you take sides? Would you leave me? Judas 2, I hope you realize he left you too and just remember that. One day he thought about us both, and he said, 'Can I do without them?' He thought about us both—separately, and then together. After a long while (hopefully) or a short while, he said, 'Of course—off with their heads—nothing to it—who needs it—travel light!' So you see Judas 2, he moved on. We are his past. And he has let us go naturally, as the leaves on a tree.

The Quiet of the Birds

'He bid me take love easy, as the leaves that grow on the tree;
But I, being young and foolish, with him would not agree—'

Anyway, let's try and sleep, old Judas 2—and I'm sorry trying to influence you like this—they say divorced parents try and do that to their children, I'll not do it to you, Mr Judas 2—you needn't take sides if you don't want to—and you can go on forgiving Rohan or anyone you like. And tomorrow you and I have serious work to do.

And you and I are going to listen to our music again. Teleman and Vivaldi and then the well-tempered Claviar.

Mark can't go on spoiling us, she thought as she lay in the dark—I have to do something and soon. That's all there is to it. She thought of the first evening, arriving at Old Cypress and finding a note from Mark—'Wish I could be here to welcome you, I hope the long journey didn't feel too long. I've had a fire lit in the living room and the master bedroom and had all the rooms aired. Velu has left you candles in the kitchen cupboard and something to eat—tomorrow will feel better—when the sun comes out and you've had a night's rest. Welcome to your new home.'

For many days the house stayed aloof, very cold, hostile. Endless bending over trunks, books so familiar, now seeming not hers at all. Cupboards not closing, shelves odd, out of place. The old aga smoking and smoking without really cooking anything not even heating anything—but one day it felt different. Distinctly different. Curtain up. Rocking chair near the fireplace, rugs beginning to belong to Judas 2.

Perhaps she had come home.

But not the nights. Not the dead of night. She was afraid, heard voices. Sounds.

Saw shadows move. Wished she had learnt to pray—she hugged Judas 2. We have followed too much the devices and desires of our own hearts—I wish morning would come.

The Bad Times (Contd.)

One day as they walked Mark said, 'Is it all right if I ask you some questions, just a very few?'

'Yes, a few, of course.'

'Is your husband coming? I mean, when is he coming—it's now you need a lot of help so I wondered—not prying, just asking.'

'No, he's not coming. He's not following after or anything like that. I'm here. I've come to stay. About help—well, I'll unpack and uncrate slowly, perhaps you know of someone who might help with the heavier stuff? I don't mean to impose. Truly. Perhaps your Velu might know of someone who might help with the heavier stuff, do you think?'

'Yes—I think. And if it's all right with you, after work I could drop by and help. I'm quite good with nails and hammer even an old aga that needs starting with more than a kick, that sort of thing.'

'Yes, soon. I'll ask you. You are very kind—'

'Will you, rather are you, always so formal? Don't be. It's often such a waste of time. Anyway, I'll wait for you to ask me. Don't be too long, soon winter will come and before that you should be properly set up.'

'Yes, before winter comes, and thank you.'

Another day, on his way into the nearest town, Mark dropped by to ask if she needed anything and when she said a hot-water bottle he said, are you feeling the cold already and she said, yes, and he asked if she was sleeping all right, and she said, more or less, but sometimes she woke at odd hours and heard things. He said, what kind of things, you mean the wood creaking sort of sounds? And she said, not-in-the-house sounds but outside-sounds. Like people playing-tennis sounds and Old Cypress creaking. Silly, of course, but it had happened several nights. Even Judas 2 heard it—heard them. Mark said, why don't you come into town with me now, we could talk and you might see other things that you need. Bring Judas 2, he'll like the drive, and so she had gone with him. Judas 2 had his head stuck out of the window—looking amazed.

The Quiet of the Birds

Soon she said, 'Judas likes it here, he's always had a raw deal. For a big dog he's never had any space—where we lived he couldn't ever roam free or run, his walks were sedate up-and-down-the-lane kind of walks—dodging garbage and wild cats and filthy crows and the children would call out, "Here comes Judas's mummy!"—They loved him and always wanted to hold his leash for a bit—but he never liked them much, he really likes it here, he has the garden, unbelievable freedom.'

'Do you miss it then? I mean what you have left—the lane and the children calling you Judas 2's mum?'

'Yes, yes I do, it was so many years, no other reason. Anyway, the children in the lane were beginning to grow up—some had just started karate and some were learning ballet so anyway soon they wouldn't have had the time for Judas 2 and me. I shall buy a toaster as well. I've just decided. We—I—love toast and I've never got round to buying one—amazing how lazy one can get. I mean to be lazy like that, selective lazy.'

'Wait till you see our "everything" shop, it's a real "Ye old shoppe" with marvellous wood floors that creak and counters with the most amazing things—home-made jams and chocolate fudge and hot-water bottles and socks with clocks and toasters and books by Mrs Gaskell—'

'No! You're just making it up as you go along, aren't you?'

'Well, just wait till you get there and you'll see it's true, and I'm glad you're going to get a toaster. Also they have strange things in large old glass jars—we're nearly there. About those sounds you hear some nights, voices, are you frightened? Or do you manage to get back to sleep? And Judas 2—you said he heard them—what did you mean?'

'Exactly that—Judas 2 hears those sounds and those voices, they are playing a game of tennis and they call out—'

'Here we are then—Judas 2 is allowed in with us—I told you it was a remarkable old shop—now for your toaster and the hot-water bottle. Why is he called Judas 2?'

'We had a dog called Judas—he was bitten by a Russell's viper—many years ago.'

'I am glad you have Judas 2.'

The Old Tennis-Court

One day Mark said, 'Why don't we try and deal with the old tennis-court, I've been thinking about it, it seems a shame not to try. I mean it's there, isn't it? And if it's unusable tennis-wise, you can still put it to some use because we'll have cleared it of years and years of nettles and brambles and goodness knows what. I notice Judas 2 has become quite fond of that part of the garden.'

'Yes, he has and always comes back really filthy when he's been rooting about there—but about the tennis-court, I never thought to touch it somehow—I mean when Rohan decided not to come, that is.'

'Don't you play—?'

'Ye-es, I do and I don't. It was really a passion of Rohan's.'

'But if the court proved usable would you play? Are you fond of the game?'

'Yes, yes, I am, do you play? I didn't think to ask. You do so much else, but do you?'

'Yes, I used to play quite a lot in college, but here all these years it's been too far, somehow, to go for a game, so I gave it up. But I'd start again—if you would. And then there's Anand—it would be good for him—let's give it a try, anyway.'

'But won't it be a fearful lot of work? I mean, work on the court—won't it?'

'Well, we'll soon find out. It has a wonderful natural boundary—the old wall and then the tree. We have a heavy roller down in one of the factory sheds and there's any amount of gravel—it will be a red gravel court. Really, it seems a shame not to use it, I mean, there it is, waiting. Let's give it a try. Of course, you'd tell me if you hated the idea because it reminded you too much of things you want to forget, or pained you too much, you would, wouldn't you? I don't want to push you too hard—'

'Yes, I would. Tell you, I mean. And, thank you, Mark, for thinking as you do—'

'Anytime—Radha. For you. Anytime.'

'I suppose partly you're trying to rid me of night fears—sounds from the tennis-court—?'

'Yes—partly.'

'You know Mark, the person who really will be pleased about this is Ram Swaroop, he's been itching to clear all the tangled stuff and the bushes, he hates a jungle—he doesn't think much of my idea of a garden.'

'Don't I know it,' Mark said, 'he loves clearing, he loves clipping, chopping and mowing, he loves very neat flower-beds with edges clearly demarcated, you know the kind of thing, if he had his way he'd make a bird sculpture of your Old Cypress! Be firm with him—he's a very knowledgeable mali—but don't let him bully you or touch the way you want your garden—'

'I want a clearing-in-a-forest sort of garden.'

'Right. You tell him to help you achieve exactly that, all right? About tomorrow, you haven't forgotten, it's the Saturday I'm taking you and Anand to our famous game sanctuary—we'll leave very early and come back by nightfall. I feel certain you will like it very much, and if we're lucky we might see a tiger or a leopard—apart from all the other game.'

'Yes,' she said, already excited. 'I've only been once to a game sanctuary when I was very young. I remember being frightened of the silence—what do we take—I mean, what shall I—?'

'Nothing, nothing, Anand and I have arranged everything. Anand has never been you know—I suspect he's coming because you are!'

Very early next morning they arrived to fetch her. It was still dark and she was worried about leaving Judas 2.

It felt mysterious in the jeep, warm between Mark and Anand, enveloped in a kind of cocoon—all round the light darkly mauve and the headlights on. Gradually she felt like a child again, the day not quite begun, neither night still nor day yet. What delight hid, unknown, behind each bend in the road? The jeep wound round bends and slowly, very gradually, light touched trees and bushes that had been there all the time. It was magical. Radha began to hum and Mark completed the old tune. 'Oh,' she said surprised, 'it's an old favourite. I thought not sung any more, before your time!'

Anand half-asleep woke with a startled jerk, 'What? Where are we? Are we there? I don't want—'

'Go back to sleep, Anand. What's it called then? That old tune—the one you were humming?'

'I don't know but it has such a quaint story to tell, I love it—about a boy called Willy who goes acourting, every day he is asked about his beloved's skills and Willy is so proud about her spinning and her weaving and her baking and then in the last verse, which goes,

How old is she now, my boy Willy?
How old is she now, Willy won't you tell me now?
"Twice six, twice seven, twice twenty and eleven—But
she is too young to be taken from her Mamie."

'That's the final verse. I hadn't thought of it for a very long time, maybe it was this setting off on an adventure so early that reminded me—made me remember. When our son was little we often went down to a village near the sea and we'd sing this song on the way. He loved the words, he's twenty-seven now. That's where Judas was bitten—by the snake.'

The sun was high in the sky now, the hillscape very different. They stopped for coffee and sandwiches near a break in the hills from where they could see a deep gorge far down, water cascading down, deep green, deep green silence—all round in the near and far distance, violet-blue hills.

'We're nearly there now, it's our lucky day. We are going to see a lot of wildlife,' said Mark.

'How do you know? Why do you think we'll be lucky?'

'Just because. Also I saw a marvellous blue kingfisher just now—it flashed past Anand's left ear. That's how I know! Ready everyone?'

Later, much later, Anand was to tell the doctor, 'I was frightened—it was a lonely, dark journey and when we stopped for breakfast a dark bird flew close by me, a death bird, it chose me, not Radha, not Mark, it chose me. And then we drove down to death valley—it was waiting for me. Everything was dead—near a small stream there was a dead skin, or pelt, of an animal—the others didn't see it. Only I saw it, it was waiting for me. Like the yew hedge in my garden—Ram Swaroop was not frightened of it, only I could see what it was, it was death all the time, hovering, waiting at every turn—even on the way to the sanctuary there was a greasy, greeny-black sort of hut shaped like a wigwam—doctor, you do understand me, don't you? Radha was interested because she had never seen such a strange shape and when Mark told her we could stop and take a look she was intrigued. But I knew immediately that it was a bad thing, again a death thing, an evil thing. I was afraid and stayed in the jeep. I tried not to look, though I knew what lived inside that evil, smoking tent. But I couldn't stop them—how could I—if I told them they would guess how afraid I was, they would guess everything and write to my father. I was so afraid because I knew it was part of the black yew hedge in my garden—it was part of the message that came every evening in the mist. But I couldn't warn them—what would I have said?'

When they got back into the jeep Radha said she'd never have thought that the strange hut could have been put together to extract eucalyptus oil, was that the way it was usually done? And Mark said, it was one of the more primitive ways, yes. And simple, really quite ingenious—to build a tent wigwam sort of shape entirely of eucalyptus leaves and a slow burning fire inside and huge bowls or vats to collect the pure oil.

'Interesting, wasn't it? I wish you'd come with us, Anand, didn't you want to see? You are lazy.'

'So you see, doctor, that's what they thought because that's what they saw, but I knew different. It was a death hut, it was waiting for me, if I had gone with them I would never have been able to come out again. It was the same colour as the yew hedge—and that smoke coming out of it was another kind of mist, waiting for me, for me. And then we went on to the sanctuary—I couldn't change anything I couldn't make them turn back. I was chosen—marked—the only one. I was so afraid.'

And Radha had thought, what more can this marvellous day hold for us, it's been just as Mark had said it would be when he saw that blue kingfisher flash past Anand's ear, oh the very air seemed green, and there was a wonderful stillness sometimes only our footfalls and the sudden clear call of a bird; there was a clear stream with large, rounded pebbles and we paddled our feet and it was so clear and so cold we cooled our beer bottles in it—small fish darted past the brown, shiny, wet bottles, the most ordinary things had turned into new images of happiness. We found a silvery skin in the water—a water snake perhaps. Mark laid it out in the sun to dry and said I must take it back to remember this day. It's odd but I think I saw, or half saw, Anand push it back into the water—he said it was an accident. I don't think it was. He didn't want me to have that beautiful thing. In the late afternoon we went for an elephant ride deep into the jungle. Our elephant was called Durga.

And Anand told the doctor, 'When the sun was nearly gone we went for an elephant ride, it was to be the grand finale to the day according to Mark because he said now we would see some big game. Our elephant was called Durga and our mahout was a cruel-looking man, I didn't like him and he guessed who I was, he took us to the deepest part of the jungle, it was not a jungle at all it was death, it was a kind of lunar landscape—dead burnt-out trees in a desert, trees charred and burnt out, skeletons hung everywhere—and these dead white-yellow shapes that were once trees. And the deathly silence, doctor, it was so quiet—only two sounds in that long, long ride the susurration of dead long grass when the elephant's huge, padding feet brushed past it and the loud terrible thwack and again thwack when that evil mahout beat the elephant on the head, it seemed between his eyes, so close to where I was sitting—and that poor Durga just went on and on and we never saw any wildlife—how could we—it was all dead like the trees, like the grass, like the birds—there was only Durga and the mahout and us—I don't know why Mark or Radha didn't say anything or do anything—we went on and on in that deadness.'

On the journey home, as the jeep took one of the hairpin bends at the crest of the mountains, their headlights picked up a shape. Mark turned off the engine and they watched a beautiful large cat move across the road then turn—great eyes in the headlights, great beautiful cats' eyes—and spring into the jungle. Radha said, 'Oh Mark—like you promised—we did see some wildlife! How beautiful she looked—'

The Quiet of the Birds

But Anand told the doctor, 'The terror never stopped even when we left the sanctuary. On the way home death stalked me—death looked at me at a turn in that dark road. It had waited all day and found and looked at me—pretending to be a leopard.'

About Mark

Mark was good at most things. At the beginning she realized he was good at all things useful. Shelves that wouldn't hang straight, crooked nails, uneven stone flagging, drainpipes clogged with last autumn's leaves, the aga in the kitchen—most things. He worked very quietly and unlike most people who are good at useful things he didn't irritate her, didn't ever make her feel she was bad at most things.

She missed him the evenings he couldn't come.

One day she said, 'Tell me about you.' He was oiling a stubborn cupboard door.

'Very little to tell—'

'Tell anyway—when did you come to these hills, to this tea-estate?'

'Oh, I came here a long time ago, I was Anand's age—in fact I lived in his cottage—in our family, to use a cliché, we've always been in tea.'

'Your family—and where are they now?'

'There's really only my mother now. I like it here very much. Always have, right from the beginning, that's why I'm sometimes unable to understand Anand. In fact, I wouldn't be anywhere but here. My mother feels I'm lost now.'

'Why lost? Doesn't she like it here? Or doesn't she like it for you?'

'No, not quite that, she's always been used to this sort of life but then there was a family. She'd like me to start a family—she thinks it's easy. I think it's very difficult. In the early years she'd bring friends, you know with daughters—or photographs—sometimes even lists of names. She thought I might get to like someone, she thought I'd be unhappy otherwise. She likes people to marry. Then she's happy. She doesn't believe I'm settled yet. I'll never be more settled, I tell her—it's over fifteen years that I've been here. No other life to live, I tell her. She can't and won't understand that.'

'And now—?'

'Oh, she still comes on her annual visit, she still feels anxious—but things are better now, she has begun to come just to be here with me. I like that. I like her enormously.'

'That's nice.'

'Yes, I like her visits very much, because there's a lot she likes to do—in fact, apart from this worrying about seeing me settled, she's an unusual mother, I think. She loves walking—I mean really walking—she reads a great deal—so, in fact, there's never a worry when she comes. In fact, I have often wondered why it has taken her so long to realize how and why I like the solitude that comes with the territory, so to speak—I obviously take after her—'

'What does she say?'

'She says that's different because she had known the—"other". And now has this—the quiet. The extreme solitude.'

'Yes, I can understand that.'

'About Anand, I mean, she's met him only once. She told me he'd not last. I laughed at her because he had only just come, not settled down at all. It was wrong to decide from that. But now I think about it, about what she said, and it does trouble me. Not a great deal, but I do watch him. I do think about him quite a lot.'

'Let's go to his cottage and take him for a walk, bring him back here, do you think we might?'

'Why not? He might even come. Seeing it's you—I think this door is done. It won't stick—I'm sure it won't. Also that silly squeak has gone. Wrap up.'

It was cold out—but very nice. They walked quickly. Anand's cottage was in darkness. They unlatched the gate and went in. It made an odd sound in the darkness.

'Anand, Anand,' they called out just in case. After a while they heard his voice. Disembodied.

'Here, I'm here, what is it? Who is it?'

He was at the far end of his garden, in the dark, near the hedge.

He seemed pleased to see them—only he also seemed odd, standing there in the dark, his cottage in darkness. 'Would you like to come, a short walk and back to my place, we'll have something by the fire? Come—do.'

'Yes, I'd like that, only I have to watch this hedge—it's about now that it happens—I can't leave now.'

'What happens? Is it prowlers? Jackals? What happens to the hedge Anand?'

'Something—I'm not sure yet. That's why I have to watch. I have to wait.'

About Anand

One day she told Mark, 'There's a bird that comes every day and picks away at that perfect Easter lily—every day, ever since it opened completely. I've watched for it—it leaves a single small feather in return. Judging from the feather it's a very small, very plain bird. I feel so angry because it's destroying something so perfect but I can't do anything about it—because I really do understand why the bird is so destructive, after all there's a whole garden of things to choose from, why this most perfect flower—so white with those slashes of scarlet just painted on and with such a beautiful name, amaryllis. The bird doesn't really need to eat it, does it? The bird can't become the lily. Jealousy. It's jealous—I suppose pecking away at it makes it look so much less perfect. Anyway, where do you think we ought to put the bird-bath? Mark, are you listening? Do you think near the old copper beech or don't you think the birds will come there? Do you know I saw one morning, very early, a jackal. Really, it was a jackal—and to come so near—I was worried for Judas 2. What could a jackal do to Judas 2? Or is it not a worry? I know so little. I must make a list of things for you—all the things I mean to ask you and tell you about—there's so much—I'm sorry, do I exhaust you with all my questions? Is it all a most frightful bore? But you can take your time, I mean go through the list as slowly as you like, you know, I'll keep adding things. All right? What would I do without you?'

'Oh, you'd manage. You'd manage very well. I can tell.'

'But I'm so glad you're here.'

'I'm glad too.'

'Is Anand all right? I dreamt about him last night. Sometimes—quite often—I worry about him, I'm not sure why.'

'I'm going to see him, would you come with me, let's look him up, all right? Let's go now. I made him take a week off. He looked tired. He looked terrible.'

'Yes, let's go now—very now.'

With a sense of strange urgency they left Old Cypress and walked quickly down the road to Anand's cottage. Even from the gates they could see Anand at the far end of his garden staring at something.

'Oh, Anand, what is it? What are you staring at? Tell me or tell Mark—what is it—what?'

'I can't see what's behind this hedge. It's a yew hedge and it's so dark and heavy it shouldn't be here, it belongs in the graveyard, I can't see beyond it and I have to if I'm to manage—'

'But Anand does it really trouble you, because then—'

'Yes, yes, of course, I think about it all the time, I don't like it, it's so tall—dense—it makes a darkness. I don't like that—the sun never comes through and it traps that terrible evening mist—and it keeps coming at me—all the time. It waits for me to get back from work and then it comes for me, the hedge comes and the mist comes. You don't believe me, come inside the house. It's there as well.'

They went with him into the little house—on the round dining table they found a place laid just for one—a meal uneaten—and in the bedroom a bed unslept in, and all the lights on.

'Look, there it is behind that cupboard and there under the bed and behind the bathroom door! Can you see it, can you smell it?'

Yes, yes, they said, and now we are here and so lie down and try to rest, we'll bring something to help—

'I don't want anything except to kill that hedge before it kills me, Ram Swaroop refuses to do it because he says it's old and beautiful, he refuses to cut it or cut it down, so I shall do it because I can't bear it, it's taken over my whole life and I can't see anything.

Even in the game sanctuary it was there.'

It's all right, they said, it's all right.

Mark went to fetch the doctor saying, 'Stay with Anand. Don't leave him alone, I'll be back as soon as I can, poor bastard.'

She made him lie down and sat with him and he talked and talked about that thing and loneliness and not being able to see the sun and now there was no sun it had killed the sun and was waiting to kill him but he would kill it first and would she help him, would she, would she and when, because they would have to hurry and had she got an axe they could start soon before the hedge killed him. He was sorry—he was sorry to be so much trouble to her and to Mark but he hadn't told anyone how awful things were—and it was terrible to be like this to feel like this—he didn't dare sleep in case it came for him while he was asleep, the hedge, that dark thing, would she please look out of the window and see if it had moved and thank you for staying with me—that time when she had come and they'd had tea with Mark—that long-ago time he had been so happy so pleased that she was coming to live here and so near him in Old Cypress but she'd taken so long to come—why had she taken so long? The hedge had grown and grown taller and taller and now she mustn't go away again, was she going? His mother didn't know—nobody knew—about his fear. He hadn't told his mother because she would have told his father he was a failure. His father would think he was a failure. She wouldn't, would she, tell his father? He wanted to know if she thought he was a failure, no good at anything? But he was afraid, really, up here in the silence and the loneliness he was afraid. He heard that hedge in the night and sometimes even in the day, could she heard it?

Try to rest, perturbed child, try, try.

You won't go away will you?

No. No.

He was afraid to close his eyes. It might come.

Didn't you like that little tea-party that long-ago time at Mark's?

So long ago—the sun never comes.

But it wasn't so long ago, perhaps it was. In soul time, in despair time it was a long, long time. Why she had been happy—she and

Rohan. Then. Odd. After seeing Old Cypress they had gone to Anand's cottage and then gone back to Mark's for tea. A warm room with a fire in the hearth and the curtains drawn and Velu as amazing as he had sounded when Mark had spoken about his prowess at scones. It had been a magical evening, the friendliness and the warmth and the scones and the smell of woodsmoke and the wonder that they had found Old Cypress and now it was theirs. But. There had been a hidden and dark thing. Not just that fear that Anand had—but. The fact that she hadn't known about Rohan's woman. And Rohan was hiding his dark secret, and Anand was hiding the terrible fears he had—hiding them from Mark and his mother and his father, so there they all were. Nobody knowing about anyone else. Nobody with intuition. How could she blame Mark for not realizing about Anand's deep, terrible fear? Each of them had had something to hide, something to pretend about. She herself, who had always prided herself on her awareness—her sensitive awareness about things—she had been proved the biggest fool of all. She had not been aware of the slightest hint of anything between Rohan and his 'chick'. They'd all been together in the firelight, friendly and warm, laughing and talking and together— or at any rate pretending so well—to be so happy together. So much for intuition, so much for good simulation. What worlds away—what worlds undone—and all less than six months ago. Not possible. Don't think. Don't think. Don't think about yourself. Think only about Anand. Hold his hand.

After what seemed hours she heard a car-door slam. She heard voices. Anand said, 'Don't go, don't leave me. I wish I was like Mark, he's not afraid of anything. He's alone and he's not afraid. Ever.'

'Don't think like that, it's just that you're not well. Soon you'll be fine. Now that the doctor has come. Everything will be fine. You'll see. I promise.'

'Are you ever frightened?' Yes, oh yes, often I am. But now we won't let you be alone, all right? All right. We'll all be together. Hang together. Please God let Anand get well again. Make him not be frightened. Let him find some light not darkness all the time. Let him make it. Please.

Flora and the Bird-Bath

Come on dog, old faithful, best friend, grow old along with me—
not yet though—why must you keep sitting near that crate, why
not one of the other ones? She came and sat down close to the
crate and watched Dog crouching even closer—what is it? What?
What are you watching, waiting for—ears very keen, hair bristling,
what? And then she saw what it was. A squirrel in the crate—a
very small face emerged through an opening, expression watchful,
disappeared again. Dog, even more watchful, sprang. Two paws
atop the crate quivering with the insult, barking. On the crate in
black paint she saw—'This Side Up—Handle With Care—Flora,
Bird-Bath'. That time with the dog sitting next to her she'd packed
them with great care and not expertise in old newspaper and soft
old clothes. Well, they'd have to come out now. Clever squirrel—
I'll do it today—now. Why on earth did I wait so long—because
my heart with rue was laden.

Once, long ago, Rohan and the child on a Saturday morning
disappeared not taking her—she had thought for a hair-cut or some
such thing. Appeared again having combed Chor Bazaar and found
these two. Dusty, cobwebby and perfect. 'Flora' they had instantly
named the first. A marvellous woman in marble with one great
wing and one most delicate hand holding a lily—broken lily but
clearly a lily—this most perfect woman set in an old heavy frame
out of which a lizard came startling them all—'It's for you Mom,
for your birthday, it's for when we have a garden, Mom.' Time—
God, that was years ago, the child now twenty-seven, then what?
Still little, still able to shout with excitement, still hug, still hold
one's hand. So what did one feel then, feel now? Rohan ever so
slightly embarrassed, shuffling his Saturday-chappalled feet, so
pleased at having found such perfect presents, knowing how pleased
I was, feeling so loving enabling me to express what I felt. That
was Flora. And then with a flourish—that golden, raining-gold
Saturday—emerged out of the boot of the car—'Close your eyes,
Mom, don't look don't look till we tell you'—Bird-bath—
perfection, pure genius for them to have found such treasure and
now she had a garden. Find the pliers, get on with things. Start.

Good old squirrel for making her realize it was time to start unpacking. My birthday came and went. All our birthdays came and went. A family. Find the pliers. When Rohan had finally told her about his 'chick' she'd said, 'Dog is mine he comes with me and Flora and the bird-bath.' 'Naturally—they're yours, after all—' He could have meant anything—tone-wise he'd never given much away. She had persisted, 'Would you like to keep Flora and I'll take the bird-bath?'

'Yes,' he had said abstractedly.

'Yes what—? Will you keep Flora?'

'No, no, I don't want her, for God's sake I don't want anything—'

'Except my life—except my life,' bitterly she thought now, and hoped she had said then. And now Flora and the bird-bath with its two perched, ready-to-fly birds. She would put them in the garden, near the far wall, and real birds would come to drink—at last. When did time pass? When did time happen? When?

Letter from Radha to Her Son

It's been a very long time since I wrote to you. But then I can't really remember when last I had word from you. When you were much younger you used to get rather embarrassed when your father and I quarrelled—we always did, quarrel I mean, but those were important quarrels. Necessary. I suppose what has happened now between us has made you feel you can't communicate with either of us—I do hope not for too long. And don't feel divided. I suppose what I really mean is, don't put it off for too long. I miss you. Especially now. I don't think sons should die before their parents. I mean children. A young boy, man, died in our hills and it has just happened and it has distressed me greatly, enough to make me write to you. I miss you and if you felt like visiting—it would not put too great a strain on either of us! Do you think? I know how busy you are, always. But. Permit me to use that old cliché. Life is short. I suppose a lot shorter than we think.

The boy was called Anand. I mean, the boy who died. He had a father, unlike yours, who pushed him into a way of life that was really impossible for him. He got lonelier and more and more lost. Then he became very ill. Now he is lost. He is lost to us. Us is Mark and me.

You might like to see Judas 2. Also what Flora looks like and the bird-bath—in a garden.

You don't have to come—but seeing as we were once quite good friends—why not?

Why not indeed! Ay, there's the rub. I shouldn't think your father would mind, in fact, knowing him, he'll be rather relieved somebody is checking on how I'm getting on—as long as it's not him!

Do come—if the spirit moves you—

There are some good walks—the weather's very nice when it's nice.

Very quiet.

Also there is in my back garden, near the tennis-court, a very old cypress.

Love, of course
Mama

Letter from a Dear Friend Who Wrote

This morning a letter—how could a friend know, exactly know, however dear, dear, dearest friend know enough to write: 'Loss, I think is an opaque pane of glass in a window, vista lost, but also, in direct contradiction, it is a winding pathway into the past— think you will, of course you will, but try, try my friend to stay buoyant—all the days, early days till now, where memories and Rohan whom you loved—love—cling like burrs. Just keep going, live ordinary days, slipping, sliding, ordinary days and you'll work it out. Bleak days for a long, long time—but remember why you are there in those hills you chose, and live. Live all you can. Soon.'

That's how the letter went and she read it several times and then folded it very carefully and tucked it into the pocket of her shirt. She went down the steps and into the garden and to the swing that Mark had set up for her—this was her own swing. She had told him that once on a journey to another hill station they had stopped at a small hotel just before the ghats began. While Rohan was busy filling up petrol and checking the water she had seen a little, bright, fussy playground. There was a slide with sand to land in, a see-saw, a miniature merry-go-round and, her best love, a swing. There were no children around and she had gone and sat on the swing with the lovely sense of how she would swing really high and then come rushing down with a familiar feel of fear in her stomach, when a man in a red and white uniform came up to her saying rudely and rather loudly, 'Perhaps you cannot read—see that notice over there.' She had left the swing feeling silly and sad and angry with the odd notice that hung on a railing. The notice said, 'Children Below The Age of 12 Years and Adults Above The Age Of 12—Strictly Not Allowed to Play.' Spoilers of fun she had thought and anyway what on earth did they mean? She'd gone back to the car and told Rohan about it, spoilers of fun she had told him, and he had said, 'For God's sake, act your age.' After a bit she'd stopped being angry with Rohan and the notice but she hadn't forgotten. That long-ago time. Standing in the garden one day she had told Mark about it and he'd said, 'Everyone needs to, wants to, has to, once in a lifetime have a swing of their own— and I know a perfect place for yours. Come and see if you agree.' And it was perfect, of course, between two of the trees quite close to the old wall in her front garden—so she had sun and she had shade and Mark had said she could read there or do nothing there because that's what good swings were for. It was a very good swing. She sat down and began to swing, first very gently kicking her feet but feeling the grass and then a little higher and higher and then really high with that wonderful feeling of fear and exhilaration in the pit of her stomach. 'And I ride'—yes I ride, she thought. Oh and I'm lucky, I'm really lucky, and I've just realized it, I've been stupid and selfish and a misery. Here I am swinging, sometimes so high I can see over the wall. And what do most people have as they grow older—what do they have for the vistas stretching ahead—I mean, as they grow older and older, not really needed by anyone in that very real sense any more, what? Living with their grown-up children—more than a little unwanted—facing a smaller and smaller space, trying to be unobtrusive, making oneself invisible, finally not even a room of their own, a part of a room—sharing and not wanted, baby-sitting in a flat, gazing out of a window or a bit of a balcony—one dusty potted plant and a teeny bit of sky—upwards a kite, a crow, a cloud and downwards people hurrying—people running-off-to-work, or back-from-work sounds. Apart. Not wanted—a bit of a bore if truth were told. And then the next stage and the next. I'm lucky, she almost shouted. I am. I have. A home. A garden. Trees. This swing. The sun. My limbs and the use of them. Sky. Old Cypress. And later, much much later, if it's a cane or a wheelchair, I can be everywhere still, not a bother to anyone. Worrying about help at lifts and stairs and at traffic lights. I'll be me and so near there'll be Mark (because he's going to live forever) he'll look in from time to time and see that all is well. Truly, this is the life. Freedom, and I don't and won't depend on anyone to be sad or happy. Me. And I have friends. And I am a friend to some. On my own terms. They like me. I like them. There'll always be books, there'll always be music. So it will all work out. The letter was really saying 'Hang in there' and I will, I am. Doing just that. So it doesn't matter about the old tennis-court, nobody will play there any more perhaps. But they did play there once. So it's a legacy. And if I hear the sounds of people playing in the dead hours of the night I'll not be afraid. I should be happy—they are happy sounds—people happy, calling out to each other, friendly, playing-tennis sort of sounds. I hear them. So they are calling out to me. Happily. They lived here. Now I live here. They are as important as I am. They don't resent me. And Old Cypress protects me, protects us all. Living, I must go now and tell Mark about this. He'll be busy but he'll understand that this is important. So I'll tell him. And he'll know. He'll know exactly what has happened.

Reply to a Letter from a Dear Friend Who Wrote

Dear friend you thought to write—thank you. You must know, of course, that I mean much more than thank you. Also, I could not write for so long, though I meant to and now I am. Writing, I mean. You wrote to me of loss—you wrote of memories that cling like burrs—of trying to remain buoyant. How did you know, how can you know so well? Thank you for knowing and for writing as you did. It is summer now. But then it was still autumn and a long bleak winter. It is over now, I mean the very cold and most of what went with it. Unpacking was bleak and lonely but my home has begun to seem lived in and Judas 2 has begun to have his favourite places in the sun and in the shade and close to the fire when I light it. Do I make it seem idyllic? It's because I leave out what's bad or sad or very bleak. Already we have a death. What's worst is the nights. No one to talk to when I can't sleep or wake in fear. No familiar person next to me in bed. Familiar hand, familiar comfort, silly old jokes, old habits. No one to share things with. Also there were strange sounds in the night from the tennis-court at the back and the tree that names my home never looked too friendly at night. But. It's summer now and the sun is so friendly and bits and pieces of the garden look ready for you to see. Why not come? If the spirit moves you. I mean it. The garden isn't quite what it will be soon but in a strange sort of way it has began to take shape, soon I shall feel a healthy, instinctive anger if anyone should steal a white hibiscus just opened (my side of the wall) because it's mine. I enjoyed planting it, so the rewards are mine. Also, I cannot bear to mow the lawn in one miraculous corner near the old wall because it's thick with daisies—I don't want to see their lopped, chopped heads flying—even if Ram Swaroop disapproves (he's my one-hour-a-day mali shared with Mark). So whatever the rules about manicured lawns—that corner is snowlike grass. I think my garden at best will be like a disciplined jungle, no, not jungle, a clearing in a forest. To rest, to breathe, to be at peace. Sometimes a white pigeon comes and drinks from the bird-bath—why not come?

Now I will learn the name of ferns and wild flowers and weeds. Now I will learn to recognize birds. Also their calls.

Now I will do many things.

I might bottle fruit. Bake bread. Make jams. I might. I might think about Anand. I might try to grieve less. Think about death less. Listen to music and not be sad.

It's odd though, it's not all gloom now as it used to be. Of course, sometimes, some days, it feels a bit bleak. The prospect before and after—but that might happen anyway. Sometimes I'm quite peaceful—peaceable—happy, like now. Quite content to look at the sun creeping over this wall and the difference it makes to the moss growing on it out of its old crevices. It glistens. Of course, sometimes when birds come to the bird-bath I do hear an excited voice calling out, 'It's for our garden, Mom, Pop found it, I—I helped him find it, it's for your birthday, Mom.' Well, that's natural too. Nothing really lasts. But it did. For a long time. So. That was the nature of our days.

Now this is the nature of my days.

'Sometimes it gets a wee bit lonely in these hills especially towards evening—but keep your eyes firmly fixed upwards—on the trees and the hills—you'll be all right then.'

I remember the woman who got into the train when it started to climb—that's what she said. She knew.

She said it like a warning—she said it like a benediction.

I try hard—sometimes I fail. Most times.

Because, well, because.

The poets say it best, remember that Carver fragment?

Fear of anxiety.
Fear of having to identify the
body of a dead friend.
Fear of running out of money.
Fear of confusion.
Fear of waking up to find you
gone.
Fear of death.
Fear of living too long.
Fear of death.
I've said that.

Pigeon

And as it had been a very cold winter, or rather she had been cold all winter, nothing would warm her. When she was invited to the conference and she realized she would be warm there, really warm in the sun, she said, yes, she would go. She would get away for a while and be in a place that was warm. She would store the warmth up for all the days to come. Yes, she said, even when a few cobwebs of doubt crept in. Yes, she said, brushing them aside and away and not naming them. Yes, I will go because quite soon I will be a spent force, quite soon they will not ask me any more, so this time, because it will be warm there, I will go. Yes, she decided, and started to pack.

She packed very neatly, very carefully, always. The sheaf of instructions had referred to the weather there—'During the duration of the conference the weather will be warm, sometimes hot. Because it will be summer. Our summer is warm. Sometimes thunderstorms occur. Then it will turn cold. Sometimes very cold. Delegates are therefore advised to pack accordingly.'

She had refused to believe the 'very cold' of the instructions but had compromised by packing her raincoat like a good, careful delegate. She was that. A good delegate to conferences, always had been. Never any trouble to anyone. Had always done her 'homework', always checked and counterchecked lists, made lists, checked maps, dictionaries, encyclopaedias, made more notes, consulted phrase books in the language of the place she was going to, underlined in red certain phrases, memorized important words, read up all sorts of information and prepared herself to meet what she would meet, see what she would see and sometimes prepare for the surprise of something not planned (this was rare). Anyway, the place she was to go to would then become very real to her before she got there—sometimes became rather less real to her while she was actually there—and then recede and be something that he had never participated in at all. She had, of course, always brought something back from the place: a shell, a bit of coral, a pressed leaf, a pine cone, a smooth pebble; once when the place had been particularly bleak, an ashtray from the hotel room. So many conferences, so many different places. She was always invited. She contributed. She participated. She went. The shell, the bit of coral, the pressed leaf, the pine cone, the smooth pebble, the ashtray, proved that she had been. She never knew why she was asked. In her field she was something of an expert. This only she knew. She spoke very little, listened a great deal. Perhaps this was why she was asked.

She finished packing as the voice from the inner room called out, 'You are packing. Well, and where to this time? Is it far or very far?'

She told him.

A day or two later she left.

In the aeroplane she read a guidebook she had found about the place, and turned to 'Museums and Art Galleries'.

Soon blankets were being handed to the passengers and little pillows, it was chilly, people were going to sleep. She read:

The Icon of the Self-existent Saviour from Anchiskhati: the sixth century centre section is the most ancient example of Georgian icon-painting. The embossed gold setting belongs to the latter half of the twelfth century and was created according to the inscription by the hands of Bek (Beka Opizari, the celebrated Georgian goldsmith).

The next page was about the Pectoral Cross of Queen Tamara, and then she came to what she was looking for:

The Icon of the Mother of God from Khakuli; this unique triptych was made in the first half of the twelfth century to frame the enamelled Icon of the Virgin which dates from the tenth century. The setting is embossed gold; the side-pieces are gilded silver, and the triptych is set with precious stones and enamel. It is 197 cm high and 202 cm wide when opened out.

The small reproduction was in black and white—compelling enough, though, to make her close the guidebook and close her eyes, and see it. The icon from Khakuli, the icon of the Mother of God, the icon she would soon see. 'Only connect'—the phrase came to her now—what was the connection and why had it come to her just now? Elm trees, birch trees, Howards End, what was the link, what was she trying to link together? 'Only connect'— connect what?

The icon made her feel odd, what was it? Khakuli, Anchiskhati, pectoral—not chest or breast. Why pectoral? Was it because only the face and the hands were dark, everything else white or what was it! Mother of God, self-existent Saviour, what did that mean? —how could anyone be self-existent? Why did the Mother of God look like that? Where was Khakuli? Was it a place, was it an old monastery, where was it? Why . . . Oh not now, she protested, go to sleep. She fell asleep. She woke up many times. Shifted her position. Smoked a cigarette. Closed her eyes.

And then it was time. She gathered her things. Herself. She moved. Down a ramp. Another country.

Then a hotel room. A bed, a lamp, a closed window. In the bathroom a notice—'Turn the tap indifferently to left or right'. Another country.

And the next day would be the first day. She did not really look at anyone on the first day of the conference, not even when all the delegates were formally introduced to each other. But she was aware of him. The conference unfolded like all the others she had attended, perhaps this one was more tedious because she seemed to be waiting for something. Also, it was warm. Very warm. Often oppressively so. Papers were read. Many papers. Questions were raised and some were answered. Discussions sometimes arose out of the papers read. There were the coffee-breaks. The lunch-breaks. The afternoon sessions. The tea-break. The short wrap-up session. Dinner. Coffee in the lounge. Good-night. And then to bed. And so from Monday to Friday. Five days of doing exactly the same thing. Of being rounded up. Herded together. A herd. 'My cries heave herds long huddle in a main', and why think of that just now? And then Saturday. The 'free day'. Not all that 'free'. Sightseeing. The no-work day. The day for being herded around in a different way. So far they had known to the minute the exact programme for the day, so that even after dinner in her room she daren't do anything adventurous, not even steal out of her room and down the stairs and out in case she wasn't ready or prepared for what was planned for the delegates.

The structured exactness from Monday to Friday. They all moved towards the door that said 'Out'. Even that was in four languages. So you couldn't cheat.

Anyway Saturday. The day for seeing what had not been seen. The elegant tour coach with deep, long windows and deep seats with comfortable armrests and high backs and a packet on each seat drew into the portico. Even the packet was not a surprise though. Inside was a guidebook and a map. A scratch pad and a pencil. The tour coach had a cheerful guide for the guided tour. 'Good morning, ladies and gentlemen! Today we will become good friends and you will see our beautiful city and its ancient environs, and become a friend also of our great city with its great heritage. As we drive out we will move into the avenue of first importance in our beautiful city. Observe on your left the spacious Town Hall, and on your right our spacious Prison. As we move on we will come to the Great Museum of our city. Here we will halt for forty-five minutes so that you may see and note all our great treasures of the past. You will see something of our ancient heritage. Though much has been stolen, much has been recovered and returned to its rightful place.'

The coach stopped.

'Now we will all get out and visit our Great Museum and return to our seats in forty-five minutes.'

They all got out and waited while the guide counted heads. Like a herd, she thought. We are actually being counted. I wonder if anyone's ever got lost, run away, screamed, shouted and jumped out of a window. Then they moved. All together because they were the right number, no one was missing, no one was hiding in the coach, crouching, refusing to come out. No one of the herd had to be prodded, poked, told to 'move along'.

They moved automatically, already counting the minutes, through the great gates, up the carpeted staircase, and then heads bent desperately to guidebooks, looking, counting, Gallery 1, Gallery 2, gallery after gallery. Would they make it back to the coach to be counted? Forty-five minutes, the guide had said, not sixty. Exactly forty-five, like a constitutional in an early novel—'Ah Miss Bennet, shall we take a turn in the garden? Nothing too strenuous, I do feel it is so good for one. Shall we turn at the next elm and return through the rose garden—a little walk not too long and just right, after a meal and before retiring, really sets one up—does it not?'

She realized she didn't have all that much time left for what she really wanted to see. When she reached 'Art Treasures' she found him there and the Icon. Both should not have come as such a surprise—perhaps she had not expected the lurch in the stomach because by now she was familiar, was she not, with the experience of seeing him every day, Monday through Friday? And the Mother of God Icon had to be there, and was, only it was different and the same.

He said, 'This is very special, is it not, this one? Do you know it through reproductions? Have you waited a long time to see it?' She nodded. She could not move. It was as the guidebook on the plane had told her, the bit about the jewels and the enamelling of gold also of silver, and the Mother of God wore white, her head was covered in white and the surrounding area was white and only the face and the hands were the colour of skin, ordinary human skin, skin and then the white of the cloth drawn over the shaven head of a widow. It was an unusual icon, very real, very sad, very human. A small woman in white with a knowledge about children, about her son. Two brown hands outstretched, reaching out, touching nothing.

A slammed door. An end.

It was time to get back to the coach. It was now taking them to the old city, out into the country, climbing gradually towards the mountains. And then the coach stopped—something seemed to have gone wrong with the engine and everyone piled out and stones were found for the rear wheels and then people stood around talking or just stood around feeling pleased at an extraordinary, unplanned halt and did not quite know what to do with this bonus. The sun was very warm overhead, some sat on boulders by the roadside and some stood in the shade of a tree and the man said to her, 'Shall we walk into that old field—we will know when the engine starts again—' And she went with him, crossing an old field with the earth in hard clods and mounds and weeds and old roots, and she counted six poppies and picked one. And then an old wall and then a kind of gate and then a barn—an old wooden barn leaning curiously sideways but intact with two old elm trees near the door and an upper window hanging half-open on its hinges. She sat down on a bit of a bench and he sat with her and said, 'Perhaps I do not have much time because that driver will soon mend the engine and we will all go back to the hotel and tomorrow back to wherever we came from.' She waited, twisting the poppy in her hands slowly. And he said, 'In the museum there was only one icon that was true. It is the only thing in the world that I would steal, to have, to possess, to keep, so that I could look at it when I wanted to, also because it is like you. She looks like you. She has a pale, drawn face. The skin is stretched tight over the cheekbones from the strain of knowing what is going to happen long before it has happened. She will not always be serene, she cannot be. She does not accept her destiny. So she is like this. She is like you.' It was the longest speech he had ever made. It was the longest she had ever heard about herself. It was so much and she wished she had watched his face as he made it.

She was still looking down and the stem of the poppy was all twisted in her hands. And there was a silence. And he said, 'If you were a vain woman it could be said that you were aware of how your cheekbones look at that angle with the light on them, and that was a reason for not saying anything. Or if you were an arrogant woman it could be said that you do not look at other people not even at someone who speaks to you, because they are not worth looking at. But you hear me. You can hear me and recognize what I am saying to you. Other people do not come into your thoughts very often, you are tired of them, you are tired of thinking about them, of having been absorbed by them, you choose not to allow that to happen any more. You are not vain, I think, and you are not arrogant. There is another reason, and your head is still looking down and that poppy will drop from your hands but you will not speak. You will not look up.' He waited. She waited, but knew that he had stopped and knew also that he would never speak like that again and knew that the moment was over and that she must live on it for a long time. After a long while or short, he said, 'I did not mean to interrupt our walk and your life so let us go back. It's time.'

A kind of wind had started up and the two bare elm trees sounded different in the wind and she could see that everything was the colour of ash, the wood of the old barn and the window swinging on its hinges and a bird flew out of the window and then another bird and she, startled, called out, looked up. And he said, 'So it is birds that you allow, that you accept.' And she said, 'I have a great many pigeons in my backyard. They are mine, I have had them for many years. They are mine.' He said, 'Why pigeons?' And she said, 'Cats do not care at all and one might make the mistake of caring for them, and dogs care too much so it becomes difficult in my life because I go and I come and when I go—' she stopped because she did not know why she was telling him all this, she did not want to share with him what a dog did when you started packing a suitcase or what a dog revealed when you came back. And he said, 'Go on.' 'But birds may care or may not, they will not show you, they will eat and sleep and fly just the same when you are there and when you leave and when you come back again, there is no burden of anxiety, on either side. Do you know what I mean?'

He said, 'I know what you mean.'

And she said, 'Every year, once a year, I read Jane Austen. Birds are like that—clear, clean, controlled. To fly is to be precise. The way pigeons fly down for grain, the way they pause, their poise even when in pain. Balance, poise.' She stopped again because she realized she was talking not only about pigeons or Jane Austen but about a need in herself. The wind quickened and a small rain started and she thought, we must hurry back, this is summer rain and I have packed a raincoat, but it is in the hotel room and soon it will turn very cold, that is what the instructions told us. 'Our summer is warm, sometimes very warm. But sometimes there is rain. Then it will turn cold. Sometimes very cold.' We must go back quickly, she thought, and they did. The next day she left.

When she got back the voice from the inner room said, 'You have come back.' 'Yes,' she said and unpacked. The poppy from the field had fallen by the old barn so she had nothing this time to prove that she had been. Nothing to go with the shell, the bit of coral, the pressed leaf, the pine cone, the smooth pebble, the ashtray. Just as well, she thought.

A week after she got back she got a parcel—the message said, 'I could not steal the "white" icon. I am sending you two pigeons. Perhaps they will outlive us both.'

She put the two grey pigeons with her other pigeons in the backyard. She looked after them and looked at them. They were quite different from the others. Quite separate. She did not want to think about the message—she had thought she would forget.

One day she got up and went, still in her night-clothes, to the backyard. It was a definite, decisive movement and moment. She knew exactly what she was doing and did it. She took one of the grey pigeons in her hands and stroked his feathers and then neatly wrung his neck. And then she took the second pigeon and did the same thing to her. They had never been given names, just 'pigeon'. And now she would forget.

Allegra

Letter 1
Allegra to Her Mother

Mama, by now you must know what has happened. He must have told you. Perhaps the hospital has. Mama, you know me well, you know me best, you know my way of trying to explain my need, to make my need clear mostly through an indirect way— Miss Williams taught us that a long time ago, 'Through indirection direction find.'

Mama, if a marriage fails, in so many communities, in so many religions, the woman returns to her home, to her own parents. I think it is the most humane thing, don't you? I mean, if a marriage is failing, perhaps even before it really has ended, it's far better. Except in one religion or perhaps two. Then a life is so distorted, put through so much pain and humiliation. I can never forget Fatima. Mama, you remember Fatima in school and all she went through?—she lived in the same house to which her husband brought home another wife—you can't have forgotten—how she shrank at her own shadow—she was made to feel so ashamed? The failure, I realized then, is always the wife, she is always the victim. She always has to remain in her husband's house—under the same roof. She has to suffer and or wrestle with her demons of anger and outrage and sadness in the public gaze. She must allow the newcomer into the house, she must, by her presence, cause her husband to be constantly reminded of a shared past. The bed their centre of things said, of things done. It is unnatural. The West is much better at handling this unnatural burden. The woman is freed.

She goes her own way and tries to make something of her life, of herself. Is not made to feel every breathing moment that she is a miserable failure because one man found her wanting. Why should she have to remain in that house? Even if she hides and crouches and makes herself a shadow, however shadowy her outline, she must still have her own distinctive smell and sound and feel.

Mama, I ramble because I am not writing this letter to you but calling it out, saying it, pleading it, and my kind Mordred is taking it all down without a murmur because she is truly kind and because she believes this is very good for me—to have so much to say and to want to say it. Therapeutic, no doubt, the first victory won. I shall now get better. My mind at least is intact. And that is true. Alas! My nurse is patient. She does not say she is tired, so could we stop and start again tomorrow? She knows perhaps that I have no other way to beweep my outcast state. And that is my state, whichever way you look at it. Outcast, I lie on this surgical bed, cannot see much or move, or feel. I really cannot. Mama, move at all. And this is why there are so many more hours in my day–night to think. Bear with me. All the earlier bit and thoughts of Fatima must not make you think the very worst—that my husband has already abandoned me. Far from it. My husband has not—not yet—stopped liking me or loving me. But this must change—and it will change—quite soon, to resentment. How can he see me day after day like this? Just now he is possibly still in a state of shock, but that will wear off. When that happens he will realize what has really happened. And then his life will stretch out before him—he will see years and bloody years of me unable to do anything. And he will be so hideously reminded, so graphically reminded that he can walk, stand, sit, lie down, get up. Run if he wants, bend. He is untouched. Mama, he has been told that I will never walk again. Or run or stand. I will not climb trees. And later, when I am much better, or rather the best that I will ever be, I will be carried to a wheelchair and carried back to bed.

Now that's all said. I am assuming that you know what happened. That ordinary day. The day it happened. He was driving the car. No matter what the doctors tell him, or the specialists tell him, no matter what the nurses or I tell him, no matter what his reason tells him, he feels that by that one basic fact—or truth—he is damned forever. He was at the wheel. I was not. He was driving. I was not. I was badly hurt. Am badly hurt. He is unhurt. So guilt, Mama. Guilt, that worst of all cankers. Guilt will dominate his relationship with me.

Just now this guilt makes him so gentle, makes him so very tender—as if I will entirely break if he touches me. He moves from this bed and goes to the window—to draw the curtains, he tells me—and he stays there looking out and I hear Mordred saying, 'There, there, sir, you mustn't, don't fret yourself, you'll need all your strength to help the wee lass!' And she must say so because he cries bitterly at the window, staring out at the rain. Bleakness. But soon it will be impossible, and not just for him. Just now it is as desperate for him as it is for me, but soon it will be different. First it will be resentment, the round his life millstone, and won't that become hate or something worse? He could throw away photographs, letters, he could change everything around in our home, banish memories along with mementos slowly, slowly. But with me here all the time—his life ruled by hospital hours day after day and then month after month—he will change, he must. Mama, I am his guilt—and we are neither of us saints or even unusual, extraordinary people. And I—soon, when the pain is less, the other pain will begin.

As I said, not being a saint or a martyr I will soon start to blame him, will I not? Hate him, hate him for the things he still can do and I cannot. I am, after all, the result of what happened and though he did not mean it to happen, I am the result. He can choose a book from the bookshelf, he can make love or not, he can choose. Mama, he can choose to do nothing at all if the spirit so moves—and I will not ever do these things. Those silly nuns, I can hear them still, 'Never say cannot; never say can't; nothing is impossible; it's just that you are stubborn and won't try.' I wonder what they would say now if they saw me. They were talking about me always failing in maths, what would they berate me with now? I cannot do anything on my own. And when I am better, the best I will ever be is I will lie when carried to bed, I will sit when carried to my wheelchair, I will be wheeled in my chair and then learn to wheel myself. That will be the extent of my recovery. Mama, help me to leave here as soon as I can. Help me to not be here for too long. While there still is a great deal of caring and love and being in love, help me to leave before I am left.

And you are not to blame him when you grieve about this thing that has happened to me.

No matter what he thinks, no matter what he has written to you, he did not do this. A freak thing. No blood. No breaking. No wound that shows. Not then—not now. Not a single crushed bone. Nothing. A freak, a wonder, a horror, a jolt, a sudden halt, has caused this rack I am on now. Rack. How medieval, what shades and degrees of torture hath caused so dire, so grievous, so moral a ceasing up. Such a consequence. Such an absurdity on a warm sunny day—'How can an infant die in spring when butterflies are on the wing—warm-something,' I can't remember. And such a sky— Mama, that's all we did. It was a warm day, a really warm day after such a winter, it was nearly hot like home and it was a holiday. Everyone got out, how could anyone stay indoors on such a day? We didn't. We drove and drove on the main road and then off it and into one of those tucked-away country lanes and into a field. All of it a cliché. All of it out of travel posters for Spain, for Italy, for the South of France. Except it was England. A few miles out of London—well quite close to Stonehenge—I suppose that means a few hours out of London, I remember thinking how the scale was different. Stonehenge somehow, when you read about it or think about it or see photographs of it . . . And then we came to this bylane, country lane and this field and parked the car, and I, huge, as they say, with child, lay on this warm grass and stared upwards and thought of the skies of home and that lucky ol' sun with nothing to do 'cept roll round heaven all day', and I remember thinking about Stonehenge, Tess and about the Easter Island Gods and whether the scale would be different there as well and then I went to sleep.

There is no such thing as premonition, I mean, that day there was nothing. Nothing at all. It was still warm when I woke up, the sky was still blue, the grass still warm and all was well, it felt well, and we found a place with some chairs out under trees and we had sandwiches and beer and we set off for home. Mama, the something that happened, happened then. I don't mean just then but after a while on the main highway. We were talking and we were not talking and somewhere on that road it happened.

I feel suddenly very tired, so tired, and a bit frightened. So I will stop now going back, backwards. I will write to you again tomorrow. My nurse says 'Yes, of course, tomorrow', she must be so tired too of writing all this for me. Isn't she kind? I mean she could have shown in so many ways that she would not write all this for me, not day after bloody day. I like her very much. I like her name. She must have an unusual mother as I have. Her mother named her Mordred, not because she had wanted a son but because she liked the name, because she loved the story of King Arthur and never understood why you shouldn't name children as you pleased. Often Mordred's aunts and uncles call her Maudie for short because they don't understand her having the name she has, also, some of them never could understand why Mordred did all that he did do. Anyway, I like it, don't you? I have told Mordred that you, my mother, have something in common with hers. You, after all, did name me Allegra. Enough for now. Next time I will tell you— tomorrow I will ask Mordred to write about that road. I will finish. Soon. Allegra.

Letter 2
Allegra to Her Mother

Mama, I have not written to you for several days or for a long time. Mordred says this does not matter, soon I will want to again, not to fret about it. I have wanted to and have not been able. But today I awoke from a dream about our home, I mean real home, our home on the island. I was crying a lot in the dream. I thought I would be crying when I awoke. I was not. There was so much movement, the trees near the shrubbery and the special tree— Mama, you have watched me and trees so often—climbing up them, higher and higher, you passing up things for my tree house and you often watching me jump. I have flung myself into water, learnt handstands in the garden—remember? And then whenever we went to the beach—oh you remember that, don't you Mama? Mama, are you listening? Often you worried while you watched, was it that you thought I might hurt myself, damage myself? You were anxious, perhaps you wondered if all that activity was seemly in a girl? But nothing untoward happened, did it? All those years nothing wrong happened. To my body. Nothing, not so much as a sprained ankle. All that violent jumping and diving and falling. So why now? A tiny odd movement/moment/displacement—of a second. How in a second, or less of time could my body not be ready/braced/braced and ready, for that jolt or bolt that came? That is all. And that is everything. They say that's all it takes. A tiny second and a displacement of the spine. And it is my spine that I never ever thought about, took for granted, thought would last forever. Mordred, who always tells the truth, says that there is no possibility of putting right what has happened to my spine. No way to repair, no repairing my only spine. The others say things less definite. For instance, they say the wonder is that I can lie. Do they mean that I can lie and do lie and stare and stare upwards? Or do they mean the wonder is that I am not dead? Soon, they say, offering me so much, I will be able to sit in a special chair and then even be able to work it myself, the chair. When I have learnt, or unlearnt, a great deal, they say, I will be ready to leave. Soon, they say. When is soon? I ask them when soon will come. I am not being impossible and I do not ask them for anything but an approximate idea of soon. They say soon. Only Mordred tells me something through inversion. She says to try not to fret—she tells me that it is now July.

Meantime, I lie here in this bed in this room in this hospital. They come to wash me, to change me, to eau de cologne me, to powder me. 'No bedsores,' they say. 'We can't have that on top of everything else,' they say. I can feel nothing. They change my sheets. Often. What a luxury it was at home, every Saturday. I can feel nothing. To be more accurate Mama, nothing below the waist—it's all waste below the waist. Now there it is, said aloud, and written down by Mordred.

But my having said it does not mean that I have in any way accepted it. Not yet, because it is too enormous a thing to grasp. Also that jolt did not impair my mind, not at all. So memory and all stay with me to curse me, to remind, to keep everything very near, very intense, still. Everything seems to have happened just to me and near me or around me—it has not happened to other people, to anyone else. When we read about earthquakes, volcanic eruptions, about floods, fires, typhoons, tidal waves, hurricanes, there is somehow, even in the news photographs that we see, a feeling that people huddle together—children and their parents, or a dog or cat or goat or teddy bear, pots and pans, a rocking chair; there seems a togetherness, a huddling togetherness which must help somewhat. I mean it is not utterly alone like a drowning, a suicide. Mama, do you know what I mean? This thing that has happened—it seems to me that something so shattering could not happen to just one person. It would have felt, I think, less unbearable, less cold, less absolute, less lonely, if it had happened to at least one other person. We could have swapped news for one thing! No, I mean this, I could then have shared a sameness with someone. I would not be so separate. I am quite quite separate. I am like no one. I am outcast. I am an outcast. 'I cannot trouble deaf heaven with my bootless cries.' Sometimes I hear the peculiar sounds that only pigeons make. Mama, you know the sound I mean? A moaning. No, that is not the word for the sound—sounds—that they make.

Really I do hear it, or them. I wonder where they are or where the sound—sounds—are coming from. The sound is so real, the sound is so sad, the sound is so much in pain, in travail. Is that not a real word, like no other, Mama? Travail, travail, and Mordred comes to me, comes close to my bed and tells me not to weep. Not to weep. I did not know that I was crying. I did not know that the sound of moaning was me.

This letter goes back to the beginning. Help me to come back home, Mama. If you told them that that is what you want, it would help them to make up their minds about allowing me to make the journey.

They say the journey is too long. They say I cannot yet make such a long journey, so far, the way I am. Mama, tell them my roots need rain. Mama, tell them that Time will only be my friend if I can come back to the first place, the island. Tell them. Tell them that when the journey is over I could stay in the hospital on the hill. The War Memorial Hospital overlooking the cemetery. The fine old hospital where you had me, where Papa died. You could tell them about the hospital, how it has always been there, almost all your life and mine almost entirely, tell them it is our view from nearly all our windows. Tell them that there I will look out of a window at the sea and the other islands. Tell them about the windows that look out to help wounded soldiers get well, to help sick people get well, help dying people to forget. Tell them. Write to them. You tell them of our island. Tell them that there I will breathe again, look again and see. I will see the sea. Here it will not happen. Here there is a wall.

Not the whitewashed walls of our island, Mama, but a real wall—a dark wall. There is a dark, dusty sort of creeper on the wall trying to reach the top of the wall. The rain rains on it. The rain rains on this wall and this wall is the only thing outside my window. It is all I can see.

Now that I can be carried to my chair near the window this is what I can see. When the rain rains on this wall it looks even darker, it drips and drips, this wall. When the wall is wet it looks dark, when it stops raining it drips, this wall is never dry, I do not know how this dark wall looks when the sun shines on it. The sun has not shone on it since I was brought to this room. Of course, the sun has risen each day and gone down each evening but it has not shone, not given any warmth, since the day of the drive into the country when it happened. Mordred says, 'All you see is the wall, what about the cherry tree?'

I say, 'What about the cherry tree, Mordred? What cherry tree?'

And Mordred says, 'There, see, there you go again, selecting what you see, what you want to see, deciding that there is only a dark wall and a dusty creeper, shutting out the rest, really removing it, like in a photograph you cut out the bit you don't want, the bit you don't want to remember, you're doing a real cut-and-paste job.'

Mordred is rather more firm with me now. Often quite stern, does not allow too much moping. 'Dredging it all up, not much future in that,' she says. But she has never ever said the one thing that would make me hate her in spite of all she has done for me, been to me.

If she had even once said, 'Pull yourself together.'

She hasn't.

I like her. You would like her.

But I have been thinking about the term she uses, Mama. 'Dredging —dredging it all up!' How does one stop that, after all it's all going to keep coming back, what else is there except the past? All of one's life is there, the present is within these four walls and that dark wall outside the window. Perhaps when I come back to the island and to you there will be other things to think about. Of course Mordred has started to read to me but it is still difficult for me and for her. Music is impossible. Almost all the music I long to hear makes me unbearably sad, really sad. Mordred says, 'We'll wait—don't fret yourself, soon you will listen again, it won't run away, it's constant, it needs time.'

So you see really, if my mind were blank, really blank just now, blanked out completely, for a few months say, I might heal better or start to heal, concentrate without interruption, on getting better. Now I keep thinking of lost lines, bits and pieces of things read, music heard, colours I have seen—have worn—the touch of things, touch of people, longings, yearnings. I want to come home, Mama.

I want other walls.

I want walls that shine with blinding whiteness.

I want whitewashed walls shining because the sun shines on them. Where creepers get to the top always, somehow, and then down the other side of the wall—always.

Tell them—write to them. Tell them I must come home. Tell them that home is our island. Tell them and they will believe you, they will listen to you because you are whole.

Because you are not maimed, not broken, not wasted from the waist down. Because you are my mother.

They must and will listen to you. I promise after this one thing I will try never to ask you for such a difficult thing. Never.

After the first shock of seeing me as I am I promise that I will not be a further burden to you. The War Memorial Hospital will look after me. You need not see me. Or see me only when you wish to, want to, need to, whatever. 'Selfish to the very end,' you will think. Will you? Mama, sometimes I have a very bad dream. Two dreams really. The one runs into the other. I want to tell you about it/them. They recur. They are really one dream. Mordred says to stop now. I will.

I will tell you the next time Mordred and I write to you.

Please write to them again and again. Please.

Allegra, waiting.

Letter 3
Allegra to Her Mother

Mama, I had a dream and then I had another one, do you remember, I mentioned them when I wrote—spoke—to you last, do you remember? Well, I must tell you because they keep coming back— they become one dream—and I am frightened. Mordred says I can now try and tell you. That I should tell you now. Because Mordred thinks about things very carefully. I trust her and will try.

There is this lonely stretch of beach and I am walking on it and the beach is familiar, it is our bit of beach and there is a dog playing in the sand, really playing, as a child would play, rolling over and over in the sand and lying in the sand and kicking it about and quite oblivious to everything around—there is just the dog and his joy in that warm sand. And suddenly, dreadfully and horribly, two wild dogs rush from behind that strange formation of four great rocks and furze (you know it) and fling themselves on that playing, unaware dog and I watch, I am unable to move, it is so near and I am so frightened, so horrified, I can't move even though I can see, almost feel, what they are doing to the dog. They hurl themselves on him and it is so dreadfully planned, they must have been watching him playing in the sand, watching from behind those four great rocks, and known exactly what they were going to do. And they knew how they were going to do it. Mama, I have to try and tell you most carefully about it otherwise this dream may never leave me free again, ever.

From behind those four great rocks that rise out of the sand that you and I have always known, suddenly two wild dogs rushed, raced and pounced on the dog who was playing in the sand, playing more happily than a child. It happened swiftly, with a furious planned swiftness yet I saw his terrible fear before he disappeared. Felt it. There was nothing of him for seconds, except little sounds from him and dreadful sounds from them, and sand everywhere, furious, kicked sand and one of them was at his throat and mouth clutching there and clinging, even being dragged for a bit, but not letting go and the other tormented and bit the dog, now his back, now his paws, and then his stomach and he tried and tried to break free from those brutish two and little sounds were coming from him still and he tried and tried not to die and the little sounds were not coming any more and the sand stopped flying and their great growling also stopped and only then did they glance at me before they went back to the four great rocks. And I had not moved—I had watched, I had wanted to move forward, rush forward and if I had they might have let go of him and run but I was afraid, my distress for the dog, my fear for the dog, my hate for those brutes, did not make me do anything. I was so afraid and they were such snarling, brutish, bullying, killer dogs, and I did nothing and they knew my fear of them was larger than my love and pity for the playing dog in the sand, for the dog playing in the sand.

They knew my cowardice. They knew me. And I knew that caring, even desperate caring, does not help. It is impotent. I was impotent. Mama, you have guessed by now that this is not just a dream. It happened that long-ago day to you and me. You cannot have forgotten. We are walking along our stretch of beach and we watched that little dog playing in the sand, and when those two came at him you picked up a bit of brushwood/driftwood and went for those wild things. You rushed and yelled at them, thinking only of the poor, hounded, harried-to-death dog and the terrible, uneven struggle. You did not allow your knowledge of the two brutes, and what they might do to you, to stop you. I was there, Mama. We were together, Mama, and you know that I stood there, I did not move, could not move. Remember? Remember you waited for just a second or two but when you knew that they were too much, too horribly much for the dog, you rushed forward. You yelled, you shouted and went for them.

With that bit of brushwood/driftwood you ran to help. You must have been afraid too. They were, after all, wild and fierce, unknown dogs with no rules in their fighting. They were killers and you were going to thwart them. You went. And I stood there. That day you must have realized something about me, about myself. I did not move. You rushed forward. Do the same now. Please. Please, Mama.

The days do not contain this dream. The days have reading and being read to. You taught me to read. I mean really to read. You said that never ever was there a substitute for it, never a vacuum, never a loneliness that couldn't be dealt with. Learn to read, you said, devour what you read, learn that it is second to nothing, to nothing, you said. But it is a reminder, Mama; it is memory Mama, it cannot be erased, it is one's most inmost being. And what you started Miss Williams carried on. Perhaps it was all for this eventuality, perhaps you both knew this was what was going to happen to me so I would need something to fill loneliness; make loneliness. Miss Williams and the year of the Sonnets—bits and snatches—things I had not remembered in years come back now— 'When I consider everything that grows/Holds in perfection but a little moment'—oh, I know this leads nowhere. I will stop. I will stop before Mordred says I must.

Stop before Mordred says, 'Don't fret yourself.'

Or before Mordred says—or before she says—

I will write to you. You will write to me and you will write to them. Soon. Allegra.

Letter 4
Allegra to Her Mother

Mordred asks me about Miss Williams. She wants to know about her. Mama, do you remember Miss Williams? The English teacher? The last two years at school? My English teacher. I think of her a lot. Just now I think of her a lot. Do you remember her? I feel sure that you do. I remember you once said I was very lucky, you said what a difference it made to have at least one real teacher in one's life, and if this happened when one was ready for it, then it mattered for all the rest of one's life, it changed everything, one was never ever the same, and how terrible for the children that it didn't happen to; it had happened to you but only for a very short time. You had got married, just when everything was beginning. You got married. But you told me, and often, that Venice was your real teacher, that that was where you learnt most things that mattered for all of your life and that you realized it at the time. You had needed to go back there but had sensed even then that you never would. And you did not. You could not. Venice had to last you. Did it, Mama? Did it last you? Do you have it still?

But what was I saying? What was I trying to tell you? Yes, about Miss Williams, that I have been thinking of her a great deal just now. There we were, our group, our gang in our school uniforms, our ankle socks, our flat shoes. The year of *The Merchant of Venice*, of *Hamlet*. The year of such excitement, such newness. Such a lot seemed happening for the first time, we couldn't name it, we felt it, we all felt it, I mean our group, but it must have been Miss Williams. This newness we expressed in such ridiculous ways, we were so silly. We had no other way, not yet, not then, not that first term with her. We'd pounce on each other in the locker rooms hot and sweaty after games, tired after gym or netball or whatever, shouting, 'Well met, well met on the Rialto.' We were in love with 'pray you' and 'prithee sweet' and 'by my troth' and 'it well becomes' and 'betimes' and 'beseems' and 'behoves' and 'sweetings'. We loved these new words, this new terminology. We loved Miss Williams. 'Rest, rest perturbed spirit,' we would say when we were tired, when we were sad, when we did not understand our anxieties.

She opened up so much for us and we could not tell her, could not express our gratitude to her. We learnt early that the people who mean the most to us might never be thanked. All we ever did or said was, 'Rest, rest perturbed spirit,' or 'Leave her to heaven,' showing off, quoting madly, inappropriately, wildly, hoping she would notice, doing our best term papers for her, only for her, hoping she would realize how much she meant to us, hoping she thought we were special too—to her—and that all this wouldn't end, would just go on and on. But the last term of all came and with it the best and the last. She came into class and said, 'Yes, now I think you are ready to meet the man behind the mask, behind all the masks.' And she started the Sonnets with us.

After that, glimmerings of torment, shadowy dark ladies, and bits and pieces of *Hamlet* would come to disturb and sadden—'It's bitter cold and I am sick at heart'—we did not, we could not understand and we did, we did not understand and yet we must have had glimmerings, and that's why she must never forget, or almost always remember—

Ruin hath taught me thus ruminate,
That Time will come and take my love away.
This thought is as a death, which cannot choose.
But weep to have that which it fears to lose.

And now when I ask what is outside my window and my nurse says 'nothing', then I know that she means—
'That time of year thou mayst in me behold
When yellow leaves, or none, or few, do hang'—
And I think of you, Mama, and I think of the Sonnets and I think of Miss Williams and I think such long long thoughts. I must come home. I would like to find her. Now that might be another reason you might suggest to my doctors, you might tell them or rather suggest to them that it could prove important to their patient, to your daughter, that she find her long-lost English teacher, that she find her and thank her, because at the time she hadn't done that, she had meant to really, but had not known how to, but that now she would be able to, given the chance, and this the doctors

could and should realize the importance of. Mama, you do see, don't you? Were we not fortunate to have had Miss Williams? I mean, we might so easily have never met her, might so easily have had Mrs E for English those last two years—always reducing everything to grammar and spelling and punctuation and scansion. It was luck, luck, it is luck, isn't it? So much is luck, who you meet, who you don't meet and then whether you meet them at the right time or not, who smiles across a room, who says just the thing you need to hear. So much is luck. Why, I might not have had you for my mother.

And you might think but you would not say—or you for a daughter.

But it was Miss Williams I was telling you about, or trying to, and the way she looked to us as she taught us, thin she was, strands of greying hair always escaping from a bun low on the nape of her neck. Do you remember, Mama, that year, how I was trying to grow my hair again? Well, it was to try and get it to look like hers. You must have wondered because it was so inconvenient in terms of the rest of our lives—all that swimming and tennis and netball and that sudden craze for our version of baseball. Steel-rimmed spectacles, the only teacher who came to school on a bicycle—we waited anxious, peering, till her familiar cycle came through the gates. She would get off and wheel it in—and I can hear the familiar grating sound on the gravel of the driveway—then fix the chain to the wheel, then take out her books for the day from the wicker-basket carrier, 'the sun on her arms and her arms full of books'— neat legs, neat skirt—walk up the steps and she was ours. That awful feeling when she didn't come. Was she late, or was she sick? When did we realize we loved her? For a long time I suppose we loved what she taught us, she telling us what we wanted and needed to learn and hear and share that year. How did she know? How do you always know? I mean you, Mama?

But when did we realize we loved her? I don't think we ever told her. I don't think we ever thanked her. I mean really thanked. What doors she opened, what thoughts she made us aware of, the colours, the shapes, the sounds, the seasons, the changes. All the things we were close to and closed to she taught us to be aware of,

The Quiet of the Birds

things taken for granted she made us see again, feel again—and everything through what she told us, taught us, the connections she made us make. Really, that whole period, how can it have been just a year or a year and a bit, everything was different! Everything was changed for us—utterly.

Once she said, once she curiously emphasized, 'Through indirection direction find.' I mean it was there all the time, there in the text but she kept bringing us back to it or extending it or—oh, I don't know—I suppose making us feel its importance in all sorts of ways. Only connect. I remember that that whole year those of us who took 'needlework' rather than 'cooking' had Miss Williams as a bonus—bliss really—hateful needlework, pricked fingers and blood and ink mess on our chaste altar-cloths. I mean, this is what we were learning to embroider till we were demoted to ordinary tray-cloths and tea-cloths and aprons with boring chain-stitch and feather-stitch instead of what the nuns liked most—'shadow-stitch'. This period in the day was transformed by Miss Williams because she read to us while we stitched away and pricked away. The nuns had told us that our English teacher would read to us 'uplifting' work, words that would move us and stir us. Thank God, it was Miss Williams because she chose *Villette*—and how we loved, and how we suffered. We were not in love, any of us, with anyone, but we were all Lucy. And because we were Lucy we loved and we suffered silently. With Miss Williams reading to us we listened and we wept, on those dreadful tea-cosy covers and tray-cloths we wept and waited; we felt demure, we felt intensely, we were loyal. And because Miss Williams had chosen to read *Villette*, I mean chosen it rather than what the nuns probably had in mind, we naturally decided that Miss Williams had a long-ago love and that she too had suffered and wept and waited. She too was Lucy. For a long, long time after that, autumn would hold a kind of desperation and we would think of that term, of Miss Williams sitting very quietly, head bent over an old, green-leather, gold-tooled *Villette*, and all of us heads bent over the leaves and flowers we had somehow managed to embroider, and all that was contained—held— in the sound of her voice reading, reading what we wanted to hear, what we could not bear to—

It is autumn—
The sun passes the equinox; the days shorten, the leaves grow
sere; but—he is coming. Frosts appear at night; November
has sent his fogs in advance; the wind takes its autumn moan;
but—he is coming.

What happened to Miss Williams, I wonder? I remember after we
left school we couldn't bear the thought of her teaching other girls,
sharing things—the same things—with them and of course assumed
that she would miss us because we did so much. I mean, miss her.
She did say to us, 'Look me up—now don't forget—come.' But we
were shy to, did not want to impose, thought that perhaps she
said it to all her school-leaving girls and we did not look her up.
We did not forget, but we did not go. I wonder what happened to
Miss Williams. Mama, do you think you could ask at the school?
Do you think you could find out for me? I would like to know. I
would like to be sure that she was—is—all right. The nuns would
know.

Mordred now allows me to sit up quite long spells. She helped
me to write some of this letter—actually to write, I mean, not like
all the other letters which I spoke to her. She says that now every
day, if I want to, I may be allowed to. The doctors say it's all right.
Not too long, but for a while, every day.

Do you remember that old record we had, or have, it must still
be with the others, about September? It's odd to hear it after such
a while—Mordred hums it and sometimes sings snatches of it; do
you remember it? Something about the leaves turn gold when you
reach September and I haven't got time for the waiting game but
these few precious days I would spend with you, these precious
days I would spend with you—do you remember? Remember? An
old 78?

There is a wall outside my window. I told you about it. It is the
same room. But, here outside the window, my window there is a
cherry tree. In May, Mordred told me, it was thick with blossom,
pink and pale, pale pink-white blossom. In May I came to this
room. This hospital room with 'this bed my centre'. I asked her
then what she could see from the window, asked her, and she told

me that the cherry tree was waiting for me to look at it, covered as it was with flowers. I am at the window now in my new 'centre', my very special wheelchair, and the cherry tree is there, but it did not wait for me. It is quite bare. It is time to come home. It is time.

Write to me. Please.

Find Miss Williams. Or find out about her. Please, Mama.

Allegra

Letter 5
Allegra to Her Mother

Mama—you have not asked and I am grateful. But I also realize you must, Mama, want to know about my husband. I have not spoken of him for a long time. I will now, and then not again, all right?

You remember what I wrote about him and what I felt was sure to happen, I mean about guilt? Well, I mean, it more or less worked out like that—don't imagine just because I felt it would that it hurt less. But really guilt is worse, truly much worse, than any other form of punishment. And it's a funny thing, Mama, but I was made to feel as guilty as he was feeling. The lying there, day after day, for him, was such torture and pain and sadness—and then it began to change. You can't miss that kind of change on a familiar face, on a beloved face. I mean, the way you can see it on a face when someone is beginning to love you, there's no mistaking that—it's there. And it's as surely not there when it's gone and something else replaces it. Pity—resentment—disgust—loathing, yes, even loathing. My God Mama, that is something not to be borne. I did not have to bear that when there was all the rest to bear, did I? He could not bear the sight of me. He could not bear to see me each morning made so carefully ready for display, sponged like an infant, powdered, cologned, pretty nightgown, hair tied back—yes, neatly—and by one particularly enterprising nurse, even ribboned!

That would be the morning visiting hour. His coming in, my being made ready for this hopeless event. His leaving. My being left. And the evening visiting hour exactly the same. Except that it was longer. Except that it was evening.

And this day after day then week after week and then a month and then two months; May became June and June became whatever comes after and by now, of course, there were some very slight changes for him to get used to. For instance some light relief—now, for part of the visit, I would not be lying in the surgical bed but be sitting in my surgical chair, and he could wheel me to the window and we could both look out of the window or he could look out of the window, and I could look at him. Or I could look out of the window and he could look at me. There was so much he and I could do—now that we didn't, or couldn't, seem able to talk; converse with each other any more. Anyway, when I looked out I would see the dark wall—the one I have told you about, there is no other—and he—I think he must have seen the unendingness of his life stretching before him bleakly with me like that wall always there. Clearly, unlike Mordred, somehow he did not seem to see the cherry tree that she always saw and spoke of. One evening something snapped. It was an evening like any other. No more dreary, no more hopeless.

It was the same—the window, the wall, me in my wheelchair. The same. And I said:

'Please, tomorrow, don't come to see me. Please don't come in the morning or in the evening. It is always going to be like this. No better. No different. Please don't come.'

And he said, 'Only tomorrow or not ever again?'

And I said, 'Not ever again,' though I had not thought of saying that before.

And he said, 'All right.'

And he has not come again.

Mama—if the child had lived. I do not say if only the child had lived.

There is a difference.

So this is the best.

I mean this is how it happened. Exactly.

The Quiet of the Birds

I wish it had happened differently—
I wish he had surprised me—
I wish he had said—
I wish—
I know—if wishes were horses—
I need a letter from you.
Write to me.

Mordred must think something out all this. Must wonder. She has never spoken of it. One day she might. I am still got ready each visiting hour. Morning and evening.

P.S. We never really give enough credit to young Browning with his yellow gloves and his courage, imagine saying to a crippled older woman, and not just saying it but meaning it—

'Grow old along with me!
The best is yet to be—'
My love to you
Allegra

Mordred to Allegra's Mother

Ma'am,

This letter is very difficult for me to write and I know the suffering it will cause you. You will forgive me for the way I write and the content of this letter when you recognize in some small measure what your daughter is living through and grieving for. Truly.

Your daughter was to have had a child in less than a month when the accident happened. Her doctors fought very hard to save both lives. The travail—there is no other word, Ma'am, to convey the torment and pain your daughter went through—I have been a nurse for a long time, and I have seen much in that time. It was a desperate labour and a terrible birth—death. The child was a girl.

Your daughter will not regain the use of her lower limbs and her body is still so traumatized that it cannot be medically stated yet whether she will lose even more. The extreme damage to her spinal cord paralysed everything below the waist.

That she has borne all this, or rather, that she has survived all this, is a miracle, and Ma'am I am not a believing, church-going person. It is a miracle, but there is no hope, no question of offering hope about her regaining the use of her lower limbs. It would be wrong to offer such hope, you will forgive my bluntness. It is my medical bluntness. Her doctors know that I am writing to you, and they write to you whenever you write to them, asking them about your daughter.

It is five months since the accident, we do our utmost for her; but our utmost now only means we try to make her as comfortable as possible. As free of pain as possible. But the comfort is so cold, so minimal, that I must again write bluntly. If she were a dearly loved animal I would not have hesitated about putting her to sleep, putting her out of her extreme suffering.

Her grief she shows without realizing it. She speaks very little—in the beginning not at all. But, gradually—through the letters she speaks to you and this is very important to her, and for her—there is an easing, however slight.

It is unusual to look after and try to bring solace to someone who has withdrawn so completely. There is so little we can do. I suppose if we were priests or nuns we would feel less ashamed. We have not their confidence, or their indifference. I realize, Ma'am, that I am expressing myself clumsily.

I do not agree with her doctors who are of the opinion that your daughter should remain here under their care and my care, in this hospital, in this country, because the accident occurred her. I do not agree with them and they know that now. I have made it clear to them and they told me I could write you about my 'medical-psychological-human opinion' since I have had much closer contact with the 'patient' than they have. Also, now it is over five months, and there is nothing to gain for her here any more and much to lose. No operation, no further therapy, can help regain the use of what she has lost so why should she be here? She must be where she wants and needs to be. Not here. We can prepare her for the long journey. All the mechanical/technical/marginal preparations necessary we will manage, and teach her much that is necessary for her to learn for the rest of her life.

I ask you to help her. Help her to return.

You have the right to feel that it is not for me to write as I have done. I have grown to care, to respect and to love your daughter, and to understand some of her fears and needs.

She wants to go home. She needs you and so you must help her.

I remain,

Sincerely,

Mordred

Mother to Allegra

I think, Allegra, it is now the time to tell you about Venice and not just because you have told me so much, but of late I have thought that only something unusual, a grief, a parting, a separation, a death, a crisis, makes people talk—I mean really talk, really tell each other the things that matter; they never seem able to do it otherwise and it's such a pity because so much time is lost, and who was ever given enough time, anyway?

Relations, relationships, most of them working in a vacuum or at cross-purposes, so much unsaid and so little said in a whole lifetime. Oh, of course, sometimes, but very rarely, it's seemingly perfect (a drink helps!) and the moment is perfect but a drink ends and it's all worlds away again. I remember, Allegra, there was just such a charming moment in a play when this very young girl introduces herself to her new governess by giving her a book saying, 'Here's the book that explains me.' I do wish we all had a book like that, to give to people who mattered—matter. A book that really explained one, told one, shared one. Think Allegra, how simple things would be, it would all be there in the book, everything—every blessed little or big thing. I would not have had to wait so long to know how much Miss Williams meant to you and how deeply; and then mostly it's too late—I mean how many people have a crisis or whatever, so that they can speak, can tell, can ask, can share what's deepest, dearest? And you might never have asked about me and Venice. So Venice. The 'book that explains me'—mostly, partly.

I will at least try. Make of it what you will.

Suddenly I get cold feet.

Plunge.

Remember Allegra I was seventeen.

And now turn the page.

I am going to start with your favourite sentence as a little girl—
'Once upon a time . . .'

I will tell you about the island I came to, or rather was brought to.

It was very far from my home. I think that is why your father took me first to Venice for our honeymoon. To prepare me, I think he felt, to learn about how far I was going to be taken, and how cut-off I would be and what water was going to feel like and what an island would feel like. For all these reasons, I think, he took me to Venice. I say I think this was the reason because you know he never did explain very much except he did once go rather far, that is for him, in explaining that there were many more cheerful islands, actual islands, real islands, that is, 'a piece of land completely surrounded by water' kind of island, but he felt I would learn a great deal more from this unusual place to help me later on. I trusted him, of course.

There was no one else and I was very young. He was right—if not for the same reasons—still, right and wise. Venice was an initiation into many things. It was my first knowledge of my husband—in that sense my sexual initiation (what an awful term!) and my first exposure to a hundred other things, undreamt of. Like what? Like light, like shade, like water, like pigeons, like mosaic, like fresco, like silence in the afternoons, like bridges over canals, like water, like church bells far and church bells near, and little islands with huge churches on them and dark cool interiors of churches and water lapping and water dappled on old walls and slime on old walls and huge squares suddenly and light and dark canals with dark water and openness upwards but strange, still, claustrophobic walled gardens, old palaces, canal walls, footsteps on cobble-stones, sun on cobble-stones, the dark shine of ages on cobble-stones, little windows and no light and large dark canvases of paintings in interiors of no light, or little light, showing huge wings of angels with bad news or good, and dark spires of cypress trees and light through olive leaves and deep reds of gowns of kneeling women and men with dark heads and faraway hills with the menace of clouds ready, ready for something to happen and the frames of these huge paintings, dark, carved, gilded, hanging wood, downwards frames, heavy with stories, with textures.

Where I come from, where I had lived till now, I had never seen or felt such things before. And it all came in this way to me in Venice, on my honeymoon, away from known life, away from the only people I have ever known and loved. And I was now with someone in Venice and alone. I say alone, because I really did not know your father, I only knew he was from a faraway island and that after our time in Venice we would go, he and I, to that faraway island. I did try and ask my mother about when I would see her and my father again but she did not tell me except to say, 'Soon— soon, we will be together—soon.' And because I did not want to think about it too much, I mean about separation and distance and about how all this was suddenly happening to me I put it off, I switched off, I let myself think, 'Another time is beginning and they will keep; they will wait for me. They will not change. I will not change.' There had to be another time, of course, or I could not have borne the sense of loss I felt. So I made myself believe this and that is how I came to be in Venice—very young, alone, and with someone who was now my husband. And I could not ask him either about all these things that troubled me, how could I? I think your generation is very lucky—I think you ask all the time, you demand to know, you are not tentative and shy with the people you know or love. You ask, you are bolder than we were, than I was. You would have asked, you would not have let it worry and trouble you and cause you the agony it did me. If only I had asked from the very beginning, 'Why am I being married so soon?'; and/ or 'Why am I being married to someone I do not know?'; and/or 'Why am I going so far away when you know it is so far?'; and/or 'What is being married?'; and/or 'Are you not apprehensive about this marriage, about this stranger from a faraway island that you are marrying me to?' I tried to ask but needed help and I thought I would be disappointing them by asking, would be making them unhappy by asking, because these were not just questions—were they? They were a pleading for my life, a pleading that things should not change just yet, and I was afraid that my asking would sound as if I did not trust them with what they were doing, and that it would seem as if they did not mind my going away, that they did not care that much any more. You see, Allegra, how young I was? I was young enough to consider love and care and trust and security in those terms. I did not ask. Anyway, being very young my sadness was extreme, I thought it would not pass, would not change. I felt in terms of melodrama, I suppose, I thought I would never see my mother again, that I would never see my father again and that it was forever. As it happens, happened, it was. I never did see them again. It was my mother, you remember, who had said, 'Soon, soon we will be together again, as we were, soon.' You are quite right, Allegra, to allow yourself to be wary of that word, to allow yourself to worry about that most evasive of words. After I had lived on that faraway island for a long while I met so many, many women who told me that they had never seen their parents again once they had left home—after that very long journey—and really, it was very long in those days. You must realize, it was usually a complete break. And letters, the only lifeline, took such a long long long while. These women told me how, often, a parent would be ill in one letter and be dead long before they got the next. Letters were longed for and letters were dreaded in almost equal measure. But, Allegra, it was Venice I was telling you about, was it not? So I will start again. I mean go on from where I stopped about Venice. The food, Allegra, it read so beautifully on a menu, just an ordinary meal. I found an old '*menu del giorno*' in my letter case:

Antipasto; Giuliane di sedani n maionese, sardine, prosciutto
cotto burro olive
Maltagliati alla sorrentina
Suprema di tacchino dorato oppure
Costata di manzo ai ferra
Patate mignonette
Zucchini trifolate
Formaggio o dolce
Frutta

We had come by water to this unusual place—the sun shone on the water and Venice seemed to emerge out of the water. It was magic. I was bewitched. The menu I copied out for you was to make you realize how charmed I was, how I must have preserved just an ordinary menu to help me later with the sound of it and the colour of it: that *tacchino* was turkey and *prosciutto* was ham and *zucchini* was baby marrow, and that when I wanted beans I should remember to say *fagioli* and not *fragole* or I'd get strawberries instead. Yes, Allegra, it was charming, day after day, with vegetables that sounded like fruit and fruit that sounded like flowers and we ate at little tables under striped awning, sometimes close to a curved bridge over a canal or in a square dominated by the facade of a church and sometimes a priest going by or a flight of sudden pigeons and the wines such lovely colours and the bread, I loved the bread.

And then the weather changed. One day the sun did not shine.

Venice is different when the sun does not shine. Venice is another place. I suppose all places are different when the sun stops shining but when it happens to Venice it is very strange, very dramatic. A complete change of stage set, of colour, of music, of atmosphere. It deepens, it becomes shrouded, it becomes death-like. Mists and vapours rise out of the waters and stone changes and the shape of the prow of the gondola changes, and the curve of the bridge over the canals changes; everything stops feeling familiar and the sounds of the great bell coming from San Marco feels as though it is coming from a far island and the grain that is thrown to feed the pigeons lies wetly and even the wings of the pigeons sound different and you feel that the piles that this city is built on might sink and disappear and the strange way it came to be built becomes believable for the first time, where before it was just facts in the tourist guidebooks. I became fearful and filled with dread. I felt that now this strange city of water could slip back into water, that this city built upon the mudbanks of the lagoon with canals instead of roads, this city of the Oriental, the Gothic and the Renaissance everything, would quietly sink back, drown, and the water would cover it over. I learnt much in this changed season. I think I do not need, really, to spell out all the things I learnt—but I think the main thing I learnt was how tenuous most things were, how light and shade and space could all change, how a mood could come and go, how joy was short-lived and sorrow rather longer, how inarticulate most emotions would always be and that perhaps that is why there is painting, that is why there is music, that is why there is the written word, and great architecture and sculpture, because human beings could never—would never—be able to communicate through the spoken word—at least not the things that mattered most deeply or most truly. And so only by looking and seeing, by listening and hearing, by watching, by silence, by not clutching, by not yearning for the needed words, any ache would gradually heal.

I know now that this was why your father chose Venice rather than a more cheerful island—look how quickly I learnt, how richly I learnt from my teacher.

Venice, and then this very different Venice with no sun and only rain and mist, gradually filled me with less dread, with less intense foreboding. We stayed in a very quiet pension and though its entrance looked out on water and an island with a large church, our windows looked down on a small walled garden, tranquil and overgrown with tangled grass and weeds and wild flowers. Against the moss-covered wall were two cherry trees and an old gnarled apple tree. A little before dusk a woman would come and sit in this garden; she would sit close to an old stone bird-bath. No birds ever came. I grew to depend on this garden. I was like the woman who sat there each evening.

Then one day the sun came back.

We crossed the water to that small island with the large church. The church was empty, but for a woman, quiet in black. And someone was playing *Jesu joy of man's desiring*.

You know now why you have an odd name. I am tired of so much remembering. You must be too. I wish you were with me. Soon.

Mother to Allegra

And you progress, my Allegra, do you not? I too am writing again to you, because it's time now to carry on from where I stopped last time in Venice.

The month was over and we boarded the ship for my husband's home, his island. I think during the long sea voyage I still felt that I was going on a visit to a strange place, I felt that Venice was where I now truly belonged and that now I was just going to pay a visit, going to a temporary residence. I would be a visitor—one who visits. And I had such a long time to think because in those days the voyage took us through so many waters, seas, oceans. After Aden and Ceylon more seas and more oceans. Sometimes great stretches of water. Sometimes a single seagull would rest for a while on the rail of the deck, as white as the furrow the ship made, and I would think of my pigeons in Venice, and mostly the sea was calm and the sky was calm and I would sit in a deckchair while day followed day. It seemed a suspended time and I seemed also to be in a suspended half-dream or half-real state, unable to distinguish what had ended or what was about to begin. I think that's when I found a dictionary in the ship's library and I looked up the word 'visit'. I felt that its meaning would explain my state of feeling strangely suspended. Allegra, this is what I found. I had copied it out and it was with that old menu, remember, and some photographs:

> *Visit* v go, come, to see (person, place etc.) esp as act of friendship or social ceremony: stay with or at; (Bible) punish, avenge (upon) afflict (n) call on person or at place, temporary residence; occasion on going to doctor etc. for treatment, doctor's professional call. (n) (esp) migratory bird as temporarily frequenting place etc.

Strange word I thought, that starts fairly simply, innocuously— friends and friendship—becomes a little ominous—visitation, doctor, punish, avenge, migratory bird. We are at fault if we overstep the boundaries. I had made a visit to Venice and I presumed that the visit had not only changed me somewhat or utterly and irrevocably, but I had assumed or been presumptuous enough to believe that the people, persons, person, place, encountered on that visit—the women in the walled garden, the women in the church, the waters, the smells, the sudden disturbed lizard, the Bellinis and Tiepolos, the pigeons—all these things, all of them, were also changed utterly because we had met, encountered, come across, blundered upon, chanced upon, visited.

And when I sat in my deckchair now, or when I walked the decks and stared at the unending sea, I think I began to realize that this was only one of the many delusions; things to prop up my own need for a sense of permanence in impermanence—just one more delusion. Imagine thinking, or really believing, that we change other people or rather that we make a change or cause a difference in—to—other people when we encounter them. I had changed nothing—no one. I thought a great deal about my mother and my father. I wondered if they thought of me, and what they thought. I am glad that they did not know my thoughts. At eighteen I had these thoughts. At eighteen I thought I knew how we change nothing or rather so very little as to be of no significance in other people's lives, as in a landscape that remains the same, no impress at all. The grass when you get up from lying on it, the footprint in a muddy land—all will seem untouched in just a little while and that is why to live very near the sea is to be able to learn this truth much quicker. I remember your father, who spoke to me less and less, said this once—'The sea is so far, the sea is so always there.' The sea goes out and the sea comes in and it will always do this whether you are there or not. And no matter how elaborate or beautiful the castle of sand you build is, there is nothing to protect it from the sea; to think that the sea will not destroy it because it is yours, because you built it, is vanity. Just the print of your foot in sand reminds you of your own mortality. Oh, Allegra, I'm sorry to go on like this—I talk so little to anyone that it's sheer luxury to talk to you—but as I was saying the ship, the ship was taking me away from somewhere to somewhere else and if this voyage, this journey, was long and strange and lonely I remember wondering what that other voyage must have been like for those who had gone before to the island, herded and crowded in the holds of ships, airless, a hundred years ago, like cargo, like horses—to fight in fields of mud and slush, far from things familiar—or like Africans in chains to fields of cotton or tobacco; except these went to fields of sugarcane. And with one thing binding them all: thoughts of home, thoughts of fear of the unknown, sickness, homesickness, a kind of petrified stoic fear ruling everything. They say, Allegra, that there is a great difference between slavery and indentured labour and of course the ones who can make these fine distinctions and even tell you all about how vastly different bonded labour is have never seen these things or allowed themselves to think too deeply about the implications. But some might see, or rather feel, areas of closeness. All three imply a binding, a bond, a written contract. An agreement binding an apprentice to work for a master; then the being transported thousands of miles away from known things to an alien land, an alien people, an alien landscape, food and sky; always the sense of great distance, the knowledge of miles and miles of sea separating the unknown from the known; the panic and the stricken understanding that you may never ever go back and you did not choose this, no element of choice entered this contract, this bond, this agreement; but it bound you all the same. You and your kind—forever. Allegra, I thought these thoughts and many others and I listened to the talk of people in the lounge and in the dining room and in the library and in deckchairs and walking the decks and often the talk would be about this island and its past, its history and its mystery; its chiefs and its beauty and fire-walking and Methodist churches and beaches and seas and its coral and its fields of sugarcane and its great trees and flowers and fruit and its people. What about its people, what were they like and what did they look like? And what would we be in their midst? What were we to them or they to us? The island was theirs, the land was theirs and we were not going there on a visit. Those others—years and years ago—had not gone on a visit or for pleasure. They were taken there. To work. Bonded, branded. And now I really knew this, I mean, now I was truly alarmed and felt it was not just facts and figures or encyclopedia sort of quick information, but real. Real lives—lives of real people—generations of people, compelled because of history, to live in a certain way. Forced out of one context—dislocated, changed, removed—for other people's greed and trapped. I suppose all this must get rather boring, Allegra, but I do so want to try and recapture it all for you, most carefully, what I felt then, and all that that voyage out meant. Also, of course, you did ask me, didn't you? And I have never been asked about how I saw this rather unique experience, how I felt about it all; so now it's all coming untidily, spilling out like this. Anyway, I can't see or feel you yawn! Then there came days when I felt dreadfully sick all the time and the only food I could manage was green, sourish apples and jelly—and the jelly came in lovely colours, some of the colours I have not seen since, I mean in a jelly. A kind of green and a kind of purply-black with lights inside. Sometimes the sea was very rough and lots of people used, suddenly, to leave the dining room. I did too. Sometimes the sea was as smooth as silk and I would still feel most terribly sick and it was jelly and green apples and the ship's doctor said, 'Yes, my dear, it's a baby on the way, not a shadow of a doubt—' So I was told I was to have a baby. That baby was you, Allegra.

The decks would be swabbed wetly and the missionary couple would ask how I was feeling 'dear girl' and the ship was taking me from somewhere to somewhere else and I was not ready for anything. And we reached Perth. Many people left the ship there. We did not. Others did not. The missionary couple did not. They were going where we were going. They didn't seem afraid. Of course, they had prayer. They prayed quite a lot.

Sometimes when I walked round and round the deck I would come upon them kneeling, heads bent, close together. On the bare boards of the deck.

Mother to Allegra

Allegra, you asked me in your last letter to enquire about your English teacher, Miss Williams. I went to your school. I spoke to Mother Superior. She is the same—older, of course—and the fear you felt when you were older, you would still feel. In that way she has not changed. Her amazing glass-blue eyes are the same—no kindness has reached them even now. I think she would still force you to eat meat and stand watching you, crying and afraid. She still has a fierce limp, she still has that cane to help her limp and to help her rule with fear. Lilies, that special beeswaxy smell, lacy bits and pieces, a high polish to that wonderful floor, sacred pierced hearts everywhere, silence, the feel of a lower order of nun waiting behind a door or a little side chapel waiting for an order or just waiting in case there was something she would have to do: speak to the gardener about cabbage or the carpenter about the west door that creaked during prayers or ordering fresh candles for St Jude. Allegra, do you remember when you first encountered Rumer Godden? I remember how I loved you, specially whenever you liked or loved a writer that I liked or loved. Anyway, I went to ask about Miss Williams. I waited in that little anteroom just outside. I think that's one of her little 'to-create-fear' strategies as well. I was, I must confess, a bit fearful waiting for her to see me, realizing how sick with fear you used to be waiting to see her every time you failed in maths. She kept me waiting. She had no one with her. When I was finally allowed to go into her room she did not look as though she had been praying. She just looked like someone who enjoyed a bit of power. She had for years and years, after all, kept little girls and older girls in fear in that anteroom and their parents as well, I daresay. She must be at least seventy years old but looks—looked—like an SS officer of about fifty-five in her white, starched, nuns' medieval garb with the same dreadful—beautiful—ice eyes.

'I understand you wished to see me about a former member of our teaching staff?'

'Yes,' I said, 'Miss Williams, the senior school literature teacher.'

'Why?' she says. 'Why would you wish to know about her?'

'Because my daughter, Allegra, asked me most particularly to find out if she was well.'

'Really, how extraordinary, and why specially Miss Williams, and after all these years?'

'I understand she was an extraordinary teacher and my daughter is most anxious to find out how she is.'

'You intrigue me,' she says, 'I mean the term you use, as though there was something remarkable about Miss Williams.'

'There was something remarkable about her, did you not realize? She was greatly loved besides.'

'Realize, remarkable, loved. No. Not till you used these terms to describe her.'

I said rather rashly, 'Did you really not have an awareness of what a remarkable teacher you had in your school, or rather, have? She must still be here. Still teaching?'

To which this cold woman, nun, Mother Superior says, 'Remarkable—in what way—remarkable?'

I felt at this stage that she would never, anyway, have realized, sensed, known anything at all about the quality of mind or heart or scholarship or love of subject, of her 'lay' staff member, so I let it pass. But I did ask her if she herself taught. She said, 'Oh yes, of course, we are a teaching order.' I did not ask her what she taught. I cannot pretend to have cared enough to ask. About Miss Williams she said that when she had reached the age of retirement she had been asked to leave, she had hoped for an extension but their religious order did not believe in changing the rules for lay teachers. I asked her how long nuns went on teaching and she said she did not have the time, really, to discuss their policies.

'Someone in the office outside might have Miss Williams's address.' A bell rang. She got up. I got up. That was a room I was glad to leave. And that was a woman I was glad I would not have to meet again. Ever.

I realized after I got home that she had not asked why you, after all these years, had wanted to know about Miss Williams. She had not asked about you, what you were doing, where you were—nothing. Nothing at all. Not even formally—as a principal of a school where a child had grown into a young person. More than ten years and she had no curiosity. I am sorry, Allegra, that all those years you were in an institution, in the uglier sense of the word. I did realize, but also, I did not. We didn't really have the choice on the island and I did not want to send you far away and have you only for the holidays. So I thought, or rather hoped, it would work out in the end or in the balance—that you would have the awful and the good. I know that when you were little you were very sad in that school, you would come back somehow burdened with sadness and a kind of dread about the next day and the next, till the joy of Saturday afternoon transformed you and you were so happy Sunday morning and all the way to after lunch—and then you were different again because of Mondays. I thought it was all that hateful arithmetic and then algebra and geometry and failing in these subjects and being made to feel stupid all the time about them. And then when you began to be good at sports and had your small group of friends I thought, hurray, now it will be all right; now will come the good times and I was right because then came Miss Williams. And she was your 'good times'! Anyway, all this comes to me because I thought about your Mother Superior and about how cold she was, I mean apart from everything else. I could not very easily get rid of the feel of her. I realize that I felt a sense of dread somehow, as though she had destroyed something. She coloured the day. My day. I felt that perhaps it was something to do with Miss Williams. She could not hurt you any more. Or me. So I went to the address given to me by the school office. I went to look for someone precious to you. Someone precious to anyone who truly encountered her. Someone I wished I'd had. And I thought now I might because you asked me to, and then because of that Mother Superior and what she had said, or perhaps what she had not said. I think she resented Miss Williams. I think she was deeply jealous of that kind of person and her gift, of her special gift of love and understanding of all that she read and the way she could impart it and share and teach. Of course, this must have made her feel great guilt. They aren't supposed to feel anything overmuch, are they—nuns, I mean? Not love, not hate, not pain, not grief, not tenderness. So when they encounter these things in others or in themselves it's terrible. I think your Mother Superior was jealous, was envious of Miss Williams. Also, of course she recognized, she recognized, I think, what Miss Williams was and what she herself could never be. Most of us live wanting to be like some aspect of another person, and we desire this in lesser or greater degree. The way a person looks or is, oh, all sorts of things, like your own beloved Sonnets. You remember when he says, 'Desiring this man's art, and that man's scope,' remember? How does it go? Oh, Allegra, it's from the same sonnet that that dreadful line you used in your letter comes from, you wrote—

I all alone beweep my outcast state.
And trouble deaf heaven with my bootless cries,

And look upon myself, and curse my fate,
Wishing me like to one more rich in hope,
Featured like him, like him with friends possest,
Desiring this man's art, and that man's scope,
With what I most enjoy contented least.

Anyway, I'm sorry, Allegra, to go on about that wretched Mother Superior instead of Miss Williams. It just shows, though, how people like that can really upset one; I mean they too linger. I wish you were here with me. And you will be. Soon. I'm sorry I used a word you dislike at the moment. Soon. But I really do mean it, in its most hopeful sense—in a short time, not long after the present or a specific time—early, quickly. I'm going to stop now, writing I mean. In a little while I will again. Please thank Mordred from me for being with you. Thank her from me for being there. I will write to her and not just because she troubled to write as she did to me. Thank her please, Allegra.

Your mother

Mother to Mordred

Dear Mordred,

I know you would want to know what happened to Allegra—and why she has stopped replying to your letters. She loves you—I know that very well. After she got here she seemed to adjust—I say seemed. She joyed in her old room, looking over the waters to the other islands and spent most of the day in her wheelchair in the garden. One day her old teacher, Miss Williams, came to see her and after that came nearly every day—they spent hours talking and reading together. But one day Miss Williams spoke to me about how unhappy Allegra was. Deeply unhappy. Also, she had asked to see the undersea kingdom that she had seen so often when she was a girl. Allegra became rather persistent about this so one day Miss Williams took her in one of those glass-bottomed boats we have in Fiji to view the coral and the fish.

Long after it was dark I realized that they would not come back. They did not come back. I do not think it was an accident. I only hope that before it happened Allegra saw the coral branches and the wonderful coloured fish and flowers of those deep clear waters.

I know that Allegra could not bear to live. But that is not the same thing as wanting to be dead. I hope she was not afraid. I think Miss Williams knew what Allegra wanted. I think Miss Williams was a very brave woman.

I think of all the hours of hope and care and love you gave Allegra in that London hospital room with the wall outside with no sun on it. I think of you with gratitude.

I think of my life and all that we invest in our children. I am quite alone now and wonder sometimes why they did not ask me to come with them in that boat to view the coral and the kingdom under the waves. I too would then not have come home to this empty house and my long memories.

You know, Mordred, this island I live on has so many hazards—snakes in the garden of Eden. When Allegra was about five there was a very destructive hurricane with a charming unlikely name like Elsie or Lucy, and I grabbed Allegra and we lay huddled together under the huge dining table and the roof above our heads was lifted clear off the house and great trees were uprooted and the sounds we heard above the sound of the hurricane were the singing voices of the Fijian women and girls, they have wonderful voices and they sang harmony and counterpoint for over eight hours. When we crawled out we were all right and we never found the place where our roof had landed—maybe some faraway field of watermelon or beach with bleached driftwood. Another time we were at a picnic on a white secluded beach and we swam and played all day long and collected some beautiful coral—like twigs, like a lad's slender, long fingers. It was just us and another group of four people. Late evening as we were packing to leave—the huge sun ready to set—a great scream started and never stopped and we saw a huge black wave, a last wave which seemed to have nothing to do with that gentle day by the sea, come out of that tranquil still water and those four people were gone.

Oh yes, Mordred, on this island paradise there is death by water and death by wind and death calling with voices from a clear underwater garden. And no traces left. No wheelchair and certainly no copy of Shakespeare's Sonnets open at beweeping one's outcast state.

But a child should outlive a parent—even in a world of unequal justice. I am much alone. Perhaps you would write to me. I would then have a great deal to look forward to.

Thanking you again most warmly,

Allegra's mother

Album

We were three, that is, before she came. It was a nice feeling. Just the three of us. My mother, my father and me. For a long time it was like that. I was not spoilt by them. Being an only child this might have happened. It did not happen, I think, because of two rather important qualities my parents had. The one was that they conveyed a great deal of affection and warmth and care without being demonstrative at all. I do not remember any kissing and hugging, but always, somehow, love. The other quality, and I really do mean that word, was a regard for work. Both my parents worked very hard so there didn't seem to be all that time spent on what I observed in some other families—spoiling. I had presents on birthdays. Story-time came at bedtime, the oiling of hair on Sundays. I had my own room, I had to put my toys and books away at bedtime—only the teddy bear given to me by my father was allowed to sit on my bed, always. I seemed to have loved my uneventful life, it was so stable, it was so ordered. It was happy. It was us three. Her coming was something of an event. For a long time before she actually came everything seemed to change in our home. My father came home from work a little earlier and did not go on long tours. We now had an ayah. My mother was not so busy all the time—she seemed to spend a lot of time sitting in a chair in the garden, she walked much more slowly and our family doctor came more often. I felt a great sense of unease. An old pram came out of the storeroom and was freshly painted. My old cradle was refurbished with new netting and soft bolsters and a mattress. It was a time of fearful anxiety. I started to bite my nails again. My whole world seemed shaken, seemed changed. I thought I could not bear what was going to happen. No one had prepared me for the change. The ayah would talk about how nice it was going to be for me to have a brother or a sister. Very subtly, my room seemed to be different. Sometimes when I got back from school my mother would not be in her chair in the garden and I would find her resting in a darkened bedroom.

One day after school I went to my mother and said I did not like all the changes that were happening in our home. I told her that I was afraid. I said I was really very afraid. And my mother said I was not to be afraid, that I was not to worry, that just now it all seemed strange, she said even she was often frightened but that once the baby came everything would be all right again. And she said I had a very special place in the family because I had come first and so I would be able to help the new baby. And I remember saying, 'But what if the new baby is a girl?' and my mother, who was always wise, realized what I was really worried about, and said, 'But that will be so nice, she will be like you, and you will share so many things with her, and you will teach her so much, and you will look after her because you are older. And you must always protect her—see that she doesn't fall down and hurt herself, rock her pram when she is crying. Just think, she will think of you as her big sister. Won't you like that? She will be your little sister.' I had not thought of the change like that at all and because I always believed my mother I began to feel much better. I would know all the answers—my sister would always come to me and I would look after her because she would be new to everything. I must not be afraid of the dark any more because she would be afraid and I must help her—always. I must give her my favourite possession. That would be the sign, the secret bond. Only she and I would understand its importance. It would be the teddy bear. I asked my father if I could give away a favourite possession if it had been given to me. He thought about this gravely and then told me normally one never gave away a favourite possession, especially if the giver was still around, but, he said, this was an exception because there was a very important significance attached to it.

And then I waited. The house waited. The garden waited. One day she was there. It had happened. I had a sister. Our family of three was never the same. How could it be? Everything was different. My mother had said, 'She will be like you,' but she wasn't like me. Not then. Not ever. Because I waited. She was never afraid of the dark. She never bit her nails. If she fell down she picked herself up long before I got to her. She hardly ever cried. Nothing about her seemed to be the way my mother had said it would be. Still, I was the 'big' sister. She was my little sister. I must always protect her. So I gave her my teddy bear.

This childhood, this adolescence, had to end and it ended violently on rather more than just the political front. When Partition came and my father had made his choice, my sister made hers as well. My sister did not come with us. Everything was sadly ready in the hall and in the front and side verandas, crates of my father's books, and crates of glass and crockery, and most of the furniture and one most beautiful carpet. And my sister disappeared. I mean she ran away. It doesn't lessen the shock knowing who the person is. I knew, and had hoped she wouldn't do what she did. I asked her several times if she imagined that she was in love. She objected to the word 'imagined' and didn't answer my question. Once she had asked me if I had ever been in love. I lied to her, and said, 'No, of course not, except perhaps with people in books.'

Old sepia coloured photographs in the family album of those long-ago years include many of our home with deep cool verandas and steps leading down to a garden, cane and rope garden chairs, little girls in awful frocks and socks kneeling in the grass or sitting on a swing. Some with our parents. My sister always on my father's lap, I, stiff, plain, awful legs, awful hair, straight hair. Later, the same straight hair in plaits, legs now longer but still in unbecoming clothes and my sister—quite different. She looked different. Right from the start (if we take those photographs as being the start). Her hair was not straight. Her eyes were a colour that had never occurred in the family—'ever' said my mother—and she was willowy—I mean even though she was not tall she seemed to be. I could have disliked my sister. It's been known to happen. Just for looking the way she looked, I could have resented her or hated her. But I didn't. Oh, a long time ago I had accepted that I was a lesser mortal—not inferior, but distinctly lesser. At the age of five she refused to eat meat. At the age of seven she refused to have her hair oiled. At twelve she refused to wear any colour save white. In our family all these things were considered rebellious. She was punished and sometimes very severely. But in spite of my father's anger and my mother's tears my sister won all her battles. All this I watched and wished I were like her. But I wasn't. I was I, and she was different. That's all there was to it. And as I said earlier, even the photographs show this difference. The old, browning, patchy photographs. Before I close the album one photograph draws my attention. Perhaps it says it all. Again it is the garden. I am standing with a favourite ball ready to play with my large old dog but he is patiently guarding a small sleeping form on a durrie.

My father worked very hard and long hours and often was away touring for weeks. His return was always exciting, always an event. Sometimes we were allowed to stay up late when friends came. My father was very fond of poetry, of music and one of his friends was a musician. When he came there was always a great deal of arguing and 'political talk', but this man had a singing voice of great beauty. Often he would explain the words to us, often singing again and again the songs we liked most. One song in particular—it is a very famous poem—'Love, Do Not Ask'. '*Mujh se pahli si mohobat, meri mahbub na mang—*' A few Sundays ago a magazine section of a newspaper ran a translation of that poem and as I read it I thought of my sister's face as my father's friend translated it for us, for her, so many years ago.

Love, do not ask me for that love again...
Once I thought life, because you lived, a prize
The time's pain nothing, you alone were pain;
Your beauty kept earth's spring times from decay
My universe held only your bright eyes
If I won you, fate would be at my feet
It was not true, all this, but only wishing;
Our world knows other torments than of love,
And other happiness than a fond embrace

This was the person I meant when I asked my sister if she imagined that she was in love. He was my father's friend. He was my father's age. He did not dress like my father. His hair was much longer than I had ever seen on a man. Even my mother liked him, for his warmth and his charm and, of course, for the voice that sang those songs. But my sister fell in love. And that made all the difference. And then he died.

Her telegram was lonely and seemed to emphasize how far away she was—had been—still was. I tried hard to get to her. It wasn't all that easy. I managed. I think I persisted largely because of that lost-seeming telegram. It didn't say much but I had it with me when I finally got to her. If her telegram seemed lonely and lost because it read, 'He is dead. He died. There is no one. Could you come? Ismat', the reality was far worse. She wasn't there to receive me when I arrived—how could she be?—she didn't know when I was arriving, if I was coming at all. It seemed strange to come back to a country where I had been before, to a city where I had lived before. When we had all been young and all been together. A family. Some of the old houses I passed in the taxi from the airport could have been our home when we lived here.

It seemed strange. It seemed familiar. The taxi-driver didn't talk so I could think my thoughts. And prepare. Somehow be prepared to see my sister. It had really been such a long time. For the people we really love the most we seem to spend the least amount of time with. I wonder why that seems to be possible. I suppose we think they'll keep. Wait. Forgive. Understand. Not need explanations. Or something. I could sense we were nearly there. And there we were. The taxi drove away. And I thought, what is she now that she was then? What risks we take. She was—is—my sister. I may blunder. May not know at all what I do or say. May do and say everything wrong. Make things worse. For her. She may wish she had never sent a scrap of paper that asked, 'Could you come?' All this was silly. Futile to worry so. I had come. And I was here. So I went in.

The front door was open. I thought of that only when I was inside. And then wondered why she hadn't heard the taxi draw up and stop and the slamming of the door. Surely she would have heard all those sounds? What I probably worried about was that the front door was open and she had not come to see who it was.

Had not come to see if it was me. How devious are our thoughts.

It was dark and cool and empty where I now stood and remained dark and cool and empty as I moved from room to room calling out my sister's name. It was a large house with deep verandas, and the chiks swayed and knocked, and in some of the rooms the ceiling fans turning and kept turning with no one to switch them off. I found her, of course, in the end, and she was quite alone in a corner of her walled back-garden. She did not say very much then and not for several days. I wondered if I had made a mistake coming. Wondered if she had meant me at all in the telegrams. I felt so useless to her in her grief. She was quite alone in that large house except for an old woman who cooked for her and lived somewhere at the back of the house. My sister looked ten years younger than me. She was that. She still wore only white. She was very thin and she was very beautiful. She walked endlessly in her walled garden, round and round it, and I walked with her. We walked to the farthest corners where the shrubbery was deep and dark and smelled of deep and dark and of mogra and memories. Our mother had always worn mogra in her hair. And we walked to the small marble fountain with a few leaves in it and no water, and we walked round by the sunken rose garden and the roses were opulent and sensuous and growing exuberantly with no care at all. And then we would walk back and forth and round again till I felt she would drop with tiredness because I felt so tired but she seemed unable to stop so I just trailed after her and so it went for many hours each day, and the days were many.

She didn't talk—I mean not really, not for all those days—and then one evening while we were walking she stopped by a strange cactus sort of plant and said, 'Tomorrow I will show you something that perhaps you have never seen before, something you will never forget—and you will be glad that you came all this way, and there could not be a better way than this to thank you for coming all this way to me, for me. Because I do thank you and thank you, but I can't seem able to say anything, not really, not yet.'

The next evening she dragged a garden chair and a durrie to the cactus-like plant and we watched and waited for the Star of Bethlehem to happen. I did not ask her and she did not tell me how often she and he had watched the extraordinary star happen, but this time he was not with her. I was with her when it happened, or almost. Hour after hour, minute by minute, it opened and opened with a delicate penetrating scent and a waxy, thick whiteness—a whiteness with a glow like old ivory so that as the evening wore into night it glowed, really glowed, so that we needed no other light to watch it by. My sister sat on the durrie and I on the chair. She did not seem to move. I know that I dozed for a while and woke with a start and she had not moved at all. I watched her absorption in the still opening flower and then I could not watch any more even though I wanted to so much.

When I woke it was with such a feeling of desolation, such sadness as I had only once known when our mother died. Then a sound. Two sounds. There was a bird-call, very dear and persistent. And the other sound was that of my sister crying and crying because it was dead—it hung obscenely dead, that incredible beautiful star now like a goose, with its neck twisted and wrung and very dead.

I'm glad my sister wept and wept and thought she was weeping for that flower and its brief absolute perfection, its short life. I'm glad that flower lived and died when it did because now my sister began to sleep a little and eat food as though it was food and necessary. And now sometimes she spoke, or listened to me when I did.

I said, 'Come home—why don't you?'

She said, 'What home? How do you mean home? This is home. I live here. Home is where you live.'

I said, 'You come back—come and live with me.'

I said, 'Please leave this large and empty house.'

She said, 'It is my home.'

She said, 'It is large and empty now—you cannot know.'

I said, 'I know it is your home but just now it is too large, it is too empty. It is a house. It is lonely here now. It is not good for you. Perhaps you could come back here later on.'

She said, 'How later on? It's too late now. It's been my home for too long. Do you know how long?'

I said, 'I do know how long. Very long. Since you were seventeen—long, I know that.'

She said, 'Twenty-five years long. Nobody has much longer than that in one home, in one life. Do they?'

I said, 'Come with me when I go, please. We would go together. It won't be so bad.' I was pleading for several things and hoped she would not know.

She said, 'I cannot leave here. As you said, seventeen when I came here. I am not twenty or thirty or even thirty-five years old now. I am over forty. That's a very long time in my life, in one place. It's what I know. It's what I am. Can't you see that?'

I said, 'But it is so empty now—only you and the house.'

She said, 'And the garden. Its emptiness I will get used to. It will take a little time. I shall stay here. You must not worry because you have seen me like this. Soon I shall not be like this. You must not worry, please.'

In the night I would hear her crying. In the dark the sound of her crying. Outside, the garden waited for it to be morning. I did too. In the morning, as we walked in it, I would persist. I would say, 'Please don't close your mind to it. Allow yourself to think about it. Come with me when I go.'

And she said, 'I cannot leave, or go—please try to understand. You stay if you like—as long as you like.' This is how we spoke to each other—when we spoke. One day she spoke first. I mean, she asked me a question. I was so surprised that at first I did not answer her. I was so pleased because I felt she must be better now, perhaps she would not cry in the night, perhaps I would not hear her crying when I woke in the dark. She repeated the question. 'Did you think when you came here that you would take me back with you? Did you have that in mind when you got my telegram?'

I said, 'No, I don't think I thought that, I mean, I just thought of what you said in the telegram, no further than that. Why? Do you wish I had thought that or planned that far?'

And she said, 'No—it's strange but a longish time ago if you had asked me or persuaded me I would have come.' I was stunned by what she had just said, so I waited. And then I said, 'Why? Why would you have come a longish time ago? Why would you have wanted to? I mean then and not now?' She wouldn't say anything for such a long while that I thought, I've lost her again, she was going to say something—now she isn't going to say it, or repeat it. Perhaps she didn't say it at all. And then she said, 'It was about the time that he started calling me by my new name, the name he gave me. And it was then that his wife left him. For a long time she stayed here even after we had been married. I think she must have felt I would go away again from where I had come. But his calling me by the name he gave me must have hurt her with a sense of permanence; my staying here she had only seen as a kind of threat, not something lasting. Till then. It's odd. A name. Once there is a name—it's like an endearment. It hurts the one left out. Do you think? Do you think that's why she left—then and not before?'

I said, 'Perhaps, I do not know. How can I? But you go on with what you were telling me.'

She said, 'There isn't very much left to say, I mean the only time I wanted to leave was when she left. I know it was ironic. That's when I should have been most contented. Because now there was only me. But it was then I remembered you most acutely, and what you said to me. Once. Do you remember?' I said No, though I did.

So she said, 'It was when you asked me if I imagined I was in love. I was upset at the use of that word because of course I was in love by then— "fathoms deep"—and you knew and you knew who it was. And you said to me that long-ago time, "You can never make happiness out of all the unhappiness you will cause." You said that and I remembered it when it was too late.'

I said, 'Come now, now you can come.'

And she said, 'No, not now—it's too late now to undo any of the unhappiness.'

I said, 'Do you still have my most favourite possession?'

And she said, 'Yes, of course.' She went away out of the room. She came back with it. It was torn at the neck and it seemed mended several times. An old, torn, knotted bit of the original ribbon still hung, a sadly rusted safety pin tried to keep the stuffing from falling from one of the paws. Two white shirt buttons for eyes.

I said, 'You still have the teddy bear after all this time.' And she said, 'You gave it to me.'

The next day I left.

African Bird

El's Monologue
Looking Back

Well, if you really want to know, I mean really, as I know you do, unlike these ghastly new nuns who keep coming, six at a time, to see me as though it might be too much for them to bear singly—how it happened, my leg, the leg, the leg that once was— you I'll tell because you and I, dear, dear En, we've mostly told each other everything, haven't we? I mean, a long time ago but an important time, that long-ago time and for a long time when we were little, then when we were growing up, and then when we were young. That's a long time—and you were my dearest friend in all the world—do you remember that? How we used to say that? We had to say that to each other like a charm—against the enemy nuns. Remember?

To start at the start it really was my fault—not acknowledging the big D—my D is how I have always ignored, refused to accept, minimized the importance of, absolutely hated to know—my diabetes. I had it, of course—I am stubborn and selfish but not quite stupid, and I refused to allow my life to be cluttered, messed up, with injections and testing my urine, for God's sake, every day and every day and weighing my food and stopping this and not eating that—of course, now and again, I did refuse a third chocolate, or that second helping of apple tart with an extra dollop of cream—I thought, like fear of the dark, it would just go away. But clearly it didn't.

Do you remember En, when we started thinking about such

things, when we were about fourteen or fifteen we decided one day that you might turn out reasonable looking but that I was going to be an absolute knockout? 'Mixed blood,' is what you said, explaining things. 'mixed blood often results in astounding beauty.' Sort of best of both bloody worlds—is how I put it. Well, it did happen—I turned out an absolute stunner. You went to college.

Anyway, among my endless list of vain thoughts, helped along, of course, by what everyone confirmed, were my feet. Yes, truly En, my feet. Remember, right through school those awful socks and awful shoes, winter and summer—shoes for walking and shoes for games and shoes for church on Sundays? Well, we never really looked at our feet most of the time, did we? So it felt as though after one's thighs ended, lower down came knees, lower down calves, and then lower down socks—and shoes. We never saw them, did we? Not really, because even bath nights were such a nightmare with queues for hot water and nuns breathing all over us. But when I did notice them, as feet go, my feet were as my grandchild says describing anything she thinks is pretty or beautiful—tops. I loved my feet and I looked after and at them and they were my vanity of vanities! My feet—what a lark, En—if those ghastly, pleasure-destroying nuns had ever guessed what was to come, short of chopping them off, they would at least have worked on their usual list of punishments devised specially for 'little girl-children far from home' to destroy such wicked, wicked thoughts. What do you think En? Ten Hail Marys and ten Our Fathers kneeling on the freezing floor or Confessing in Front of the Whole School at Assembly or Not to Be Allowed to Walk with En in the Crocodile for the Rest of the Term-Year or Ever and Ever, or No Tuck from Home—or which one, En? Or do you think all of them—to really emphasize wickedness and the meaning of punishment? Or maybe not one of those—perhaps one of their more ladylike, more seemly, more fastidious, punishments. I take it, En, that you haven't forgotten those? Needlework for their wretched charity sales! And when they sold all our blood-sweat-and-tears where did all that money go, I wonder? We weren't exactly charity students were we, En? Or orphans or illegitimate babies, were we? Anyway remember those dreadful napkins and table-cloths and altar-cloths and tray-cloths and handkerchiefs with messages of doom at the edges instead of lace:

'Be good sweet maid and let who will, be clever.'

'Silence is golden.'

'Leap before you look.'

'As you sew—sow—so—so shall you reap—weep.'

Chain-blood-stitch, stem-blood-stitch, knots.

Anyway, to get back to my feet, about two years ago I was having my usual pedicure and the girl nicked my toe, just a little—a slight nick and I was sharp with the girl, but it happens, and I forgot about it. I was trying a new colour—'Copper Ice', lovely name, don't you think En?—and a super colour, sort of coppery-bronze, hot but cool, shining but subtle. A couple of days later I stubbed my toe, the same toe, against a stone step—you know how it is—pain draws pain, and it hurt rather a lot but I neglected it. I know I was careless but I've always not bothered as long as I am having fun—and I was having fun, it was my winning time, week—I just couldn't stop, I was winning and winning and I did not stop to bother, though I do remember putting a bit of medicated plaster on it, and every now and again being rather aware of it. Pain yes, oh yes—but nothing to what came after, in such small beginnings came my end, you might say—oh well.

To cut a rather long, agonizing story short—I have no foot, I have no leg. As beastly Mother Baptiste would say, 'The Good Lord gives and the Good Lord takes.' It was all my fault—nothing to do with the Good Lord—but I hated the mistakes the doctors made—they meant well, I'm sure, but they botched it up—I suppose I expected them to perform miracles—save my toe, save my foot, save my leg.

I remember at the time, that long time, when nothing was clear—I mean when everything suddenly was clear—that it was not just my foot but my leg, my length of leg would have to go—that I used to dream a dream, almost every night the same dream, till I was afraid to sleep because of the dream. You will notice, En, that I don't call it a nightmare.

There was a small horse—perhaps it was a donkey or mule—

The Quiet of the Birds

and it was in the drawing room, so incongruous in that setting of card table and potted plants and books, a small donkey standing on the drawing room carpet and I was in the room and I could see what a man was doing to that small animal and I said no and no till I was crying and crying with the kind of pain that crying is like in a dream, helpless, impossible crying. The man was making a hole in the donkey's back, it was a deep hole already, but the man kept making the hole deeper and deeper and the pain was terrible and the small donkey was trying to break free and could not move and I could not move to help him and the man hacked away and there was blood and I said stop and stop but nothing stopped and then the hole was ready and the man looked up at me and said now the first hole is ready for the wooden stave—now it will fit— and I could do nothing as in all dreams, all nightmares, nothing at all even though he had said quite clearly the first hole is ready and I knew he meant that he would start on the next hole and I was howling and knew the agony of pain that that small donkey would have to bear standing on the drawing room carpet, bear all over again, and I screamed, 'Die, can't you die and then you won't feel anything?' But nightmares are not like that, they follow real life rather closely, don't you think, En? Oh, En, I'd give my eye teeth for my leg—really, really.

Anyway, I'm here now. And so are you—quite by chance after so long a time, what a lark, what a strange thing after forty years, is it that? Can it really be—it happens in books, I know. I am so glad it is you—dear En.

El's Monologue: 2
And Now

And you sit there so quiet, En—and, of course, you must want to ask a million questions which you won't, of course—but one. And how is it with me now? That is your question, isn't it, En? So like you—no futile, silly, wasteful questions, just the one. And, of course, it allows me to tell you nothing or everything. Do I like it here after the big city—am I getting to like it? Has this lonely stretch of beach and sea and bit of lane become, for me, home? Yet? Or is it still just a place of exile, a place to hide and wait—for so long it was clearly that—a place for my ugly festering wounds to hide. Remember, En, that cruel story about Philoctetes on that small rocky island, the other sailors just left him there, his wound was smelly and repulsive and they couldn't stand it? Well, he couldn't stand it either, it was much worse for him. En—do you like those old Greek stories—I don't really mean the word 'like'—I hate them, they are so close, far too close, aren't they? All the really great ones remind us of ourselves, don't they? I mean some aspect of ourselves too close for comfort—reminders of nothing really being outside the pale, nothing. Those old Greeks, they weren't afraid of anything, faced it all, made you face it too. Imagine writing a play, En, about the stench and repulsiveness of a wound that won't heal, disgusting to everyone, and it is the central point of the play, isn't it? The image that's there right through—disgusting wound, festering wound, smelly, pus-filled wound leaking year after year, of ragged, crude bandages; not healing and rags hanging out to dry stained—oh, it's there all the time, and I'm so glad. Philoctetes refuses to make peace with that awful Odysseus with his tricks and lies and deceit. For a long, long time, En, I thought that was why I was here, I mean so that I could be out of everyone's way, I mean everyone to whom I might be a repulsive embarrassment— you know, En—even those who meant well. I could tell, or rather feel, that they were wondering what the leftover stump of my leg looked like—they would have been shocked at how much worse it looked than even their imaginings!

My imaginings! You see, the damn thing wouldn't heal for ages, then when it did start to heal, it didn't neatly at all—each flap of skin refused to do what the doctors had said it would, or ought to do—so there was skin and mess and more skin and everything was really what was left of my leg and that's the bit only I felt so strongly, sadly for—how could the others? It was after all not theirs. My 'D' and gangrene and years and years of my own folly had ended in this—and, En, I was well into my fifties by then—so my leg, or rather my stump, made me howl with its horribleness and, open or covered, it was there all the time in everything—till the surgical leg came and that was the next horror to face, which, of course, I refused to face for a long time—it was so heavy, really heavy, I hated it. It's not a leg, it's a fresh affliction, like a bit of unwieldy furniture I drag around all day, rather when I can bear to pretend to walk. In the villages round here, I've seen myself in the cattle they hobble with a heavy wooden post and when the beast tries to run he drags this fifth leg so horribly, so painfully—I feel and look like that, dragging this huge encumbrance, not a leg, not a help to movement. But kind strangers are to send me a 'lighter leg' from America—can you just see that, En? First a sort of old-fashioned store-catalogue of legs arrives, pages and pages of legs—different sizes, measurements, colours (tick the one suitable for your needs), and then the leg's arrival—it hasn't arrived yet. At the customs— there's something to imagine! Earnest customs officials tearing off all the outer packing and finally coming to a leg—'It's a leg.' To get back to what you asked me, En, how is it with me, now? It's been a long haul through such black times I thought I'd never come out again. Black, nothing despair, bottomless pit. The why me bit and rotten, grey gloom day after day, never lifting. I wouldn't allow my hair to be washed or brushed, I wouldn't allow anyone near me—and I could not sleep. No matter what I was given I could not sleep, so the black thoughts got worse and much worse till I only wanted to be rid of everything, my life. But it's not all that easy no matter how determined one is and how clever one becomes—remember Miss W explaining about shaking off this mortal coil? Remember, En, dear Miss W—those nuns must have helped her to shake off hers. How they disliked her mainly because we loved her and also, I suppose, because they could never hope to teach us the way she did, explain things the way she did. know things the way she did—wasn't she a marvel? Do you wonder, En, why nuns as a breed keep entering into this that I am trying to share with you? It's because you of all people must remember what they did to us when we were so young and couldn't protect ourselves—people keep starting societies to prevent all kinds of cruelty, don't they? I wonder what prevents the start of one against nuns. I suppose partly they have a kind of beauty (attached to what they wear) and that starts the myth, or perhaps everyone has met or heard of one good, really fine nun so they think that the norm, or a kind of fear carries over into adulthood like I suppose a very cruel parent and that silences a person who has experienced the cruelty. Our lot—Mother Cecilia, pretty, delicate, and Mother Baptiste, large and white. If they hadn't been so cruel we would have learnt so much more in those years apart from fear: in our own way, in a Dickens/Brontë sort of way, if we'd spoken up or written about it, we and hundreds like us, they might have been exposed. Yes, 'our lot' could have helped so many little children sent up to those schools in the hills. It's well-known that priests and 'Brothers' have brutalized little boys but with nuns it's much more difficult to make the average person realize what they are or can be like. Poor us in their care, in their loving Christian care! Christian values, Christian virtues. Balls, I say, or the three C's— Christian Cruelty to Children. Or, more specifically, our society would be named 'The Society for the Prevention of Catholic Cruelty to Children'. Think how we could help the next generation of children from suffering the terrors that pursued us into the rest of our lives—it really does in nightmares, doesn't it you? And in other forms it's warped us, hasn't it? Oh, En, why don't you say anything—you and I shared it, knew it—have you shaken it off? Have you forgotten the anguish hidden behind those weekly monitored letters—'My Dear Mummy and Daddy. How are you? I am very well. The nuns are very kind to us and we are going to have a nice time for Easter . . .' Remember how they never allowed us ever to write, 'I miss you very much, I wish I could come home.' I mean, even children on a happy holiday away from home are allowed to write that, say that.

And you are so patient, En—after today, don't be—slap me down, I don't mean to be so obsessive about nuns, it's as though the long-ago times we shared brings out this hate/trauma/fear again and those six giggly nuns descending on me yesterday—strange. You'd think as far as I've come there would never be another nun in my life but, as they said, sweetly smiling when they weren't giggling, 'We're bringing Father with us next time to bless this house, dear, keep your holy pictures ready.' Looking around and seeing only my lonely Sabavala 'Nuns' and my nude eyeless woman

The Quiet of the Birds

near the staircase. Keep your holy pictures ready. You remember En how those long-ago harpies of ours used to give out 'holy pictures' as prizes for good conduct as though we had attained the holy grail—not that you and I got all that many? Impossible pink-white, beatific Virgin Marys rising from nowhere and ascending into fleecy clouds, gold edged; angels with Anglo-Saxon curls—I'm sure they had a special printing press down in the basement for bringing out these holy horrors with a text over the door reading 'Suffer little children to come unto me'. Suffer, of course, being the operative word. But En, I've been here such a long while now, why do you think those nuns came last evening? Six of them fluttering like seagulls, but without their grace, coming to visit. (To bring you cheer, dear.) I wish I had set Aly and Sheba at them and their earnest Sunday faces. (My what big dogs you keep—do they bite?)

Why did they come, En? And then you. I grow old and superstitious to boot—and you, have you accepted growing old? I hate it, this whole growing-old bit—I hate it in others, in myself—it's humiliating and defeating when there's so much else to deal with, all the changes, all the steady inexorable deterioration, there's no way to ignore it after a while. Hair and teeth and skin and movement. Of course with me because of my leg, or not having one, movement went first, but it emphasized for me the rest. Oh, I know what you are going to say—and it's probably true, that I still look wonderful—but it's all so much more difficult, takes so much time—and I look out from this balcony and I see day-trippers running on the beach, jogging, doing handstands, swimming. All effortless, all young. And I can't stand them. I hate them, I hate me. Oh, say you do too, En. Do you hate growing old, do you sometimes wish for it all to happen again? To have another go at it? I suppose not, not really, because it would be the same, the same mistakes, the same losses, the regrets always coming too late. No, it's best as it is. All in all. There was, during my very 'black' time, a doctor rather different from the others and he said I should leave my well-known life, my familiar life, because I was not, any more, a part of it and the black grieving for it would never change or leave me, that I must go to a life that was quite different, to a place that was quite different, and I would get well again. And when I told him I was coming here he said to look at the birds and learn from them and watch them.

I wondered at the time what he meant, for a very long time it made no sense to me. But when you asked me how things were now—you meant very now, didn't you En? This place is my home now, is home in a lonely, alien sort of way—that doctor, the one who said that about birds, knew or must have known this place very well. When I first came the silence frightened me and when I looked across the water and saw the city and its lights I longed to go back, but very slowly, as I lay on my long chair, hour after hour, I realized I was not waiting to go back but waiting for other things. Sometimes a tree lizard immobile for an hour on the casuarina tree staring upward waiting, just waiting, and I would wait and think, that's me—I am both tree and lizard; and sometimes a bird circling in that quiet sky—circling and waiting and circling and ready to strike downwards, hidden but ready; and every day there is the setting of the sun. Here by the sea it's different every day but the silence is the same once the sea has swallowed it up. And sometimes young wrestlers from the village horse around on the beach and leave messages in the sand written with their fingers and then filled in with shells—'God is great/Love is here.'

The sea is huge, En. When do you leave? Will you come, En? The sea is always there.

African Bird

The voice tore through the sound of the casuarinas. Tore through the sound of the sea.

'Mum, Mum, oh Mum he's laid an egg, an egg Mum, can you hear? Are you listening, it's never happened before, Mum, don't you see? Not just to him but in the whole history of bird-life. Are you coming . . .? Oh, come on, he must be suffering terribly because he's a male bird—don't you see, a male, its been known to happen with fish, but a male bird isn't built to lay an egg—are you coming, Mum, just anything might happen . . .?'

'All right, all right, you don't have to scream, I can hear, I'm coming, you don't expect me to run, I take it? As for suffering, let him suffer—there's always a first time! In fact, it's a shame it's not the first human male giving birth, God I'd love to see that since you mention suffering and since you also mention not being built to lay an egg—who ever gave you the idea that we were built for suffering that particular pain? Let me tell you as usual it's a myth spread by men for men and for women to believe—and which I'm sorry to think even my daughter believes . . .'

'Oh Mum, that's the stupidest thing I ever heard, even from you! Even you know it's in all the medical books and books on anatomy and the . . .'

'Watch it, girl, are you calling me stupid? Who do you think wrote all those medical books and books of anatomy and spread the word for us dumb females to believe? We've been brainwashed right from the word go—and before that—and we've never questioned it ever, we've just gone on and on believing and accepting that we were the ones who had to have the babies. Anyway, didn't it occur to you sometimes that men have done such incredible things—experiment and change and research and oh, on and on— how come they never ever conceived of the notion that they could work out some way to have men suffer the bearing of babies? Why not? They go into space, they go deep in the ocean—they walk on the moon, they play around with the heart, they give you different coloured eyes, they . . .'

'Oh, Mum, will you stop that. Think about Thika.'

'Don't interrupt—it's just what I am doing—I'm thinking about Thika. As I was saying men could figure out ways to make all these changes but not that one change! Not them, not that particular change—too clever by half. When they realized how dreadful all those months and months of carrying a baby, getting larger and larger and all the other changes and all it involves—and then the unspeakable end to those nine months, they must have said, 'Right, that's something we don't need, that's one area we are never going to change, even tamper with—never.' They knew that their threshold for pain, for sustained suffering, was low. You'd think they'd want to improve it—but not them, selfish buggers—anyway here I am at last, so let's look at that bird—Good heavens—it's going to lay another and there's yet another—oh poor, poor bird, most foolish bird—you fooled us all, perhaps you are a female and not a male—but everything about you is male—you are a parrot from Kenya and your name is Thika and the female of the species is drab grey. Anyway, your mate died on the flight out (I'm not surprised, what with the distance and the homesickness involved), you are a male parrot from Kenya and you are a marvellous gun-metal grey bird with splendid scarlet tail feathers—you have to be male, everything about you is male as described in the books about you, the literature about you, you are the male bird and you have laid not one egg but two and there is a third to come. Oh, poor bird, you look terrible, you look exhausted, you look in pain, and you can't understand what's happened, what's still happening—be brave, be like a Christian soldier—bear up sweetie—I mean bear down, it will be over soon. I know you can't believe that now but it's true. And when it's over you won't remember the agony—really, none of us do! Real suckers—that's why we do it again! And again! And why didn't anyone tell me this was happening? Why didn't anyone call me, he must have needed me so much, I mean she must have needed me, what were all of you doing, thinking about . . .?'

'Oh, Mum, be fair, we've been screaming our heads off for you to come ever since we realized, but you were under the casuarinas today, quite the furthest you've ever managed to reach, much further than you normally manage to walk, so it took a while—but now—I mean what do we do now?—he, I mean she, refuses to sit on the eggs—I mean, it's against nature, he or rather she should do that naturally. Mum, it's nature, it's natural to sit on your new eggs and warm them till they hatch, but he won't, I mean she won't, just look at her, look at him, he hates them or hates what has happened—he's going to break them! Oh Mum, do something, you have to do something, he's yours so you must know what to do, you always know what to do, so do it now—they are all going to die or be killed, can't you see . . .?'

'Yes, I see that and you can stop screaming and carrying on—agitating him even more—just stop it . . .'

By this time the group from the casuarinas had arrived,

The Quiet of the Birds

pretending they hadn't heard everything—first, Chris with Aly and Sheba—jealous knocking against his legs pushing each other to be closest to him. And Ronnie came, not quite sure he was part of the family during a crisis, which this clearly was. And Dean came already planning how he'd write about it to his family back home (he wrote to them every night, a kind of journal he had told us, we hadn't asked and it's not something you can easily guess). And we came—we came last because we didn't really belong, we had only been here by the sea for a little while and we were shy and thought that all this was very private, was family, was extraordinary but still not quite for outsiders to participate in. We were outsiders, pale from the city, silly from the city. And now this. We all crowded around, not meaning to. Wanting to help, wanting to understand, not knowing how, faintly ashamed, faintly awed. Excited. We waited. Orders we would have followed—immediately. We would have run if El had shouted 'bandages' or 'ice' or 'warm water' or 'cottonwool', 'towels'—anything—but El said collectively, 'Don't gawp—go away—think how you would feel, she or he can't bear everyone staring at her—him—at a time like this—she's not an exhibit in a zoo, at a fair—go away. I'll stay, and I'll tell you what's happened, but go for now.' We went, dragging our feet—sheepish, feeling reprimanded. Rightly. Ours had been curiosity. And El knew this.

For a long while El's voice followed us. Except it was a different voice. This voice of El was low and sweet and consoling and the voice said, 'Now then, sweetie, sweetie, Mum's here, don't worry, we'll see this through—can't you bear it? Can't you bear them, then?—Do you hate them, then?—Do you feel trapped or something?—Do you feel your life's over, then?—Do you feel now this mill-stone is round my neck and I won't have it—I'm not ready? I know that feeling sweetie, but don't worry, you'll get over it, we all do, now come on, sit gently on you eggs. Sit. Try, I know you feel odd because you've never done it before. But there's always a first time even for us—even for you. You don't think it all comes naturally to us, do you? It does not. Now get on those eggs will you, go on try, there see, it's easy, nothing to it if you don't think about it, and nobody is watching so not to worry—even if you are a male bird. Think how lucky you are not to be in some Kenyan jungle with all the other birds watching! Here there's just you and just me. Now sit, sit dammit, sit on your eggs, hatch them, learn to care. Learn to see things through. That's it. Now stay there—get used to it—the feeling that they are yours—you can't chicken out, oops! You're unique, you'll be the first male in the world to care right from the start—not just later when the kids are fun. You're going to make history. Think of that. My arm's aching, do you think you could manage alone now? Okay. Take it easy—now you're on your own, you're going to hatch three parrots on your own—just as you bore them all on your own, and then you'll feed them, and they'll grow and you will have done it all on your own. That's as far as I'd go for now—because afterwards, when they are really grown up, it's another whole story which I feel is best left shrouded for now. One step at a time. One pain at a time.'

In the meantime the men were being sullen. Feeling dismissed from the scene, not just sullen but inadequate, somehow. They were back near the casuarinas where they had all been earlier on. Their chairs were there, just as they had left them. But nobody sat down. It seemed too casual an act, too soon. But they were kicking stones, kicking shells, humming. Being men this mood was not going to last very long. But while it did they looked disconcerted, just kicking, just pretending not to care. The sun was huge, blood red, in just a short while it would be in the water.

Then Chris said, not looking at anyone but stooping to stroke Aly and then Sheba, 'I shouldn't let it worry you—El doesn't mean to shout, to be rude—it just comes out that way. You've got to remember what she's been through, and come through, and even though she doesn't want us to remember or make allowances, still it's very hard, she takes things very hard. And really it's touch-and-go even now—so, well, cheer up.' Nobody said anything.

Then Ronnie said, missing the real point, 'Look I don't claim to know everything or even a great deal, but there are a few things I do know also I may be a marine biologist by training but nobody is going to tell me that that bird is a male bird, and that it can or rather that it has, laid an egg. It's not possible.'

And Dean said, 'I say, hang on—after all there are more things

The Quiet of the Birds

under heaven or something than are dreamt of in your etc. etc.—'

And we didn't say anything.

After a while El came to where we all were. She came steadily. Purposefully. Like an exotic African bird. But she'd been crying. We just had to look at her face once to know that. Her chair was still there from earlier on and she sat down. And we waited—pretending that we were not—for her to say something—or the first thing. Even Ronnie didn't say anything.

And then after a while made even longer by the sound of the waves and the wind in the casuarinas El said, 'And when are you going to put up our huge brass lamp? Chris, you remember I asked you to do that a while ago?—To put it high up on that eucalyptus branch over the main dining table—you remember how we thought that because it was carved, cut out, it would shed a kind of dappled light and look incredible? I wish you could imagine it. If you could imagine how it would look you'd remember to do it—I'd do it myself if I could still climb a ladder. Soon it will be too late, the rains will come, then it's useless, we won't sit out. Nobody will sit out—useless—it's all useless—that damned bird! That bloody, vicious, angry bird smashed all its eggs. Broke them—smashed them!—there is nothing left but thin bits of shells and a fearful mess. How could he/she, bloody unnatural bird, selfish bird, hateful bird. Men. I thought we could have been two of a kind—unnatural, different. A club with two members. Thika, the male African parrot who laid three eggs—and me. And you know what I'm famous for? El—the one-legged Mum. Well, anyway, why is everyone so quiet? Did I say something to upset anyone? Surely Chris has already explained me, already told you not to mind me, not to mind anything I say or shout or scream. That it's still touch-and-go—with me? Hasn't he told you all that? And he's right. He nearly always is. Yes, it's touch-and-go—still—with me. And that damned bird let go—survival, endurance, that's the name of the game. Isn't it?'

Even Ronnie realized it was a rhetorical question—and it was suddenly dark, really night. No light at all.

One Summer Meeting

'I was told you might be here, so I came. Do you come here to pray, to be quiet, or to hide?'

'No, no'—the eyes still very young, the green he remembered now greyish, beautiful still—'No, I did not come here to pray—but to be quiet—yes—perhaps yes, to relive memories of this chapel, rather in this chapel I have memories—we met here quite often—very often really, when we could not meet anywhere else—and obviously we could not meet anywhere else. I mean, where else can you meet in this small village where everyone waits—I mean, surely you can feel it—can't you? Don't you feel the weight of it in the still heat, in the air? The weight of waiting—even now? Perhaps someone behind a blind, someone behind a slightly displaced curtain—no, not curtain, this village doesn't go in for curtains, it's still a very conservative village in every way, I should know, who better-burnt child, you know? No, we still stick to our blinds, our shell-blinds of a thousand eyes, watching watchful waiting eyes—our ubiquitous shell-blinds. So old and ever so true to our unchanging habits, beliefs, no, we won't change, we like our hours watching without seeming to from behind our shell-eyes.

'As I was saying—or was I thinking?—someone perhaps even now saw me come in—goodness and it's not Sunday, why ever to chapel on a weekday? Someone saw you come in—and why not? They mean no harm, they have nothing to do, they have nothing to make them feel alive—so they watch, and they wait and that summer, certainly, they were truly rewarded, they had something to watch, and us to wait for—but that's not the way I meant to tell you—no, I'm getting it all wrong—it wasn't like that at all—that summer, not quite like that for a long time. Let me start again—all right?

'We two—once we had met, where could we meet? We could

not walk on the beach where we had first met, we could not walk together on the main promenades—too public. We could not really meet at parties—again too public—so where? We could not go away anywhere, could we? And it was very important. I'd like you to know that, and never to forget it. You were very young when it all happened and there was no real way then for me to make you try and see how important it was. But now, since you have come to me, I know that it is something that I would want you most deeply to understand. True, nothing of your pain or outrage or fear can be undone—but still, for the record, as they say, from me to you. All right? We met in this chapel—in the afternoons.

'I was, I suppose, a visitor to the village because, after all, we did not live here all the year round—though we visited every year at the same time—for so many years we had done this, still we were visitors. There were advantages, I suppose. It was not difficult for me to ask for the key to the side entrance to the chapel. "Special prayers" is how I put it—very special prayers—and I meant no disrespect—after all it was my key to a kind of haven/heaven. Yes, it was. The little priest was touched, I think, because I made it very clear that I loved this chapel so much more than the big church— "I cannot pray there well, not so well," I said. "Of course, I will always be there on Sundays for mass but for real prayer, may I have a key to our chapel, Father?" I said. I think the "our" in that appeal was what made him give it to me, in fact he soon found me a spare key and when I think back, I was not entirely dishonest with him. I really did love this small chapel, its cool darkness, its quiet. I really did pray here too—not just for some form of forgiveness—but in gratitude. Also for a way—I mean some way that could be found—I prayed for that too. Do you know, I mean, can you see a little of what I mean? Whatever people told you about me then or later I was not a destructive person. I did not mean to destroy so much, truly—I suppose that has been said so often—"did not mean to". . . I—anyway, I knew it was true then and it is still true now.

'I did not mean to hurt you.

'Also, of course, I could not think—imagine—that your father could really carry out what he said he would. I hoped that he might put you first—above everything. You were so young. He might have kept that in mind—he could have tried. For you.

'But he minded in the worst sense, I mean, in his pride. His pride was hurt and that is the worst sense, isn't it? And not a personal hurt—I was only a possession, one of his possessions. In that sense he minded so much; in terms of the shame—not personal shame, you understand, but that peculiar shame attached to the family name—standing—society—scandal—other people! Never just me and him as a unit. Never me in relation to him. Or just him. Or just me. Don't you see, then we would have talked or argued or agonized, tried in a small human way, talked about errors, human errors, mistakes, what lifts the heart, what breaks the heart? An error, a mistake—if not forgiveness, at least understanding, or if not understanding, a recognition of human need or want or joy or sorrow—one cannot refrain from everything, one life to live! Remember, I must have my life in my time—who said that?

'But he would not talk, he would not listen. He said only one thing. And that you heard. I know you heard. You heard him say— "I will never speak to you again—ever." You were outside that closed door. You heard him say that, didn't you? And you could not have been frightened as I was because I knew that he meant it coldly and absolutely and that he had closed all the doors, all the human doors, and I hated him for his lack and I pitied him. It was a serious lack—he lacked humanity, he lacked thinking, caring that you were a child, a small child, and that should come first over every other consideration—surely.

'You must have thought it was like the games you children used to play, your threats and your punishments—"I'll never speak to you again" or "I'll never play with you again" or "I won't be your friend again, ever" and of course you meant it, at the time, always with a fierce anger or a fierce hurt, but also you knew that it never lasted, not for long, not for very long.

'You must have been frightened as children are when they hear the raised voices of their parents—or the cold, very quiet voice of your father as you heard it that day, but I'm certain you never thought he meant it—I mean not quite—the way he said it. But I knew that he did mean what he said. Oh yes, I knew that he would

The Quiet of the Birds

never, never speak to me again. Cold rage—very cold your father's anger—steely, absolute, unbending. He would never talk things over at the best of times—and these were, after all, the worst of times. He had made up his mind and he would never change. Oh yes, he was considered a very strong man, a very disciplined man— an honest, straightforward man and of course a clever intelligent man—but joy? That's something he never had, or lost when very young—I mean, before he married me.

'I'm glad I am spared having to agonize over that as well as everything else. I did not ever know joy in your father. He never showed it, nor did he express it over anything—not music, not sculpture, not growing things, not birth, not a sunset or sunrise, not me, not us—never ever.

'Anyway, I am straying. I was telling you that we met in this chapel—in the afternoons. I don't know who told you father, it could have been anyone or no one. I mean, anyone behind one of those shell-shuttered windows like eyes, like eyelids lowered—and you never are quite sure if a person sees or just observes the scene without anything clear emerging—shuttered eyes half reading or half asleep or praying or dreaming or looking and remembering and then reporting, who knows, how can one ever know? Everyone looks innocent, everyone looks guilty.

'Or maybe it was me. Maybe I changed—you know, happiness is as difficult to conceal as real unhappiness—do you know this yet? So I might have changed, so it was noticed. Or your father remembered the Winged Victory in that gloomy museum—I don't know. But he said he would never speak to me again—ever. And he never did. Premonitions never really stir one at the right time or serve as a warning—or we simply do not interpret them rightly. Being only human—how can we? There were times, though, very soon after we were married, that should have warned me. But then, except for being frightened, what could I have done?

'Your father had work that took him to Greece; he took me with him. And it was in Greece that both incidents happened, I mean both the strange warnings that I should have recognized, understood, remembered. I will try and tell you as closely as I can remember—all right?'

'But the man, Mother? What about the man? The other man, I mean? I should like to know about him. Aren't you going to tell me? You haven't done that—yet.'

'I thought that by inversion that is what I have been telling you all this while—amazing that you should not have realized. Anyway, why do you call me "Mother"? For a moment I couldn't think who you were talking to; all those years ago it was "Mama"—always, there was no other term for me and now you say "Mother". Anyway, if it's your formal term for me I should be grateful that you still think I am—I mean, your mother. Anyway, you say I have not said anything about the man, the other man, the other-than-your-father man. I have, only you haven't been listening—not really. So I will tell you in a different way and then go back to Greece. Well, he was like a sun-bird—no, no please, please don't interrupt again—I know what you want to know and I am going to tell you in the only way I know, so even if you don't want it told in this way I really can't help that because it's the only way that I know. It happened to me and you just asked me to tell you about him. You said—"But the man, Mother—what about the man—the other man—I should like to know about him. Aren't you going to tell me? I mean something—anything—anything at all about him"—so now you listen even if it's difficult for you to see him as I did because it will still be better than the way you have been told—or imagined—for yourself. If you interrupt again I shall not say anything that is important.'

'When you speak to me I shall listen, even though it hurts me; even if you say things I cannot understand immediately or for a long long time. But I will listen and try to hear you—"like a sun-bird"—is how I will try to see him.'

'Do you know the sun-bird? Have you ever seen one?'

'No,' he said, 'never. Or if I have seen one I have not known its name. Is it a very spectacular bird—I mean a name like that—?'

'No,' she said, 'very small, sparrow-small—but its breast is a lovely yellow, bright, cheerful—and the male sings excitedly while pivoting on its perch from side to side and opening and closing his wings and tail, sings "tityou, tityou, tityou". Oh, to see it and hear it is such joy. The sun-bird flits about, he is full of movement, he is here and then he is there and you watch him—before your eyes he flits about and away. In vulgar terminology my bright, high-stepping man did the flit—moved to another summer. To another summer's diversion—it's happened before but it happened to me; well, I suppose you cannot be like a sun-bird and not break hearts. Or move them or change them and make dead things live or things never dreamed of come to life—I mean, the sun-bird does not pause, cannot pause, is compelled to move. That is its nature and, alas, you cannot make him behave differently or make him cause less damage, less devastation, just as you cannot define his quality of quicksilver joy, cannot make him create less light, less sudden beauty. I mean they are created for this specific reason. Do you see?'

'Perhaps I do—I don't know. But where—or how—when—did you meet this man?'

'Oh, you were with me and so was your father—he came high-stepping over the dunes on one of our walks. We were always together—that you surely remember? Don't you? That suddenly he was there? Of course, he was with other people but suddenly everything changed. It did. Even now telling you about it, that first meeting, all those years ago, I can describe only in ridiculous terms something very specific that happened. I'll say it anyway, the sudden stopping of the heart, an inability to breathe and then, as suddenly, a recharging: you breathe again, the heart is working again but everything is different—the air smells different, colours are unusual, if you could taste your skin then the familiar taste would suddenly have become unfamiliar. The sea-sound had changed and your small hand in mine must have sensed something —surely. Can you not remember—make yourself remember? You do, don't you? You look so appalled—but you did ask me—didn't you? You seemed really to want to know—or was it just—?'

'Yes, I did want to know—and I did not interrupt you this time. If it is the way I look I cannot help "my look" as you speak. Shall I look away from your face while you are speaking? Would you prefer that? But something is unfolding and I am watching that— also I am listening to your face.'

'I am glad. I like what you just said. That you are "listening to my face". When you were very small, a very small boy, sometimes when I was telling you a story, or reading a story to you, I would look at your face as it was listening—it was a listening, wandering face and I loved that face because it was so different from your everyday face. It saw, your face saw, what I was reading to you or telling you. It saw colours and shapes and smells and happenings. It was not like your face at family meals, or your face as it went off to school, your face when it came back from church or your family-visits face. It was none of those faces, it was different.'

'And so was yours, Mother. Your face as it was telling me about your sun-bird—man—was different and perhaps I was seeing a face not seen by me for a long, long time and now remembered—your face also looked different—I mean, as you put it, very unlike your "everyday face".'

'Well, I'll go on then, shall I? Where did I stop, what was I saying . . . ?'

'You were telling me—or reminding yourself—about the first meeting, about the familiar becoming unfamiliar, colours and sounds and taste of skin and a hand in your hand—mine. Mine, my hand, my small hand in yours that, too, in one moment, became unfamiliar. You did not need it any more, you are so able to convey that time and what you felt, that time and what you did, that time and what you forgot. You are indulging yourself when you talk about a small hand in yours—it was not a disembodied small hand, it was mine—it was me and you forgot that completely. I wonder that you can recall it now, and speak to me of it—how Mother—how?'

'Because you come here after years and years and hours and days and ask me about a certain time. If the great meaning and singular importance of that time involves areas that hurt you—then acknowledge them—you ask me and then you want me to edit my telling—if you are upset—or if you are aggrieving—then grieve all you can, it's a shame not to. Who said that? Anyway don't say in your father's tone—"How, Mother, how?" It's too late for how. Earlier, when I was trying to tell you of my life and all its denials, trying to tell you in a different way, you stopped me. You said, "Tell me about the man, the other man"—well, what

118   *The Quiet of the Birds*

do you want? You are a man now, not a small child and, unlike your father, you seemed to want to know from me about that time in my life, in our life, in our family—what happened. What comfortable or comforting things did you expect to hear? So why can't you bear to hear? To hear me? Or did you come here to me with your ears already filled with what you thought or hoped I would say? Is that it? Is it disappointment, then, that you are feeling? Was I supposed to say, "I'm sorry, sorry that I met a man who was like a sun-bird, sorry that he filled my days and changed my ways, sorry that he made me feel that I was beautiful, that I had things to say and share—worth listening to, worth sharing—" Well, I will not say it to please you, or to fit your idea of what is seemly or right for me to feel or say to you—but I missed you very much. I missed you unbearably—that was the greatest loss—the only loss—the grief that could not be denied and was denied me. I am tired, angry. I suppose I'm not used to you or anyone really. A person is entitled to becoming rather set in certain ways—I told you I have grown accustomed to silence—I mean, I don't really talk to anyone so you are an intrusion and I am exhausted by you and my trying to tell you what you have asked me. I am not being impossible—I had years and years of adjusting to your father's ways—of not talking, of not describing, of not sharing anything—and now I am not going to adjust to anyone—not you—not anyone.'

'I'm not sorry, Mother, about what I said—I feel like that—I shall repeat it, I shall say it again: How Mother? How?—there I have said it again. It's not so bad, really, is it? After all, it made you say what I wanted you to say in the first place—'

'Really? And what was it you wanted me to say, as you so crudely put it—"in the first place"—as though you had the right to cut through everything else I have tried to tell you so that you could dismiss it all and find just the one thing—the one selfish thing. And you said I was indulging myself. My God, men, you men—I was free for a long time and I had grown fond of it. I now realize—I know what you wanted to hear me say—I may be many things but I am not yet quite stupid—"But I missed you very much—I missed you unbearably—that was the greatest loss—the only loss"—

there it's said again and meant again. But before you hug it too close as the only truth remember that that too changed—life and the living of it does go on. The heavy unbearable loss may last and last but it changes and one day it is not there any more and you are free of it. Your father I did not miss at all, except for realizing how many years he had deprived me of myself by coldness, by sternness, by such a lack of laughter—truly we never laughed about anything. I used to hope that when you were at school you would laugh at anything or nothing at all so that it could last you for the hours after you came home. Tell me, did you become friends with your father? I mean do you like him now? Are you easy with him?'

'Why do you want to know, Mother? Mother—would it make you feel better or a lot worse?'

'How—better? How—worse? You really ask your questions as though you were my enemy—my friendly enemy—are you?'

'Am I what? Enemy? Friendly enemy? It's odd how we talk to each other—don't you think it's odd? To answer your question about my father—you will be upset because—yes, he and I are friends—and I call him Papa. And you are close to crying because you wanted me to say that he was impossible in all those ways as he was to you—as he was with you. You wanted me to say that he was not my friend—that I did not like him, that I was not easy with him—and that I called him Father. I am glad I have hurt you. I am glad that I have made you cry. Mother, shall we talk to each other again? When you have stopped crying—shall we? It's your turn again, because I have answered your questions, haven't I? Only I answered them truthfully, but—if you—'

'Oh, do be quiet—leave me alone—I was alone and you had to come and disturb me—and my crying should not add to your feeling of triumph; it will pass. It will not happen again to bring you even a moment's pleasure at having caused it. Are you waiting for anything? I mean is there anything else? I am tired. I am not used to visitors.'

'I shall be going soon—and you are right. Not just because you are hurt by what I said—but right in calling me a visitor. I am a visitor. I'm glad unhappiness has made you acerbic rather than the other things it can do to a person—but that's just by the way— you were starting to tell me about two incidents, "warnings" you called them, about Papa in Greece. Something that happened there. I was impatient and interrupted you, but please tell me, it must have been important, relevant. Please—we may never meet again— or I may never visit you for another twenty years. Can we afford that again, do you think? Perhaps you wanted to warn me about myself through Papa. Was that it? Was it? Is there something about me that reminds you of him?'

'Yes, there is something about you—you look very much like him— it's something—it's something else. Anyway, I shouldn't marry if I were you. You don't like women, do you? I mean you don't really enjoy their company, do you, or rather you feel odd, don't you, when you are with them for long. I'm not sure I'm right, it's just a feeling. Anyway you can tell me if I'm wrong. Am I? Am I wrong?'

'No, you're not wrong. I once asked Papa to tell me about you and he said you were a bitch. He said it shamed him to have to use such a word but that is what you were, in essence. He said women like that, like you, should never be wives nor should they become mothers. I asked him why he had married you. He said that he had not wanted to marry at all but had somehow been prevailed upon to do so. That is all.'

'Prevailed upon to do so—oh that's rich—sounds very like him and is that all your father ever told you about me? And you—did it satisfy your curiosity about me to be told this? Only this—just this? Had you no memory of me—that added up to a little bit more? Had you no memory of us, little things, anything? You were little, but not that little. I thought we enjoyed each other—that long-ago time. Anyway it does not signify—'

'Yes it does, as you put it, signify, but you were not there, you had chosen to be somewhere else—here.'

'Yes—as you put it so simply—I had chosen—somewhere else— here.'

Leave Taking

'You are going now, of course you are, I have kept you long, have I? You were always free to go, as you came, unasked. I am not ungrateful—I'm not sure gratitude is quite the word I mean—anyway, I have kept you so long—but after so long a time it did not seem, rather did not feel, so long to me it was not really long, was it? I will not say the obvious things but perhaps you will know that I have said them already—have I? But you must not forget anything that I have told you—or that you have asked me—now you know something and I too know a little of you. We will not intrude on each other's life—lives (is it?) but to quote a dear friend, "Don't ever forget that one line on a card is one line of a life. And as such, much." So just a line on a card—with no strain attached, mind you, as so often happens to sons with mothers—because you and I are nicely poised—being so separated there is choice. You can even visit if you like or not—visit, I mean.'

'You mean, Mother, we two, now, still have a choice?'

'Of course we do. We managed without each other for two decades—then you came to visit me. We talked, we listened, you were curious, we hurt each other, we upset each other—at best we were interested in each other. But that is all. We are not yoked to each other—don't worry about that at all. If we liked each other enormously then I think we would most certainly have to meet again. But for the other formality—yes, I think that is the word I need—I mean the rather more slender thread that binds us—mother–son, son–mother, blood—is a myth, created by interested parties. Blackmail of the emotional kind we do not need. I do not need a crutch and nor do you. You are bent in a certain way and you would like to feel it is due to me that you are what you are. It's too convenient, though, and even if I did feel a little guilt I do not intend to do anything about it. I like my life. For the years and years that I didn't, for the lonely years and the sad years and the years of real despair and blackness there was no help—so now that I am all right and I have earned the right to my selfhood, I do not need anyone unless there is laughter or joy or even just a comfortable rightness about a person—I do not want or need anyone.'

'But you will miss me now, now that we have encountered each other and you are protesting so much, you are so vehement in your denial that I suspect you—I think you mean the opposite of what you have said, what you are saying and—'

'I shan't miss you because I don't know you too well, or perhaps I mean I only know what you have told me, just as I have told you some things. But soon after you leave and go back to your other life, first you'll sift what I have said and some things you will believe and others you will suspect did not happen quite the way I told you—and why should you believe all of it? I will do the same with what you have told me and I know that in the balance I will always like you less for not choosing me to live with rather than your father. Also if that is unfair because you were only a child, there is something you said that will always remain with me and it will fester and take over completely. I hate what you said about your father, that you liked him, that you were friends, that you called him Papa. Also, of course, you meant it. I mean, you didn't just say it to hurt me—but it's very late now, you must go, which is another way of saying that I must go, I want to go home and do the things I do every day at this time.'

'And what do you do at this time that is so important—'

'What you are really asking or implying is what can it be that is so important when you are here—that it is unimportant really, compared to your having come, well it isn't as it happens. I mean, it's much more important and more constant—and I don't have to tell you what it is but I will—because you won't understand anyway so it signifies nothing. At this time, every evening, I water the plants in my garden.'

'Really? That is what you do, at this time every evening—and it can't wait?'

'No, why should it wait? It's what I do. It's what I do and it's what I like to do at this time of evening.'

'You have a garden, Mother? Your own garden? I mean a garden implies a certain kind of house, a certain way of life—is that how you live?'

'Yes, that is how I live—in a large old room of a large old house. The house is closed, boarded up, except for this one large room, my room, which opens out into a small, walled garden—this is mine. The room and the garden and this small chapel can also be said to be mine—does that answer you? I mean, does it answer your—"is that how you live?"'

'Yes and no. There were other things implied in my question, like—and now you are always alone, are you? I mean, don't you see anyone, talk to anyone, I mean no one at all? Is that possible? Who owns the house you live in? Don't you meet anyone connected with the house?'

'No, I don't—not really. I am answering your questions backwards. I meet no one connected with the house. I pay for my room and my walled garden to the nuns who look after the old lady who owns the house. Her sons all live in other countries, so that is the arrangement. Sad for the old lady but good for me and the nuns I imagine. The old lady I would have liked to have met but the nuns feel it would be indelicate. I have no wish to argue with the nuns on this. It would involve talking to them. I do not like them. Nuns I mean. The sons I hope I never meet—for obvious reasons. As for your other questions—of course, that is possible. You don't have to be so alarmed by the thought, or make it seem so dramatic. I'm certain there are more people in the world who do not talk to anyone, and I don't mean converse, I mean talk at all. More people than do—talk, I mean. Haven't you noticed, around you? You are not entirely unobservant, nor all that young surely, not to have noticed or sensed this? Old people, and very old people, that sort of person. They are talked at sometimes, have things said at them as though they couldn't possibly have anything to contribute or contradict. I'm only giving you an example, mind you, to jog you, stir you into realizing that it's not so extraordinary at all.'

'It is extraordinary, Mother, and you don't convince me at all with what you say. I think you—'

'But I don't say anything to convince you. I've said this earlier and I repeat what I said, I am not sufficiently interested in you to care to convince you—you said something and I merely said something, that is all.'

'I know you want me to leave, Mother, to go now and that is why you are rude—or no, not rude, but dismissive, which, I think, is much worse. But since I shan't be coming again may I not ask you just a few more questions? Please? Not idle curiosity. But— how shall I put it? Let's say something in me wants very much to know.'

The Quiet of the Birds

'What in you wants to know, I wonder? Anyway, since you won't be coming again, all right, ask. Tomorrow life will go on as usual—as it has been before. So not much to lose or gain.'

'You make everything sound so peaceful the even keel, no rumbles, no threats—nothing. Is your life really like that?'

'O, you are so literal, you are, you know. And I, as usual, making the same mistake, expecting you to be different. Why on earth should you be? Of course, there are rumbles and threats—your words—of course things aren't on an even keel all the time. I'm not dead, as you can see—I imagine that is the only time things will feel on an even keel—don't you agree? I have things happen that disturb me immeasurably. In my walled garden a tree died ten days ago. It died in three days. It had been a part of my life for a long time—eighteen years. And one day all the leaves crinkled up. The next day the crinkled-up leaves turned a sick yellow. On the third day all the crinkled-up, sick, yellow leaves fell and fell and I knew it was dead. It had never looked like that before. It looked so dead. I cried a great deal—for the tree and for my helplessness. Three days is very sudden in a tree—in a man. I mean in a well tree and a well man. And I thought someone had poisoned it. It was so sudden. No other reason occurred to me. How could it? And at the small shop where the three roads meet, where I buy things I need, a man, not of this village, asked me if I needed any help. He was out of legend or myth this man. Very old, with a length of dirty, grey beard and a long plait of dirty, grey-white hair. At the end of the plait was a bit of pink ribbon. Yes, really pink! He said he travelled about doing odd jobs though he was best with growing things. I asked him if he could help me with growing things that died; he said he could. I took him to my walled garden and he went straight to my dead tree. He looked at it for a while and then he said it was dead. I told him that I knew it was dead but that he must do something about it. After all that is what he had said in the shop, and that is why I had brought him here. And he said, yes, that is why I am here. And he worked at that tree every day for three days—worked very long hours for three days—and on the fourth day he did not come. To work at my tree, I mean. He came only to say that he was going away and that I must watch and wait. I felt he was deserting us, the tree and me, and he knew I was thinking that. He went. But I did what he said, I waited and I watched. The tree. I wish he would come back because today there is a change in the tree and it is because of him. I did not thank him. But nobody knows him or where he comes from so he may never come this way again. To be thanked and to see whether the tree came to life, coaxed back by him.

'So, you see, even my life is not without event! Not without threat or rumble. It has sickness and death and chance encounters—even people to talk to—have you ever talked to an old man with a pink ribbon at the end of a plait of dirty, white hair? A man who could raise the dead?'

'No, Mother, I can't say that I have. Thank you for telling me about your tree—truly. And now there is just one question I want to ask and mean to know and then truly I will go. Mother, it's about the beach. That particular stretch of beach. Do you not go to that place any more, where we used to go every evening—and where you first met the sun-bird?'

'No, I don't go there any more. I did for a long time after you went away with your father and then even after—as you called him—the sun-bird—went away but two things happened on the beach, on the same stretch of beach that was ours, that was familiar. I took those as meaning something and I don't go there any more.'

'Mother, would you tell me what happened—please? I really want to know because that stretch of beach is one of the clearest memories/pictures in my mind, in my head—of us three, my hand in yours and Papa, please tell me and then I will go.'

'All right, I will, because you used a term almost from when you were little. When you were a little boy you would say "Tell me a picture-story" and you meant a story that you could see. So I will give you two "picture-stories", both are my life and me. Low tide about five-forty-five in the evening, our usual time for a walk and the usual stretch was as smooth as silk but at every step dead fish lay—white, upturned, dead fish at every step or second step—countless white dead fish, I could not count them but I thought it would stop but it did not. A perfect sky and a perfect sea and dead fish, and finally, when the quiet horror seemed impossible to bear, an old green bottle and a dead seagull. And think, all the time there was a more not less than perfect sunset spreading and then suddenly darkness. The other picture-story I found even more frightening. Perhaps you might remember the pair of dogs that used to come running down from behind one of the sand-dunes every evening—do you remember? As we passed that way each evening, with a rushing and barking—excited and almost tumbling down the dunes but always managing to stop just short of the sea's edge? And they were rather like children (not you of course) when first they are brought to the seaside, excited and rushing to gather up all the excitement contained in sand and sand castles and sand pails and wooden spades, shells and the first wave. They were, this pair of dogs, a part of summers in that village by the sea—an integral part. Always there, at just that point, always excited, always rushing—pointing out our own wretched staidness, our upright, measured walk, taking the air. One day long after that summer I walked that way alone—when I could bear to begin going where we as a family or rather where you and I went every evening, your hand in mine, and as I reached that sand-dune I heard the excited barking and something came down that dune— a sideways moving thing—it was one of that inseparable pair of dogs, hideously maimed. Both hind-legs broken and somehow mended on their own, giving the creature a strange sideways movement—can you see it in your picture-story? Both legs smashed and mended, crudely bent, but moving. Dragging itself sideways, quite fast downwards making strange markings in the sand, body and legs down to the sea's edge. It had such a sense of its territory— its area, its meaning. After the first horror I felt like that dog—and I am like it. Not dead. Not nearly. Not yet. So you see pity needn't keep you awake either—luckily you've seen me—so no reason and that's two things eliminated—pity for ageing mother who lives alone—and I-ought-to-do-something syndrome. No need—go free. I am quite free so you should be too. There is a smell of autumn, though, that we do not have—perhaps it's the burning of the leaves. And now you must go. I shall stay for a moment or two.'

Four Friends and a Wedding

They had very little in common—if you really thought about it.
Anyway, why should you really try and think about it? Really
thinking about it feels like trying to analyse it—and who needs
analysing things all the time? Rare things work. This worked. Had
worked for quite a long time. They were very good friends. As in
most good marriages they didn't seem to have anything, or too
much, in common. But there you are. Good relationships are a
mystery. Now this analogy—four good friends and a good
marriage—why did I think about that just now? Yes, I know.
Because this story is partly about a marriage. Only partly though—
mostly it's about friendship. About four friends. I was the mother
of one of them. They were from different schools. So it didn't
begin there. Later, in college, they met. They all took quite different
subjects, so there wasn't even that—I mean the same lecture rooms.
Not one of them was absolutely sure what to major in, but they
were all 'into' film one way or another—discussing or watching or
reading books on 'four great European directors'. Only one of
them did a film appreciation course and that was mainly (not only
but mainly) because of a girl who was not just keen but quite sure,
in a very committed sort of way, about her future. That was the
thing about these girls. They knew for certain what they meant to
study, and they knew why and how. They made notes, they drew
up charts for study—with dates and deadlines. They made reading
lists and knew about evening courses. They knew exactly about
their futures. This was alarming for the four boys. They spent many
of their Friday stag sessions discussing their own lack or seeming
lack of direction. 'What the hell, yaar,' they said, 'how come they
are so sure and we are not?' This went on for a long while. Not
just through college but into their working lives as well. They all
worked, mind you. They weren't too certain what they were

working at, what they wanted to be working at for the rest of their lives. They said, 'You can't expect that, yaar, there'd be something wrong surely if you knew for certain for your whole life.' 'You'd have to be some kind of nut or Da Vinci or Bach or my Mom, for instance,' said one of them, 'she knew what she wanted to do—teach, yaar, and she knew what she wanted to teach as well—at fifteen! But she doesn't count—she's an oddity, but our girls how come they are so sure? How come?' They all fell in love more or less while they were in college, mind you that's not the term they used. They liked girls and some rather more than others. They went steady for a while, and then a longer while and it seemed rather less frenzied than our own, or rather, our generation's, falling in love—which seemed fraught and sad rather than happy most of the time, a lot of it seeming to take place in the mind and not in actuality, wild imaginings, letters written and never sent, conversations with the beloved out of books of poetry—the actual person never met, perhaps never knowing. Ah love! Ah youth!

Not with these four friends. Girls streamed in and out of the house making coffee and finishing the sugar and making friends with the dog. It all seemed so relaxed—I wish it had been like that for us lot. When they weren't meeting they were phoning each other. For at least six years I don't remember a single phone call being for me. I took messages of course. From Tanu and Anu and Phiz and Rash and Yas and so on—'Meet at Sundance at eight otherwise Gorai at M Braganza's'—or, 'Jam says no way' (I would say—is that all) 'Yes Ma'am, just say Jam says no way'—not one of them seemed to have a complete name. I wonder why parents bother. About names, I mean, if this is how it all ends. Anxiety-ridden months and weeks before the child is born. List one for 'If the Child Is a Girl'; the other, 'If the Child Is a Boy'. And then Maya and Vatsala and Mirai and Valsa and so on—and the other list, Ravi and Aditya and Rohit and Rohan. All those lists. Well thank God for small mercies. Think if one of ours had been named Vatsala, by now she would be called Vats or Vat, Vat to do?

Anyway, after eleven years and some months there was despondency and excitement in more or less equal measure in the boys' camp. One of them decided he was going to get married. He knew who he was going to marry and the rest knew, too. They were shocked. The even keel seemed unnecessarily to be swerving off course. They were pulled up short: 'What the hell, yaar—why get married? Even my Mom said given the choice she'd not do it again so why does he have to get married? Nobody gets married any more, yaar.' They seemed unmindful of the fact that in season or even out of season, every club, playing-field, ballroom, empty space—double-bedsheet size—always had two large gold and red velvet Ramayan-sized thrones and neon or fairy lights and shehnais and circus horses trained to become bridegroom carriers. Our trendy boys hadn't noticed this, of course—theirs was a different world—a great padded-shoulder-jacket world of Sartre and Stevie—not Wonder but Winwood—and cool chicks. And into this had come this wedding. Not an outsider wedding where they sometimes had to go, 'Family, yaar' pouring themselves into ethnic chic for the occasion, bored but finding the 'puris smashing, never get them at home, yaar'—but one of the asli in crowd—one of the inner four!

Except to Ravi it was not inevitable. Our four, rather three now, wanted life to go on and on as always with only very minor changes like maybe a different job, hairstyle, a trip abroad, a new girl, but marriage—impossible to conceive of. Even a single earring sported by one of them was taken fairly easily in their stride. But this was different. Anyway, they knew that they had to be a team. They knew that Ravi must never guess the way they felt. So things were given priority status. Things were on a war footing, so to speak. Operation Wedding. They closed ranks, they began to help to make it their wedding—a memorable, once-in-a-lifetime, gang-of-four-managed wedding. They worked very hard but seemed to be sleepwalking in the month just before. The one in charge of creating the invitation threw himself wholeheartedly into the project working so hard on it, spending whole nights on the intricacies involved, that he all but lost his job. The others not having been given anything specific were hanging loose yet always on the ready—'You know you can count on us, yaar—for anything, you first have to tell us.' The actual wedding seemed to be falling into shape without their help though; they were all to be witnesses so the planning of what was appropriate for them to wear took up a great deal of time. None of them had been asked to be witnesses before; they were aware of the honour as well as the solemnity. Also, they realized their huge shouldered jackets might not be quite the thing though they planned to have them ready to slip into the minute they felt things were more relaxed. Their parents reminded them that they would not be the cynosure of all eyes—that would be Shalini—so why not take it easy. This was said gently and over several weeks so no offence was taken—if meant. They then planned the stag event—the surprise party they were giving the night before the wedding. They decided on a party in a harbour launch with music and familiar things that had always been part of their long friendship. When the launch proved astronomical in terms of their budget the three decided, well, even if it's a tradition we'll have to break it and anyway it's still only for all his close friends, chicks included. So that's the way the bachelor party of four 'opened out'—as they termed it. Opened out. You have to hand it to them, their terminology was colourful, was immediate, was unusual enough for one to have to ask them to clarify. To ask them what they meant. I suppose that's why they went around with dictionaries when they were in college. To clarify what we meant. They simply hadn't understood us. They were luckier. In terms of dictionaries. We had to grope. Or ask.

Their launch was done up with coloured streamers and paper plates (That's part of the deal, yaar) and was called 'Party Lines'—one of their more enterprising acquaintances was doing this during the nights; he was 'into' computers during the day. I, by now, was feeling left out so I was given charge of Perfect Ice and tracking down their favourite Marx brothers films ('for old times sake, Mom'). For all their looking like old-time gangsters they were really very sentimental. A minor crisis. Shalini said she couldn't come to the pre-wedding day party (I wasn't surprised), she said she hadn't known about it in time and her mehndi people needed her for eight hours. They were trying something new—not just her hands but her forearms as well. But then, of course, they couldn't uninvite the other girls so, anyway, they took this in their stride. They didn't really have a choice. Dawned the day. Not the wedding day. The day before. It was a weekday so everyone went to work as usual. Late afternoon Ravi turned up with the wedding invitation—the final creative scroll, silk and handwritten, with a little wooden knob and ribbons no postal system would take charge of; which was why poor Ravi was hand-delivering them and had at last reached our home late afternoon, the eve of his wedding. He'd been doing this every evening after work—and being such a thoughtful, old-fashioned boy each visit meant standing in a doorway, tilting sideways with tiredness, then a glass of water, then the handing over of the scroll and smiling and then the cheerful waving of the hand with, 'I hope you and uncle will definitely come.' How could a person stay away? I was told that the last scroll was delivered five minutes before the actual wedding, this may just be hearsay but it's true, Ravi was rather late for his wedding. It's called putting first things first.

Which is what I should be doing. Putting first things first. When I first met Ravi he was a very tall sixteen-year-old boy. He stood in a doorway leaning slightly to the left and that's how he always stood.

He was standing thus, waiting politely to be asked to come in, I did, and he did come in and moved to a bench where everyone shifted and moved up for him and he shared a book of Prose and Poetry (Eleventh Std), with a girl called Shalini. For the next five years Ravi and Shalini shared the same bench in different classrooms and they shared the same book. Of course, the book changed— that first day when he was sixteen and she was also sixteen the poem started with 'Had I heaven's embroidered cloths', and five years later it was a very bleak poem by Hardy, 'Only a man harrowing clods/in a slow, silent walk'. Ravi always looked very confused when faced with poetry—less with prose and later, greatly at ease with photography which became his life and work. Shalini was a tiny girl and later she became a tiny woman. Ravi seemed never to stop growing and now at twenty-seven, he was as tall as a tree and still stood in doorways listing slightly to the left. By now I realized why he stood like that—it was because he was so tall and all the people he loved the most were very small—first there was his mother and then there was Shalini—he was constantly bent slightly sideways, either listening intently or caring or loving intently.

So Ravi was late for his own wedding but that comes a bit later. Something happened before that. And it was this. Little omens and portents if you think like Hardy or like most of us Indians. Perfect Ice hadn't turned up with the ice and there was a whispered phone call about blood and could you bring a bandage. So my son says to me, 'Don't gaze out of the window, Mom, that won't make Perfect Ice turn up quicker.' Which was his homely way with The Watched Pot Doesn't Boil so I said I knew that and then he said, 'I'm running late,' and I said, 'I can't think why you are having this party at all when you know Shalini is not coming.' 'Well,' says my son, 'we are having it and I'm late so could you look for the bandage, knowing you it's going to take a while finding it?' Not liking that last bit but knowing how futile it was to argue about it considering the state his room had been in since 1980 when he had started being against anyone coming into his room, I started looking for the bandage. I knew it would take a while since I had put it away safely and forgotten where. Before I found it there was another phone call, again whispered, and yet frantic sounding and my son shouts—'Have you found it, Mom, because Gautam is bleeding to death from the sounds of it?' And I said, 'Where's his mother?' and my son says, 'He doesn't want his mother to know, because it's his bike again,' and I said, 'How will he hide it if he has a great bandage on it?' And he says, 'At the rate you're going he may never have a bandage.' Which I felt was cheeky considering it was my bandage and I was wasting a great deal of time looking for it. In the meantime Perfect Ice turned up with such miraculous looking ice I wanted to have a party of my own, and then I found it. The bandage. It was in a neat cardboard box marked 'Nepal trek'. The neat box had trekking boots, safety pins, rope, a tin-opener, a prayer about 'going placidly amidst the noise', a book on 'Back-packing in the Cotswolds', and a bandage. What years ago that trek—don't think about it now, think about the child bleeding to death. 'Oh,' I called out, 'remember that trek?' 'Who could forget it? At least it's over—that's the best part.' 'Yes, but remember, remember the snow?' 'Remember tearing through the rhododendron forests, our ankles and feet bleeding with leeches hanging on?' 'Oh, but think of the good parts.' 'Yes, like it rained all the time, anyway Mom not now some other time and oh yes I'll take the Savlon cream just in case, shall I? Oh and Mom before I forget, tomorrow for the wedding you will try and look nice or at least like other people's Moms.' 'Yes,' I said, 'I'll try hard not to look as if I've just taken the dog for a walk, yes I'll try. Have a good time, I hope it's a lovely party. It's a splendid idea and Ravi has three very good friends.' He preened a bit at that and left. I started to think about what he had said about looking nice the next day—were things really that bad? I remember once, when everyone was at least fifteen years younger, how one of the boys had a mum everyone talked about—she walked about wearing a sari-petticoat done up with pins and a great Alsatian on a bit of string. I started looking for a sari. It all seemed very tedious suddenly. Suddenly I felt old.

But the pre-wedding surprise party didn't go off all that well. In fact it was 'a bloody disaster, yaar,' they were to say later, 'but how could we know?' Yes, true, how could they know? The launch looked beautiful as did the coloured paper plates and the streamers and the booze flowed, Perfect Ice was perfect, familiar music, familiar girls, old jokes and then Ravi disappeared; he just disappeared. He was found, of course—how far can you lose yourself on a launch making its way to Butcher's Island or somewhere? But he was with someone no one had seen before. She was an outsider. Who had she come with? Nobody seemed to know. Later it turned out she was somebody's outstation cousin— she had looked quiet enough—not the kind to rock the boat— she'd been sitting all by herself at the edge of the launch, staring at the water, not eating or drinking and that's where Ravi had found her. And that's where they sat most of the night together, staring at the water, sometimes they talked and she told him about what it felt like to live in Kashmir, how she'd lived there all her life. And now she didn't know where she'd live. It was over for her—Kashmir was finished. It would never be the same. And Ravi sat with her and thought about her and thought about what this must all feel like and Ravi was sad and Ravi could think of nothing else.

Except the girl. The girl that nobody knew. Except. Who had gatecrashed the party. Of course the friends resented her. How could they not? She had changed everything—it was not any more their party for him, their farewell party for him. The thing was she had made it her party—the party that Ravi would remember now because of her. The most literate of the four said, 'It's like *The Great Gatsby*, yaar.' 'That's all we needed,' said another. 'Might as well wind up,' said a third, 'Ravi danced only with her. He really wasn't there for anyone else.' Someone said, 'Thank God Shalini isn't here.' Another said, 'That's the whole point yaar—if only she had been here this wouldn't have happened.' But they weren't so sure about that either.

Anyway, the closeness they had striven for was gone. They felt vaguely unhappy. 'It keeps reminding me of something,' said one. 'I told you it's like *The Great Gatsby*. I haven't read it yaar.' 'So what, you've seen the movie—Redford and Woody Allen's bird, remember?'

Someone raised a toast 'to Ravi and Shalini', but there was no joy in Ravi's eyes—truth to tell he wasn't there for them any more. The party ended earlier than they thought it would. 'Long day tomorrow,' said one and felt silly immediately. 'Take care,' said another. 'Don't be late tomorrow—remember you're a witness.'

Ravi left with the girl. The cousin never materialized. Years later he said, 'It wasn't my fault, she just turned up, I had to look after her, how could I know?' Which was also true.

The rest felt hollow. Empty. They felt defeated, and more than a little disturbed. They couldn't think about it. And there was still tomorrow. Because tomorrow was the wedding. The girls thought about *Jane Eyre*. They didn't share this thought with the boys. They were afraid they might say, 'Jane who?' or, 'Not now, for Pete's sake!' So they kept quiet.

The wedding was a routine, dreadful affair. The witnesses were on time. The bride was on time; also her family. Since she was wearing long sleeves nobody could check whether the mehndi which included her forearms was really worth it or not. It didn't seem worth following that particular trend of thought. They thought it, anyway. You can't stop your thoughts, can you? The heat was unbearable. All around the roads had been dug up, getting to the wedding had been like the First World War—there was a smell of hot tar, the monsoons were round the corner, the gulmohurs were in furious flame. Ravi was late. But he came. Pale and quiet and tilting slightly to one side. 'Sorry,' he said. They signed their names. 'Sorry,' he said.

A tiny crack in an eleven-year-old wall. Nothing would fall apart. The centre would. Would hold.

English Girl

Park Bench

Sophie lived on a street lined with cherry trees. They were a marvel when in blossom. They were not in blossom now, it being winter. Even had they been in blossom, Sophie would not have noticed.

Sophie had had the flu for a long while. She had taken a long while shaking it off. Longer than usual. She was up and about though she felt odd, disoriented somehow. Her Aunt Meg rang her every day, 'Just checking, Sophie darling—did you sleep all right and have you an appetite yet? Wrap up warm and try and get out a bit even if it's just to the park. Don't get broody. Promise.' One day Sophie had felt terror at her kitchen window. She'd been shelling peas at the window and thinking only of the task at hand— a blue colander, the peas green, and her finger. But, suddenly, the feel on her fingers was wrong, it was moist, it was slimy, it was horrible. When she looked down she saw it was a fat green caterpillar, green and moist, fat and snug between two peas, and she felt sick and frightened at the unexpectedness of it, like a step which isn't there on a familiar staircase or like looking up through the friendly leaves of a tree to find a gecko looking back at you, shadow on a wall, face at a windowpane. She'd flung away the bowl of peas and felt so afraid that she'd got her raincoat out of the hall cupboard and rushed out of the house thinking, I must do something, I really must, and I must do it quickly before I am set in this mould forever. Because there are people who live alone and feel like this and it stays with them forever. Always. That I should feel such fear in quite ordinary things—and that I feel, still feel, that I cannot go back and climb the stairs and fit the key in the lock and finish shelling peas in my own kitchen—it's nonsense. But I can't bear it and I can't go back, not for a while, anyway. Soon I shall get back to it and manage if not perfectly well at least adequately. I shall soon get to the park and I shall sit on a bench and try to think this out—because really it may still be as Aunt Meg says, the after-effects of flu. My life feels awful just now. I keep thinking this can't be really all that there is to my life—years and years of just this—no change, ever. Impossible. But what I felt just now in the kitchen is frightening because I refuse to embark on a life where, apart from night fears, fears might be contained for me in such friendly places. Day fears. In the park I'll think. She turned in at one of the smaller gates. In this grey season within and without the park at this odd hour seemed strange. But it is only, she thought, strange because this is not the time of day I would usually come. The hour is odd, I'm usually doing something else, so I must not worry. Usually she had with her her great bag and usually when she found a bench she took out the book she was reading. So that, even if she did not mean to read it, it was always a comfort to know she had it there with her. But today she had rushed out, with no great bag—its familiar weight dragging at her shoulder—and now she was here and she found a bench and she sat down feeling odd, exposed, wondering if the park attendant might ask her to leave or something; she felt so odd and was certain it showed. After a while, when she realized that nobody in the park was going to do anything dramatic to her, she felt better, she began to work something out. What I need is a change, she thought.

Sometimes with a change a person improves, or at the very least, things look different, perspectives seem to shift. Yes. Even before I fell ill I was stuck in a groove. Perhaps everything is stale now in my world, too long at just the one thing and all that went with it too, of course. Still just the one thing and time slipping by and then the flu badly, at a sad time.

That was it. Or partly it.

I am very miserable, she thought, now that the illness has gone there is a sort of grey aftermath. Yes, now that I have said it to myself for the first time, I realize I am really deeply miserable, as though, yes really as though, I have nothing, I am nothing. I have no life to live. Just now, I am nothing, I am as grey as this season with no name, when summer is over and autumn is over and winter is about to come but hasn't. Grey waiting season.

No season.

'Sophie, it is the flu—for a long while after a bad bout of it a desolation sets in. You enter into a bleak no-area sort of feeling. Are you listening to me, Sophie darling?' her Aunt Meg had said. 'It passes, though you feel it will never go away, it does, believe me.' Her Aunt Meg had said. 'It doesn't do to brood about too many things when you've just had the flu, makes things seem very black, but you just guard against thinking it means everything, or that that's all there is to life and you've had quite enough, thank you very much! Are you listening Sophie love? Because, Sophie, I can see that you're pretty deep into it, you are, aren't you? It passes, trust me. Just when you think it never will, it goes away. Do you hear me?' her aunt had said.

Part of Sophie did believe Aunt Meg, but it hadn't passed, it hadn't gone away. Her aunt had said that to her weeks ago. Ages ago. And now she was in the park.

Sophie loved Aunt Meg because you could count on her never saying things other people said when they were trying to help you or advise you, like: 'You're as young as you feel' or 'Things aren't so bad, every cloud has a silver lining' or 'Pull yourself together' or 'Think cheerful and you'll be cheerful' or even 'Wear happy colours—no more greys or browns, and, heaven help us, never black! Try pink or buttercup-yellow.'

Sophie looked up and saw an elderly woman with a shopping bag. And Sophie thought she seems part of a life. This woman with her shopping bag will buy what she has to and then she will go home and then she will cook a meal and then she will eat it and she will wash and dry the dishes and put them away, and water the plant on the kitchen shelf and then she will wind the clocks, listen to the news and the weather forecast and then she will go up to bed. She has a cat and she might allow the cat to sleep at the end of her bed. No, perhaps not. Perhaps the cat is put out last thing—and then the light on the landing. And then to bed. I'm sure she folds her dressing grown neatly—it's a royal blue Jaeger, to match her hot-water bottle.

Sophie felt almost soothed about a life so well ordered. The life that she had gifted the woman.

Sophie heard the sound of a guitar.

Unmistakable sound.

It sounded far. It sounded quite near.

Sophie stood up and moved in the general direction of the sound. If someone, she thought, could play like that, in the park and in the cold, I must see who it is. The sound was not like the usual familiar 'accompanying' sound you heard all the time in the summer in the park—small groups sitting on the grass, lying on the grass. This was quite different. I must see the person who plays like that, she thought. She came to a group of trees—under one of them, a bench. And then she saw a man with his guitar. His head slightly bent towards his guitar; he seemed to cradle his guitar. He was a young man. For a while Sophie stood very close; and then she sat down.

He did not seem to mind her sitting there because he did not stop playing. Sophie thought, people always have a way of making you realize that you are in the way, that they feel you are an intrusion, that you have invaded their privacy. And Sophie thought, this man didn't do anything at all so it must be all right my sitting here on this bench watching his hands, his fingers, play as he is playing his guitar. And I shall stay here till he stops. I hope he does not stop. At least not for a long while. I feel very sad at his music. I feel greatly at peace even though I feel sad.

After a long while he stopped. Sophie got up and started to try and say something, but he said, 'I shall be here tomorrow. Will you come?'

The next day she left her house and walked straight to the bench under the trees.

Already he was there. She said her name was Sophie. His was Rui. She had never heard this name before. He said he came from Goa. It was very cold in the park. He played his guitar a long while, also he sang. Sophie did not understand the words, only the mood. Later he translated the song for her. He said, 'Sometimes it is just a mood—the words are just about a longing, for the soil or for the feel of my land. In Portuguese there is a word, *saodades*. It's a simple word, it means a great deal, perhaps it's a simple word which makes it difficult to translate. Anyway, *saodades* is a favourite word with which the Goan likes to name a feeling about Goa, a kind of nostalgic longing and deep belonging, yes, that's what the song is about.' Sophie said, 'Have you been a long time away from your home?' He said, 'Yes, a long time.'

When she got home she rang her Aunt Meg who said, 'Sophie you haven't done this in such a long while, you must be better, are you better? Is that why you called me, darling?'

And Sophie said, 'Yes, yes, that's why I called you Aunt Meg, I felt what you said I would, one day quite suddenly, you remember, you said it would go away and it has, really. I feel different, the awful feeling has lifted. Thank you, Aunt Meg, thank you so much for telling me it would.'

Her Aunt Meg said, 'I'm so glad darling, has anything else happened?'

And Sophie said, 'I'm not sure yet but I'll tell you soon.'

And her aunt said, 'Take care.'

Conversation 1

One day Sophie said, 'And London, what has it been like for you here? You've never told me, except for the park, you love this park. But where do you live?'

'I'd rather not think about where I live. I escape from it every day. A Bed-and-Breakfast place, narrow little gloomy room with no bath, in Bayswater, do you know that area? Sophie, it is awful! Hotel facades quite Victorian, quite elegant, single room no bath and gloom and smells—little babies learning to crawl on the landings because the rooms are so small and their mums feels that they will never walk if they don't learn to crawl. It is gloom and doom and dark, it's why I come to the park every day, so in a way I should be grateful to my B and B in Bayswater or I would never have realized quite the meaning of your London parks, never.'

'But it's freezing here in the park, bitter, so cold and the thin cold rain and—'

'But, Sophie, it's much colder in my room in Bayswater, truly. I prefer this cold in the park, and then there is the sky, and there is the grass and trees, and I can feel my guitar, and oh yes, the lake reminds me of home—so my friend Sophie, do you see? Have I answered your question about where I live, and why I come to this park every day? And now of course it has even more meaning—'

Sophie said, 'Why does it have more meaning now? Why? Do you mean because soon it may be spring, that spring will come, because I feel that too, now, in the air, or something?'

And Rui said, 'No, that's not what I mean, though that may also be true, I mean, quite simply, that one day you came to this park, and through the trees, to this our bench and now you are my dearest friend in all the world. That's what I mean, Sophie, that is what I mean. Do you understand?'

'Yes,' said Sophie. 'You have said what I have wanted to say, and been meaning to say, and now you have said it. Thank you, really, thank you.'

'But Sophie, I have to go back home now—I have been trying to find reasons for putting it off—because though I want to and have to—I have been putting it off. Can you understand that? Sophie, can you see that kind of mad faint-heartedness?'

'Yes, I can and do understand it—I am like that when it's something very important. The other things, of course, I don't dither a bit.'

'Come with me, Sophie. If you will come with me I could show you what I love, what I miss. Come to my home, Sophie. You have been ill, you have been unhappy, you need the sun and you need the sea, and I need you to come with me. Could you do that? Would you want to do that? Could you think about such a journey, Sophie?'

Sophie said, 'It takes my breath away, but yes—I could think about it and, yes, I would want to do it and I would find sufficient courage for such a faraway journey if it meant coming with you. Yes, Rui.'

'Sophie, I don't think you will regret it—it is so warm in the

The Quiet of the Birds

sun; you will love the sun and you will love our beach, our village is about ten minutes from the sea, you can swim every day and never feel cold and you will live in our house and I will take you to see everything I want you to see and everything you want to see. With you I could go back tomorrow, I mean, very soon. The things I fear would disappear—come to feel unimportant anyway, compared to the things I love, and miss, and long to be part of again.'

Sophie said, 'Will you write to your mother? I mean she will need to prepare, you have been away such a long while, she won't welcome the idea of a stranger in a home that has been without you in it—for what is it now—four years?'

'Yes, I will write to her and say I am coming home and that I am bringing with me the best friend I have in all the world—she has to be happy. Anyway, Caridade will be happy and she'll start cooking the moment she hears—or at least fattening up the piglets— '

'And who is Caridade, Rui? And is there room for me in your—'

'Caridade is Caridade—you'll see when we go home. I can't describe her. She's always been there—she's kind and she's thoughtful and she's loving. You'll soon see. She will love you as I love you. As for room for you, of course there is. Room for you, rooms and rooms for you, things locked up will be opened for you, if you don't like my sister's room, you could have the spare room, and if you don't like that you could have my room and I'll move into my father's study. Oh Sophie, there is room. For you.'

'Rui, I only meant—'

'I know what you meant, of course I know, but it will be all right. Look, let's not think about certain things at all, or we'll never go, certain hurdles we'll meet when we get to them, all right? We'll go together, it will be new for you and it will be new for me showing you—it gives me such a wonderful reason for going back— I should like to show you my home, my land, where I come from. The smell of it, and the tastes and the old walls and arches and chapels and the deep red stone and the paddy fields and salt pans and palm trees, and the cashew palms and the areca palms and the islands far and near—and always the sea or calm inlets, water and heat and whitewashed houses and churches and roadside crosses and a profusion of bougainvillaea, pink and magenta, loading down walls and arches and gates. Sophie, you cannot begin to imagine what it is like! Only think of that—don't think about the other things—not now. Just think we are going—you and I are going—you will come. You must come. And don't worry—no strings attached, as you say. No strings, naturally. Unless—'

And Sophie said, 'No strings, naturally. Unless, as you say—and thank you. Yes, let us go, and very soon.'

Conversation 2

It was very cold; they sat close to each other for warmth and trust and, by now, much affection. This is how they were every day in the park. When she joined him he would play his guitar and sing and always explain the words of the song to her. One day she said, 'We have an old song rather like that, it goes something like this—

In the sweet season, my fate is bitter
The month of May has changed into winter;
I find the nettle when I look for the rose;
You are free whereas I am fast bound.'

'Yes,' he said, 'all the best songs in all the languages of all the world have really the same meaning—I will try and set that to music for you.'

When he tired of playing they would talk. Sophie asked him many questions and Rui would tell her many things. One day she said, 'And Rui tell me about your family—I mean, you seem rather alone even when you say things about Goa, and then you mention your sister's room or your father's study, you don't mind me asking, do you? Do you mind? There is so much I want to know.'

In the pause that followed she said, 'It's just that you are rather like an only child a lot of the time, you don't mention other names or things said or done in a family—I mean, just quite ordinary things—I feel I have told you so much about my Aunt Meg that when you meet her you'll feel you already know so much about her whereas I—'

'Of course you're right, Sophie, and of course you . . . I don't mind your asking me, you can ask me anything at all, I mean that, truly. Do I have a family? Yes and no. My father died before I was born. My mother lives in our family house in a village in Goa. A long time ago I had a sister. Not now. Not any more. That's my family.'

Sophie said, 'How do you mean, not any more? Do you mean she went away, do you mean she died? Rui, is she dead or dead to you, or what?'

'No, she isn't dead—that's the trouble—I mean virtually she is. Look, Sophie, don't mind me, it's just I'm not used to talking about her. I haven't talked about her to anybody for so long, I mean, perhaps I haven't to anyone since I was very young. She, my sister, was ten years older. When I was five she went away from home and then, though we visited her sometimes, she never came back home to live with us. She was very important to me. She was my friend. I waited for her to come home. I waited for her for a very long time because nobody had explained to me that she was never coming home. When we visited her it was difficult to ask her, there were always other people there. I was afraid to ask her in case she said she was not coming. I could not understand why she would not come—I thought that I was as important for her as she was for me—so things were never the same after that. It was finally Caridade who told me not to wait. She told me that the 'Order' that my sister had joined was a 'closed' one—is that the term you use here? Or is it called 'cloistered'? Anyway, she'd become a nun.'

Sophie said, 'But do you mean that at fifteen she wanted to become a nun—she actually chose to become one over anything else in the world? I mean, she was just a child, a girl. Rui, isn't that very unusual? I mean, it's true every now and again one reads about someone having a vocation—rare times when someone chooses something so drastic, so very young.'

Rui said drily, 'Where I come from it's very seldom like that—you have a very romantic idea about nuns and priests. It's something chosen for you. Like deciding that you'll go to boarding school or whatever!'

'Oh, you're just joking, you can't mean that,' Sophie said. 'Are you saying that this was decided for her by someone else—when she was so young? Do you mean a parent? Is that what you are saying, Rui?'

'Yes, that is what I'm saying. Precisely. That's it. In Goa the nunneries are full. The seminaries are full. You don't imagine every one in them has a vocation? Sometimes they are even referred to as factories! Dear Sophie don't look so upset—so shocked—because it's true, really.'

'But Rui, not fifteen! That's far too young. By any standard. Surely, I mean, I do realize that in certain centuries, in certain countries all sorts of things were happening—but not now—surely not in this century.'

Sophie was so agitated that she got up from the bench and stood in front of Rui. He looked up at her saying, 'But Sophie— Goa is a different country—and a different century, for many things. You read a lot, think a lot, don't you? What about India, what about child marriage, what about sati, what about Muslim countries? It makes me angry, it makes me depressed, but it's all still in this century, isn't it—isn't it, Sophie? Please sit down again, near me, give me your hand. I know why it feels really bad—it's because you never thought to know someone whose family might contain such a reality—that's always a shock, isn't it? Perhaps subconsciously you like me less—perhaps blame me somehow for allowing something like this to happen to a dearly loved sister. Though I know I couldn't have done anything about it at the time, I do feel guilty, I do feel terrible. So of course I can sense your feeling of outrage, and it is that, isn't it Sophie?'

'Yes, I suppose, partly it is that—but partly I'm thinking that unless there really was a desperate reason why—why that for a girl of fifteen? Your mother, Rui—you have never spoken of her. She had to make all the decisions, didn't she? You say your father died before you were born—she was alone with a ten-year-old daughter and a baby. Maybe, maybe she couldn't manage, couldn't cope or something. Rui, why do you think she decided that for your sister? Didn't you ask her—I mean when you were older, didn't you ask, you must have wanted to know, you did, didn't you? You did ask?'

Rui said, 'Yes, I did ask and, yes, I did want to know.' Sophie said, 'And—and what did she say? Rui what did your mother say?'

'She said it was what my father would have wanted—and that soon it would seem even to me the wisest thing in the given circumstances—that it was what my sister also wanted and that was all.'

'Did you accept that, Rui? Did it make sense to you?'

'No, Sophie, of course it didn't make sense—but it was an answer that made me realize certain things about my mother—things I can never forgive—things I shall never understand.'

'Even now, Rui?'

'Yes, Sophie, even now—perhaps more now. Perhaps it's why I left my home.' Sophie looked up through the branches of a tree where still there was no hint of a leaf and thought, it's very important to me that he is saying these things, perhaps he's not really sharing them with me so much as somehow needing to speak, that's all, speak out, get it said. So I must not mind this momentary feeling of separateness—I am not just a stock or stone. I am not just a sounding board. She looked back at Rui and said as if there had been no pause at all, 'Why do you say that? Why more now?' And he said, 'I suppose distance and being away so long has made me think about my mother, she is difficult to think about when living in the same house. Anyway, I realized her answer didn't really make all that much sense at all. Perhaps what I should have seen in her answer was merely that she had decided that my sister should enter a nunnery—that's all. I mean, when she said that it was what my father would have wanted what did that make my father? What kind of a father is going to express that kind of wish for his only daughter? I mean, when she said that it was the wisest thing in the given circumstances, what did that mean? If it had been a large family, many daughters, many sons, one might consider that it could have been an economic problem he was helping to deal with, that he was dying and what would my mother do? How would she manage? I mean, that happens all the time in Goa. But none of this was true. We had money, we had a large and well-appointed house, as they say. And there was just my sister and me.

'And then, Sophie, almost as an afterthought my mother had said that it was what my sister wanted—I can't hide behind the fact that I was too young to question some of what she said. So why didn't I? So why didn't I ask? Why did I just accept what my mother said? It's just an excuse to say I was stunned, shocked. Just an excuse to say that I was sad and sick with loneliness for my sister. If I really loved her and missed her then why didn't it help me to find out why my mother had decided this for my sister. It isn't really a legitimate plea, is it Sophie, to say I was too young. Perhaps I'm weak. Put in another way, perhaps I was afraid of my mother.'

'But that's not unusual, Rui. Many children are afraid of a parent. It's a pity, it's unfortunate, often it is tragic—but you can't decide it's because you are weak. Anyway, it was a long time ago, when there was no way you could have done anything. If it happened now don't you see you would do something? Of course, you would. You can't chastise yourself forever about how you did nothing when you were just a boy.'

'But Sophie what about later? What about when I was not a boy? Why did I ask Caridade and not my mother? It troubled me always when I was no longer a boy. At twenty-five I left home rather than confront my mother. I long to go back. But, I'm still here. It's been four years—I haven't been really happy except for meeting you. I need to go back; I find it difficult to go back; I long to go back; I'm still here. I am afraid of my mother. Also, I think I hate her.'

A little wary and weary, Sophie said, 'You love your mother—excessively. Let's walk by the lake. Let's just walk and walk. May I carry your guitar for a while? Come on, Rui.'

Sophie and Rui stood up and left their bench and walked towards the lake—clearly some things could now not be said. But in an odd sort of way I'm glad, thought Sophie. Fearful, but glad. And Rui thought, I think I could go home—now. Yes. And I shall.

The lake was placid, no colour, and looked cold. They walked and walked and soon were warm. And Rui stopped suddenly and said, 'You came to me in winter—you are my girl in winter. Come home with me, Sophie. You come.'

Conversation 3

A few days later they went to tell Sophie's aunt Meg. They went to tell her the news, to tell her about their plans. In the kitchen, making coffee, Sophie said, 'I am going Aunt Meg—shall I—Aunt Meg— do you think that—?'

And her aunt said, 'Don't think so much Sophie—go. Don't wait worrying. Don't mull over it, grab; seize. Remember what we once read together? Anyway, he likes you enormously and clearly you do—how can you wait? Seize it, say yes, with all your heart—'

'Yes,' said Sophie, 'but—'

'There aren't any buts, not just now. They may or will come later. Always do—raise their ugly heads, unfortunately. But for now "live all you can—it's a shame not to" remember? Oh Sophie, go,' her aunt said.

Sophie hugged her closely and said, 'Will you be all right? I'll miss you.'

'Of course, I'll be all right and, of course, I'll miss you too— enormously, and I will be here if you come back, or when. All right. I'll keep. But Sophie, recognize when you are unhappy, don't wait till it's too far gone. Act. As you have when you are happy. You are doing something about it. Even if it means coming back, it's no failure. Promise? Promise me, Sophie—all right?'

'Yes,' said Sophie. 'Yes,' she said.

Arrival

The excitement held for a while. 'It is as you said, Rui! It really is! The water and the islands and the very deep red soil and rock and the whitewashed walls and churches and the massed bougainvillaea. My God, Rui, it is beautiful—even more beautiful than you said it was! And it is warm, it is so warm! I'm so glad we came, aren't you? I can't believe we were so cold just a few hours ago. I know you said it would be warm but it's still such a shock—I shall turn brown quickly. I can't bear to be the colour I am, I shan't wear these awful shoes any more, I can't wait to get them off, and when will we go for our first swim? Rui, you're so quiet, I'm sorry to go on like this. But I'm so excited. Are you all right? Are we nearly home, I mean, is your village quite near now? Are you worried— yes you are. Hold my hand.'

Very late that first night she wrote, Dearest Aunt Meg—we are here—I mean, we have arrived. It is as Rui said it would be, but it is also something else. From the airport the road is marvellous, it winds and seems to go up and downhill and has the sea always on one side and an island called Sao Jacinto with a lighthouse and church at its highest point, also a village you can see through the trees. Remember when you took me to Greece and we went to the islands? The feel of water and whitewashed walls and boats and people at work with fishing nets and the heat? Well, here I am reminded of that, but it's different. The smells are different and the architecture is different—it is like but not like.

It is very green, no grass, but the earth and rock are a deep terracotta red and the dust makes the bushes and trees have a kind of red film on them. Though the sea and inlets of water are everywhere, still it looks parched. There are large white churches and small white chapels everywhere—but you don't have church bells at all! Quite soon, after the airport, the road passed a very high white wall, very high and all enclosing, and on the wall painted in black I read in large painted letters, 'Cloistered Carmel' and Rui turned away when I wanted to ask him about it. He has a sister in a closed order. I wonder if his sister is in there. You would love the pink and orange and magenta of the bougainvillaea, Aunt Meg. They grow in such profusion everywhere—over gates and porches and walls. Not over Cloistered Carmel—that was rather menacing—stark white and the black of the lettering. I must still be jet-lagged as they say, because some of what I saw was so very clear and yet some hazy as though it wasn't something I had really seen. Rui's village seemed very far from the airport. But perhaps it felt like that because it was so varied, and it was very warm—we crossed an expanse of water twice, once over a vast bridge and once by a charming ferry. I loved that, we got out of the bus and stood near the railing of the ferry—breeze and lots of people and motorcycles—Rui must have been so excited—it made him very quiet and tense. Finally we reached his village. It is idyllic, Aunt Meg. The road wound downwards, paddy fields on one side and salt pans on the other and in the very near distance a huge church through the palm trees. Very white, but so big for such a small village. And then his house.

Letter 2

Dear Aunt Meg,

I'm not sure whether I ended my first letter to you. Anyway, Rui says, he posted it to you. What I had meant to say at the end of the letter was that Rui's house deserved a whole new letter. It's quite extraordinary, like no house I have ever seen, let alone visited or now lived in, for a whole week. Are you well, Aunt Meg? We both send you our fondest love. And now the house. Oh, interruption—I'm writing this propped up against a huge, rounded rock formation, sitting on the softest sand imaginable, shaded by an old, twisted, bent palm tree and all around, if I look up from what I'm writing to you, which I do frequently because it's so superb, is sea. Sea and more sea but broken by an island and in a small sort of bay, a white boat. It looks quite close but it isn't really because I have tried swimming up to a sort of platform near it. I haven't managed to reach the platform yet—I get suddenly a little uneasy some distance from it. But I shall do it quite soon because the water is so calm and so beautifully warm and should I tire I'll just float. Remember when you and I used to swim in Greece how it always looked perfect—that extraordinary blue—and yet it was always rather cold, wasn't it, and close to the rocks rather slimy and black; seaweedy? But here it's not like that at all. The water isn't as blue, but it's perfect in every other way. Hardly any shale, no really jagged rocks, no slime and warm-cool water—

overhead a perfect sky. When it gets too hot, this palm gives enough shade and there's a light breeze off the sea nearly all the time. And this beach is just about seven minutes from Rui's village. I come here every morning if Rui is not taking me to see something, and I stay here many hours, which brings me back to the house. I suppose it's the scale of the house in its setting that is so daunting—because when you leave the rice fields and the salt pans and the great church, the road curves down into what is really a dusty, narrow country lane with a small sort of village common, part playground, part dusty trees. There are some very thin and dusty stray dogs, a few very small houses and then this high washed-white wall and tall wrought-iron gates with stone pipelines on the side columns. Very little garden in terms of the size of the house—with a kind of gazebo thing in the far corner with trailing, pale-pink bridal creeper, a few massed coconut palms, one great pink and white cassia tree, a wild almond tree, no grass. Then a short flight of steps and two stone seats and the great wooden front door with a lizard for door-knocker. Extending on both sides of the front door strange shell-blinds to what seem to be many, many windows. You step into a very small hall with a very high ceiling, potted plants in vast ceramic pots, and then into what you could only call reception rooms—not drawing rooms or living rooms but like eighteenth-century rooms for soirees or yes, formal reception rooms. Very formal, high walls with family portraits, great carved beams and intricately carved, high-backed or winged chairs and carved or marble-topped tables and lamps with domed glass; doors and panels inset with deep coloured glass—wine coloured or deep green and topaz. My bedroom looks out on a private little walled-in courtyard with a single tree and flowering bushes. There is a very high, carved four-poster bed and a ceramic basin and tall water jug (mine has blue flowers); there's a chamber pot under the bed and one immense cupboard, one door of which is highly carved and the other set with a mirror full of grey shadows. At the back of the house a kind of deep veranda looks into a central courtyard-cum-garden. The outhouses and kitchen and storerooms are at a lower level—you just walk into an area that has a very deep well, two papaya trees and one very old shade-giving mango tree. Caridade hangs the washing up here and draws water from the well and grinds the spices in this courtyard. There is no running water and no electricity. Rui's mother does not want a major change to be made. Of course she does not use the palanquin covered in dust and cobwebs that I saw in one of the outhouses—but everything else seems set in another age. The shell-blinds keep the intense glare out, but the only time it is cool is very early in the mornings or late evenings when the blinds are open. It is an older way of life in nearly every detail. Dona Gabriela uses an ivory fan. When it is open it shows a man and woman flirting delicately near a garden. The man has a well-turned foot—elegantly shod. Talking of which, I can't bear to wear shoes—I have some open sandals—at the beach, of course, it's wonderful to kick them off. It can't be just that ivory fan. Aunt Meg, I know you don't like books with long descriptive passages but I have no camera and I have to share this extraordinary house with you. At night it's even larger and the many oil lamps create shadows and shapes not there in the day. Talking of cameras, rather photographs, our arrival forms a group photograph I find it rather hard to erase. Imagine. Aunt Meg: that overhanging porch with the stone seats, then the flight of steps. Rui's mother, Dona Gabriela, stood at the top step and just behind her, a little to the side, Caridade. I remembered what Rui had said about Caridade, she was so immensely happy to see Rui, she couldn't wait to hug him and her warmth somehow extended to me. She's very thin and I can't venture an age to her, essentially a sad looking woman but whose eyes lit up when they saw Rui. Dona Gabriela was rather different—the camera might or might not have picked up her expression. I could not see it when Rui bent to embrace her but when he introduced her to me then I did see her expression. Of course, I hadn't expected her to be ecstatic—why should she be— she hadn't seen her son for close on four years and here he was and with a stranger. But I had not counted on such coldness. She did not pretend to be even faintly pleased. Anyway, Caridade's eyes had lit up when they saw Rui and for now it's quite enough. Maybe the sun was in Dona Gabriela's eyes when she saw me. That might account for the expression—or lack of it. Dona Gabriela speaks to Rui in Portuguese. He has tried to include me, by replying in English, but it doesn't work very well. From the little she has said directly to me I suspect her English is excellent. Rui has not once played his guitar since his return. I miss that profoundly.

I must stop writing. I shall swim now and then get back to the house.

My much love—keep well.

Sophie XXX

Caridade and Sophie

One rather late evening Rui and Sophie returned from a long day spent in the island of Sao Jacinto. Sophie had wanted very much to go there ever since she had had a fleeting glance on the very first day from the airport. It had looked so green and still set in water with slow country craft passing and circling it. When she had turned back to look again she had seen, high up through massed trees, a white church and even higher, a lighthouse. 'I should like to go there Rui, may we, will we?' 'Yes,' he had said, 'of course we will.'

And today, finally, they had. It had been rather a long journey and hot, but it had been the best day in every sort of way and the island had been, strangely, even finer than that glimpse of it. Now she and Rui had seen something for the first time together. He had always meant to go and never been. Sophie called it immediately the Island of Hyacinths!

They were late. Of course when they turned in at the gate and saw the lone figure on the balcao they realized just how late. As they went up the steps Dona Gabriela half turned away from them saying, 'I am surprised that you are back at all—it is late. I was about to tell Caridade not to wait any longer, to turn down the lamps and bolt the door.' Rui said, 'I'm sorry, Mama, for being late, but surely it's not—' Gabriela interrupted him with, 'It is inexcusably late. I take it you have eaten?' Of course, none of this was directed towards Sophie. Rui went straight to his room. Sophie went up to Dona Gabriela and said, 'I am so sorry we kept you up and worried, so late—we rather miscalculated the time it would take—'

The Quiet of the Birds

'You misunderstand me. I am speaking to my son.' Gabriela spoke in English.

Sophie persisted because she still felt such a sense of the island and their day and she wanted very much to share it, or some of it, with Rui's mother. She said, 'Dona Gabriela, have you been to the island many times, I feel certain you must have because it is so beautiful—I have seen so much since I have come, but this island is finer than anything I have seen. I should love to live there—do you?'

'It is very late,' interrupted Gabriela. 'Yes, I have been to the island of Sao Jacinto. You will find that Caridade has taken the lamps to your room—excuse me now.'

Sophie said in a rush, 'Of course, Dona Gabriela, it's late, it's just that I wanted to thank you for making a day like this happen, I mean the island. I would very much like to ask you about it, just for a few minutes. We didn't mean to be so late but the ferry—'

'I am not concerned with why you are late, it surprised me somewhat, that is all. As for thanking me, it has nothing to do with me. Nothing at all. The island is there—and you have seen it. Good night.'

The snub absolute, thought Sophie. I suppose I deserved that. I'm glad it was dark, though. At least she didn't have the triumph of seeing how awful she made me feel. Rui could have warned me—perhaps he did, perhaps that's why he went to his room immediately. But how could I have just gone to my room immediately? She is my hostess. I am her guest. I did want to thank her. I did want to talk about the Island of Hyacinths. She was staring out of her dark window and realized she was crying. It's stupid to cry. It's just the beauty and the excitement of this day and I must be more tired than I realized to feel so hurt and so snubbed by Gabriela. Oh, I refuse, I absolutely refuse, to think about her tone of voice, I refuse to think of how she speaks to me, because if I do, if I do, if I really do, I shall burst, or tell Rui, or just leave. I shall have to leave—go away. That's really what she wants me to do and what I have tried to ignore and not think about. I wish it was tomorrow and I could escape to the beach, the sea. Perhaps swim to that platform. See who lived on the white boat with blue trimmings.

She heard a small sound behind her and Caridade's voice saying, 'You are very tired, you sleep now, it is not good to think too much about how you feel at the way she speaks—if you think about it, it hurts even more. I should know. Is there anything I can bring you?'

'No, nothing, Caridade, but thank you for coming to me—how did you know?'

'Oh, how could I not know? I have lived in this house so long—I know long before something happens that it is going to happen. It makes me feel so sad and helpless to think that knowing still does not help to avert it. Take today, as it got later and later I could tell from the way Dona Gabriela paced up and down, up and down, and then sat on the balcao and told me not to light the lamps—she said not to light them because you were not expected to return. Oh, please do not cry—she wins a great victory if you cry or let it upset you too much. Wipe your tears—wipe away what she said. Think only about your day with Rui. Think about the island, think about the things you wanted to speak about, think about how you loved the island, think about the dark, cool, old orchards of coconut and cashew trees, the sound of the sudden bird in the quiet, think about that old causeway, half in the water and half out and the colour of the old stone of the fort, the strange old church, and high up the lighthouse. Think of the sky and the water all around and the slow boats passing and passing. Think of—' Suddenly Sophie realized something and said, 'But you were not with us today, Caridade—you know it so well as if you had just come from there. When were you last there—you have spoken of the things I liked so much about it—when?' Caridade said, 'Yes, I have been to the island of Sao Jacinto—that is why I was so glad that Rui was taking you there today—'And Sophie said, 'But when, when did you last go there?'

'I have been there only once and a long, very long time ago, but I have never forgotten it. Even foundlings, as we were called, are taken out sometimes. I must have been thirteen years old because it was the same year that Dona Gabriela came to the Home. Three of the nuns took us, not the very little girls but us 'older' ones, the twelve to eighteen years ones. It was magical out of the foundling

The Quiet of the Birds

home with its high grey walls and dormitories; it was the closest thing to heaven that I could imagine. In fact, for a long time after that I did think of it as being what heaven was like, if I was a good girl I would get to that island again, if I did all my chores before the others I would get to that island again—one day. Clearly, I have not been a good girl because I have never been back there.'

'Oh Caridade, not once in all these years, not since you were thirteen? But when did you leave the Home?'

'That same year when I was thirteen. One day I was called to Mother Superior's parlour. I was frightened because only if you had done something really bad were you ever called there. When I got there I was wondering what the punishment would be, I was not thinking of what I had done wrong, and there was this very young and beautiful lady with Mother Superior. I could not take my eyes off her. Yes, it was Dona Gabriela. She needed a strong, capable and "good" girl to take home to work for her and the nuns had chosen me!'

'You mean Caridade that you have been with the family since you were thirteen years old—is that what you are saying?'

'Yes, that is what I am telling you. Since that morning when full of fear I went to Mother Superior's parlour with the sun coming through the bars of the window and two scarlet Easter lilies in the doorway—and my first glimpse of Dona Gabriela—she was young, she was beautiful and she was already in widow's black. Since that morning I have been with this family. The nuns chose me for being the brightest and the best! And I blessed my good fortune because I thought once I was out of that grey foundling home something good might happen—like that island, for instance! I might get back to the island—I never did get to that island. I came through these gates and up the stairs and met a little girl of about nine or ten and a new baby; the husband had died and she needed some help—'

Sophie said, 'You mean that baby was Rui—?' 'Yes,' Caridade said, 'that was Rui.'

In the silence Sophie watched several moths clustered around the lamp, half-dazed. One smashed itself against the dim, hot globe and dropped, stunned.

As if disturbed by that small sound in the silence Caridade said,

'I remember in the foundling home the girls who were plain or dark or ugly seemed to settle down much more easily to the life that they knew they would always have to lead. In the dormitories, after lights out, the sounds of those crying were from the pretty ones, the ones who knew they were, or were going to be, beautiful in spite of the awful uniforms of charity. Maybe, Sophie, it was like that for Dona Gabriela. Maybe being beautiful you have great expectations. I mean greater hope, finer dreams; that beauty necessarily gave the right to a wonderful life. Maybe.'

Sophie said, 'You are such a kind person, Caridade.' Caridade said, 'Because I am nothing else. You sleep now, try.'

Rui and His Mother

When Rui did not find his mother in her favourite room he went to her private chapel. He waited a long while. When she finally emerged she looked as usual, cool and cold. She looked at Rui with no surprise at all. 'The chapel does accommodate more than one person at a time—did you wish to pray? You look hot and bothered.'

'No Mother, I did not wish to pray—I was waiting for you to finish.'

'Then you must have something of urgency to talk to me about, do you?'

'Yes. It's about Sophie.'

'Really—and urgent? You had to wait outside the chapel for me to finish my prayers! It can only mean that she is leaving. When?'

'No Mama, she is not leaving. Her name is Sophie not "she". And that's what I want to talk about. Your extreme rudeness to her. I don't expect you to be nice to her—I gave up hoping for that ever since the day we arrived—but civility I do expect from you— it's the very least, Sophie is your guest. You are barely civil to her.'

'She is your guest, Rui. I did not invite her, I had no choice in the matter.'

'Mama, I wrote to you, I told you I was bringing a friend to Goa.'

'Precisely. You gave me no choice. You wrote to me. One letter in how many months—or is it years? What was I supposed to do—write back and say you cannot bring her to my house? This friend of yours?'

'Yes Mama—if that is how you felt when you got my letter. Is that what you really felt?'

'Yes, Rui that is what I felt and that is what I would certainly have written but I thought if I wrote that, you might not have come either. I had not seen you for over four years, you might have changed a great deal, I could not risk her telling you not to go home. I thought she might influence you enough to forget this house altogether. So I did not write. Anyway, why do you complain? Has she complained?'

'Her name is Sophie, Mama, and, no, she has not complained— not once in all this time. She is not that sort of person. Even if she is hurt by you—perhaps you have never watched her face when you have been rude to her? Anyway, she is too well bred to complain or to retaliate.'

'What amazing words you find, Rui, to describe this common English girl you have picked up—anyway she is fed and she has more than a roof over her head. What more can she possibly expect? Rui, you tell me, what more must I do for an outsider?'

'Mama, if you cannot sense the quality of a person, the quality of Sophie, I do not think I could explain it to you or even begin to define her fineness. Don't shrug your shoulders like that. Yes, her fineness. To you it has meant nothing, you are as you always are— were—no change, in all these years, no change. It is a sad pity, I must have been more than foolish to have hoped you might have changed just a little, as people do, you know, even the most hardened, the ones most set in their ways. And I suppose I felt you might genuinely like someone other than yourself. Someone different, someone like Sophie.'

'Really, Rui, what is so different about this girl—woman? What is so unusual about her that you expect me to change, me to genuinely like her? A "friend" from England—an ordinary, not unusual woman, the kind that, unfortunately, many young men from our better families from Goa bring back with them. That is all. Perhaps they tend to bring back girls from Germany or some such country—other than that what is so different about this English girl?'

'Well, for one thing, I'd say she was unusual to even try to understand a family like ours—think about that.'

'What do you mean, Rui? What do you mean by a family like ours? We are an old and very important family and it is a great privilege for any—'

'Oh do stop Mama—for God's sake—must you spin that old story even for me? I've been away but four years which is hardly long enough to forget what one has heard over and over again for most of one's life. There is nothing special about our family. Nothing at all. That it can trace itself back for hundreds of years means nothing at all—unless it has produced good people, caring people, people who had bettered the lot of other people who had nothing at all. If decades and decades ago we had in our family a fine scholar, a great and caring doctor—that's good. Or if our family had one great fighter for freedom from injustice, for freedom from pain—that's good, in fact that's very good. But, Mama, we cannot batten on that for the rest of our lives. We have not done anything at all for the last fifty or sixty years. In fact, to tell the truth, I'm quite ashamed to speak of "our family"—because what rears its ugly head is you and I—that's our family, Mama, and it's only special for a peculiar brand of separateness, selfishness and a brand of indifferent cruelty—that's all. I have done nothing with my life except grieve for something I could not understand or have. I am nothing at all. And you—what have you done with your life? Worn your widowhood as a badge to protect yourself from doing anything but harm to other people. So what gives you this rather ridiculous approach to "important family of Goa"? Do you mean in terms of the size of this ancestral home—its great age, its many superior architectural qualities, its beautiful chapel, its fine carved furniture, your hundreds of coconut trees and cashew trees and your villages and your daughter in a nunnery? We mustn't forget that, in hushed tones, others must speak or wish they too had a daughter in one of the only "cloistered" nunneries left in this land! Straight to heaven, it must gain you special entry—that, coupled with the amazing number of hours you spend praying. Special dispensation!'

'How dare you—?'

'Mama—to be slapped by you is an honour because I have managed to touch you to the quick, disturb you with something like the truth—disturb your selfish, hypocritical life.'

'You know nothing about my life, and there is nothing more I want or need to hear from you. If one strange girl you have brought into this house can make you say such things, I can only think that the sooner she leaves the better—'

'Oh Mama, why do I hope and hope that you will use your intelligence, that you will not willfully continue to be as narrow and closed as always? Think, it's not too late—or try and listen to what I am saying.'

'I listen to you, Rui. I hear what you are saying. I have listened and heard a great deal and now I am tired and would rather you left me alone.'

'No, Mama, I will finish what is very important for us to talk about. I have not tired you since I have come back and you have had four years to rest! To go back to why I wanted to speak to you in the first place, Sophie. Would you be civil to her while she is with me under this roof? The old laws of hospitality which you feel mean only food and shelter actually include courteous behaviour and kindness to a stranger. Sophie is a loving and caring person and she is a stranger in a strange land—let her not feel so unhappy while she is here.'

'So she has complained—you said she hadn't. Has she told you she is unhappy because of me? Why, I hardly see her—if she isn't with you showing her half of Goa, she is by the sea.'

'But that is why she keeps going to the sea. You make her feel so unwanted here in this house. In the beginning she was so eager to share with you the places she was seeing, she wanted to ask you so many questions about Goa and gradually she realized that you had no time for her. None at all. No, Mama, Sophie has not said anything. I see the change in her. Caridade sees the change in her. Only you see nothing. I can think of only three reasons why you are as you are with her. Perhaps four. That she is not a Catholic.

That she is not a young girl. That I like her very much. And that you did not have a hand in choosing her for me.'

Gabriela said, 'I do not have to listen to any of this any more. She is from an alien culture, an alien religion and she is not fit for our family. She is an outsider. She is not one of us.'

'Yes, and thank God for that. What you meant was a supreme insult but she is the saving of me because she is so unlike us. Must you continue to ruin and make unhappy all the lives that touch us? What are you so afraid of? Why must you clutch and hold so fast things that you know you are going to break? You won't give up the throne you occupy. But what kingdom do you reign over, Mama? You know there was once a truly great queen, some think the greatest the world has ever known till now. Her achievements were vast and solid; the times she lived in, violent and dangerous. She reigned alone and long. But even she, in her aloneness, in her hours of deepest perception, wrote on a windowpane certain lines— "I saw one night my own body, exceeding lean and fearful in a light of fire"—are you wont to see such sights in the night? "All the fabric of my reign, little by little, is beginning to fall." Mama, what about contemplating the fabric of your reign? Isn't it time?'

'Foolishness; ridiculous woman, weak woman, I have no such fears, not at night, not ever. Because I pray, Rui. Because I pray, I do not fear. What you have quoted to me is the weakness of a woman who has never prayed. Did you make it up by the way? It sounds rather like the sort of things you might set to music and sing to your guitar—?'

'No, I did not make it up—I wish that I could write a song like that—but what intrigues me is your complacent view of praying and prayers! What do you pray in your beautiful chapel? Is it still the prayers you learnt by rote when you did not know the meaning of most of the words? Surely, by now prayer is contemplation— stillness—a time to review "things ill done or done to others"— harm which once you took for exercise of virtue—'

'I don't know what you are talking about—if there is nothing else Rui, I really must now leave you—'

And Rui said, 'No nothing, nothing that you would care to

hear or remotely begin to understand. I have wasted your time. I have wasted mine.'

The White Boat

Sophie had often seen the neat white boat with blue trimmings. In fact, she saw it every day that she was at the beach. Whenever she was tired of reading or writing to Aunt Meg and she looked up and out to sea it was there. The platform that bobbed up and down quite close to it seemed a kind of anchor as well as a kind of resting place, Sophie decided, for tired swimmers. I must get to that platform soon, I know I can. And I must before that white boat sails away. I shall mind very much the day that boat isn't there any more.

One day when she swam quite close to the platform she noticed a woman in shorts hanging up some washing on a line on the deck. Sophie realized with a slight sense of shock that there were actually people living on the boat—she had somehow not peopled the boat. After that day she looked more carefully and one morning a man with a beard got into a small rubber dinghy and rowed towards the shore. Rui told her that sometimes boats that had sailed from quite far away did dock in this quiet inlet, used it as a resting place as well as a place to replenish fresh stores. So it will sail away, thought Sophie. I wonder where it has come from and where it is going. Now I have seen two people, a woman and a man with a beard. I wonder how many there are—it seems rather a small boat. I wonder what language they speak. I wonder when they are sailing back or sailing on.

When Sophie finally made it to the platform she heaved herself up on to it—triumphant, exhausted—and lay down flat and closed her eyes. I did swim to the platform—it was always here but I was afraid. She heard voices—or a voice—and then distinctly the voice said, 'I'll be with you in a moment, love,' and Sophie sat up.

She saw the woman that she had seen before hanging up washing on the deck and the woman smiled and then the woman waved and Sophie called out, 'When do you sail back or on?'

And the woman called out, 'In a week now—if all goes well.'

One Afternoon

One afternoon, as Sophie lay on the great bed with the shutters closed against the fierce glare, something snapped. The heat was unbearable. I cannot bear it, she thought. It rises and enfolds me like a great, rough blanket till I cannot breathe. Like a sauna bath trapped, and I cannot leave. She sat up and crossed to the shutters and flung them open—the opened window flung the heat back at her, the dust hung on the leaves, the leaves drooped with the heat, the ground was the colour and texture of dust, one enormous cobweb hung from her window to a far-off branch, in it caught a feather and dust. Sophie felt the sweat gather and trickle, trickle down her back. She felt it in her hair, like ants. 'I cannot bear it,' this, she said aloud, 'and I must speak to Rui. I must tell him. He has never asked me how I feel about this heat, he has never asked me how I bear it. I shall find him and tell him that I can only breathe when I am near the sea, on the beach. I shall tell him I cannot live in the interiors of Goa, they are all like museums, you cannot live your whole life from morning to night in a museum, you can love the great houses in Chandor of Loutolim or Margao, and you can admire the carved great chairs and chests from Macao. But you cannot live in them in this heat. Never.' She went looking for Rui. She found him on the balcao, his guitar on the bench beside him, staring out at the garden. She sat down next to him and he said, 'That gazebo there, Sophie, was where my sister and I used to sit and she would tell me stories, sometimes she sang to me—of course, now it looks different.'

Sophie looked at it—the pillars were more exposed than when she had first arrived, the pink bridal creeper looked withered. 'Anything would look different now,' she said. 'It's the heat. How can anything survive?' Rui looked at her then and said, 'Something is the matter, isn't it?' 'Yes,' Sophie said, 'I want to know why your mother is so rude to me. Why does she have to dislike me so much? I have waited a long while hoping that she might get used to me being here. Surely you can see it? Surely you can feel it? I stay out of the house so much—I am not in her way. Every trip you and I have she has managed to spoil by her coldness when we

The Quiet of the Birds

return. When we came back from Piedade or after that time we came from Chandor I wanted to tell her all about it, but she was so cold and so indifferent that I stopped trying to share anything. She doesn't have even a polite interest in what I have seen and how all this must be so unusual and different for me. She has never asked me a single question, Rui. In all this time. Not one.'

Rui said, 'I know—and I've thought about how you must feel.'

'Have you? Have you really thought about it, Rui? You never speak of it to me so that I would not feel so cut off, only Caridade from the way she looks at me makes me feel as though she understands.'

'What do you want me to do, Sophie? My mother won't change.'

'And you, Rui, what about you? You won't either?'

Dona Gabriela's Parlour

One particular day Sophie had been just about to leave the house as usual for the beach, stopping for a second in the back courtyard where already Caridade was grinding coconut, to pick up her swimsuit drying on the line, thinking how faded it had become in the hot sun in just few weeks—that's all it had been—a few weeks, when Gabriela stopped her saying, 'You are leaving early today, earlier than usual?'

'Not really, but I did want to finish a letter before I swam. Is there anything I can do for you? Anything special?'

'No, not special—but I thought we might talk—'

'You mean have a talk about something special? Might it wait till I came back, Dona Gabriela?'

'You mean wait till your usual time for coming back, you mean late afternoon?'

'Yes,' said Sophie, 'late afternoon as usual, unless there was something special. Is there?'

'Actually there is something important I think we should talk about so why not now—before you leave—it will not take all that long. I would not wish to spoil your morning.'

You have already, thought Sophie. You have already done that.

My whole day, I shouldn't wonder!

They went to the room that Sophie hated most in the house. The room most signifying Gabriela. Airless. Overpowering. Lace placed everywhere, covering things, protecting things, no single chink of outside air allowed in, it might cause a tiny disturbance to the portraits on the walls, to the closed piano, to the sepia coloured photographs smothered in elaborate silver frames. Why have the photographs, just keep the frames? Sophie almost said aloud and then did not—seeing Gabriela's face. Suddenly very nervous, Sophie felt like laughing out loud because this was bound to be one of Gabriela's famous confrontations—in her room for such scenes—felt like laughing because the room was so awful, because the moment seemed so important, because this awful woman was going to say the things Sophie didn't want to hear, the things that would tip the ever-so-delicate balance—something preserved for such a long while. And Sophie knew already that it was finished. She wished that she could somehow stop Gabriela from destroying the rest—the best—the very best of what was left.

She wished Rui was here. In fact she was angry that he was not. To help her. To avert or deflect some of what was about to be said. And then she thought, no, he is my dearest friend in all the world. And my dear, dear love. And this time I will say what he never will to his mother. Of course, Sophie didn't laugh out aloud and braced herself instead. For she knew that her dear love's awful mother would get what she wanted—what she always did get in the end or the beginning. Gabriela began. No preamble—she just began.

'My son is very unhappy and I feel . . .'

As all fools will, who never learn, Sophie blew it saying, 'Rui has never been happier, ever, in his whole life—if you really must know—if only you would let him be—if you—'

Her voice very cold, very precise, Gabriela continued—'Perhaps you would allow me to finish what I have to say—or at least the sentence I had begun? May I finish it?'

Sophie felt stupid and knew that that was what Gabriela wished her to look. Sophie wished that Gabriela did not look so composed, so calm, so elegant. Formidable. But she did. She sat so straight in the uncomfortable, carved, great chair—her chair, like a judge, like a hanging judge—and looked back at Sophie. Sophie mumbled something about, 'Sorry I interrupted—do forgive—do carry on.' Civilities—weakness in the face of such an opponent. Even if she did hear Sophie, Gabriela brushed the apology aside and didn't 'carry on', rather, she started all over again.

'My son is very unhappy. I feel or rather I know without a doubt why he is unhappy. You are the cause, Sophie, and because I am his mother I see things about him long before anyone else. Clearly, I have known him for a longer time than you have and I see and feel and know just how unhappy you are making him. Do you understand me?'

Sophie, realizing that this was her rhetorical style, knew that the question and the pause were not intended to be filled with an answer or even by a retort. So Sophie waited and thought her thoughts, she thought you can't really blame her as you might anyone else for talking the way she does—or thinking the way she does. Her kind of insensitivity is a role learnt through convents and years and years of hearing nuns, Superiors and others who speak like this. Then the disembodied voice in the confessional that doles out—what is it called? Absolution—forgives them— knows all—sees all—forgives all—so they never feel they need to work out anything really, like being personally incapable of hurting or harming and having to learn about accountability, about guilt, or regret, as we do, or feeling sorry and sad about what we need not have said or done. Years and years of hearing voices sounding as if God spoke to them personally is what makes Rui's mother speak like this—she and her ilk just assume the same mantle—and that's it. They never hear other people talk or converse. They don't read, hardly laugh or think anything is funny—so how can she be blamed? She can't hear herself—or she'd never try—would she? Surely not—at least not to another adult. Of course, she would, thought Sophie. She's a humourless, self-righteous Mother Superior, Mother, Priest, Holier-than Thou, Important Family of Goa, Mother Octopus tentacles-a-tremble waiting, waiting—for the ever-so-soft kill as she sits in her parlour.

'I take it that you are listening to what I am saying. Are you?'

'Yes, of course, I'm listening,' said Sophie. 'Do I have a choice?'

'All right then, since you agree about my son—what do you propose to do about his extreme unhappiness?'

'Nothing at all—I don't propose to do anything at all. He's not a child—I know you wish he still was. I'm quite sure you propose doing a great deal—you are, aren't you—and I do wish you wouldn't. I wish you would leave him alone. He has to work it out. Anyway, don't you think *you* might be the cause of his unhappiness?'

'I wonder that you find it possible to speak to me, someone my age, as you have done—how dare you!'

'What odd terms you do use, Dona Gabriela! I am not your poor Caridade, you know—I haven't been pulled out of some foundling home and been made to feel your great bounty and been made to slave for you in the name of charity so that you can dish out words like "dare". If you weren't so destructive a person I might even find you rather funny or at least eccentric—but you're not. As for "someone my age"—as you put it—I think you're remarkably young, not so many years older than me, aren't you? So again it must be one of your unremarkable ploys to tame the natives—so to speak. Those you can bully. Caridade for obvious reasons and me because I am living in your house but as an invited guest of Rui. Why, by the way, don't you ever call your son by his name? It must be so tiresome to keep referring to him as "my son—my son". Like royalty. Or to make me feel that I haven't the right to use his name. He has a name—also a highly unsuitable pet name—I wonder you never use it? Doesn't it suit your role when you're sitting in that chair—doesn't it suit your tone of voice when you are trying to intimidate someone, me for instance? Might it seem soft or might it make us equals? Anyway, if you've finished I'd like to go now. When you waylaid me on my way to the sea, I seem to remember you said the talk we were to have wouldn't take all that much time—that you wouldn't want to spoil my morning. May I go now? Retrieve some of it, perhaps?'

Gabriela's hands trembled ever so slightly—her tone of voice not at all. 'Sit down—I have not finished—'

Sophie said, 'I'd rather stand now—and I'm sure you haven't. Finished, I mean. Also try saying please if you are trying to be even mildly persuasive—occasionally. A difficult word, it's true, for someone not used to using it. But useful. Rather like thank you. Even if you don't mean it, it's useful and polite—it can be used as a kind of ritual which may both mean or not mean anything. Like your own custom of touching your cheek to another's cheek—first one and then the other—both sides. I was so charmed by it when I first came. I had thought—hoped—it meant real welcome to a stranger, a true salutation. Alas, how wrong I was. Anyway, since I'm leaving—no, not the country yet, but this room—you might practise the word on Caridade—that will be an unusual experience for her, will it not?'

Gabriela almost stood up. 'Come back here at once—who do you think you are?'

Sophie stayed where she was and said, 'No one—myself. What you really mean is how dare anyone speak to you as I have. I dare say it's a shock to your system. But it's good for you and you've a pretty stout system I'd say—though you do the "fragile" bit rather well. Look, why are we behaving like this? You're not fifty yet— and nor am I, yet. You're not a girl—nor are you a young woman— but somehow you remind me (I remind me, too) very much of the worst, most insecure aspects of those two phases. You grab and hold and cling and don't give in or up about anything. What will you be at sixty if nature keeps you alive, sorry, I mean I was reminded of an irrelevant rhyme. Rui has shared so much of his life and his memories of when he was growing up that I feel I know you—I never wanted to believe many of the things that agonize him still, but after meeting you I can believe all of it. Dona Gabriela—what you have done to your children, no, don't interrupt me—of course, Rui, has told me about his sister—he's my very dearest friend in all the world, he's told me most things that have mattered to him—and why should it surprise you? Have you never ever had a very dear friend? Being widowed young happens to a great many women—it is not your peculiar right or privilege— and I'm not being harsh. You did not have to deny yourself every pleasure and joy once you were widowed—in doing that you really maimed those so close to you. Why don't you have close friends or any friends at all? Why don't you read or listen to music or help anyone in your community? You never had to work, you had money, you had this house, you had your land—and you had your children. My God! I thought I was a mess, but meeting you has been a revelation. At least I have never consciously tried to hurt or deny or destroy another person—and that is all you have ever done. When you sit here in your chair, in your parlour, do you think about your daughter? Notice, I didn't say "imagine" her life. She wouldn't be where you have put her if you had an imagination. All I asked was if you ever thought about her. Ever since Rui told me, to hear the sound of Pilar or Santa Monica makes me sad. Because you chose that way of life for her—you denied her what you don't even begin to love or appreciate. You denied her choice. Doesn't it ever trouble you? Not even at the hour when most of us are vulnerable? Suddenly waking in the night and not being able to sleep again—or sometimes at twilight or when you're weakened by illness? What, never? Ever? And you sit there now talking about Rui and my causing him to be unhappy? Oh yes, I have thought about your family a great deal—how you have ordered it so neatly to your own advantage in the role you had decided for yourself. She couldn't have put up much of a resistance—being so young— but this one, Rui, is putting up quite a fight, isn't he? And you can't bear that, can't stand it. He wants a life other than the one you want for him, that must contain him. That's it, isn't it? Your plan isn't working, and since you won't blame yourself and you don't dare frighten him away again, you've decided to blame me, decided that I must go—don't you see that, you stupid woman? He escaped from you a long time ago. Long before I met him. Didn't he tell you? Or didn't you ask him? I only met him five months ago. In a park. He was sitting on a bench playing his guitar—longing for the sun and home. It was very cold in the park. He'd been away from the sun and his home for over four years— you should have rejoiced when he came back.

'I rejoiced when I met him. No! Don't you interrupt me. This, I will say; this, I will finish saying. It's very important for me to say it—and for you to try and listen.

'I rejoiced when I met him. There, I have said it again. And you hate that. Even the day he came back, you, after all the years he had been away, could not rejoice at his homecoming! All you did was show how you disliked his bringing me with him. And every day since then Rui has tried, I have tried, God knows how hard, but you not once, not ever. What a lot you have undone in so short a time!

'That day in the park, just a chance meeting, my need as great as his for a friend at a time of great loneliness, what a quiet wonder that was! That it should happen—not in a book—but to me. And in all the days that followed he made me realize so many things, made me feel why he longed to go home again, in spite of everything. He didn't, I suppose, say all that much but he conveyed such longing and love and pride—and he wanted to show me everything and make me feel it too. He wanted to come back and try—really try—to salvage what he loved—in spite of you. Did you not sense any of that? Didn't you feel any of it? You said, because you were his mother and clearly had known him longer, that you could see things about him long before anyone else could. If only you could hear yourself, "My son is very unhappy, and I know why he is unhappy. You are the cause." But you can't hear yourself, rather, you will not—it's the only role you've ever played. If only you were just a bad actress in a very poor, melodramatic play you would harm no one. But in real life it's rather different. Your lack of any critical sense about yourself has caused so much waste, so much damage. None of which can be retrieved. Not now—perhaps not ever. Why don't you throw open a few windows in this room—let some of the outside come in? Why don't you unpin your hair? Why don't you take off your shoes and walk in the sand and feel it between your toes? And while you're about it, why not try wearing another colour? After all, you aren't in mourning still, are you? I should think it's your children who you have doomed to wearing that colour—not you. Try!

'Oh, one last thought before I really do go—why not listen, I mean really listen, to the words of some of the songs your son sings? He wouldn't have to translate them for you as he has for me. He's really gifted, you know. It's not very often you meet a musician like him. It's not just that incredible voice—it's that he can interpret other men's songs and compose his own and need never have an accompanist because of what he can do with his guitar. Surely you know all this? Why are you ashamed—because that's what you are—and outraged at what he wants to do and might finally accomplish? Is it not a career that has ever occurred in your family—ever? Does it seem too frivolous compared to becoming a priest or a doctor or a lawyer? But it's a great tradition—even you would know that. It goes back a long, long, long, long time—longer than even you can trace your family tree! Remember the wandering scholars—the troubadours, the balladeers? Are you troubled that he'll end up singing in cheap cafes, or at beach barbecues or—horror of horrors—expensive five-star places where three times a week he will have to sing while foreign tourists, lobster red from the sun, lap up the culture and the past of this land through your son—while they eat king prawns and delicately sip their feni cocktails (smell and all) finding their rewards at the bottom of the glass—the alien, familiar, red tinned cherry, skewered on a plastic white and green palm tree? Or, Dona Gabriela, is it not that kind of shame you feel? Is it a far deeper, far more primitive and basic rage you feel—what most mothers hide or try not to show they suffer—the desperation of having to let go? That Rui, unlike your daughter, will wander further and further and one day never come back at all. To you. Is it that? Is it that?'

Gabriela looked up once from her clenched hands on her prim lap and said nothing. Nothing at all. She did not need to. Already she knew the danger had passed. Tomorrow everything would be as it always was.

The stranger who had hammered at the gates would go. This she knew.

Rui and Sophie

'What shall we do, Rui, what shall we ever do?'
    'About what, Sophie?'
    'Obviously about us.'
    'What about us?'

The Quiet of the Birds

'Oh, Rui, please—you know what I'm talking about and you know what I mean. I have not spoken of so many things but surely you know they won't just blow away because you don't want to confront them. If it's painful for you it is worse, yes, much much worse for me. You might think about that. I'm the odd one out, I'm the nigger in the woodpile, I hurt inside badly and I have to hide it and not show how humiliated I feel, and all this because I felt you must understand and were biding the hour—but I think now perhaps you are not really going to confront the situation at all. Why don't you help me, Rui? Why don't you interrupt me, not allow me to say these things, interrupt me, tell me that I don't need to say any more, tell me you have been agonizing over all this and that you have reached a decision, a way out, something, anything? Rui, you know that it doesn't come naturally for me to talk like this. So, come on, Rui, dammit, say something.'

'Sophie, Sophie, yes I have reached a decision—and, yes, you are right as you nearly always are. I was hoping I would know what to do at the right time—above all hoping that the ugliness would blow away as you put it—and that I would not have to do anything.'

'But, Rui, you have done something, you said you had reached a decision . . .'

'Yes, but not one I am proud of—in fact one that I'm ashamed of, even as I am unable to do anything about it—I—'

'What, Rui, what is this decision you have made? And why are you ashamed of it, just tell me—you have to tell me if it's to do with me or you or us, and it sounds rather frightening your saying "decision", somehow momentous or final—is it, Rui? Are you sure you don't mean it's a plan, or an idea or a problem we could share, thrash out, together?'

'No, Sophie—it's a decision and it's this. You and I will live in this house. You will have to learn to live here. I live here. It is my home.'

'But Rui—'

'No wait, Sophie, you must allow me to finish. I know what you were going to say—that my mother lives here—isn't that what you were going to say? Well, it's true and it is what I was about to say—that you and I will live here no matter what.'

'You mean, Rui, I'd have to get used to your mother disliking me—get used to her hating the fact of me—the fact of you and I meaning something to each other. And—all this under the same roof?'

'Yes, that is what I mean.'

'And, Rui, is that what you want me to do? Is that the kind of adjustment you feel a person could make? Could you? You know, Rui, there is so little I would not do for you, but this that you ask of me is impossible. Truly. I would and already have adjusted to many things, but not this. This would be disastrous because it would change the one that matters. It would change us both. It already has. Already it has changed you. I wonder that you could ask this of me—even more, wonder that you didn't think we two could have talked about this, really talked and thought and worked out something. Anyway, I could not live here in the same house with someone who does not welcome me. Rui, haven't you a clue about how I feel? How I have been made to feel? I thought, just that once, that you did understand—that afternoon when I finally spoke to you and you told me that you had spoken to your mother, you wouldn't have spoken, surely, unless you also realized how she behaved with me, how miserable I was feeling, and what happened? What? Nothing, nothing at all. Except the one thing I never realized might—that you would ask of me that I change. That I adjust. That I learn. Oh Rui, think, just think how it feels.'

'I have thought. I told you Sophie that this was a decision.'

'But, Rui, she does not want me here—we could live somewhere else—live on our own—'

'No, that is the point. Not in Goa. I could not do that to her in Goa.'

'What is that supposed to mean—you could not do that to her in Goa—you mean you could do that to her anywhere else but not here? But we are here—we are not anywhere else—and you say you could not do that to her—and yet you can do what you are asking of me—to me?'

'Yes, that is what I am asking of you. In Goa I would not live anywhere but in my own house—in my home—'

'With your mother?'

'Yes, Sophie—because my mother lives here—'

'And me, Rui—and me? What about me? Where does that leave me?'

'You could adjust, Sophie, after a bit it would not be so bad. I know it's very difficult now but given a little time it would not be so difficult.'

'You don't know what you're talking about—it would get more and more difficult. Not less. Surely you must realize that—you do, you must—but you don't want to think about it too much. Just try and tell me one thing, Rui—just one and then perhaps we can leave it for now—or leave it for a while. I feel sad. I feel very tired—'

'Yes Sophie—what? What do you want me to try and tell you?'

'Just this—would you expect it of yourself, Rui—if you were me? Could you contemplate what you are asking of me—could you? For yourself?'

'I am not you, Sophie. And it's not a fair question.'

'Why isn't it a fair question? When something difficult, something that normally goes against the grain is thought about for someone else surely one might ask of oneself if one could, if one would adjust?'

'Sophie, it just does not apply here. All I am saying is, if we are considering anything more permanent in our relationship, then you and I would continue to live in my home which is this one. That's it—for the rest . . .'

'For the rest—as you put it—dislike, hostility, downright rudeness; oh, everything else comes after, does it? Rui it comes first for me. And I had imagined it did to you too. You have changed, Rui, how you have changed. London was not so long ago, our park bench was not so long ago—for you to forget. You were different—in London.'

'Was I different—how? No, not really different—except somehow . . .'

'Yes—yes you were—don't you remember anything?'

'Please, Sophie, I don't want to talk about London. We are here—we are in Goa.'

'But it's relevant, isn't it? It was in London that we met, in London that we became friends, in London that we shared all manner of things. We are the same two people—you don't change because you're in another country—I mean you try not to change on essentials. How can you say you don't want to talk about London? It's where we did all our talking, all our thinking and a lot of our deciding. And now you make it seem irrelevant—'

'I think, Sophie, that in London I told you I was weak. I told you that I accept and adjust to most things—and now that I am here, after a few little sounds I have tried to make against my mother—I will once again not fight her—I cannot do it—maybe that's why I don't want you to bring back London. I thought with you with me I might change, but here I am, as I always was, unable to do anything about her.'

'And aren't you worried, Rui, that I must go—if that is how things are to be, did you really think I would stay? Is that what you thought? Did you?'

'No, not really. But it is still what I hoped would be possible—because I care for you more than anything else—however lame, contradictory, that may sound.'

'Except your mother—Rui. So that's that. That's it then—oh God!'

'Sophie don't cry—please—please don't—I can't—'

'What, Rui? Were you going to say you couldn't bear it if I cried? I will cry and you will bear something for a change—I have not cried before though I have wanted to, so often, but thought it would be so awful for you to know just how unhappy I have been. But, really, I couldn't give a damn just now about you and the strange things you can't bear. Perhaps you need just that. To bear and to care and not just make these useless little sounds of pain. This crying is just outward—it will pass. But what you have caused, what you have undone—how will you bear that? Tell me, Rui— don't you feel better already now that I've stopped crying? Of course you do—now you needn't feel so bad, already you can start feeling less guilty, and allow yourself to forget—remove yourself just enough so that you take centre stage again with, "I am weak— I can't bear to fight—I like things to be as they always were—I adjust to everything—I accept most things."'

'Stop it, Sophie, how can I—'

'You see, there you go again, I, I, I. And I won't stop it—what do you mean stop it? Stop what? Stop talking—or rather what you are. Your mother is so strong only because you are so weak. And she is so strong because she knows just how weak you are— she has always known and she has played her cards so well about me—about this visit of mine. She knew that she could be as cold to me as she liked, as rude and as hostile as she liked, because she knew you would not really do very much about it. And she was so right. I wish I had been there when you spoke to her about her behaviour to me. That must really have been interesting—for her, I mean! I wonder what you said. I can imagine the scene the way I would like to have seen and heard it played—but it must have been rather humiliating at best so I'm glad I was not there. It must have been cold, precise, and devastating. Anyway all this—points to no end.'

'What will you do now, Sophie? I would like to know—'

'Ask yourself what you will do now, Rui. That's far more to the point. And why should you want to know what I will do? Just to cushion your own slight discomfort? To feel that I'm taken care of? Oh, Rui I'll land on my feet, never worry. Anyway, why worry now? I mean, if you haven't before. Stop indulging yourself even now. What a habit it is with you. Like breathing. Do you think you might go? I mean, please leave me alone. Your mother must wonder, if she doesn't know already that is, what all the fuss is about! If you're beginning to feel sorry for yourself, don't. You'll recover. You're almost there already. If I could despise you more I might love you a lot less. Anyway that's neither here nor there. Please go. Go.'

Beach

As she walked away from the house to the beach, Sophie remembered what Aunt Meg had said on their last meeting, 'But Sophie—recognize when you are unhappy—don't wait till it's too far gone. Act. As you have when you are happy. You are doing something about it. Even if it means coming back—it's no failure. Promise? Promise me, Sophie.' It was unlike her aunt to make her promise in that way. So Sophie had promised. She wondered now why her aunt had been so firm. Had she had a premonition?

Nonsense. Knowing her Aunt Meg it had just been common sense—as opposed to Sophie's usually taking so long to face the truth about things when she cared a great deal—and her aunt knew that Sophie really loved Rui. Of course, she must also have realized that going as far away as she was going she was obviously going to face far more physical and emotional shocks than mosquitoes, heat and extremely spicy food! So in an odd and rather devious way Dona Gabriela had shaken Sophie into realizing that, of course, Rui was extremely unhappy and that was why Sophie had been uneasy and uncomfortable and unable to name what she felt herself—unhappy. So selfish Gabriela had got what she wanted. She had scattered her enemies. Sophie must go. Rui would not know how to move. Would not know how to hurt Sophie. Rui would not speak. Rui would not analyse what his mother was all about. Nor would he break with her. Four years ago he tried, he had gone right away, stayed right away, but in the park on that cold bench in the cold season he had been miserable—longing for the sun, longing for home. It was not so much that he had met Sophie—she was just a catalyst. She had happened to be there, just then. That is all. Which is not, thought Sophie, to minimize the importance of what they gave each other, felt for each other—but. But. I suppose we each needed a great deal and imagined not just that our needs were identical but that no matter what it involved we would see it through. Old habits die hard. And if one of those habits was Gabriela I suppose it would be difficult. And everything that was said in her parlour—on my part, anyway—was wishful thinking. I said what I said for Rui and me. Rui should really have said it. Sophie had reached her favourite spot on the beach. She changed her faded costume and spread out her towel between two tall rocks and the familiar, dead-looking palm tree. Her book and her half-written letter to her aunt. I shall finish my letter or start a new one and then I shall swim out to that yacht again. That's what I do every day so I shall do that today in spite of everything.

Dearest Aunt Meg, I wonder why I don't feel more let down or why I am not as hurt as I should be with Rui? Maybe I will be later on. I suppose he's different. Maybe, I hadn't thought much about just how different a person is in his own setting. Or, maybe, I wanted things so badly to work in a particular way that I hadn't worked out the implications of certain things at all. Specifically his mother. It's too late to change Rui. Also, I don't think, Aunt Meg, that I'm that important to him—I mean, for him to move heaven and earth. His mother is set in her ways, she is both heaven and earth to herself and also to him. I cannot blame her entirely. Not entirely. He is a weak man in the face of his mother. Or rather, he's weak when his opponent is his mother. I do not wish to spend a large part of my life fighting other people's fights. Anyway, much as I care for Rui, his mother I do not, nor ever could, care for. He is inextricably bound to her. Eventually I would lose every battle and every petty skirmish. It would rub off on us too. We two do not form a multitude. I do wish we did. Ah, well.

I'm tired now. It's been a very bad morning. Too much thinking. I shall swim and float and drift. I shall also make up my mind. To do what?

But, she thought, as she swam, I wish Rui even now would say what he must for himself, if not for me. But he won't. I already know that he will not—or he'd have said it already to her, not left it to me to be made to say it. Sophie turned on her back and looking up at the blue, very blue sky said aloud, 'At most he will run away again—that's what he will do—and then he'll come back again. But not with me, not with me. Because, and that's the truth, he's not going to make a stand for me or for a separate life for him and me clear of her, here. Ever. So it's not going to be a brave new world. For Rui and me. Or for Rui.

Leaving

Early next morning she left the house. As she made her way to one of the outhouses to say goodbye to Caridade she realized that it must have rained in the night. There was such a fresh smell to the air and earth. The washing line was quite free—just a faded swimsuit hung there. As she hugged Caridade, she said, 'It rained in the night. You know why I am going, don't you?'

Caridade said, 'It always rains on the eve of Good Friday—it must. Even the heavens cry for the pain on the cross. And, yes, I do know why you are going. I wish that you could stay here in the house.'

'But you do understand, don't you, Caridade? You know why I am going; you know that I want to be with Rui?'

'Yes, I do understand, also I know why you are going even though you wish to be here, it is difficult for anyone to live in this house. I have no choice. But if you come back—I will be here.'

When Sophie reached the beach there were two early fishermen washing their net and an old woman looking for crabs among the wet black rocks. My bit of beach, my group of rocks, my best old palm tree for shade, my bit of sea and sky and my island close by. There was no movement yet on the boat with blue trimmings. Sophie sat on the rock to wait. It was still very early. But soon the heat would rise and rise and envelop everything. Not everything.

Not quite. Once Rui had taken her to see his favourite church. It was rather far from his village—beyond Ribandar, beyond Velha' Goa, beyond St. Quentin and it had got hotter and hotter and she had almost given up caring about where they were going. And Rui had said, 'Just a little further, Sophie, truly, we are almost there and you'll be so glad you saw it,' and she had said, 'But I can't breathe any more, I shall faint or die or something.' But then, at the end of an old road, they had come to a steep rise with steps cut into the hillside and the sharp, sweet smell of ripe cashew fruit and at the top a huge church, grey and very old, with a charred stump of a tree and two very small boys roasting something on a fire.

And Sophie thought, they had looked at us as if we were the first people they had seen in a very long while but we could not have been because cut deep into the old walls of the church we read 'Rosa loves Anton', and 'Dilip XXX Sudha 2.3.88.' 'Barbarians, vandals!' we had said as we peered through a barred window because the big main doors were locked. And as we peered into the deep darkness we could see dimly the great altar and feel such a coolth that was almost cold rising from the depths of the church, and a musty, rotting smell. Old-wet-damp-of-ages smell, peeling-walls-and-rotten-wood smell and cold. She had shivered momentarily and Rui had said, 'Didn't I tell you, Sophie that it would be worth seeing?'

The sun was quite high now in the sky and the figure from the white boat waved to her. She stood up and waved back. She thought, Rui knows where to find me. He has not come. Long ago in the park he'd said, 'No strings attached—unless—' Perhaps I will cross his mind, sometimes.

The small rubber dinghy was quite close and she waded out to it and got in as if in a dream. As they rowed out to the white boat with blue trimmings Sophie said, 'Thank you for taking me. Will it be a lovely day for setting sail, do you think?'

Two Postcards and a Letter

Sophie got back to rain. Thin, cold, English rain. Her street looked familiar, and not. Seemed the same, and not. The cherry trees had been rained on and blossom lay thick on the pavement. Not pretty. Like snow when it stops being magical. Slushy, muddy, trampled-on snow. Blossoms not pale pink not white. Dirty. Her letterbox had only two postcards and a letter. From Aunt Meg. From Italy. She saved them for later. Nothing from Goa. The plant on kitchen shelf—dead. She opened windows. She made up her bed with fresh sheets. She cried. I'll read my letters. I feel so awful. I'll think of that later. She went to her living room and stared out of the window. Her rust japonica looked all right—it had survived the winter. Good. She thought I wish it would stop raining because I would feel better able to cope if it would stop raining. I'm a fool. My moods arrive or change with the weather and what it does to the landscape. I should have learnt by now that danger and sadness come even in the sun. What was that Elizabeth Jennings—'I feel I could be turned to ice! If this goes on, if this goes on—' and then later, in the poem, something about stone. Yes—

'I feel I could be turned to stone,
A solid block not carved at all,
Because I feel so much alone. I could be grave-stone or a wall.'

But it's not the end of the world—it just feels like it because I'm back where I started from. Somewhere there through the trees is the park, and in that park there is a bench. What worlds away. I shall read my letter. I shall look at my postcards. I shall put first things first. This is first. A letter from Aunt Meg is first, two postcards from Aunt Meg is first. She was there from the start, she was always there, everything else that happened to me has come later—much later. Even Rui.

Aunt Meg is—good parents, caring always, seeing one through everything. Aunt Meg is—good friend, loyal through everything, Aunt Meg is—allowing risks. Aunt Meg is—through sickness and health. Aunt Meg is—lasting. She is Aunt Meg. Sophie opened her letter.

Darling Sophie, as you see I am here—it kept raining so I left for where I knew the sun would come out and if it did rain it wouldn't be dreary and cold and bleak like London. Also, as you have always known if they cut open my heart etc., they would find engraved upon it the one word, Venice. I know you're back by now. I know. So know my plan: Even before you start unpacking, pack again or come as you are. There. Trust me. Just come. As the travel posters, say, COME TO VENICE. As I say, please Sophie, come here. I'm at the same old pension—I was here nearly thirty years ago, I was then the age you are now. It's changed a great deal but for the essentials—the things that make Venice important—it is the same. It is still the city that I consider mine. Sophie, for you it will be neutral zone—not your land and not Rui's. I know you know what I mean. Anyway, for a while it will be a dead zone but come here, darling. You're too near your park—is the bit outside your house just squashed cherry blossom? London is awful just now, rain, just the worst time of year for anyone, for anything. I think this city will help you decide—one way or the other. Anyway, it's a better place to wait for letters from Rui. Or for Rui. You will, of course, leave him a forwarding address. In the meantime, don't think—just come.

My much love, Meg XXX

P.S. I realize that you are folding up the letter, also you are wavering a bit, thinking it's impossible, so I will add a few bits and pieces to help you decide. We will eat at little tables with red check tablecloths in a sudden square where sometimes a pigeon and sometimes a priest will hurry by. We will drink wine, sometimes close to a curving bridge over a canal—or sometimes we'll just walk and walk and a church we want to visit will be closed so we'll eat bread and cheese on the stone-steps till the church opens and then we will see the one Bellini that will change our way of thinking about darkness and light. Meg.

The first postcard said, 'I rowed past this, the Palazzo Da Mula yesterday. I didn't go in. Saving it for when you come. Hurry. Love Meg XXX'

Sophie turned it over to a strange palace seeming to emerge out of the waters of a canal, misty, strange, with a draped gondola waiting and great tall windows, all closed.

The second postcard said, 'Look, darling, all this might sink and disappear, I can't prop it up forever, hurry, love Meg XXX

P.S. Here in the late evenings somebody plays Bach and Albinoni on the great organ—'

The photograph was of a church on an island—a great sense of isolation and a feel of something seen over a great space of water. Why wait, I shall go. Aunt Meg is right. And Sophie went upstairs.

Why wait here, is what Aunt Meg meant. And she's right.

The park is too near, the bench and trees and lake are all too near.

A cold water B & B in Bayswater is too near.

It would all be self-pity if I stayed here just now.

It would all be wondering about the postman. Hating Sundays— no post. Always, it's all one's pride, in the end. That's hurt. I thought I came first. For a long while I didn't think that. And then I did. Anyway, I don't. Come first, I mean.

I put Rui first. Above everything. So.

I shall still wait for a bit, but not here. I shall go to Venice. I'll wait there.

Rui has to write—one way or the other.

Rui must come. Why not? After all I went.

Anyway, I shall sleep on it. Tomorrow I shall decide what to do.

Rui might come. Why not? After all I went.

Anyway, I shall sleep on it. Tomorrow I shall decide what to do.

An Ending

Most of that night it rained. Most of that night Sophie thought many thoughts. Among them Sophie thought, even ghosts disappear—think of people after a flash flood, after an earthquake, a cyclone. They're in shock for a long time—those photographs of them in the newspapers—sitting on heaps of rubble clutching a doll, a bit of a pram, a bathtub close by—they get on with their lives, eventually. I feel curiously suspended in time but it's a phase. A phase passes. Soon I will do the things I have to do. Ordinary things. And then I will start doing the things I like to do—the things that gave me joy—much joy—the life before Rui happened to me. And then will come the next phase—I will be able to put it down to experience. A thing that happened—a thing that mattered enormously—that really did happen. Not something half-imagined like falling in love when one is very young, or falling in love with the idea of a person. This was not like that. I really liked Rui. I really loved Rui. I really did go all that way with him. I really did think through all that time there that in spite of everything, or because of everything, we two would be all right. And I'm not a romantic. Even now when I think of certain things I don't give them a romantic colouring—I mean so much was damnably unpleasant: that heat, that airless house, that rude, impossible, alien Gabriela, a strange, changed Rui, months of living with ghosts out of legends and myths undreamt of, things said and heard—it became my life and it did seem that there was Rui at the end of it somewhere—somehow. Rui and me. I'm not a very vivid or special sort of person in any way. Rui made me feel I was for a while. Nothing much to be gained thinking like that—we are what we are. Anyway, I'm lucky—it did, all of it, happen to me. Soon I shall be free. I shall read again and listen to music again and walk in the park and enjoy my garden again and my friend, Aunt Meg. Soon I shall be free.

Sometime in the night the rain stopped. Sophie woke early to sun. She swept the soggy cherry blossom from her front steps and threw away the withered plant on her kitchen shelf. It died from neglect. I let it die, Sophie thought. Things do—die—she thought. She made herself coffee and wrote a letter to Aunt Meg.

Dearest Aunt Meg, it was awful to come back to rain, but your letter and postcards were waiting for me. Thank you for writing as you did. Yesterday I decided to come to you in Venice. Today I know that I cannot come. I shall not use you or a 'neutral zone' to cushion myself against whatever is to happen. I hope one day you and I will be in Venice together—but not this time. I know that being you, you will understand why I have decided to stay here just now, and wait here just now, in my own home. Today the sun has come out. I hope you have sun for the rest of your stay. I miss you. Take care. Love Sophie.

P.S. I miss Rui terribly, perhaps he misses me too—but perhaps he cannot act on that. But Aunt Meg darling, he has to now, doesn't he? Anyway, if he does not come or write, it's best for me to pick up the pieces of my life here. I wish I could feel great anger rather than this heavy miss for him, but I don't, not yet. I think men are made rather different from us. Do you think? Love. S. She folded the letter and crossed the road and posted it. Now that's done. Tomorrow I shall go to the park, not today.

Sophie went back to her house and made a list of things she would need now that she was home again. Note to the milkman. Bread—butter—eggs—fruit—flowers—vegetables—shampoo— Tide—orange juice—cheese—newspaper. That's enough for today. And she set off feeling insecure down the so-familiar road to the shops she knew so well. But the pavement felt odd and though she had her list she shopped stupidly, having to retrace her steps several times. The money in her hand felt unlike money she had handled before. There's nothing really the matter—it's just that I have become a bad traveller—not like the other times because I always had Aunt Meg with me. I will adjust perfectly well in a day or two. Anyway, though it does not signify—I hope. I hope there is a letter when I get home. I won't look in the letterbox immediately. She unpacked her shopping and put the flowers in water in a blue jug and read a bit of the newspaper and then went out to look in her letterbox. It was empty. I shan't mind. After all, it's my first real day home. And Rui doesn't know I'm back yet—for certain. It was a silly reason to have worked out but it sufficed. There's always the next post. And then there's tomorrow.

The next day she walked to the park and straight to the bench. She sat down and looked up at the trees. I hope he misses me. I don't think he's going to write. I don't think he's going to come. She was watching a leaf stir—of course, it wouldn't fall. It isn't the season. Soon it would come round. And I shall be here.

There were no leaves then. When he was here. Once she had said, 'It will be lovely here when autumn comes—sitting right here where we are—above us the leaves will turn each day to a red and gold and brown—of course it will be turning cold again but a different kind of cold from this.' He had not said anything but it was not a cutting-her-off kind of silence, not one that made her feel that she talked too much, or that he wasn't interested in what the leaves would do when autumn came to this park, but a comforting kind of silence. So after a while she had said, 'Do you have a clear distinct season like autumn in Goa, I mean when the colours change?' And Rui had said, 'No, not in Goa—not really.' He said, 'But I know what you mean, the changing of colour through one tree in my garden at home in Goa—a wild almond tree—it has leaves that turn from green to a glowing red, bronze and then brown and then shrivel and die—large leaves.' When he sang songs about autumn he thought about just that one tree and he knew what it meant, also there was a smell he associated with the season he didn't really know—through Caridade burning the leaves. She would sweep them into a great pile and then set a match to it and the leaves both dry and slightly moist would burn slowly for a long while and he loved that acrid, woody and leafy smell.

And Sophie said, 'Leafmeal,' and Rui said, 'What?' and Sophie said, '"Though worlds of wanwood leafmeal lie": Hopkins, a poet, wrote about the fall, about autumn and trees un-leaving and he—well, it was his way really of trying to help a little girl come to terms with the death of things, she is weeping for the leaves at autumn—leafmeal is his word—he uses that word.'

After a while she had said, 'I wonder if you will be here in the autumn,' and he had said, 'Perhaps we two will be somewhere else watching a "pretend" autumn, with just the one wild almond in the garden in Goa.'

Sophie got up and walked to the lake. The sun shone. She heard the voices of children as they played. Sophie heard, 'You are my girl in winter.'

So I was, thought Sophie. So I am. And now it is not winter any more.

Antonio's House

And once upon a time in a little village called Arpora there was a lady called Angela and she built a house near a small chapel and she built a kitchen and two large bedrooms and a large sitting room and a dining room and a room for the altar and the saying of prayers and a balcao to wait on.

And she went to Cucolim in her carriage and that was many miles away but she was happy because the workmen made beautiful, carved four-poster beds and chairs and tables and cupboards and they carved apples and pomegranates and animals and birds and they polished the carvings so that Dona Angela could see her face in the apples and pomegranates and she was very pleased.

And then she went to a hill called Guirem and got some beautiful basket-work chairs for the little garden with its four great pillars and great basket-covered bottles for the wine.

And then she went to Bicholim and ordered mud pots, some large and some small, to cook in and some so that water would be cool to drink. And then she went to her mother's house and took a crucifix and statues of the Madonna and her child and St Francis and St Sebastian and St Antony and put them in the altar room.

Then, when the house was ready, she carved a beautiful front door and the garden door and the front door key was large and hung by a red cord and the door-knocker was a metal lizard and she decided on a lizard because a guide had once told her in Portugal that gargoyles help ward away evil spirits from the churches and why not her house, she thought.

And then she realized that the windows needed shutters so she had them made of seashells cut square and set in wood so that light and sun filtered through like mother-of-pearl.

And then the house was ready except for a lovely green parrot placed on the roof instead of a weather-vane which would have been useless anyway because there was never even a suggestion of breeze in Arpora. And on Sunday she got into her carriage and went to church and gave thanks for her beautiful house and prayed that nothing but happiness would follow all the people that lived in the house all the days of their lives. And next door to her house was another beautiful house but the husband died and haunted the house and nobody dared to live there though smoke came from the chimney and Angela prayed for this house as well because it was next door to hers and, indeed, shared one of its garden walls. And then Angela got married and had four sons. And she named them after distant cousins, hers as well as her husband's: Francisco, Jeronimo, Antonio and Fernando and they did not care at all for the beautiful house she had built for them. Except for Antonio. He loved the house and said, 'I shall always live here and I shall marry and my sons will live here too.' But his brothers said, 'As soon as we are old enough we shall leave here and this gloomy, dark Arpora and we shall never come back.' And when Jeronimo grew up he said goodbye to his mother and went to Portugal and never found peace, and Francisco went to Mozambique and became a doctor and brought peace to some people, and Fernando became a priest and went to Angola and became a prison chaplain and tried to tell prisoners about the pain of Jesus Christ at a time when they were uncaring of everything except their own pain, and Antonio went to Bombay and said, 'I shall come back.' And he studied hard and longed to return to his own home but this took many years.

And one evening in Bombay, when Antonio worked very hard, he was taken to a large house called Villa Rozario with a beautiful acacia tree that lent into the top window and two chickoo trees and one wild almond tree and there were lots of carriages in the driveway and chandeliers to light up the darkest corners and a marvellous fruit punch for the young people. And the daughter of the house was called Eugenia and she wore a wondrous dress of white and cream lace and pearl drop earrings and played the piano and sang like an angel and all the chairs were covered with needlepoint done by Eugenia and Antonio fell in love with her but he was only a poor student and her parents said, 'No, no, our daughter will marry a rich man,' and so Antonio went away and hoped one day that he would be rich and could marry Eugenia. And one day he heard that she was married to a fine rich doctor and so Antonio went away sadly to the wars, fighting many years in Africa till his hair turned grey.

Yet he said, 'One day I shall go back and marry Eugenia and take her to live in my house in Arpora and we shall have a fine life there and she can go to church every Sunday in my mother's carriage and she can sit and sew in the garden like my mother.'

And Dona Angela stayed in her house and locked up the sitting room and the dining room and lived in one of the bedrooms and prayed in the altar room and the carriage got rustier and the horses wandered away and the grass got longer and longer and the hinges of the gate got weaker and the shutters remained closed and dust hung everywhere and soon the bats came because they thought that the house was empty—they never heard a sound from Dona Angela's bedroom. And one day when she had waited longer than anyone ought to wait, she gave up waiting and died and Marialena's father had her buried in the cemetery of Arpora.

And one day, years later, when Antonio was fifty-five and Eugenia was fifty her husband died and Antonio went to Villa Rozario and he climbed the stairs and knelt by Eugenia as she sat sadly by the window not sewing but staring at the pale blossom of the acacia tree; and her hair was now streaked with grey and her dress was black, not white lace, and he knelt by her side and said, 'Will you come with me and live with me and be my love and though I do not have a "fine white court by the side of the sea", still we could be very happy. Will you come?'

And Eugenia said 'Yes' and they got into the ship with sixteen large trunks full of Eugenia's dresses and sixteen hat-boxes full of Eugenia's hats and soon they came to palm trees and white beaches and Eugenia was happy and free and then they moved further inland to lonely avenues of trees and green paddy fields and wonderful great white churches and Eugenia felt happy and free and then they came closer to Arpora and suddenly the wind dropped and the earth was dry and the trees were small and gnarled and the houses were not so whitewashed any more and all the pie dogs of the world seemed to lie like shadows everywhere and Eugenia began to feel less and less free and happy. And then suddenly the carriage stopped and there they were, at Antonio's mother's house, and the huge gate fell on its side as they touched it and all the leaves of many autumns lay in the garden and up the stairs and an old glove lay on the balcao and the key would not turn in the lock.

And Antonio called out many times, 'Mama, Mama,' and a small white cat wandered out through the leaves till a young girl called Marialena came running and said she would take them to where she was and they followed her to the village cemetery and there she lay in the ground and her headstone read, 'Here lies Dona Angela who died of long waiting.'

She had waited so long for someone to live in the beautiful house she had built. And they swept away the leaves and placed a bunch of flowers at the grave and then they went back to the house. And this time the key turned in the lock and they went in, Eugenia and Antonio.

And they then just stood there and the portraits on the wall of a doctor, a priest and a man who had no peace stared down from the walls and the cobwebs lay thick everywhere and the cane chairs were all broken and the great cross-beams were eaten up by white ants and the mattresses had fistfuls of silk cotton falling out and the Madonna looked much sadder and could hardly bear the weight of her son and all the saints' wounds gaped wider than before and Christ on the cross sagged with the weight of pain and years and great bats flew everywhere. And Eugenia sat down and said, 'I cannot live here, it will be like dying.' And Antonio sat down and wept and the small kitten came and touched his hand and he said, 'Eugenia you must do as you think best, but home is where you start from and I started from here. I shall stay here.' And Eugenia got into the carriage with all her trunks and hat-boxes and went away, but Antonio stayed in his house and cleared the cobwebs and mended the chairs and got rid of the bats and opened the shutters and cut the grass and swept away the dead leaves and washed the glasses and dug out the wine and lit candles and the altar smoke rose from the chimney and Antonio was happy. He had come home.

Three Lives

And once in a time not long ago in a small village in Goa in a large house with a large garden with a wall around it and a great iron gate, there lived a family—a father, a mother and a daughter. Nobody ever came to their house and they never went anywhere except to church every Sunday.

And because she loved her mother, she always believed her mother, believed everything her mother told her, always. Her mother told her many stories. Her mother would say, 'Virginia, come, I will read you a story before you go to bed.'

And she would go to her and sit very close to her with her head on her knee and her mother would adjust her skirts, black and silk, and touch her coiled hair gently. She was very beautiful and her smell was like the orchid from the garden outside the house— pale mauve and delicate. And this smell came through the shell-panes through which the sun filtered—rain never. This faint perfume came through and sometimes the moon. 'Why are the windows never open, Mai? The garden might come into the house then.' And her mother said, 'No, for our lives we need the window closed and what we need of the light and the outside comes through the shells. It is enough. The other would be too strong to bear.' 'Where do the shells come from?' she would ask. And her mother would say, 'From water, from the sea, from the beaches, from the water's edge.' 'And can we go there where the shells come from?' And her mother said, 'No, they are from far away.' 'And have you ever been to the sea where the shells come from?' And her mother said, 'Yes, only once—never before or since.' 'But when did you go and why do we not go there ever?' And her mother said, 'I went there once—in a carriage with my mother. It was my mother's fortieth birthday and we went to the sea in a carriage for a picnic and we drove for many hours and it was very hot and there was dust on the leaves and my mother was very excited, as I was. And after many hours we turned a corner and there was the sea and we got out of the carriage and my father grumbled but it was my mother's birthday. And we never went again.' 'But why, why did you never go again?' And she said, 'The picnic was not a success. My mother was greatly upset. She cried.' After a pause she asked, 'But do people cry when they are forty, and when did she cry, where did she cry?' And her mother said, 'Yes, people of forty do cry—my mother was forty and she did cry and that day when she got out of the carriage and saw the sea for the first time on her birthday when she was forty—she saw the sea and its colours, and she saw shells on the beach and she cried and my father said, "But you wanted this long and hot and dusty drive on your birthday." And my mother said, "You should not have kept this from me, this secret, this sea. It is now too much for me, but you have known of it and kept it from me till it is too late." And I could not look at the sea or the shells, only at my mother's birthday face when she was forty, and crying.' 'And was that the last time you saw the sea?' And her mother said, 'That was the only time I saw the sea . . .' 'And is that why we have shutters on the windows made of shells?' And her mother said, 'Yes to remind us and help us forget—the colour and smell and sound of the sea.' 'But it is there outside, isn't it? Will it always be there?' And her mother said, 'Yes, do not fret, it will keep. And now, Virginia, you must go to bed.' And she kissed her mother and when she lay in bed she hoped and also prayed that when she was big she would be tall and beautiful like her mother, with always this faint perfume about her and her hand with the two rings touching her coiled hair gently though not a hair was ever out of place so it may have been a habit or a memory of when a wisp had become misplaced, and she wondered and had once asked her mother if she went to sleep and woke in the morning with hair always beautiful and just so and her mother had looked startled and then had said, 'Virginia, don't be silly,' and so she knew that even her mother could be ruffled sometimes and she wondered if it had anything to do with Pai, but how could it? He was so old, she could not imagine he could make even a leaf stir, so how could he stir her mother? She must remember to ask Candinha.

And in the mornings or long afternoons Virginia would go to Candinha when she was dusting the great portraits or cleaning the lamps or in the dark kitchen stirring a blackened pot and, 'Candinha,' she would say or rather ask, because Candinha knew a great many things, 'what happens outside, Candinha?' And Candinha would say, 'How do you mean outside?' And go on dusting the portraits or trimming the wicks or stirring the pot. And she would say, 'Outside, you know, outside the house and the garden and the wall and the iron gate and the name of the house in marble.' Candinha would say, 'Oh, outside there are people who walk about and talk and laugh and sometimes wear no shoes, and skirts swing, and people dance, and hair is free or in plaits, and there are people eating mangoes and juice running down their chins and there is the market with fat sausages all strung together and fish still in their shells, bread warm from ovens and green mangoes for pickling and red chillies and water pots—earth red.' 'Yes, but why don't we go there? Can't we go there, Candinha?' she would say though she could not see life outside clearly with her father and mother because they only went beyond the gates on Sundays to church in the carriage.

And she did not like Sundays because of church. But she loved one of the statues of one of the saints because he had a worry line between his eyebrows and dark circles under his eyes and she loved him because she realized that he worried, so he must be nice, not like the other statues. And on one of the side panels there was a nativity scene and Joseph looked so very old and she had asked her mother once, 'Is he Mary's father?' And her mother had said, 'Sh, sh, hush Virginia,' because it was in church and in church you could not ask questions and so later she asked Candinha, 'But is he Mary's father?' and Candinha said, 'No, Joseph was her husband, not father,' and she realized that it must mean that all wives were very young and all husbands very old. And she hated church because it was so always the same—the silent, upright journey in the carriage—and she knew what their three heads must look like from the rear of the carriage—and then as they approached the church courtyard and steps, her father avoiding a pig, very large, with the same, upright distaste as when the younger of their two priests (the one who came from Sailgao) was found dangling from the end of a rope and her father had said, 'But why did he do it here?' and her mother had said, 'Perhaps it was worse for him, here.' 'How worse?' her father had said, and her mother had said, 'The emptiness or the panic was worse,' and her father had said, 'Do you speak of your own life or do you speak of the priest's?' And her mother had said, 'I speak only of people's lives, that is all.'

And their three heads, her father's greying hair and back kept rigid—unbending—by a high, starched collar and the dignity of the family pew, and her mother's black, beautifully coiled hair through the lace veil and her own straight and long and held in place with a ribbon and long streamers—and her head nodded three times with sleep before church was over. And everyone else had so many children, only their family was just three people, and always other people looked at them silently with what looked like pity, except the brave ones who retied her ribbon saying, 'My poor child and no one to play with—yet?' And those braver even than that, to her mother, twisting the knives ever so gently, 'And little Virginia, does she get lonely—perhaps a little brother or—?' As though there were endless possibilities for filling little Virginia's loneliness. But her mother who was also capable of endless duplicity, or courage, which is often the same thing, could vanquish such enemies, 'We have each other sometimes and ourselves always.' And her enemies fell back, but with head held high saying, 'Donna Maria is still beautiful, but far too thin. Do you suppose she eats anything—I mean, besides her husband?'

Virginia loved her mother. Her father she did not know and he did not seem to care whether she knew him or not—from this not-caring over the years she had guessed that she was a disappointment to him. He had wanted a son not her. And she asked Candinha, because she knew what was outside the shuttered windows and the jackfruit tree and the two slender palms and the mass of dusty bougainvillaea and the great iron gate, she asked her, 'What is outside, Candinha?' And Candinha said, 'Life,' and she said, 'Oh, that must be different,' and Candinha said, 'And death too,' and licked her lips as if eating a mango. 'Yesterday, the girl-bride from

Benauli was bitten to death by a snake. Some say, by her old husband. Anyway, she died and the wedding feast was all wasted. All that family silver newly polished and the great casks of wine and feni and huge cauldrons of sorpotel, all the blood and guts wasted. And now she is already in her grave. Everybody went to the cemetery. Someone heard the bridegroom say we will eat the wedding feast as a funeral supper, which was an unnecessary thing to say, some felt, but, some tried to look less happy than they felt at the thought of the feast that would not be wasted. Only the girl's mother wept quietly into her handkerchief but nobody bothered about her.' 'But Candinha isn't that a very sad story?' And Candinha said, 'You asked what was happening outside and I told you, life and death, and sometimes they happen together. Anyway, it may be a happy story.' And she said, 'Do you mean for the bride or the groom?' and Candinha said, 'For both,' and closed her lips very tight and she said, 'Why, why Candinha?' and Candinha said, 'Why, the girl-bride could not be happy with such an old man and so she is better off dead and the bridegroom—what does he lose? He never knew her anyway, so within a few months or some weeks they will find another girl for him—there are many girls waiting to begin to live behind shell-shuttered windows and they will come to be slaughtered.' And again Candinha stopped, and then said, 'Your Mai will not like me telling you these things so do not ask me, stop asking so many questions. Now, I must clean the silver and a million things. Your Pai has a guest this evening and he is staying for dinner.' And she looked sadly at her and left for the long, dark kitchen, black with smoke and the smell of damp and years and piglets that scuttled and fell into the courtyard in small heaps looking for their mother.

And her Mai called out for her, and retying her ribbon and touching her cheek gently said, 'Virginia, today an old friend of your Pai's will dine with us. You must answer the questions put to you and smile and be careful not to show your knees. It is very important for your father. You must do as he wishes.' And she said to her Mai, 'I will do it if it is your wish: is it yours, Mai?' And she watched her Mai's mouth carefully as she said, 'You must not ask this, you must feel it is for the best—your Pai wishes it for you and that is all,' and turned away, but in turning allowed herself a thought: 'As there is no other way—it must be for the best.'

She wandered into the dark garden which had one miracle in it under an old tree, every year—just once every year, suddenly there seemed to be great hanging fronds of mauve, out of an old grey tree that did nothing the rest of the year except just be there. 'Orchids,' she was told when she asked. 'Is that a miracle, Candinha?' And Candinha said, 'No, those are orchids. Miracles are one thing and orchids quite another. Your Pai when he was a young man brought them back from Macao because he had seen them there but they had never flowered here. Year after year he waited for them to flower but it never happened till he brought his bride home. Your Mai. And then that year it flowered for your Mai and it has flowered every year after that.' 'So you see, then it is a miracle.' But Candinha was firm, 'No, this is an orchid.' 'But it flowers only for one person and not for another, surely that is so extraordinary, that is so unbelievably special, that is a miracle?' But Candinha would not see the logic of this, so she said, 'All right then, perhaps if Mai went away and it stopped flowering would that prove a miracle?' And Candinha only said, 'Your Mai has never gone away, never, so now leave me alone there is so much to do for the guest in the evening and you go on with your eternal questions about orchids and miracles, eternal questions.' Since Candinha never sent her away unless something was wrong, she knew something was wrong so she went away to her Pai's study. She went there only if she knew for certain he was not there. She found no answers in the dark room smelling of books and snuffed out oil lamps. She twirled the old globe on its stand and saw countries and oceans of the world turn slowly and then faster and faster. She did not hear the door open and close but a voice came saying, 'Your Pai will not like you to do that, Virginia. You are troubled and that is why you are doing that. Please come to me.' And the globe turned slower and slower and stopped and she rushed at her and was held very close and she smelled the familiar smell and thought, how, how did her mother guess that she was so troubled? She ached inside and in just one day she had learnt two things. That miracles are the same as orchids and that only her

Mai knew when there was something that hurt inside without being told. And she said, 'What is happening, Mai? What is happening this evening that is so different? And it must be different or Candinha would not act so, would not send me away and you would not have found me here with Pai's globe.' Her mother held her tight, very close, and said into her hair, 'Yes, Virginia, something is happening, a kind of change.' And she said, 'Are you going away, Mai? That can be the only change that could cause this hurt inside me. Please do not go away.' And her mother said, 'Do not distress yourself. I am not going away.' And she said, 'Do you promise that you are not going away?' And her Mai said, 'I promise.'

And in the evening a carriage arrived. She heard it while Candinha was helping her to dress. And Candinha said, 'Hurry, he has come.' But she went down very slowly and felt the wood hard against her hand and smooth, one step and then another and then another slowly and then after a while no matter how slow she went there were no more steps and she crossed the hall and stood against the door of Pai's study and she rested her head against the wood and she heard voices behind it, three voices, low, and a great sadness filled her again and now she recognized that what she had felt all day was sadness, and she pushed the door gently open and went to where she knew her mother was sitting and heard her father's voice saying, 'Ah, this is Virginia. Our daughter.' And she did not look up or at anything at all, and her mother said, 'Go to your father.' And Virginia thought suddenly of the piglets running out of the kitchen into the courtyard and said, 'Of course, one of them will be killed for the table at Christmas or Easter,' and this dropped into the room and the silence, and then she looked up and there was an old man like her father, a big man like her father, an unsmiling man like her father—a man so like her father that it could have been her father standing, waiting. And her mother said, 'Go to your father, Virginia.' And she went. And her father put her hand into the other man's hand and the strange man took it and held it and with his other hand trapped it, would not let it go, and smiled with his mouth, only his mouth, and she could not free her hand till a buzzing sound made her call out, 'Oh it's caught, Mai, there is a moth caught in the lamp, Mai. We must help it.'

Then the man let her hand go and went to the lamp and there was the moth, dead in his hand, grey-streaked with dull yellow, and he showed it to her. And she said, 'You were rough with it and now it is dead, my mother saves them, helps them fly away.' And her father said sharply, 'Enough Virginia.' And her mother said quietly, 'It might have died, anyway.' And the man said nothing, only wiped and wiped his hands and looked at her and wiped his hands and looked. And when Candinha came to tell them that dinner was served she did not look at her, only at the man. Virginia watched her mother's hand, lace at the wrists, lace falling over her wrists gently, gentle fingers crumbling bread and the smell of the creeper through the shutters.

And later she wrote to her mother, 'You, I cannot forgive, because you knew and you lied to me and you said you would never go away. My father behaved as only he can behave. He could not laugh or smile with his eyes or ever, even once, tell me a story or take me for a walk holding my hand, so he would not find it wrong to give me to a man like himself. Except this man is not my father, he is what they call in books, husband. When he touches me I do not allow myself to scream, because I never once heard a scream for you, Mai, but there cannot be on this earth anything more ugly and more full of pain than what he does to me. I do not cry or scream because I realize that this is what Pai did to you. I wonder how many days, months and years this can be borne without dying. You said to me that your mother cried when she saw the sea. I do not care any more if there is a sea. I have never seen the sea. Candinha said the outside world had two things— living and dying. She did not tell me that they are the same thing. I had thought that they might be separate. You broke your promise to me. You went away. And though I will never come again to you, I know that the orchid has stopped blooming.'

And when the letter was read Candinha saw the fingers tremble that held the letter and she did not have to ask if Virginia had written and Candinha saw her give the letter to Virginia's father and he read the letter and said, 'I did not know that all these years you had taught her to hate me. I thought it was enough to be hated by one person.' And she said, 'Even now you are not troubled by what you read, by what you have done.' And he said, 'She is only a girl and soon she will not mind so much or she will hide what she feels better; it is after all a lesson we all perfect, one way or another, and if Candinha wishes to change the plates she may do so without pretending she cannot hear what we speak of.' And she said, 'Virginia will never learn it, never. She will die of it.' And he said, 'No one dies of it. You learnt it and my mother and your mother before you, and soon Virginia will have a child also, and she will also learn. Of what do you complain? What is it that is so terrible?' And she said, 'My whole life, its nothingness. I have never been anywhere, I have never known anyone. I have never laughed. I have never known anything. Virginia has never seen the sea. Now she will never see it.' And he said, 'You have a house.' And she said, 'It is four walls. It is not home.' And he said, 'There is no difference. It is a house and you have a garden and you go to church. What more do you want? What more can a woman need?' And she said, 'Do you remember that young priest? Do you know why he hanged himself? Did you ever wonder?' And he said, 'I never allow myself to wonder. He was a fool, he had no faith, he knew nothing, he should have waited, he was young.' And she said, 'My mother was young, I was young, Virginia is young. That priest was young. We all hoped, we all waited for something beyond four walls. We all hoped for something other than a prison. We thought there would be more to living, more to a life that must be led.' And he said, 'He was a fool, as your daughter is a fool now— but she will not mind so much in time.'

And she said, 'Once I was a girl and I minded always.' And he said, 'Yes, but you learnt to hide it very well, and this Virginia will learn. That is all.'

And the orchid dried up and the dry fronds made a small sound like a moth's wings caught in a lamp, or in a man's hand.

Partly Living

And we got to Clare Road in Madras without much trouble. The trouble really began when we realized we had to go in at the gate and face what we had to face, not just feel we had achieved something getting to Clare Road in Madras without turning back. It was a large house set in a great garden and the garden had two mango trees, two chickoo trees, one champak tree, one guava tree and no grass at all. It was a garden of dust, no grass, only dust and a mangy bitch with two tiny pups in the dust, but by then we had reached four marble steps to a deep veranda with two cane chairs and a table and a swing. The swing swung gently as though someone had just got up from it or it had a life of its own because no leaf stirred. And we climbed the four steps and waited on the veranda hoping nothing more was expected of us, but then the silence was very quiet so we called out 'Alison' and waited and then called 'Alison' again and an upstairs shutter creaked and a voice called, 'Yes? Who is it? Is it someone for me?' And we said, 'It's us,' and she said, 'Who is us?' And then when we said who we were, there was a silence, and then a kind of muffled, joyous shout and coming-down-the-steps sort of sounds and the front door opened and it was indeed Alison. She hugged us and we kissed her and we wanted terribly to cry because though it was Alison it was Alison as she might have looked at sixty which all right if you are sixty or even fifty. She was painfully thin and pale and her hair was in a long, blond-streaked-with-grey plait with dirty string tied at the end of it. She wore a loose housecoat, cheap flowered cotton with all the colour washed out of it except a faint lilac, it looked grubby and so did her thin neck and her bare, blue-veined feet.

And she said, 'How did you come, how could you know I needed you to come, and after all these years? I knew this morning that something good was going to happen but I couldn't have dreamt anything as good as you coming.' And we felt stupid and ashamed and sad and thought of all the years between when we might have tried to come before—before this happened to Alison—this looking sixty when she was our age. And, of course, then, we said the wrong thing. We asked her to come with us, now, at once with us. We were stupid and should have realized she wasn't a stray puppy we could feed and bathe and make well again just because we loved her and felt so sorry for her. And she seemed cross for a while, and hurt, and said, 'Come with you? How do you mean? This is my home, people don't just leave home. I mean they live there and they die there.' But she thanked us, and we asked her if she was alone and she said yes, except for Vishnu. We didn't dare ask her who Vishnu was, we hoped so much that it was a child and she said, 'Would you like to see Vishnu?' And we said yes, and she took us down the steps into the garden and round to the back of the house where there were four large stables and she called out, 'Vishnu' and then 'Vishnu' again and out of one of the stables came a large, old elephant, ungainly and wrinkled, the same colour as the dust which was everywhere. He came straight to her and touched her most lovingly over and over with his trunk and she stroked him and spoke to him and he looked immense and she so tiny next to him. We were shocked because it meant everything we'd heard was true and also shocked because she was so very small next to Vishnu and she had said they were alone now, just the elephant and Alison.

We went back to the veranda and we sat on the cane chairs and Alison sat on the swing. After a while she said, 'Only Vishnu's left—all the others died because Ram died, they really did die of love for him, but Vishnu's waiting for me, I shouldn't think he'll have very long to wait now. But, really, he is wonderful, I'd hate him to go first because then I'd have to worry about what to do and maybe where to go. I can't go back to England, there's nobody left, and here I'm all right except every so often when I get rather ill, and then I know what to do, I just go to this hospital and they look after me and Vishnu waits for me—elephants must have wonderful memories because sometimes I'm ill for rather a long time but he waits and doesn't seem to hold it against me—he's always very loving in his welcome when I come home again. Do you want to see my house?' Downstairs there was a large living room and all the walls are covered with photographs and drawings and paintings of elephants and everywhere, except the kitchen, had elephants.

Up the stairs and in the bedroom, it was all pen and ink or sepia or charcoal or photographs of elephants. It was staggering; it was frightening, because it was an obsessed feeling—just this creature everywhere. In the bedroom there was a large four-poster bed, beautiful old brass, and every wall, and table, was elephants. 'Ram did all the paintings and all the sketches and the photographs are by me, do you remember when I first came to India I could hardly hold a box camera?' We went down again and we sat on the chairs and the swing and she said she knew we were worrying but we were not to worry because though it all seemed rather lonely, she'd had rather good times in her life, and really awful times as well, of course. 'Remember David? Oh, it was so super being married to David and all those children, it was odd enough, wasn't it, how whenever I loved a man I always left with masses of stuff left from his earlier life, like David's five children and Ram's four elephants? It was strange David wanted to marry me but what fun we had. I was younger than three of his children and on holidays in Skye we had seemed to own the island and we all chased the sheep and always laughed rather a lot, that was nice. I can't remember laughing very much later in my life. And that was ten years of my life and David fell in love with Susan—have you met Susan? She wasn't very nice with children, but I suppose David must have loved her because he chucked us all up for her. It was shattering for me because, really, I wasn't equipped to do anything, a job or anything. And then I came to India. It was awful till I came south and started learning dancing and started photographing things and then decided on elephants, stone-sculptured ones, till I met Ram. Ram owned four, he hired them out for religious processions and marriages, and he loved his elephants and they adored him and, really, I fell in love with Ram because, really, only a really good man could be so loved by those elephants. Really, they would stop feeding if ever he went anywhere and that's why we never could go on a holiday. He liked my photographs and said I ought to start on real elephants now, like his, and use them in a book and he'd help me. And then he found me this house and I found the brass four-poster bed and he moved in, and of course the elephants, and we built the stables. The only problem was he was married and his wife made an awful fuss which was a pity since she did not like Ram and did not like sharing him with elephants and you had to realize that you couldn't dream of having Ram unless you shared his elephants, you just couldn't have him alone and you couldn't be jealous. Of course, people weren't very nice to me, in fact, they were very rude, called me dreadful things, but we were very happy and I hardly left the house and garden except for once when Ram took me to a temple near the sea and the elephants in stone were incredible and we were very happy. His wife was on a pilgrimage and we were carefree and only sometimes worried about the elephants at home. And then a few days before we were to return Ram picked up a nasty, rusty nail deep in his foot and didn't tell me about it—it was very bad and he was in great pain and he died. When I got back, of course, everybody blamed me and I was very lonely; but I could not go away because you don't just lock up and leave four elephants all alone even though life seems all finished—I mean, you do see, don't you?'

And we mumbled something knowing we'd probably have left.

'So while there's Vishnu I'll be here. I just hope he dies first so he's not left all by himself. I get rather tired sometimes and I long for Ram and the life we had together but there's nothing to be done about that—it's over. When will you come again? Don't leave it too long. It's so good to see you—will you come again or is it all too awful? I mean the dust and these chairs—but there is Vishnu and the trees and we could have chats on this veranda. The swing was Ram's favourite place. Sometimes when nobody has been on it it sways, it has a life of its own—but come, promise to come, now that you know I'm here—promise? Remember Caitlin Thomas—leftover life to kill? I am partly living—promise to come.'

We were such liars, we promised.

Because It Is My Nature

And one night after twenty years, or rather twenty-two to be painfully exact, with his mouth on hers, he said, 'I love you, always remember that, sometimes it may not seem so to you but it will be true—okay?' She was shocked because she had said so to him so often and he never—and by then she had assumed he didn't love her or, if that was too bleak a thought to contemplate, that at any rate, he did not believe in saying so—like not believing in letters—the writing of them or the need to receive them, so that now having heard them say so she did not dare to say anything, did not in fact, answer in case she had not heard right or been dreaming for a while, but such a surge of joy and hope and love went through her that she could hardly breathe. But, in the meantime, he flirted outrageously and she was helpless with sadness and there was nothing she could do about it or him and one day when he saw how unhappy she was because of him he said it was like the old story of the scorpion and the crocodile, and did she know the story? She said she didn't, though she did, and he said there was a scorpion and he wanted to cross the river so he asked the crocodile to help him across. The crocodile took him on his back and they were nearly there but the scorpion bit the crocodile. As the poor, drowning crocodile thrashed about for the last time he called out to the scorpion, 'But why? Why did you bite me?' And the scorpion said, 'Because it is my nature.' 'Because it is my nature, because it is my nature—is that a plea, or an excuse, or an alibi, or it is a justification? A justification for most of the hurt inflicted in this world of humans? But how can your wife bear it?' she asked.

And he said, 'She doesn't know.' 'Does that make it easier for you?' she asked. And he said, 'Well, how would I explain you?' And she said, hardly above a whisper, 'But I am not one of your flirtations, am I? I am your serious one.' And he said, 'Of course, you are my serious one, but I met you too late and now let's not talk any more,' and fell to humming and singing and said his music lessons were going well and that Anila was a very good teacher and an interesting person. She said, 'Promise not to find her too interesting because she's beautiful as well,' and he said, 'Promise.' Anila was his music teacher and she had pale green eyes that sometimes looked pale as ice, as washed-white glass, she was very lovely with a woman's ample, slightly-running-to-fat kind of figure, her hair light brown in an untidy bun and a wide marvellous mouth and smile.

The first time I saw her I said to him, 'Promise not to flirt with her.' And he said, 'You are silly—but yes, I promise.' He was right, I was silly. And I was miserable most of the time and it was misery most of the time loving this man—and now I was nearly fifty and should know better than to cling and demand and whine. And I was very grey and running to fat on my thighs and stomach and hardly a memory of once being quite an attractive young woman except from photographs or a chance remark overheard or remembered, but certainly nothing in the mirror ever told me that any more except my eyes—yes, sometimes, my eyes looked rather nice. That was all. And he, on the other hand, looked like most good-looking men, better now than twenty years ago; he was tall and though thickening around the middle, ageing did not present the same problems so immediately or so unfairly as in a woman. Really, it was so loaded against a woman—she felt more, and she had to have the babies, she aged more quickly, she suffered menopause more acutely, oh the list was endless, on and bloody on. Men were more attractive in their forties, women merely trying to relive their youth, women should give up gracefully even though their more meaningful relationships seemed rather often to begin then. For men, the forties and fifties meant a new kind of excitement, for women a new burdened sadness—I was growing old, everything told me that, but I still felt like a girl, still wept bitterly on a day of real or imagined grief or hurt, felt so young when happy, felt so young when sad. Really the same things made me weep, my insides had not changed at all—rainy days, a weekend ended, a tree cut down, a leaf turned brown, loving a man, losing a man. A man changed inside, a woman never changed, it was how she was cursed; 'it was her nature'.

I thought of Anila again and thought why she would be attractive to a man or why even I found her so. She was divorced from her husband who had married again, she had a small child she was bringing up, she lived alone, she taught singing. She sang very well. She was out of the ordinary, and she was also rather beautiful with those eyes sometimes green and sometimes pale as washed glass. She had been through a lot. And this business of teaching classical Indian music suggested so much more than, say, learning the piano or the violin. I wasn't quite sure why, it seemed more languorous, more sensuous, perhaps it had something to do with sitting on the floor together. You and your teacher sat on the ground and your teacher had an ample, womanly shape and your teacher had eyes like pale glass. And stop it, stop it at once, that way lies madness. Obsessed and stupid—obsessed with love, obsessed with desire, obsessed with longing and so going round and round the mulberry bush and ring-a-ring-of-roses, everything going round and full circle but not stopping. I wonder when the worrying stops, will it stop, does it ever stop? Will it stop if he commits himself? But surely he has. Surely in this, at least, a man is like a woman? When a man makes love to a woman, when a man sleeps with a woman he loves, surely that is a commitment? Surely, surely. To lust after, to have lusty thoughts, to commit adultery, to have adulterous thoughts, adultery in the mind, all degrees and degrees of the same thing. It all comes to a kind of completeness when first you actually lie with, lie on, the body you have loved, you have dreamt of a thousand times. The texture of skin in the dark different than in the light, the trust in the flesh and the thrust; the smell of skin, the taste of skin. Surely this is irrevocable, an irreversible step, a kind of promise, a finality, a commitment? Isn't it, isn't it? But something niggled and nagged. It's different for a man. A man goes to a prostitute, a woman doesn't, it's all different. Some men are different. This is not a brutish man, this man was sensitive to your weeping when first you broke your marriage vows, knew what it meant for you to drop all your clothes and be naked and most shy and gradually lose that shyness. All right, then, he has known your body and its needs, he has known your breasts and your mouth, your skin, your hair, smelt you, felt you, felled you. But the voice nagged—in the dark everyone in the same, you are not special, you are not different. But the things said and done are surely different, razor-sharp different—never possible to repeat with another person, different. And then one night she dreamt a very clear dream. In the dream he had married Anila. The dream was very real, and very terrible and very sad, like the music of the shehnai, and she woke up crying. All next day the dream, and the heavy, sad feel of the dream stayed with her, so as she always had shared her dreams with him, she told him about this one, told him exactly as it had happened. And he stared at her as if he had never really looked at her before, and she was frightened as she had never been before, and a second before he told her, she knew.

Down and Out, Washing Up
with Gladys

And in May I needed money. I was leaving Cambridge in a month and I wanted to buy Bach's Mass in B Minor and St. John's Passion and I needed at least six pounds. I started looking for a job. Tripos week was over and a lot of people had left already but all the summer students had come up to Cambridge. It was sad and lonely, one was finished with examinations, with tutorials, with essay writing, with hunting for books and articles in the stacks; finished with gowns, with making it to Hall, finished with sherry with one's tutors, with everything that had made up one's life for two summers, two autumns, Michaelmas and Lent and Easter and Enid Welsford Elizabethan Drama Wednesdays from eleven to twelve, and Levis on Fridays for Practical Criticism and Daiches on Milton Tuesdays ten to eleven. Friends, real friends, gone. Faraway Australia, faraway US of A, faraway Scotland, faraway London, faraway Finland, faraway because it was all over. Suddenly fend for oneself. Look for a job.

I got a job. New restaurant called Soup Kitchen at four pounds a week, breakfast and lunch thrown in; washing dishes. They had been very nice and said I could serve in the restaurant, but all the other girls were wonderful looking: tall blonde Swedish or tall dark Italian girls in black trousers and pullovers and I was petrified at the thought of dropping cups and plates or getting the orders wrong. They probably thought I would look decorative serving soup and salad in a sari.

I turned up on Monday, wearing trousers and an old shirt, feeling nervous, after all it was my first job and I was afraid. At seven, I had a steaming mug of coffee and wonderfully crusty rolls of bread and then, at nine, the morning crowd of breakfast people started arriving. Just before I disappeared into the pantry I noticed that the only bit of decoration in the Soup Kitchen was a huge, but really huge, photograph of a hungry crowd getting soup from a vast cauldron. For the rest, the benches and tables were very clean and the knives and forks and spoons had nice wooden handles.

I was given a huge apron and a pair of rubber gloves and steaming hot water and a ten gallon tin of detergent. There was a kind of hatch between the pantry and the restaurant and the girls in black, serving, began to dump the dirty plates and cup on to this hatch. The morning crowd was not too difficult to manage but about twelve the lunch crowd began. The hours that followed were hectic in the way a nightmare often is—you'd never imagine so many plates in your life and you'd never realize how fantastically dirty, dirty plates can be. Bits of butter and limp lettuce clinging to it and cigarettes stubbed out in egg yolk. Horrible. I couldn't bear to use the rubber gloves so my hands were beginning to burn and peel with the hot water and that nameless detergent. But I couldn't use the rubber gloves, they felt slimy and strange, like some undersea jelly fish, and I never used them though I lost four successive lots of skin.

At about two, the crowd was really at its cruel height and I thought I'd never get the plates washed as fast as they were needed and the tall Swedish girls and tall Italian girls by then just seemed to hurl the plates down and the forks and knives clattered and the gramophone played and the noise was deafening. The cook, a large kindly man with a very large face—very red—said not to worry, tomorrow there would be help in the form of Gladys and things would look up considerably. I wondered about Gladys and hoped she'd be nice, but not too efficient. I also wondered if she would use the gloves. Anyway she would be someone to talk to and take one's mind off the general murkiness. There were two huge refuse bins, I forget to mention, the cook told me 'one for the pigs' and the other 'not for the pigs'.

At four we stopped and closed up shop till seven when the evening shift began. And then we back-room crew sat down to our lunch. I must admit on that first day it tasted wonderful, a cheese omelette and a garlic salad and marvellous bread. I was so tired but very proud at the end of my first working day. I cycled by way of Knapwell Wood and lay among the cowslips and tried not to think about greasy eggs and the smell of wet nicotine and all the other generally revolting aspects of eating, rather 'after eating'.

Next day I arrived and there was Gladys with the most spectacular yellow hair I had ever seen, it seemed to shimmer and shine in that damp pantry and she was very proud of it, 'just had it done' to give herself 'a bit of a lift', she'd been 'that low' recently. She put on the nasty gloves straightaway and seemed on the whole to be a cheerful sort of woman so I supposed the 'new' hair had done its little bit and I wished I could do something spectacular to mine so that I could stop the strange-end-of-everything feelings that I had. We started work and I must admit she was the most remarkable talker I had ever met and she said it was very nice to have someone to talk to—'much better than radio,' she said—I don't suppose she minded my not having said anything besides 'oops' or 'look out', or 'oops' again just as the occasion demanded. I can't say she was the best 'washer up of dirty dishes' I had ever met but then I had met so few and, after all, one 'can't have everything' as Gladys kept saying. She urged me to call her 'Glad' but I drew the line there. I was not ever going to call anyone 'Glad'. About noon I knew all about her, by one I felt I had known Gladys and her husband ever since I was six. Gladys had three children, three girls, and she'd started another and Bert was 'that fed up' he said he knew nothing about it and had taken on so 'oddly' that she'd decided to get rid of it. She said that the next day she was going to do something that was bound to work, a bottle of gin, neat, and very hot water to soak in, and if that didn't work she was going to keep jumping off the kitchen table like a 'bloomin' athlete' and if that didn't do the trick Bert would just have to lump it. I was reeling, I was stunned. I thought these things happened in 'Saturday Night Sunday Morning' not in staid old Cambridge with Evensong and the Guild Hall and daffodils and the backs and 'Davids' and Gladys talked and talked and while she talked she washed the dishes in a disgusting way, just dunking them into the dirty soapy water and not rinsing at all, they looked much worse than before she started working on them. I attempted to rewash them and she told me not to waste all that lovely, clean water on those nasty dishes. That second day was really worse than the first and I couldn't eat any lunch at all. Gladys, I might add, ate a 'great' meal.

Afterwards I cycled home again by Knapwell Wood and lay among the cowslips and thought of all things fresh and fragrant, dew, grass, strawberries newly picked, earth that had just been rained on and soon I didn't feel so bad.

Next day Gladys asked me to come home with her to help her while she got on with the 'beastly business'. Bert wouldn't be there so I needn't worry about that. Gladys's house was near the railway station, bleak and dreary as all houses near railway stations are, only rather worse, and there were three dirty children whose faces one couldn't really see for the soot marks and tear marks and runny nose marks and they all sat in a defeated sort of way on a carpet having tea messily. Gladys had the old geyser on already and quite soon she disappeared in the bathroom with the bottle of gin shouting to me to amuse the kids and to be sure to come if she was dying. I said yes. Later I realized I had no way of knowing if she was dying. By now the children had had their tea and waited for me to deal with them. I washed them and they had rather nice faces once the dirt was removed and then we played games, we played 'Hunt the Slipper' with my chappals and then 'Oranges and Lemons' and 'Here We Come Gathering Nuts in May' and then Bert came home from work and after his tea played with us too. After a bit we put the children to bed and I told them a story and as they all slept together in one bed I thought I would risk telling them 'The Little Mermaid' because then they could comfort one another when they felt sad. Well, they all cried and even Bert looked a bit desperate. So I told them 'Hans in Luck' and Gladys emerged about then, lobster red and roaring drunk, and we got her into bed as she kept repeating she thought she'd 'brought it off' but wouldn't know for sure till later. Bert said he'd walk me home but I said he'd better stay with Gladys as she might need him. I liked him and I think he knew I was feeling very sad by then. He liked children, you could feel that right off. I went to bed and I couldn't think of the green wood and the white flowers, only of the three little girls who had cried because they had felt so sad listening to 'The Little Mermaid'. And Bert.

Next day there was no Gladys so I had to work very hard and I didn't once let myself think of anything but the plates and the cups, the forks and the knives, and I scrubbed them as though my life depended on them. Only the cook remarked, 'Wonder what Gladys is up to.' I went to Gladys in the evening and she was very pale but jubilant saying everything was fine, but what had I done to the children and Bert, they were all so sad and I said it was because the little mermaid died for the human prince and he married someone else. Also, every time the mermaid moved she felt sharp knives going into her and the drops of blood fell on the ground as she danced with the prince. Gladys said she bet the old mermaid never went through the sort of pain she'd gone through and laughed. She wasn't coming to work for a couple of days, so I said goodbye. I had a couple of days left at the Soup Kitchen and then I said I couldn't work any more and went home with four pounds and could only buy the Mass in B Minor and it felt strange to think that such a week should have made this most beautiful of music mine. And now whenever I listen to it I think of Gladys and Bert and the three little girls crying over the little mermaid and her love and her pain like knives, and I think of washing dishes and the rubber gloves I could never wear. And then the trumpets come on and everything becomes all right because Bach is greater than anything else in the world.

The Quiet of the Birds

When Safia was a little girl, and then a young girl, her father always, in khaki drill bags and a cloth cap, took her into the jungle: 'Looking at birds, learning from birds, learning about birds,' he said, 'you have to—it saves you somehow—it keeps you from being sucked under, the rest is trivia, mundane—remember that.' When first he said this to her, Safia could barely understand the words, the meaning not at all. But the years have a way of passing and Safia began to see, to understand, what her father had meant. By then they had combed together nearly every inch of jungle, starting at sea level and reaching the egg-shell blue mosque on the hill. They learnt many birds. Heard many birds. Watched many birds. Safia never forgot. How could she? She was dragged around with him, also wearing most unbecoming khaki drill bags, till her legs were scratched and bitten and bleeding and for many years she hated these long, hot, extended marches and wondered what other children did—but when she was about fourteen she saw no other way of life. They would set off, her father and she, each morning, carrying cold chapattis and fruit and water, at very first light, looking and learning birds. Where they lived there were no other children—or it seemed to be so. Safia never had any friends. There was only her father and, of course, the birds.

There was Gangubai, of course. She had been there ever since her mother left. Or died. 'Long before that,' said Gangubai firmly. 'I have been with your family for a long time. If it were not for me I don't know what would happen to this family. I looked after your mother and now I will look after you. Your father is a good man but he has no idea about anything except birds. Of course, birds have their place—everything has its place—but there are other things in life. Without me you would never have any proper cooked food to eat or ever have a proper bath or a comb put through your hair, would you? Your mother said to me many times, "Gangu, please look after Safia when I am not here, promise me." And I promised your mother. Otherwise why should I stay in this lonely place? You tell me. Why should I be here? You and your father leave the house so early in the morning, sometimes it is as dark as night, and then you come back so late—again it is almost dark— but I wait, I am always here, I light the lamps. And look at your arms and legs today—more scratches, more hurts—when will that man realize that your arms and legs should be covered properly, not exposed like this, he does not know how to look after a little girl—all he knows is birds, nothing but his birds.'

'I am not a little girl—I've grown now.'

'Yes, yes,' said Gangubai, looking at Safia more keenly, 'yes, of course—now you are almost twelve, and last year you were eleven and next year you will be thirteen. Yes, you have grown and you are growing and growing—who can stop that? Even a weed will grow—but you should be growing like a flower, that's what your mother would want, but how can I do it all alone if all your father thinks about is birds?' Gangubai always talked like this so Safia hardly listened to her any more—except sometimes, when she said, 'Then where is my mother? If she wants me to grow like a flower, and not like a weed, why isn't she here?'

If Safia's father ever caught Gangubai talking like this he would say, 'That's quite enough, Gangubai, there must be lots of things you should be doing,' and to Safia he would say, 'She's a good woman but she talks too much—she should learn from birds.'

'I like her, Father—she is the only person who talks to me—the only person I can talk to—there is no one else.'

'But why should you need to talk? And why should you need anyone to talk to you? What do you think I have been trying to teach you all these years—why would I bother to take you with me every day—I could go by myself. Don't you realize that? Don't you, Safia? Why do I take you?'

'To learn, Father, to learn silence—'

'Yes, that's very good, that means you are learning. That's a very good answer, I never said that to you, you learnt it all on your own. Your mother never tried to learn, ever. I really am very pleased with you.'

'Do you think you could tell me something about my mother? I should like to know.'

'There's nothing to know about her—it's all unimportant.'

'But, Father, Gangubai says she was—'

'I don't want to know what Gangubai says.'

'But she was my mother—so I—'

'So, nothing at all. She was your mother, now she is not your mother. That's all. You don't have a mother any more. What you do have is this place by the sea, that hill with the mosque right at the top, the jungle and all the trees and the birds, the sky, enough food, and, for a short while, you have me. Isn't that enough?'

'And Gangubai—I have Gangubai, Father.'

'Yes, all right, you have Gangubai—for now.'

Her father left it at that. So did Safia. Though she did wonder. Safia wondered about quite a lot of things. But she waited. She knew there was no point in asking for answers to everything—or even some things. Like a poised bird, she waited.

And the years went on. Each like the last, and yet not quite. One day as Safia and her father walked she looked at him walking ahead of her and she saw a change in him. Or, perhaps, she felt a change in him. He somehow did not seem to be striding ahead. He seemed, somehow, tired. His legs looked thin. Or very thin. He looked older. Safia realized that her father was old. He had not warned her about this. She had not thought about her father changing—about her father growing old—because he had never looked old before. He had always walked ahead; she had never been able to keep up with him. Always at some point he had to wait for her to catch up. Not today. His elbows and forearms looked so thin.

Today she said to her father, 'I am tired and very hot, I should like to go back to the house—also, I am very thirsty.'

Her father looked at her for a long while and then he said, 'You are not tired nor are you really hot, as for being thirsty we have our water with us. I know why you want to go back; it's because of me. You are a thoughtful person. A kind person. I hope you are not harmed for being as you are, Safia. Let us go back.'

After that day, the days became different. They never went for their long walks. Any more. Safia should have been greatly relieved. But she wasn't. She realized a great change was to take place. And she dreaded it. She was sixteen. She had never been to regular school. She had never known her mother. And now she knew that something was happening to her father and she could not stop it from happening. Safia asked Gangubai.

'Gangubai, do you notice a change, I mean, do you think—'

'Yes, I notice a change—many changes. Your father is older than he was last year—suddenly he is much older. Also, you don't go for those mad long walks through the jungles together any more—also, I think at last your father is thinking of a change that involves you.'

'What kind of change, Gangubai, what kind of change for me? What has he said to you? Why hasn't he said it to me? Tell me. You have to tell me.'

'Safia, you are a silly girl—of course, he hasn't said anything directly to me but I know that he has some plans. I have been posting several letters that your father has been writing—and they are all to the same address—and they are all to Bombay.'

Safia said, 'But why should that have anything to do with me? Why did you say there would be a change involving me—why, why, Gangubai?'

'It's not for me to say—just wait and see.'

And Gangubai shut her mouth very tight. And that was that.

After that talk with Gangubai two things happened: the letters that Safia's father had written resulted in a family arriving from Bombay; and a long talk between Safia and her father. The long talk was the longest that Safia had ever had with her father, and it was not about birds at all. It was about Safia's marriage. Her father said that it was now that she must be married because otherwise she would be all alone. Safia said that she had him and Gangubai, but her father said he was not going to last much longer, for which he was very sorry but she must marry and the family was a good one and would look after her. Safia said she knew nothing about such things and said that he had taught her about silence and birds and that he could not now make her part of another kind of world. Her father cried a bit and said that he had not realized that he would not live forever. He had no real warning, and now there was very little time. Safia had never seen her father cry before. She had not realized that a man could cry. So she listened to what he was saying very carefully. Her father said she would be married here, not far away, and that after the marriage the other family had agreed to Safia staying with her father till—

Safia said, 'Till when? Till what, Father?'

The egg-shell blue mosque on the hill came in very handy. It was near enough and it was sacred enough. Safia remembered very clearly only that her father took to his bed after the ceremony and after that never really got out of it again. It was a strange memory to have of your wedding day—but it really was the clearest thing Safia remembered. The rest seemed shrouded and misted over. Gangubai wept. There were flowers—wilted and dying. Safia listened to the sound of the priest—he seemed to go on forever and she longed for her khaki drill shorts; she longed for her father to be striding ahead of her looking upwards suddenly into a tree, seeing a bird, hearing a bird, cautioning her to stop in absolute silence. To wait. Safia knew that that life was over. As she sat now she could barely lift her head for the weight of her heavy dupatta— it was alien to her, all of it, and her father had not prepared her for this. Perhaps that is why he had cried—because he had prepared her for a different kind of life and was sorry for his mistake. Or perhaps he was crying for himself. Safia hoped he had cried for both of them; for the life they had shared for all this while.

Safia's father did not die immediately. It was a long while. A really long, terrible while. From the day of her wedding it took six whole months—and Safia looked after her father and when he slept Safia watched the cobwebs from the old rafters get longer and longer, filled with dust and dry dead things. Safia told Gangubai not to touch them because she was afraid of what else might be freed from those great hanging loops. Safia wished her father would die because it was a terrible thing for him to die. Like this. When she washed his legs, and bathed his body she kept seeing that other person striding ahead of her in the jungle. The two could not be the same. For a while this helped her—because she persuaded herself that this was not her father at all. Her father would come back. He would wake her up at first light. They would leave the house, he in his khaki bags and cloth cap and she running to keep up—to look at birds, to watch birds, to learn from birds. Taking with them cold chapattis and water. But after a time Safia knew it was the same man. She realized this about the time when the sores came. First just little sores. Little sores would suddenly be there on his hands or on his arms and Safia thought they were mosquito bites. But soon even Gangubai said these sores were something else—and she brought neem leaves and made a kind of poultice of them, or boiled them and Safia bathed her father in the bitter neem water. But the sores spread and spread and the scratching was unbearable. Her father scratched and scratched and the blood ran and then they found some cotton socks and covered his hands with them and it was a terrible time and it went on and on—and as the days became weeks and then months Safia realized that her father had learnt from the birds that he had watched all his life— he had always said you learn silence from them. And her father was silent through all those days and weeks and months. He never complained. He never cried out. He waited. And he watched Safia and he knew what she was suffering. But he had no more lessons to teach her.

If she hadn't leant them yet.

His body became very frail. Safia now never needed Gangubai to help lift him or help to turn him. Safia could do it all on her own. But he was still very strong in some things. He would not allow a doctor to come near him. Once Safia's husband brought a doctor from the big city—someone well-known to Safia's father from a long time ago. But her father would not allow him to examine him. He acknowledged him and told him to go away. So Safia knew that her father was still very strong and that that was why dying was taking such a long time. He refused to die.

But one day he did. Die.

Safia had finished bathing him and Gangubai had taken away the terrible stained sheets and towels and sad white socks for his hands—to burn—and Safia thought all this would feel just a little better if he would cry out, or cry, or shout, or rage against it all. Rage against all this coming to him with hardly any warning. Not to be able to walk, not to stride so fast and climb, to grow so thin and then these terrible sores and the scratching and the blood. Why doesn't he rage against it, or me, or Gangubai. It was while Safia was thinking this that she heard a sound. It came from her father's bed. It was her father. Safia heard her father say, 'We had our time, Safia.' She waited because he had said this so distinctly.

'Do you want something, Father?'

This time her father said, 'We had our time together, Safia—'

Safia said, 'Yes, Father, we had our time together—' and she waited, hoping he would say something else to her because her heart felt so sad. Perhaps he is better—because he hasn't spoken for such a long time—and he hasn't really said goodbye—I don't think that is what he is trying to say—could it be? After a while her father said, 'Safia, now you have to go to Anwar—'

And Safia said, 'Who? Who, Father?' Again she waited. Her father said—

'Anwar is your husband, you have to go to him now, because it is time.'

After that her father didn't say anything.

Safia thought, I shan't be afraid—not yet. That isn't what he means—not yet.

But from somewhere Safia heard another sound. It was the sound Gangubai was making. A kind of crying sound, a kind of wailing.

Safia's husband was a kind and thoughtful man. He had been kind and thoughtful and patient all through the long dying of Safia's father. But Safia's father was dead and buried in the village where he had lived all his life with Safia and now Anwar said to his young wife, 'Now you must come to your new home. Now you have to start a new life, a new life with me. Now you have to leave this village and live where I live.'

On the morning that he came to fetch her, Gangubai had swept the house clean, and Safia closed the shutter and locked the door. The very old champak tree had dropped many blossoms and

Gangubai, stooping, picked up several and gave some to Safia and pushed the rest into her tight knot of hair. Three thin dogs chased the car, desperately barking, almost hurling themselves at it. Once out of the village Anwar drove fast and suddenly there was the hill with the egg-shell blue mosque at the top and Safia thought how long it used to take when we walked and climbed and listened for birds—how long, how hot, how quiet it used to be. Anwar said, 'What are you thinking, Safia?'

Safia said, 'I was thinking how long it used to take my father and me when we walked from the house to reach that hill—we would leave so early when it was almost dark and very cool and walk and walk through the—anyway, already it's gone.' Because Anwar was a kind and thoughtful man he noticed something in Safia's voice and he said, 'We'll come back—'

'When, when will we come back?'

'Soon,' he said.

And that is how Anwar brought his wife Safia to the big city where he lived.

Safia's husband lived in a house on one of the main streets that led to the city centre. There was a great deal of traffic—there was noise. To Safia the traffic and the noise never seemed to end. For many days after she came to the city she could not hear the sound or the silence of birds.

Anwar noticed that very early in the morning, before it was light, she would creep out to the balcony, waiting. When he asked her, though he knew, she said, 'I can't breathe—I can't seem to breathe.' Anwar said, 'Soon it will feel better, it's just the change—you haven't adjusted to the change—it will take a while.' But she said, 'How will it change? There are no trees here—no birds here—how will it get better?' Anwar said, 'Trust me—only trust me. Soon you will not notice. Look how Gangubai has adjusted.'

He waited. Safia said, 'Has she? How do you know? Have you asked her?'

She sounded upset because if Gangubai had, as Anwar said, adjusted, why hadn't she? Or how had Gangubai done it? Or when would she be all right?

Anwar said, 'Look, I should have done this before, I thought about it and meant to, but somehow forgot—these keys are to the terrace, no one goes there now, no one uses it; my mother did, but now not for a long time—I should have earlier—I didn't think—I mean I did and forgot—here, Safia, you take them, the last one on the ring is to the terrace.'

Her life changed that day.

Perhaps this is what adjusting means, thought Safia. That Gangubai had found some way of her own to live and I have this terrace. Anwar's mother's terrace. And Anwar knew. I wish I could do something for Anwar to show him how I feel he is such a good man and such a kind man and that I wish I was a little happy. I suppose he knows that I am not. I miss the village, I miss the birds and the walks and the silence. I miss my father. I miss my father. I wish I was there with him before all the bad things happened. I wish.

But now there was the terrace. Safia went to the terrace every day. In the beginning just for a short while every morning, very early, but gradually she spent more and more time there. Sometimes when Anwar came back rather late from work he would call and call for Safia—and then realize that of course she must be on the terrace—where else! Anwar was not a man given to jealousy, but he thought, how difficult it is to win this girl—first there was her father and now this terrace. Of course he was not to know how important this terrace was to her in all that happened.

Safia went to Gangubai and said, 'There is something odd happening—in my body.' 'Odd? How do you mean odd? Try and tell me—do you hurt, are you feeling ill?'

Safia told her.

Long ago, when Safia was thirteen in the village she had gone to Gangubai and said, 'There is something odd happening to me—in my body.'

And Gangubai had told her—not really explained—but at least Safia had not been frightened any more. And it had been Gangubai who said to Safia's father that he would have to go after his birds alone for a few days every month.

Safia had hated it then. She had felt invaded by something alien. It had to be borne, Gangubai had told her, every month for almost as long as she lived. 'It is a woman's fate, it is what she is born for.'

'It is not why I was born—I refuse to accept it—I will not.' She had hated Gangubai for a long time as though it were her fault.

And now it was five years later and she had come to Gangubai and told her—and this time Gangubai hugged her, and cried a little and looked pleased a lot and said that Safia was going to have a child. Safia said, 'No, I'm not. I'm not ready. I don't want a child—not till I'm ready. You think you know everything but you don't.' And Gangubai said, 'But you came to me—why come to me if you think I don't know? Go ask someone else.'

But Safia went up to the terrace and stayed there—much longer than usual. And that's where Anwar found her when he came back from work and had been told by Gangubai. About the baby.

Anwar was so happy. On the terrace he found her crouched near the water tank at the extreme end in the dark and he said, 'It will be all right—trust me, Safia, trust me, don't be afraid—please come down, come into the house. It is such a happy day, Safia, and I—want—'

'I'm not ready, I don't want a child till I know what it's all about—and I mean, till I am ready. Anwar, you do understand, don't you? I am not ready—there is so much—and it's all happening too soon—and I'm frightened and I am all by myself—' Anwar was hurt, quite naturally, but as always he thought only of Safia and said, 'I am here, I will help you, and I do understand everything you've said, but you'll see—it's just the shock, soon it will feel all right and you will be happy with your own baby—trust me, only trust me, Safia. Will you? Will you try? Come, let's go down.'

But it didn't turn out the way Anwar had hoped it would. As the days passed, one by one, Safia became more and more quiet and spent more and more time on her terrace. She hated being sick every morning—and yet every morning she was sick. She knew something was happening inside her body and she thought, 'My father was always a strong man who strode into the forest every morning at first light—but then something happened inside his body and everything changed, the bad times came and no one had a name for what happened to him. And so it will be for me now because my body is changing and soon I will be different and I will not know myself—' And Safia thought, 'I have always been used to my body—it had walked every day into the forest with my father, walked and climbed till I was tired and we had watched and learnt about birds. And now this is happening and I can't bear it, and why should I?' And Safia began to remember things that she had put away, except in every bad dream. She began to see her father when he could not walk any more and how his arms got thin, so thin they were not his arms any more and how, then, he became weaker and weaker and then could not get out of his bed. And then the sores came—and the terrible scratching and scratching and the blood and the white cotton socks tied to his hands stained with blood—so little warning, sores and shames and he bore it— all those weeks and months he bore it, maybe he was really showing me how we have to bear all the things that come to us—all the things we do not want—or cannot bear or understand.

And Safia would go up to the terrace and sit there for hours. Waiting. Watching. And Anwar thought, 'My good girl, she minds less and less, she has accepted what is to happen—the shock and the panic have gone, perhaps the fear. Perhaps soon she might be happy. Perhaps.'

Anwar began to come home earlier from his work every evening and go straight up to the terrace and stay with her till it was dark, hoping that, 'Today Safia will tell me what she has been thinking about all day—today she will share her thoughts—today she will say she is happy to be bearing our child.'

This did not happen—even though Safia was happy to see Anwar each evening. She did not tell him about the fearful sad dreams of her father coming to her with his hands tied in white cotton socks stained in blood. Dry dead things caught in long cobwebs swinging from the rafters. Once, it was so real to her, when Anwar was with her, and she called out, 'Gangubai, Gangubai, can't you see them, those dirty long horrible cobwebs? We, you, must get rid of them— they hang over his bed—he sees them and we have allowed them to hang there day after day and all these months.'

Anwar said, 'But there's nothing up here—no dust, no cobwebs—it's dark. Let's go down.' Anwar was troubled—but he did not know whom to turn to.

Soon Safia was not allowed to climb up the steep steps to the terrace. She began to sit by the bedroom window, staring out.

And Gangubai would move about the room doing nothing but wishing the baby would hurry up and come, so that this whole long, wrong episode would end.

'Don't put on the light, Gangubai—I can still see so many things—' And Gangubai would be quite pleased because at least Safia had said something and she would switch on the light anyway just to get Safia to say, 'Don't, don't put the light on, not yet, not just yet.'

Safia sat in the darkness because she didn't like her thoughts very much, they were strange dark thoughts and she felt the light might lay her thoughts bare. Exposed—so that Gangubai might see them and then, when Anwar came back from work, he would see them. She did not want him to see them. He would be hurt, she knew that. And he would try not to show he was hurt. Safia knew that Anwar had too many hurts from her and she had not meant them at all. She seemed to be unable to hurt him less though she liked him so much.

And then one day Safia got a fever—nobody could work out where it came from and why. And Safia and Anwar and Gangubai and the doctor knew that now she was ill. So it became linked with having the baby, and Safia was not allowed to get out of bed. At all. 'Till the fever goes away,' they said. 'It is a great risk to the baby,' they said. So Safia lay in a bed dragged close to the window and watched the tree that she could see from that window. And lying there, day after day and week after week, the tree became important to Safia. She watched it in the way she had learnt from her father. Each day the tree and the one leaf on that tree shaped like a wooden bird, and she thought constantly of her father. She thought of birds. And she thought of walking and walking through forests and heat and sometimes the coolth under some great tree and she heard silence and bird calls.

And each day was exactly the same. And each day at daylight and at midnight and in the afternoon, all sleepless, the tree was always there and the one leaf shaped like a wooden bird. And the indignity of the bedpan and the sponge bath was made easier by gazing straight ahead, past the intent face bent over her, and staring at the tree as though her body was not her own at all—and Safia just disowned it for great lengths of time having eyes only for the tree. Gangubai said to the others in the outhouses, 'I think if it were not for that tree being there, just there, near her window ... .' And Anwar, close to despair, would think, 'Thank God for that tree . . .' And Safia thought, 'If this tree dies I shall die—I shall never get up from this bed or climb the stairs to my terrace or ever get back to the village.'

And the days took a long, long time, they took their time to begin and end. Each dawn came heavy and slow and then continued to linger heavily, slowly. Safia, lying on her back through morning, afternoon, evening, night and so to the next day heavily and slowly, watched shadows on that tree and changing light on that tree and thought, 'I wish that my father had had a tree to watch as he lay month after month.'

Safia said to Gangubai, 'Do you think the baby inside me is still alive? How can it be? Perhaps it is dead of this fever that won't go away—tell me Gangu—how will we know if it is dead or still alive?' Gangubai said, 'The doctor always knows, you must not think like that.' But Gangubai was frightened and told Anwar. Anwar had known for a long time that Safia was thinking these thoughts because once in the dead of night she had said, 'Anwar the baby must die of the thoughts I have—' and when Anwar asked her about her thoughts Safia had said, 'Bitter thoughts, hate thoughts, sad, bad thoughts.' And he had tried to comfort her, telling her, 'No, no, Safia, your thoughts are natural, it has been so bad and sad for you but you have been so good, so brave, your—our— baby will be like you, like you, it cannot die now, it has your strength . . .' Safia had looked at him with a world of sadness in her eyes and said, 'What strength, where? It is this fever that is strong. It is as strong as that tree and that leaf shaped like a bird.'

Years and many years later Zubeida was to say to Aditya, 'I think if the tree had not been there for my mother I would not be here— it's a sobering thought, isn't it? She told me herself when I was little, so I thought the tree had some magic in it—later, much later of course, I asked my father what she had meant and he said that it was true, I mean, that the tree had saved her life and so I was born. Does that sound confused or odd?'

'No—it makes a lot of sense, knowing Safia! I hope the tree is still there. Her father, the tree and birds. Three things. They'd see to it that Safia pulled through—I mean that other time—'

'I wish then that those three things had helped her when she—you know—later—'

'Yes, well, but the later time—was quite impossible in every way—the conflict—she was just torn—torn apart and then it's too late, or I suppose sometimes it's so bad, nothing can help or perhaps timing or time of day, or the telephone doesn't work or someone says, "Pull yourself together," or, or, or—you know?'

'Yes, I can see that—but for a long time I couldn't see that—I just saw it as a rejection of me and my father. I couldn't see beyond that.'

'Of course—that would be the way—it's most natural and hurts terribly—as though one didn't matter at all. She loved you very much—you have to know that. And Anwar—I hope Anwar always knew that in spite of everything. It went very deep—but—that's the sad thing, that's terrible, but. This terrible other thing—this thing or rather a whole new set of feelings in her that she had never encountered before—never till then. Did you ever meet the doctor who helped her enormously? Friend, doctor, helpmate, what name for such? I have often wondered what he must have felt—after it all failed? I wonder if he blamed himself, do they, doctors, I mean. There must be so many sad failures along with all the successes. From what Safia told me about him he sounded a most extraordinary man, human. I felt a peculiar jealousy, really, about him. He read a great deal, loved films and plays, most elegant, civilized man. I think Safia was more than half in love with him.'

'I've read about it,' Zubeida said, 'transference it's called. You see when I was old enough I read about all kinds of cases, trying to understand about my mother's death. And, yes, to answer your earlier question—I have met her friend, doctor—whatever—during that search to understand. I met him rather often as a matter of fact. He is all that you gathered, only even more so. Rather beautiful looking, gentle, quiet. Marvellous eyes—disconcerting because so searching. Blue. Eyes, I mean. And hands like something you want to touch but would never dare to—hands by Durer or—who?'

'Yes, Safia mentioned all these things and a great delicate brow, never frowned at anything she said, or rather did not say—long silences because she was afraid, or couldn't begin to tell him, and he never looked impatient or looked at his watch, just waited, and waited till she could speak. Oh, yes, Safia loved him and she wanted to get well for you and Anwar and for that doctor. She couldn't bear to let him down!

'She said that he believed in her, that she would pull through no matter what, that Sushant was important but still only an episode, not important to the main thrust of her life. I don't think the doctor could have put it quite like that to her but certainly implied it. And Safia struggled away, wanting to break free, agonizing about her feelings for Sushant and wanting to be what the doctor believed. It was a dreadful thing to see, and watch, and be so helpless. She was really very ill. When she seemed better she was somewhere in a kind of dead zone for a long while. But she clambered back. And you were born and she rejoiced in you and they both, Anwar and Safia, named you Zubeida.'

'Do you know why I was called Zubeida—it's an old name, isn't it?—and right through school and college it got shortened to a name I don't fancy.'

'Do they call you Zubi for short then?'

'Yes, they do—I don't like that—'

'Gangubai decided to be very firm on the day you were to be named. She said very clearly that if the baby had been a boy then it would have had your grandfather's name, but since you were a girl then you must be called after Safia's mother. Apparently, Gangubai was very fond of your grandmother—and so that is how you were named. Safia was still a bit fragile so didn't say very much and Gangubai told her that since she had been such a beautiful woman it was a perfect name because she was certain you were going to look like her. Anwar told me all this.'

'I would like to look like my mother—do I?'

'Very much. You look like Safia when I knew her—you must be almost the same age.'

'You mean when you met her or when she died?'

'I just mean that time, that whole time that I knew your mother—that's all.'

'You were in love with my mother, weren't you?—not just idle curiosity. You can tell me—I feel that we are friends. Were you? In love with her?'

'Yes—I was. I didn't realize it though, not really till it was too late. I mean, not quite that but though it sounds dreadful somehow I always thought of her as Anwar's wife and respected all that that implied—I wish that the other hadn't happened.'

'The other? You mean the person my mother fell in love with. Is that what you mean?'

'Yes—I do mean that. I mean that.'

But this conversation was to occur a good twenty years on—so.

And Safia was to tell the doctor with the quiet hands after a very long silence, 'I really don't like the rain after coming to live here, in the village it was different. I was not afraid of it there. It smelt different, it came down different—here it is black rain. It is dirty before it lands on the dirty streets. Even my terrace is different when it rains. Feet shoe-shod are dirty and black and leave marks, nothing dries—nothing dries. The birds look so sad—so wet, they cannot fly. There is a wet woman who suckles her small baby at the corner of the street—I can see her from my window, she is never dry, her sari clings to her so wet and the baby is a soggy bundle of rags or wet newspaper. In my father's village we never saw such things. And it never stops—all night it rains and then all day, and its sounds never stop, days and weeks it goes on and on. I feel I might get better if only it would stop raining. I feel lost and wet and cold, like that woman at the corner with her small filthy bundle. Dead wet rats swirling round her bare feet and wet old newspaper and rags—do you think it will stop soon?'

'Yes, it will stop soon, you'll see, one morning when you wake it will have stopped. Or one night when you wake there will not be that sound you were expecting,' he had said.

'All the faces are sad leaning out of windows in the bus, and faces not in the bus are sad—doctor, your face is so sad too. It is. Do you worry a great deal about us all or do you worry about me?

Do you worry more about me? I don't suppose you will tell me, will you? I think the sun will never shine again. Every day there is a procession of wet people carrying a body to be burnt. I think more people die or stop living during the long rains, don't you think, doctor? Today they were carrying a small white wet wrapped body to the burning grounds and the rain fell on the body and the flowers on the body, and how will the body burn in the rain? Wet wood won't burn, what will the waiting people do, waiting for the wet wood to burn. And the mother? Doctor, what will the mother do waiting for the small body to burn in this rain that won't stop? It was not like this in the village. Everything became clean and shining, the leaves on the trees, the trees on the hill, the blue of the mosque shone and the earth smelt like earth should, wet and dark brown, and our well filled up. There it was life. Here it is all death during the rain. I am frightened.'

And the doctor said, 'Today has been a good day because you have said all these things—you are going to be better. Soon you will begin to feel better, you'll see. I am glad you shared so many thoughts with me today—'

And Safia said, 'When will I be well again?'

And the doctor said, 'Now you are well again, you just have to begin to feel better—soon. Very soon you will begin to feel better. Trust me.'

And she did soon begin to feel better. She did trust him.

In fact, she trusted him so much that she felt only he could make her better—so, that very last time when she needed him and he wasn't there—not at the end of a telephone line, not behind his neat clean desk with the glass paperweight with a snow scene inside, not anywhere for her to run to and feel he would put it all right again—she just couldn't manage, and that was that.

He was at Safia's funeral. He stood a little apart. His head bowed. His quiet hands useless.

Zubeida said, 'Was that other man there at my mother's funeral? Was he?'

'You mean Sushant? Yes, of course, as were all the group who had been in the play.'

Zubeida said, 'I hate that man, how dare he come to her funeral,

The Quiet of the Birds

how could he do such a graceless thing?'

'Look, there wasn't all that much to hate about Sushant—just as I felt the awful waste in Safia's death being caused by someone like that. I mean there was so little, really, to him. Apart from his charm, of course. Nothing really to have loved so intensely—nothing much to hate intensely. I don't honestly think he realized that there were such intensities in people, that he could possibly have caused them!'

'Then why? Why did my mother feel like that about him? Why?'

'If we could answer that one, my dear, dear girl, we would be able to save such unnecessary suffering. Why do people fall in love—it is never something anyone can see, outside of the person, I mean. To us—let's say Sushant was a charming, not enormously handsome man. He was like a perpetual undergraduate at Oxford or Cambridge. Very tall, well-spoken, if you could remember anything he said, it simply didn't matter. It was Russian translation one moment or the best way to eat strawberries another. Oh! he could charm just anyone—and I believe, not really know the effect he had. A tall young man always seeming to be disappearing down Kings Parade, his gown following behind him, he was a very fine Astrov! He really was. So don't hate him. He wasn't your common or garden criminal—he really was not. Anyway, hate is such a destructive thing, don't waste time on it. Try. You must. After all this time.'

Another time Zubeida said, 'So many bits don't fit—it's a kind of jigsaw puzzle—you think they were lovers? My mother and this Sushant person? It shouldn't matter, but seeing it was her somehow—well, you know? Ever since you spoke of him I've wondered—now I can ask you. I can, can't I?'

'You can ask me anything. But I don't have the answer. I have wondered too. Anyway, does it make a big difference—I mean to want, to imagine, to dream and the reality—once at a group party he made Safia dance with him. She wouldn't with any of us—we assumed she couldn't or didn't. But he made her. I heard her say over and over, "Only because I'm drunk I can say this, say this because I mean it, I love, love, love you—" And he said, "You're not drunk, what did you drink?"

'I always remember that. Another time, backstage during *Vanya*, with her eyes closed, I found her repeating over and over, "This too will pass, this too will pass." I thought she was afraid of going on stage and I tried to reassure her and she held my hand and said, "After a while he'll fade, fade, fade—after a while he'll fade, with luck—don't you think?" And I said, "Yes," though I was, and was not, quite sure who she was talking about. Later, of course, I knew who she was talking about.'

After a silence Zubeida said, 'In some ways of course, I envy my mother—really I do.'

'That's odd, because Safia never really knew what she was like for other people—I mean the effect she had on them—but tell me, Zubeida, why did you say envy?'

'I suppose I would have liked to have been like her—to be someone with the ability to cause people to love her and to be so unconscious about it—and you, you too—'

'But was I in love with her—or more than half in love with the quality of her? I was. I must have been. I had never met anyone like her—none of our group had—she seemed at once both older and yet so much younger. Older, because she was so contained, so quiet. She was so different from the young girls from college that were our friends—and who joined the group. She was a waif in comparison—a slim slip of a thing—and yet she had a little daughter.

'This may seem odd and contradictory but she seemed at once earth mother, virginal yet innocent, untouched though married. She was the oddest thing. Safia had this quality—we all felt but could not define. It grew and grew in me the belief that she would make a marvellous Sonya in *Uncle Vanya*—vulnerable yet able to help Vanya, be in love with Astrov and yet help Vanya in his enormous suffering about Helena—I had her read alone, also at the readings and auditions, I was there when Safia spoke to Anwar. "Good for you," Anwar said, really meaning it, grateful that I had cast her—he was that worried about her being so much alone—I can hear them now, after all these years—Safia said—

'"I thought you'd say I couldn't possible do it—or something—"

'Anwar said, "Silly, why ever not—aren't you glad because it's wonderful news—"

'Safia said, "Yes and no—and what about Zubeida?"

'"What about her? I imagine it's just a few hours most evenings and there's always Gangubai—I'm so proud of you—please don't worry and try to be pleased."

'I have often wished Anwar was not so nice. He really was one of the best. Always. But if only he had been a little jealous, a little possessive, a little demonstrative—like us. I think, if only, then— perhaps. But then that's silly. We are only what we are. I suppose.'

Zubeida said, 'You know what that doctor told me about my mother? He said, and I remember his words almost exactly, I was so struck. He said the tragedy of my mother's life was that in its too short span it had been full of things most terror-filled for her. She had had no mother and did not know where to look for her.

'She had an extraordinary father and it was terrible to lose him in the way she did.

'It was terrible to have had such a kind husband.

'It was terrible to have had a child when she was still a child herself.

'And terrible to fall in love at first sight.

'That's what he said when I asked him why my mother had died the way she did.

'He said, all those things, not just one thing, all those things, caused her great grief and she could not cope—and she tried so hard to resolve her fears and live with them. She cared too much. And always she tried to live up to what her father had told her about the silence and quiet of birds—and she was not a bird. And she felt she had failed him most desperately, and failed Anwar and failed her child. Me.

'The doctor said that my mother was a wonderful, most-delicately-balanced-on-a-tight-rope kind of person and he wished and wished that he had been there for her that last desperate afternoon. But he had not been there. He felt that he had failed her. She left a letter for me, you know, it was given to me by the aunt I was sent to stay with. She thought my mother was most wicked, often, she would say to me, "How could she, how could your mother do that to you, she didn't deserve to be a mother— my poor Anwar, my poor little Zubeida." I hated my aunt. She stopped saying it to me the year I told her what I thought of my mother—I told her she was all wrong. My aunt, that is. I said that she would never understand because she was not a wife nor a mother, and that my mother had done what she had done because she cared about us so much—I showed my aunt my letter, which I will show you.'

Aditya took the letter and read: 'Zubeida, I can't ask you to forgive me or even to try and understand but even though I have tried and tried not to do to you what my mother did to me I can't, I just can't cope any more. I don't want to leave you but I can't, I can't seem to manage—I want to be with you to care and love you, always through all your growing up—and I do care and love you, so she, I mean my mother, must have cared and loved me and yet she left—I can't bear the way I feel. I'm sad and dead already with sadness, it's pulling and pulling me, I try and try but it's happening in spite of me, it's bigger than I am, only when I am with my doctor I feel I can manage because he tells me I can—and he's not here now. I wish—' the letter ended there.

'You know, Aditya, I didn't understand then, but gradually I did and now I do. I really do understand that kind of desperate conflict. You can love strongly and still leave, it wasn't because she was indifferent or irresponsible as a mother, as a wife. I think it was because she was those things entirely, too much, perhaps. But I do wish I had known her all my life. I would have liked her so much. Loved her.'

'Yes, and I think she would have liked you very much. Now and while you were growing up. Anyway, selfishly, I am glad—that now late, rather than soon, I have met you—by chance, I could so easily not have—after all, it's all of twenty years. It might have chanced otherwise.'

'And what happened to the Astrov person?' asked Zubeida.

'Oh, he married, and then he married again, and—well—'

'Yes, that fits—' said Zubeida.

'Fits? How fits?'

'I mean, the play was a bit like their real loves—Sonya in love with Astrov and Astrov in love with Helena and everything bleak, except here the bleakness didn't end in the same way—I mean,

Sonya is really such a brave sort of person, isn't she? I don't mean brave in a silly sort of way but always thinking of other people first, I mean, clearly she worried much more for Vanya and his state of desperation, didn't she? Remember her last speech, the one that ends the play? I've learnt it by heart—I love that play—I feel closer to it than his others.'

'So you don't blame me?' asked Aditya.

'Blame you? Whatever for? Oh, I see, you mean for doing the play and involving my mother and—no, no, not a jot.'

'Do you blame me for any of it? Because I have felt such guilt— somehow as though, but for me, Safia would—oh, you know— never have joined the group, never have met—'

'That's madness—how could you have known, guessed— whatever. What could you have stopped from happening?'

'Perhaps, I mean if she had been left to live her own life—not been thrown into another kind of world—she was so vulnerable. And I did that.'

For a while they were both very quiet.

'No,' she said, 'no, you gave her many things—Chekhov and poetry and friendship and, I suppose, falling in love in that way, I mean with that kind of intensity—perhaps it's the thing that matters—I mean, perhaps it matters much more than what she would never have known. If you weigh it all against what she did have—she had Anwar, yes. Anwar and she had me. That's all. That's not much. Not really.'

After a longish pause she said, 'Have you really blamed yourself all these years?'

'Yes. Well, let's say it's never left me—never. So many years ago and it's like yesterday. I tried so hard to see you after the funeral— just see you or be with you—perhaps, talk to you or rather have you talk to me. You were so small. But you were a very definite person—I wanted to say sorry to you, very much. You were sent away. For a long time ·. .?'

'Yes, for a long time—to that aunt and then to school and then college and now I'm back—and I want to find my mother.'

'Find her? Did you say, "find her"?'

'Yes—find her, know her, know her better. Know her at all. I mean, find out what she was like, what she liked, what she loved, what she hated. My father won't or can't—talk, I mean—anyway, not to me. He keeps her behind a sort of glass case. But locked. You know. Now you can tell me some or all that you know. Because you knew her well—and you knew her at the time that is most important for me to try and feel or try to understand. Of course, perhaps you'd rather not. Please say something.'

'Yes, I will, I mean, I'll try. She was not an easy person—I mean, to know—that's the quality she had that made her so unusual. She was so contained. Only sometimes—only sometimes she'd say something or half say it and so it went—I mean, she made it worthwhile trying to know her—valuing very much what she was or wanted to be—I'm saying this so badly. I've thought so much about her—but never been asked—as you now ask me—bear with me if I seem to grope. I am groping.'

'Thank you. Truly. I am so lucky—more than lucky to have met you like this—as you said earlier, we might so easily not have met, don't you think? If you hate it here we could meet somewhere else or—I mean, anything. Anywhere. I don't intend losing you again—at least not or a while.'

'Your father wanted Safia to meet people—he knew that she was lonely—he felt that through the theatre group that I was involved with I might help her—you were four or perhaps just five at the time. I came to your house and met you both. Do you recall? Anything? We used to go up to Safia's terrace and talk.'

'I do—I do remember that—you were teaching her something, were you?'

'No, not really. I was going to do a play and I used to talk to Safia about it—she had fresh ideas about it and I lent her a copy of it and then one day quite suddenly, I realized she was my Sonya— perhaps that's why you thought I was teaching her.'

'Did my mother fall in love with you too? Is that why she died?'

'Oh, no. I wish sometimes that it had been me—one always feels one would have saved her from such unhappiness—but no, no. I was her friend. I suppose I was more than half in love with her—but then there was your father—I always was what would be seen as an "old-fashioned" man—Safia was married and I was your father's friend. Of course nothing is really that simple, is it? Anyway, I think I was the first friend Safia ever had—and I valued that. I realized how difficult it was for her to speak of things that mattered to her deeply—but after a while she did talk to me about the birds—'

'About the birds—what birds?'

'You must know that Safia's father was a kind of recluse—a bird man, living alone all his life with Safia in a village near the sea. He taught her to watch birds and learn from them. From the time she was a little girl he made her walk with him into the forests looking at birds and their habits and he made her believe that she must trust them and listen to them—even when she asked about her mother he would tell her that there was nothing to know about her mother—he said, "Trust only birds—nothing else?"'

'Do you mean there was no one else in the village? I mean, just my mother and her father?'

'From what Safia told me it was like that. Except for Gangubai— you must remember her?'

'Of course—she died last year. She never went back to her village. She told my father that there was nothing to go back for. She had promised Safia's mother that she would look after Safia—always, no matter what happened. And she said she had failed in her promise. She had let my mother die.'

'Poor old Gangubai—I wish I had tried to see her—I could have talked to her about Safia—God knows I needed to. But I found it very difficult to be with Anwar. As you said, he never talked about Safia—and Safia is really all I wanted to talk about. You see that, I mean, you know what I mean?'

'Yes. I do know. It must be terrible to be my father.'

'Yes, I have often thought that, but would you be able to try and tell me why you say that?'

'Yes, I think so—to be such a good and kind person, to be a thoughtful and caring person the way he is—and yet never to be first for anyone, always second or third or taken for granted—or ignored.'

'Not so bad—you can't mean it so harshly, so sadly.'

'Yes, I do—and I can because that's the way I feel about him. I know his great qualities of heart, I know his goodness and his caring and his love but I know he is not first for me—and he was not first for my mother nor for you, or anyone, really. And I know that he knows this and feels it but never allows himself to share his sorrow or sadness or grief—he feels no one really wants to hear it—of it.'

Aditya had asked Anwar if his group could use the terrace—their own meeting place was being renovated and he did want to get started on *Uncle Vanya*. Of course Anwar being Anwar was delighted, he felt that Safia wouldn't feel so guilty about leaving Zubeida, everything would be in her own home. If only Anwar had not been so delighted—because that is how Safia met her undoing. That happened in the form of Sushant.

There had been a couple of readings and Aditya rather pleased with the casting so far, and one of the group was to bring a friend that evening—'he's done some stuff before, you might find something for him.' The evening was momentous. Aditya found a perfect Astrov—and Safia met the love of her life.

After the reading Sushant had come to Safia in the easy way he had and sat down next to her and said, 'I'm to be Astrov and I believe you are to be Sonya—so you are to fall in love with me and I with Helena. I've just read the play and now this reading—do you know the play well? I'm Sushant and you are Safia. I'm told this is your terrace—what a marvellous place.'

Safia who knew nothing about small talk didn't or rather, couldn't, say anything. She didn't say anything at all, she didn't trust herself to. She left the terrace and went down to Zubeida and hugged her very close. She knew something had happened to her. She felt ill. She knew she should go back up to the terrace with the others. She wanted to. She did not want to. She wanted to stay there forever, hugging Zubeida. She wanted to be here knowing that he was on the terrace.

She had never met anyone like him before. For a long time after that first time she could not speak to him at all—she was so entranced. It was his way of speaking to her and watching her. So often she never answered him at all. And then, he was more tactile than anyone she had known—often when he spoke to her or was making some point he would touch her arm or her shoulder and she wanted him to leave it there. She never dared move—hardly dared breathe. He was easy with everyone—it was his way—laughing and joking with Helena and Vanya and Aditya, the director. And one day he said, 'But when will you speak to me—you never do—don't you trust me? Have I done something to upset you?' It was just his way. He flirted with all the women. He would have flirted just as easily with the men. But Safia was not to know. How could she? She had never met anyone like him. She had never been in love before.

Safia began to live for the days when they met to rehearse. She dreaded them most. But they were the only days that held any meaning for her. The rest passed in a dream of unfeeling. She hardly remembered who Anwar was in her life and sometimes as she held Zubeida she couldn't think what to say to her except sorry, sorry, I am so sorry, all this is happening to somebody else. She lived with a kind of heightened awareness—the very air she breathed was different. The clothes she now wore, the texture of her skin, of her hair. She began to look very lovely—she began to realize it mattered to her how she looked. None of these things had ever happened to her before. On the day of a rehearsal she would feel sick and excited all day. She worried that he might not come—that he might fall ill, that the rehearsal would be cancelled. Till he arrived she sat tense and unhappy. And when he did come she dared not look, often turning right round and leaving the terrace. Once it was so obvious that Aditya followed her down the steps, found her huddling in a corner with Zubeida. He asked her what the matter was—why was she so distressed, was it the part, was it something he had said while directing her. He asked if Sushant upset her in any way, that she must be sure to tell him because he really wanted her to be Sonya but that he couldn't have her unhappy in real life. That really pulled her up short—if Aditya had noticed then surely the others had as well. She told Aditya it was nothing—she said the others seemed so experienced and she felt awkward—not good enough, perhaps he had made a mistake in casting her. Aditya said, if that was all that was worrying her not to think like that—it was early days—she'd soon feel better. To come back to the terrace now, and the next time to come to him and not hide like this—it would worry Anwar, it would upset Zubeida. Also, he asked her if she would come with him when he went looking for some of the important props for the play—she'd see some interesting parts of Bombay. Safia said yes, she'd like that very much. So on the days they were not rehearsing she discovered Chor Bazaar with Aditya. They went by bus and then trudged all afternoon, looking and looking through dusty shelves and heaped interesting backyards and often came home with the magical past. Often Aditya would talk about Chekhov and *Vanya* while they walked and looked for things he needed to bring his play to life. He told her that his wanting to do this Chekhov had started because he had seen a bird-cage from a bus window at dusk when Bombay is at its loneliest—he had seen it in a dreary chawl.

Aditya began to remember that long-ago time—easily now as if it was close again. All of them young, all of youth on their side, and it had seemed to him to have contained all the sweetness and sadness and aching funniness of Chekhov's *Vanya*—no hero, no tragedy—Discuss! So that glimpse of a bird-cage in a small room lit by a street lamp made him want to do *Vanya*, he must do it soon before he lost his nerve. And he must have a bird-cage, large and gilt and with a small bird in it and Vanya must cry out, 'I haven't lived, I have not lived.' And one afternoon they found just the right bird-cage and an old-fashioned revolver, and an old Irani shop-owner lent them a real samovar, brass and heavy and beautifully wrought. Aditya said he must get heavy, dark-red wool to lie on Marina's lap—dark-red on her deep-purple lap—and dark red roses for Helena.

One day Aditya said, 'Talking of Helena, I hope she's not getting involved with Astrov. I hope it is just for the play because it just wouldn't do, there are enough problems without that one, thank you!'

That day Safia went home and cried and knew for dead certain what the matter was with her. As if she hadn't known already. She wondered if Aditya had said it really meaning Safia.

During the rains rehearsals were in a big dark house—rehearsals starting after six, after office hours, everyone very hungry and tempers sometimes a little sharp because tired, and people irritable. Some rehearsals with nobody having learnt their lines, some with everyone wishing they were doing *Arms and the Man* or something and thinking Aditya quite mad to try and do Chekhov, where, as they moaned, 'It's lines and lines to learn and nothing seems to happen and the audience is sure to go to sleep or ask for their money back.' Rehearsals—and only three weeks to curtain up. Rehearsals—chaotic with drinking coffee and talking Chekhov. Rehearsals—and someone saying, 'I say this is impossible I can't learn the lines let's do his *Seagull*—at least a bird is shot or something or *The Cherry Orchard*—let's do a play with some action.' Short, sharp skirmishes and sometimes tears—but gradually something began to happen, something imperceptible, and suddenly, with the rain outside in that dark old house, little portions came to life—nerves stretched to breaking point, little bits and pieces made magic, made Chekhov.

Things fell into shape. Costumes fit, people had their lines, single moments, Sonya's loneliness and the Professor's selfishness and Helena's boredom and trapped beauty. Wonderful moments when all their lives around a samovar seemed to be just talk—people talking and nobody listening, lonely like children who talk and talk and need to be listened to and seldom are and yet they talk and pretend it does not matter that nobody is listening, not really. Also that, what they are saying seems to have no apparent connection with anything they have said before. All lonely and all waiting like wonderful pianos but locked and the keys are lost. Old tunes—guitars untuned, soft strumming—how capture? How hold?

One late evening Aditya decided the play would be done outside in an old garden. The dark brooding twilight melancholy would never happen in an auditorium. Whispering and wafers! An old garden was found, it had an old gardener's shed in it. It was perfect—it became the garden in the estate where Sonya and Vanya and Marina and Waffles live and long for something they know is slipping away, slipping. That garden was right, old garden chairs and benches, autumn roses, exquisite, mournful roses—the colour of the wool on Marina's lap. Everything made sense. The garden, with all its knowledge of the past, people, and the decay of plants and life, all made a great deal of sense under the evening sky. There hung in the air a feel of so much that's never said and everything held to create a sense of the premonition of aloneness and lonely emptiness that will come when the visit is over—when the slender hopes die and the carriages are gone, with only the sound of harness bells left hanging in the dust.

Safia was completely taken over—she lived and breathed *Vanya*—she was Sonya and she loved Astrov and always would even when she knew that he was entranced by Helena. Aditya told Zubeida years later, 'Oh, your mother certainly was the one along with Uncle Vanya that broke everybody's heart, if they left weeping or heavy with sadness it was because she quite broke your heart long before the end with her, "We shall rest—poor, poor Uncle Vanya, you're crying—you've had no joy in your life, but wait, Uncle Vanya wait—we shall rest—we shall rest."

'And really all we could hear was the clicking of Marina's knitting needles and the soft strumming guitar.

'It was a great success, it really was, it was loved and remembered warmly. But for so many of us it meant the very near end of our Safia.'

And now, because it was over twenty years later, and because, by now Aditya was a good and kind friend to Zubeida he was able to tell her what he thought might have happened. He said—

'There is a terrible let-down sort of feeling when a play is over—

'When nerves that have been so taut are now trying to unwind—

'When the last curtain has come down—

'When the applause dies down for the last time—

'When you stop being Sonya—

'When you know that you will not see your love every day, come evening—

'Time becomes unnatural because it has been so heightened—

'Time drags, becomes unmoving—

'The telephone does not ring—

'He does not come—

'He will never come and it is the only reality, the only thing you want.

'Picture for yourself, Zubeida—picture for yourself such a time for Safia. This was the dead, dry, white relentless season that faced your mother and she had no one to turn to. And she knew that she could not bear her life, she could not bear her longing. She could not bear her guilt. Because you have to remember in all this just how guilty Safia felt.

'And it was at this time when she needed her doctor friend—it was the only time that he was not there for her. He was not in the country.

'Safia was at her lowest. Her weakest. And she was quite, quite alone. One afternoon.

'It is as difficult as this.

'It is always as simple as this.

'Those sleeping pills.

'To help you to sleep. To help you forget.

'She did not know that even the extremes would pass.

'She did not know that this too would pass.'

The Permanence of Grief

These are just imaginings, you understand. They never really happened. None of these things, except, of course, the holiday to Greece. It's the way I used to imagine conversations with him. I was able to make them up because whenever the nieces and nephews came on visits this is the way they would talk. So I had a secret side to me that could quite easily have sounded like this.

He feels quite guilty because a long time ago there were many 'offers' for me. Many and usually very respectable because we were of good standing. I was not, I'm told, without a certain grace, if not beauty. She had always rejected all of them. The last had been a widower twice her age—he had come a-courting and she, sensing this might be the last who would ever come, had taken him out from the stuffy parlour and shown him parts of her garden. He had felt ill at ease and of course she had made up her mind—also he had an ugly jutting lower lip. 'I could never get used to that.' She had said no with such firmness that he had fled—knowing that she would never do, his dead wife had been such a meek, gentle thing.

Returning to the house her brother had asked her why she was so flushed. Had it been difficult or had she been tempted? Why was she so upset—none of the others had touched her in the least. She had not answered him. And then he had said, 'If you had allowed him to court you, I would have tried to understand. But I'm glad, more than I can say, that you showed him the door.' 'The garden gate,' she said, 'I showed him that.' They had smiled at each other knowing that she could not have done otherwise. And so the years had come and gone. Many of them, one by one. Till the year they went to Greece.

Now the children are grown up.

Now they even live on their own.

Now only occasionally bring their dirty clothess here to be washed.

Now they don't seem to miss home cooking all that much.

Now there is only the dog.

Now there are only the plants on the terrace.

Other people use kennels. Someone can come in to water the plants. And the wild almond. Yes, that particularly. It's bound to miss us, it's been with us since the first child was two.

The first child is now twenty-eight. A long time in the life of a person, a long time in a plant growing to be a tree that has large leaves and has its own autumn twice a year.

That's true. A long pause while they both thought about the tree, about watering it, about all the years in between.

Lock up the house.

Travel light.

Go to Greece.

Come to Greece.

All the travel posters on CNN say 'the gods could have chosen anywhere in the world but they chose Greece'. Music.

Cut to—

Blue skies, blue seas, white ruins, olives, the islands, windmills, donkeys, Delphi, Sophocles, Oedipus, Philoctetes, the valley of the butterflies.

No putting it off any more.

No grandchildren to look after.

Let's go. To Greece.

Pause as the picture gets clearer, friends say it's not all it's cracked up to be. So what—to some Garbo is a disappointment. Sailing down the Nile to Luxor would. Not be all it's cracked up to be. To some.

Yes, well.

We know why we are going. We have known for forty years.

A few things packed, travel light.

And we're off. Almost.

And remember straight to Greece—no stopping in London to 'see the latest shows—'

No London and sitting in front of the TV munching mint chocs or Flakies. Straight to Greece, not the Cotswolds, not the Lake district, not Yeats country. Next time we'll look for his two young girls, one as beautiful as a gazelle. Which should remind us now, time is of the essence. Time. We have precious little of it left. I mean, in the active travel sort of way.

Now that we've had our teeth and gums seen to, our eyes gazed at, our cancer and other check-ups done, we've a whole year's reprieve. So.

We're not that old—the check-ups proved, also, we're not that young.

We need to walk in Greece, most of it rocky. We need to be fit. For a whole year we are fit. But the ground is shaking under our feet from now on.

So let's make hay, as they say. Let's go while the going's good. Let's.

So they did. Go. Come to Greece. The gods chose it.

From the start, it was a disaster. We left it too long and now we are not able to manage. We are not that strength, she thought. Suddenly, we are two old people. We are in a strange country and very far from home and we do not know the language. But for the first few days there was a kind of excitement. They set off with a map. They got to the Parthenon and sat down. We have left it too long, he thought, but I owed it to her. She had lived her whole life for me—and I? He felt great sadness because quite suddenly he did not know who he had lived his whole life for. He felt a great hollowness. An emptiness. Up here, sitting in the Parthenon, he felt small, and he felt afraid. There was a kind of white wind all the time—warm wind whipping up the dry brush and white dust. I do not know why we are both here. He looked at her. Tall and thin, sitting on a rock close by, gazing out, thinking. She is the human being I love most in the world. She has been my mother and my father, she has been my sister and my most dearly beloved friend.

And she was thinking, we should never have come, it was too late to travel so far. He looks old. He looks so tired and our holiday has just begun. Our travels have just begun. We have a map. There is no excitement, we are both wondering why we are here and not at home. He dare not tell me it was a mistake. And I. We should

The Quiet of the Birds

not have come to Greece. 'It was silly of me to make you come, and I am sorry. We will go back as soon as you like,' she said.

Next day, they took the boat to one of the islands, the boat was crowded and hot. The women mostly in black—the way I shall dress if anything happens to him. A smell of fish, of olive oil. I hope we find some green olives, the kind we both love and not just these black, glistening-in-oil ones. On the boat a tall gangling Irishman, Christoir his name. Are you going to Paros—I am—it will be my second time, you will like it, don't forget to come to where I am going. It always smells of bathrooms and there are terrible mosquitoes but it's cheap and the widow Despina never turns anyone away.

So we went with Christoir and the widow Despina did, in fact, take us in. She gave us her room. In spite of everything that happened, the widow Despina's room was something I would never forget. It seemed all black. The walls, the shrouded furniture, the bed. The many, many photographs of all her sons and daughters who had gone away to the new world all hung on the blackened walls looking heavy and 'Greek' even in T-shirts, sneakers and forties' hairstyles. And there was one, very dark, very sad and still and beautiful icon. The widow Despina looked very like the Mother of God in that icon. It was very kind of her to have let us have her room. It was good of her—she had no other.

Her whole life was in that room. It overpowered them. It made them half-live its aching deprivations. Its airlessness.

Perhaps it is not so to her. Like my room at home. It is a little like this. More than a little—except for the gulmohur tree just outside my window. All those framed photographs of nieces and cousins and married sisters and brothers. Recently all coloured—brilliant colours, the sun always shining or everyone robust in the snow in red or yellow pullovers, smiling, always smiling, for the one maiden aunt in India who lives with the brother who is, now was, a bishop. She remembered once, when they had come to visit, she and the bishop had their photographs taken under the gulmohur tree. It had been high summer, the tree a burst of brilliant orange blossom, the tree almost weighed down by the profusion of colour, and their two figures—gaunt, tall, slightly bent, wearing dull colours—thank goodness for the tree because the coloured film would have been wasted on them. One small nephew, asking if they were married, being hurriedly hushed and told 'silly boy, we told you, brother and sister'. But they must look like that. Husband and wife. They looked alike in the way, quite often, long married couples did. Clearly Despina thought so. Giving up her wedding room—her married room. Where she lived alone with photographs. Like my room at home. Like mine. Like my life. Lived through other people. But there is my private life. Hardly anyone knows about that. Perhaps Despina has one too. I hope so. Life would be a pretty unending one without that. Life isn't all smiling when coloured photographs arrive brightly from foreign countries. If he and I were to send a photograph of us and Christoir with Despina, say at the Parthenon, it would look as if we were having a very different kind of holiday than this actual one. Wouldn't it? This one is grey and tired, a sort of end of the road.

'She thinks we are husband and wife—so does Christoir.'

'Yes,' he had said, walking about, unpacking. 'No harm, she has no other room, there are two beds.'

Later, they walked in Despina's small garden and thought of their own at home. A barking sound near and picked up far away made her think most intensely of Judas. 'Don't,' he said taking her hand as if she had spoken of that long-ago grief. The carpet of red swept each evening into rusty heaps by Martina. The one gulmohur blazing before the monsoons, she missed that. But, one evening, like any other, no warning, none. Judas leaping and barking and getting in Martina's way, but that too was part of the ritual—her sweeping and the shrill barks and delighted leaps of Judas and then the slow bonfire, the burning of the leaves so that the smoke would deal with the mosquitoes as well as give us that smell of burning leaves. Till the evening of the snake. An ordinary, every evening ritual with no one to warn him that death lurked there too. Judas attacking a snake under a red heap and the garden rent apart with Martina's screams—and tearing down the steps thinking of him first, 'Something has happened to him, dear God, take anything, not him.' She'd had to pay for that short prayer, that wish—it had been answered in the form of Judas. Two great blows of the gardener's spade dealt with the snake, but nothing to help Judas. Six hours it took him to die. Six long hours. Very long. His leg becoming huge with the poison and his great head heavy on her lap, sitting in the garden with the swept leaves all blown around them. After many hours he returned from some far village and found it dark and her form and Judas's looking like one, except she was moaning and saying over and over, 'Our child, our only child—I asked for him to die so that it wouldn't be you, I asked, I prayed for it.'

Next day, they buried him deep near the wild almond but it took her years to realize in fact that Judas was dead. In her mind's eye she could smell him—sometimes reach out to touch him as he came towards, or curled up next to her as she sat, reading or cutting up potatoes. She felt it as real—his waiting, curled-up form outside the bathroom door till she came out, or when she'd been to the shop, or the marvellous greeting after any separation at all. Sometimes, settling down for the evening, the lamps lit, waiting for him to come home, expecting Judas to come and sit by her, scratching or just looking, and looking with his golden head cocked and his eyes so deep and beautiful. And what a waste—though big, so timid. Never able to hurt a rat or cat, since puppyhood afraid of cycles, car-horns—then why go for a snake? Stupid dog—greatly loved, greatly missed. The lonely house ached for him. As a house would for a child dead before its time.

Most evenings he'd come home knowing what she was thinking, feeling.

'Oh let go, he's gone, don't you know. Leave him, let go.'

'Easy for you to say.'

'Why easy for me—why easy?'

'Perhaps, easier, I meant, what with your faith, all the stuff you dish out at funerals—"Man that is born of woman hath but a short time to live, and is full of misery. He cometh up and is cut down like a flower." Yes, I know all that but I can't think why it's necessary—all this living and attachments and imagining it will go on and on. I'm not like you, I'm frail, I have no real belief, I believe in you—that's it, that's all.'

'Don't say that, don't say that—'

'But if it's true, why not? Why not?'

Later she said, 'Do you think it was unbearable, his pain, Judas's? I wish it could have been a great rush of pain and then just darkness—but it wasn't—it took six hours for him to die.'

'But he lay with his head in your lap, and he knew it was you holding him and stroking him so he wasn't alone—the very worst is to die all alone—somewhere far away, unfamiliar, with no one. And he had the best friend he has ever had—he had you for all those six hours.'

'Do you think he knew it was me—holding him—?'

'Of course—your smell and your touch and your murmuring to him—of course, who could not know? Of course he knew, or he would have skulked away to die in some corner.' And it was on the road back from the Valley of the Butterflies that it happened. One minute they were talking about what they had seen and the next he was down on the dusty road, gasping and then crying out. Unbelieving, she had knelt there and told him to get up, 'Get up, you have to get up now, I'll help you but get up,' she had said and he said, 'I'm sorry, I'm sorry, I can't, I can't, I'm sorry,' over and over. It was then that she knew—and then she took his head on to her lap like that long-ago other time and said, 'Don't die, don't die—just don't die on me in this country, in this country where I don't know the language—wait, wait for me, wait—'

For him there was a great rush of pain and then such darkness and while he clutched and clutched her hand he remembered that that is what she had wanted for Judas, that long-ago time, in the garden, the evening of the snake. And he thought, I hope it won't take six hours as it did for Judas, I could not bear it for six hours, and he said, or thought he said, for the first time, what he had always felt and meant to say, 'You are what's best and most mine, most loyal, most loved, don't leave me, don't let me go, let's go back to our garden, to the child we buried under the wild almond tree.' He could hear her weeping and weeping and he heard her say, 'Yes and yes, but don't you die, don't die—I've waited, always I've waited for you, so now wait for me—' And he tried and tried to wait for her but, after a while, he couldn't hang on any more and said, 'Let me go now, I could go if you would let go.' And his head was heavy in her lap and his hand was not clutching hers any more.

And that is how they were found—some hours later, the cliffs white and yet looming in the white sun, the road white and hard and dusty and a thin woman bent double over the form of a man who was quite dead.

And then the telephoning started, and she was heavily sedated most of the time with stuff to help her forget it had happened at all, but every few hours when she woke it was Christoir who heard her say, 'Why couldn't you wait, I waited for you, you could have tried to wait till I caught up.'

The house was waiting for her. Quiet. Martina on the top step. Everything very quiet. She could hardly bear to go up—into the known rooms. Empty. Of course he could not be buried under the wild almond tree. It was not sacred ground. And his funeral was not one that she would have chosen. But, then, in his field he was an important man—not just a man greatly longed for each evening at sundown by his tall, thin sister.

I came for my uncle's funeral—because I loved my aunt ever since the days I had lived in that house as a little girl. I think it was the garden that drew me close to my aunt that long-ago time. And the garden was what I remembered most clearly. As a little girl, holding my aunt's hand, it seemed a very large garden, but now I realized it was not a large garden at all but everything in it so beautifully proportioned that it seemed large—with so many different kinds of areas seeming to just happen. It never seemed cramped or overcrowded, one delight gradually giving place to the next, and so on, till you reached the door leading out of the walled garden. When my aunt's family had bought the house they had not had to add anything to it—it was huge. Many used to joke about it originally belonging to the nuns, because it had so many large rooms and also so many little small cells and its own private chapel. I really did like my aunt very much, she seemed so modern, somehow, compared to the other people who lived their lives in that part of the country. She was aunt as well as friend and companion. She was exceedingly close to her brother, the bishop, took care of this vast house and garden, saw that he ate and slept.

She had looked after him and the house and garden all of her life and now when I arrived for his funeral I realized she ought to have been much older, or appear to be much older. But except for the silver of her hair and his cane with a silver top she seemed ageless to me.

I was not a young girl any more but I did hold my aunt's hand as we came back from the funeral. It had been a vast affair, not at all what my aunt would have wanted for her beloved brother, but then he was the beloved of hundreds of people, and the church and the state saw it as a great chance to do him proud. And they did, in the way they knew best. They had chosen one of the largest cathedrals and several bishops and archbishops were part of the Requiem Mass to which they invited his family, but not Martina. My aunt said if Martina did not go she would not go either. Martina had nothing appropriate for such a grand affair but she looked very handsome in one of my aunt's dresses.

My aunt did not cry but on the way home she said, 'Christoir told us in the Valley of the Butterflies that Aeschylus had said, "This thing pours on your heart, drop by drop, until in awful grace of God comes wisdom." We asked him what "this thing" was and he said he supposed tragedy or experience. But I don't think wisdom comes. He's gone, he's dead—what wisdom in that? The only wisdom is the permanence of grief. I don't know why I believed it could be otherwise.'

After that time I went down every summer when I had my holidays to stay with my aunt. My mother would say, 'I don't know what you do with yourself a whole summer, don't you get bored, don't you feel like going somewhere else? Just don't become odd like her, that's all.' And I would say, 'Why odd? How odd?' And she would say, 'Well, if you don't know yet—,' And leave it at that.

Always my aunt would seem to know just when I was going to arrive. She'd be waiting on the topmost step looking over her garden at something that seemed beyond and catching sight of me she'd say, 'Oh, good, you're not too tired, are you? Because then we can just walk through the garden and I've something special to show you—it wasn't here when you were here last.' And so the month would go—a whole month, very hot before the rains. I stayed with her and longed to stay with her forever. Martina was much older and I helped her with many of her chores but after our evening walk in the garden with my aunt, still tall but so much thinner, pointing out various plants and shrubs, we would always, at last, stand under the wild almond tree. My aunt would say, 'They were both really buried here.' And then Martina would sweep up all the dry leaves and red flowers fallen all day from the gulmohur and make one big heap and burn it and the smoke would waft its way through each empty room. Till the evening we heard distant thunder and my aunt would say, 'Soon, it will be time for you to go away— till the next time.'

My aunt left me the house in her will, in which she instructed me to look after Martina and to care for the two graves under the wild almond tree.

I now live here always. And when, at summer's end, the sound of distant thunder is heard, I no longer pack to go away till the next time. I have become, I suppose, odd like her.

Autumn on a Summer's Day

*In the middle of my life I lost my way, and found myself
in a deep and darkened wood.*

—Dante

Dream of a Wedding

Mukta woke from a violent dream about a wedding—a morning wedding—a very pretty wedding it seemed at first, all white and gold and shimmering among the leaves. Casuarinas near the sea, a feel of sand in her new chappals. Whose wedding? Of course, Mirai's. It had been on a Sunday morning so there was an ordinary High Mass for the Catholic side of things, then the marriage service and two psalms sung, most beautifully, by a small choir—just eleven voices, but what voices!

But something was wrong and in the dream she seemed to be trying to find out what was wrong—she was trying to find Ashok to ask him because he was bound to have sensed it but she couldn't find him. The champagne was running out but that wasn't it, and lunch was running late and that wasn't it, her hair was slipping from its careful upswept look and that wasn't it, either. What was the wrong thing? Mirai looked a dream, smiling and lost like most brides and Jai looked bewildered, like a comfortable bear but smiling, through his spectacles, but no Ashok. Where was Ashok? The dream was beginning to feel desperate now. And there he was— she bumped into people to get to him and suddenly again she couldn't see him anywhere. Where, oh, where? She had to find him, something was wrong and she couldn't find Ashok and at last she called out in anguish, 'Oh, Ashok, where are you Ashok, where?'

'I'm here,' he said, 'I'm here, of course, where else would I be except in our bed—you've had a bad dream—you're all right now. I'll bring us some coffee, don't move.'

But she was loth to lose him again and trailed after him into the kitchen. She watched him make the coffee and pour it into their yellow mugs and she thought she would always miss him the most. If she could take him with her—the only wish in the world, if this could be a fairy-tale world. Then she could learn to bear all the rest.

'It was an awful dream—I couldn't find you, I looked and looked. It was Mirai's wedding. Where had you got to?'

'Probably getting pleasantly drunk, and smiling—there's nothing else you can do at weddings—anyway, don't think about it now, it's over, you're awake and here we are drinking our coffee and the sun coming in through the window. Stop frowning and looking so sad.'

'But, Ashok, something was very wrong, and I had to find you, if that feeling has come back after all these years then it must be real—'

'Well, if you persist then of course we will talk about it. Of course something was wrong—the whole thing, really, and that's really why I was getting plastered. The wedding was wrong, the marriage—it was all wrong, a dreadful mistake. She married the wrong man—you can't go wronger than that.'

'Oh, Ashok, what are you saying, don't say it, don't. How do you know, how could you know? Did she tell you, and when, I mean, there at her own wedding?'

'No, she didn't have to—I just happened to be watching her face, I'm glad you didn't see; it haunted me for years but then things seemed to have worked out so, till your dream—'

'But, Ashok, who? What? Don't leave me like this. Tell me?'

'But I have, it was the way she looked at the other man. I mean, she was marrying the wrong man and the right man was there and she knew she'd made a terrible mistake. She knew—she realized —then. It was terrible, the irony and—oh, Mukta, you usually guess everything. Didn't you feel or have an instinct then—you must have or you wouldn't have had this dream. You've stored it away all these years and now it's surfaced.'

'No, I couldn't have thought it. I'm sure I would have tried to do something about it. Oh, Ashok, why, oh why didn't you tell me, why didn't Mirai tell me? Why did none of you tell me? What a fool I've been. Was it Jai's brother? Well, was it?'

'Without a doubt, it was too important to rely on a hunch, but I suppose it was a hunch, the way of a smile, a look, the best man held her longer than many might have thought proper, but then, on the other hand, times have changed. People hug people, people kiss people at the drop of a hat. So maybe it was a hunch. But, Mukta, since you did dream about it and since you did ask then I'd say, not a hunch—alas! More's the pity.'

'Jai's brother, very good-looking, tall, slightly greying hair—yes, perhaps only—'

'You see, Mukta, you too must have thought that, must have guessed and felt awful about it and then decided when you couldn't find me that—well to leave her to heaven—not to coin a phrase. You did guess and that's why you agonized in your dream—but, Mukta it's too late now, things must have resolved themselves. Don't agonize now. It's all over. And it's not your life. It's her life. And they've made their life work. At least they've stuck it out—that must be worth a great deal.'

'But lives don't work like that, I mean, that's not it, not it at all, that's not happiness. Mirai, my poor baby—'

'Rubbish—really, that's going too far—and she's twenty-five years old. And if you feel sorry for anyone it should be poor Jai. He must know, he must have felt second-best all these years, which is worse than anything else in a marriage—' Mukta drank her coffee and thought, but it really was a charming wedding—with most people pleasantly drunk with sun and champagne and goodwill. She wondered if anyone else had realized that anything was wrong. She remembered now that when, at last she had found Ashok she had clung to his arm and said, 'Something's wrong, isn't it? What is wrong—don't you feel it? Have we, perhaps, made a mistake about the Catholic side of things or something?' And she remembered Ashok had said, 'Mukta, don't worry, you worry too much, everyone is happy, nothing's wrong.' So now she said to

Ashok, 'You see that's what you said to me then—you said, don't worry, you worry too much, nothing's wrong—so if you knew why didn't you tell me? Why?'

'Oh, come on, Mukta, pull yourself together. I had a hunch—I'd seen or thought I'd seen—something. How could I tell you a thing like that on the wedding day—our daughter, be reasonable, it was just a feeling, okay?'

'Yes, you're right—I suppose, except I wish I'd known—I might somehow have helped—'

'How? How could you have helped at that point? Nobody could—how, just think, Mukta.'

'I don't know, but sometimes there are ways of helping – just by knowing—you know—?'

'Yes, I know—but it's too late to think of that now. Truly.'

'But why didn't she tell me? My children usually tell me things.'

'Perhaps Mirai knew you too well, knew how much you'd care and worry and be sad—I've lived with you nearly all my life and I should know how you would have taken it—besides—' He said this so sadly, staring into his coffee, that she went across to him and hugged him hard and rocked him, saying, 'So long, so long, my dear love and my dear friend.'

And this is how Vivan, all of five years old, found them when he came down for breakfast—always hungry no matter what time of day or night—and always thin, fragile.

'What's up?' he said, 'has anything happened?'

'Nothing,' his parents said together, 'except you're up early and looking ready for something.'

'Yes, well I have to go all the way to the end bit of our valley—I saw some mushrooms there so I'm going to bring them back for your supper. And I have to leave early—it's a kind of expedition. I'm taking my new rucksack and a book and a torch in case it gets dark and a raincoat in case it rains or else just to sit on and something to eat, Ma, in case I get hungry and something to drink in case I get thirsty. Anyway, I'll be away for quite a while so I hope you'll manage without me.' They listened very gravely to these plans for Operation Mushrooms and then Mukta said, 'It sounds wonderfully exciting, you don't suppose I could come too—

I'd try not to get in the way too much—'

Her small son eyed her, pleased, yet trying to hide it, 'Yes, you can come, you're a good walker for a girl, but then what about Papa?'

'No, I'm all right, I want to read and potter about—be lazy—'

'All right, then, perhaps we ought to get a map in case we lose our way—no, perhaps not. Well, hurry up and get ready—'

While Mukta bathed and dressed she thought nothing could be more perfect to take her mind off her dream—in this expedition of Vivan's. She loved it with him—such things she saw – such things he showed her. Ready in fifteen minutes. Lovely up here in the mountains—dressing was so basic, so easy—trousers, a shirt, a pullover, shoes and socks. None of the dreadful tedium of saris and petticoats and blouses and things matching and durzies and hairdressers. She plaited her hair and she was ready. Solemnly, Vivan took her hand saying, 'Papa said I was to take great care of you—and bring you back safe—mushrooms or no mushrooms.'

'Thank you, Vivan, very much, and thank you again for letting me come with you.'

The Expedition

They walked downhill for a longish while not talking, and after a while Mukta realized that Vivan was stalking the only man-eater left in these hills. Ever since they had read the Jim Corbett book Vivan had become a keen stalker. Once she stepped on a dry twig that snapped noisily and sent a bird fluttering upwards in fear and Vivan said, 'Sh, sh.' She stopped a moment, finding an intensely blue flower, and put it in her book to check later in her *Wild Flowers of India* book. Then she found a green speckled feather and a very green bit of moss with silvery white flowers on it. She thought, I'm so glad we had Vivan so late in our lives—so late that she'd been warned about how dangerous it would be and then how nearly she had died but then hadn't. God! But how worth it it had been to go through all that. I just can't imagine our lives without this small boy who was, at that moment, crawling very quietly behind a bush. I just can't imagine not having him. He really is the most marvellous child. Wouldn't have missed it for the world. She would have been forty-four and hadn't had a child in almost fifteen years and most people had said it would be madness except Ashok who had said, 'Why not, if you really want one—I'll help.' Friends had said, 'Think of the gap—it will be difficult for the girls.' Endless advice: think of your age, think how old you'll be when he's nine, ten, eleven, oh on and bloody on, only Ashok said, 'You go ahead, it's your life, yours and mine and you want it and I want you to have what you want and that's all that really matters. Really.'

And she had. Nine months of unspeakable carrying of her large frame, her ungainliness and the fears at the end of it all—this baby, this child Vivan, and their lives had been like this expedition for mushrooms! Excitement and newness again. She still didn't think really about the other difficulties that people had warned about. When we are sixty he'll be in his teens—and when we are in our seventies he'll be in his twenties, and so on. Who could live a life if one thought like that? Sufficient unto the day and so on. We'll have had the best things with him and then he'll take care of himself. Look at the girls. It's not really all that long that your children need you, are with you, so. Actually, it's a very little while but somehow it has a way of lasting rather a long while, I suppose, otherwise one might think—who needs it? Vivan called out, 'Hey, Ma! Look at this nest, I think it's got some eggs in it, we must put it back, I think it must have fallen from this branch. Now they'll hatch, because we saved it, didn't we, I wonder how we eat eggs, Ma, knowing they become birds, do you?'

'No, Vivan, we will continue to eat eggs, the eggs of birds we eat are different from the ones that lay eggs, I remember Valsa telling me once, I forget the reason, you can ask her yourself if she comes here this summer.'

'We are nearly there—are you having a good time, Mama? Are you glad you came?'

'A marvellous time,' she said, 'and thank you again for letting me come with you.'

'That's all right, you're a good walker and you don't make a noise—' he said loftily. 'You can always come on my secret expeditions—you don't frighten away the wild life.'

They arrived at last in a small cave-like area, dark and cool and moist and in a corner—mushrooms. They gathered them carefully and then sat in a sunny–shady spot and ate their sandwiches and Vivan said, 'It's a pity Dog can't come any more—is it because he's old or is he sick? You won't live forever, will you, Mama?'

Though she was startled by the question she said fairly evenly, 'No, not forever—nobody can do that, but for a long time yet, but Dog is really very old and dogs don't have as long to live as we do, it's a great pity because we love him as part of the family but we know he will die before us—but why did you ask?'

'It's because you and Papa have grey hair and I have to wait a long time to catch up with you—we'll never be the same age—just now it's different—we can do nearly everything together, but what will happen later?'

And she said, 'We won't think about later, just now we will think about today and tomorrow and the lovely long summer that stretches for ages and ages, okay?'

'Okay, now would you like to read to me? Or do you want to read your own book?'

'Your book, and I'll read a little less to you at bedtime, what have you brought?'

'Mama, I brought Tarka—I know you said we should leave it for a while because it was so sad but I think I'm ready for it, especially during the day, like this in the sun—it's sadder when we read it at bedtime.'

Mukta was about to start reading when Vivan interrupted her saying, 'It is nice now, though, isn't it, Mama, because we sometimes are the same age, aren't we?'

'Yes, we are, and we'll go on for a long time having great times together—you'll see, in fact you'll get tired first, of us, you'll soon want just your own friends to do things with. The girls were like that too—we were all good friends while they were your age and when they were six and seven and eight and nine and ten, and then, I remember, they started wanting to be with their own friends. Of course it hurts a bit or rather quite a lot and becomes lonely for the parents but it's natural.'

'But I won't want other friends,' he said, 'you are my best friend and Papa is my second-best friend, a person only needs two friends, and of course Dog—I wish he could be young again.'

'Yes,' she said, 'but as a dog's life goes he will have had a good life. How did you remember about the mushrooms, I mean, you don't even like them, how did you know we would find so many?'

'Well, that book of pictures you gave me about things that grow here in the hills—and then I come here, it is my sort of secret place, I haven't shown it to anyone else.' They half lay, half sat and Mukta began to read, 'By now Tarka began to get very tired and knew he could not carry on for much longer—'

Mukta looked up and saw Vivan's face small and intent on the book and she thought, how this child of all her children should be the one who loved books in such a special holy way—she was going to have a wonderful time always suggesting books and knowing he would read them and he'd read and read all the books in all the rooms. It really was too sad this book—but since Valsa, her vet-daughter had sent it to Vivan for his fifth birthday he was very keen to read it. Often he had stopped her in their earlier readings and hugged Dog and then remarked on the cruelty of people, 'Think, Mama, how would it be possible for us to be cruel to Dog—and most of those people had dogs, didn't they, Mama, then how?'

She wondered how he would bear all the other animal books later on about the cruelty of people to animals. He'd have to read *Plague Dogs*—dreadful to contemplate so much sadness in store for him. Really, reading was a curse, reading was a blessing. Soon she began to feel drowsy and Vivan said, 'That's okay, you sleep— I'll watch and I won't let the hunters come too close, don't worry—' And she slept. When she woke, Vivan was lying awake, staring at the leaves above them and the light had changed and she realized she must have slept for a long while. And they started on the long upward journey home. Vivan said, 'It's always on the homeward journey after an expedition that I'm so glad you are with me— soon it will be dark and that's when I feel the hunters are very strong and will come quite close to harm us.' Mukta clasped his hand more firmly and after a while they were home again. In the hall there was an envelope. She knew it was the report she and Ashok had been expecting for over a month. A sudden clutch of fear. She turned on all the lights and went into the kitchen calling out, 'We're home, where are you?' She started cleaning the mushrooms and when Ashok came in and hugged her she said, 'We'll open the envelope tomorrow, now we will have mushrooms and Vivan can have grilled cheese and let's have a bottle of wine. We have had a wonderful day, and you?' She thought, as Ashok went to get the wine, well—this familiar kitchen and us and a day to be grateful for—let tomorrow come. We'll handle it—within us we contain a multitude.

The Intimation

Next morning, Mukta crept down before Ashok had woken and took the letter into the kitchen to read. It's strange, she thought, how every time there was anything of importance, ever since they had moved to this cottage and these hills, it was the kitchen that seemed the only place for comfort or shared happiness. It was a marvellous room, the sun came in, there were plants and if you looked out of the window you could see the valley below and sometimes pine needles drifted in. She loved the kitchen, it had shared much of what was important in their lives. On the whitewashed walls there were always Vivan's drawings of happenings, and messages were usually left here. All family conferences took place at this table where they ate and where often her current book lay. Of course, she had known before she opened it what it would contain, what it would say—but not quite how it would be said, how it would be written on a page. A whole life on a page. She read it and then tucked it away into her dressing-gown pocket and went out on to the veranda, and that is where Ashok found her. He knew by the droop and slope of her shoulders, what the letter said. He put his arms around her and they looked down into their valley and thought their thoughts and could not give expression to their grief or outrage or—or bewilderment. Not yet. Just now it was inconceivable—so they both thought of it as something to think about later. 'After breakfast—we'll have it outside today,' she said, 'we'll have all our meals outside now and we will have to plan things soon.'

By now Vivan and Dog had appeared and Vivan said, 'What's up,'—feeling something unspoken in the air, or maybe, because they were having breakfast outside.

'We are planning plans—we shall ask the girls to come for a holiday—a proper holiday, a whole month up here, while the weather is like this—pure champagne—' While she chattered away, Vivan wandered away with Dog, Ashok took the letter from her pocket and after reading it, folded it, and closed his eyes and hugged her and she leaned against him, familiar smell, familiar warmth, no place like dear dearest, best of my life. 'Don't,' she said, getting up with a rush, 'don't cry,' they both said together, and did. Hugging again as though only close human contact would give some kind of solace. 'Well, that's that,' she said, blowing her nose. 'At least, now we know—now we are sure. It's better than the other thing. The not knowing. Now we can plan, can tend our garden. Exactly. Or more or less—' she said, realizing that he was looking at her— bewildered at what she had said. 'I mean, what I really mean is, I'll write to the girls and we will have a wonderful holiday together, a family—aren't I too heavy for you?' this last, because she was sitting on his lap.

'No, never, I wish I could keep you here for all time. Never leave me—'

'Silly. You're not to say or think like that—or I'll be lost. And I want to be here every bit of me—while I am—if you know what I mean.'

'I do,' he said, 'I do know.'

'The other thing is. No telling the children. No chemotherapy. No operations. No hospitals. Say "promise".' It was an old game. Say promise. After a long while he said.

'Promise.'

'No matter what—'

'No matter what—'

This is what they said, Mukta and Ashok. Being unused to such things. But Mukta thought. Here we sit together as on so many mornings, the sun warm, the trees—

It's impossible—is this really happening to us—not other people. Am I saying these things? Am I saying chemotherapy as if I know, about hospitals? Am I talking about not telling the children about being ill, or very ill? Or dying. Being dead? Here we sit and a leaf falls on my plate the same and not the same. Never again the same.

And Ashok thought of a long-ago poem, greatly loved—he hadn't thought of it for years. Now the lines came back—then the whole—

How to keep—
Is there any, is there none such, nowhere known some,
bow or brooch or braid or brace, lace, latch or catch or key
    to keep
Back beauty, keep it,
Beauty, beauty, beauty—from
vanishing away?

There must be, Ashok thought. There has to be. I'll not listen or believe what's there.

'Anyway,' Mukta said, 'I shan't grow old, I shan't grow crippled, or blind. You won't have to watch each dreadful change of old age happen to me—and I won't be a burden to you or to anyone—'

'But what about me?' said Ashok.

'Oh, Ashok, dear heart, you won't have to bear so much that is awful—the slow horrible decline—think of incontinence, think of having to clear up after me, think of all my teeth gone, think of— me having to wear a scarf all the time—'

'But what about me?' said Ashok. 'What happens to me when I grow old. At least, together we'd manage. And not mind. You think only of yourself. I'm sorry, of course, I didn't mean that— except a part of it. I wish, I dearly wish we could go together wherever it is we have to go. I'll not be left behind. We could think of something.'

'Yes, I've thought of that, but there's Vivan. Vivan will be all alone. He talks of these things already. You have to be there for him, you have to. Think of him. He's so little.'

'Yes, yes, but just for a few years and then he'll be off like the girls and I'll be alone. Mukta, you have to fight, you have to stay alive, you can't just go.'

'Of course, I'm going to fight—I'm going to fight and try all I can—it's just that I'm not going into hospital, and I'm not going to be operated on. I'm going to stay here with you and our life together as long as I can, and that's what we'll be left with—not hospital smells and quiet corridors and visiting hours and fear, fear all the time. Here we will be together as long as we can—do the same things, live as we have and not change anything as long as we can—after that—well, great things have been known to happen, you know that. It might happen to us.'

'Mukta, you're already facing death without me—that's what you're doing. And I don't even know how to think about life without you. What about me?' Ashok got up and stooped to pick up an old rubber ball and called out, 'Dog—here—' and threw the ball.

'You're wrong, I'm not facing anything yet, I'm just talking, pretending I will know, just planning. I was always good at planning, that's all, it doesn't mean a thing. Alas!—I only wish it did.' Mukta said this so sadly. Sadly. She looked like a little girl. Ashok went to her and hugged her. 'I'm sorry, I'm sorry. I'm selfish. It's all so new, so unreal.'

'But there is Vivan. That's real. And he's such a small boy. We always made him feel so much older, treating him like an adult. But don't send him to boarding-school—keep him with you. Don't let him be alone. Perhaps one of the girls—I don't know. I shouldn't go rattling on. Stop me. Oh Ashok! A million things. So many things. How—how?'

'We'll find a way. First we will drink our coffee, and then we will walk. We have worked out so many things while we walked. Come. Let's go.'

Three Letters to Three Daughters

Mukta wrote three letters to her three daughters. After writing nothing for a long time, just gazing down the valley, she finally wrote this.

Mirai dear. It is such wonderful weather and Papa and I and Vivan were wondering if you would like to spend a month of this summer with us. We would love it and you would enjoy the forest and valley very much, I know, once the long journey from the plains was over. It must be very warm now or fearfully hot and dusty in Delhi. Do come, darling girl. Dog grows very old and wheezy and knocks things over not with his tail as he used to but because he doesn't see awfully well any more. Maybe Valsa will be able to help him or advise us about what we should do. Just bring some comfortable clothes and walking shoes and a 'perhaps' pullover. If Jai is not fearfully busy he would be very welcome. There is, as you know, plenty of room. Come. Our love to you both. Of course, your Ma.

My dear Valsa. It is such wonderful weather that Papa and I were wondering if you might like to come and spend a month in these hills this summer. Perhaps it might be possible to leave all the dogs and cats of Bombay and come. Dog needs a bit of good medical advice and Vivan has turned out extraordinarily keen on birds and the flora and fauna of this region. You would enjoy him greatly. Just throw together some comfortable clothes and take a rest. We can promise you a peaceful holiday. It really is very beautiful here. Come. Your Ma.

Suzy love. Your exams must be over and since this year you are not back-packing in the Sayadris you might like to come to our hills do some walking here. The weather is superb and it would be nice for us to spend a month together—a whole family. We haven't been that for a long time. Papa and I and Vivan and Dog look forward very much to your coming. Perhaps Valsa and you could travel up from Bombay together and then meet Mirai for the last lap. Any of your 'with-it' trendy clothes from Fashion Street would liven up these hills and us. See you very soon. Love from your Ma.

A day later Ashok sent off three short letters to his daughters. He didn't believe he was breaking his promise to Mukta. After all, he wasn't telling them anything, only putting a little pressure—just in case. He merely said that they were to be sure to come as it was very important to their mother. She didn't often ask them for anything. He counted on them—they were not to disappoint her this time.

After Mukta had posted her letters she thought of a hundred reasons why the girls might not be able to come or come together. 'Oh, I'll be sad and then I will be cross. If they give me silly excuses I know just what I will say: "Well now, it amazes me the reasons you trot out. How come you can't spare me and your father and your brother just thirty days of your lives. If you knew how much that is in terms of what I am likely to have left of my life—you'd come pretty sharpish."'

But that was blackmail. They had to come. Perhaps they would.

Fears

One day, shelling peas, she found she was thinking about obituaries. And then she realized she was thinking of her own—Dearly loved wife of—, and mother of—and the date.

Clearly, I am slowly going mad. Who ever thought like I am thinking. She went to Ashok who laughed and said, 'It's quite normal—I do it all the time. Mine and yours. Look, I even came across one that suits you very well—I'll read it to you. It was on a second-century BC grave:

Stranger, what I have to say is little;
Stand forward and read thoroughly. This is the ugly tomb of
a beautiful woman. Her parents called her Claudia. She loved
her husband with all her heart. She bore him two sons, of
these one she loved on earth, the other she placed under the
earth. She spoke with charming speech and also moved with
graceful gait. She served her house; she spun wool.
I have spoken. Go.

'Oh, that is beautiful—you'll have to work very hard at mine, won't you?'

'Yes,' he said, 'I will. But not yet—not just yet.'

She thought, what can he say in my obituary, there's nothing to say. Not a good housewife. That's certain. Let's say, erratic. Spontaneous. If he mentions it at all. But loving her home, her four walls, her roof, her garden. Yes, he could put that down if he liked. Anyway obituaries were for the birds. Only they knew. It was private.

Anyway, just live—live all we can. Live as we have lived. Live as if we never knew. Live as if we did know. As we do. Know.

Some days Mukta felt terrible in the morning. She didn't want to get up. To get out of bed. But then Vivan would come to the bedroom door looking eager as only children can, about the prospect of a new day and all its fresh adventure. And Mukta would make a great effort. I'll have to do this every day when the girls come or they'll guess something. Because, always, till now, always she had got up early, very early, before any of the others were stirring. I'll manage, of course I will. It's just a question of pretending—some mornings, more than others. That's all.

Who needs bed, anyway? I'll have enough quite soon—bed, I mean. So now get up and get on with things. Now.

Mukta carried on just as before, counting the days only for the girls to arrive. So she walked and looked and read and read to Vivan and every day she gardened. But one day as she pottered about the garden she thought, here am I, watering the garden, and cutting and pruning even putting in new seeds, drying others for later and labelling for next year and the next, and I'll not be here. Next year I'll not be here. I'll not exist. There'll be no sun for me, no water, no food, no Ashok, no Vivan. She ran into the house and found Ashok gazing out of a window, doing nothing. She ran to him and as they hugged close and warm, he said, 'I know, I know what you were thinking, because that's what I was thinking, and I cannot bear it, it's impossible.'

Mukta asked, 'How can I garden and plant seeds and water them when soon I shall not even be able to run into the house and find you—I shall be so lonely—what will I do? What ever will I do?'

'Let's walk, let's go for a walk. It's warm in the sun, it's still light,' Ashok said. As they walked they thought, this is how we will cope. We will take each day as it comes and we will try not to think much further. We will walk and eat and rest and garden and plan, each day as it comes, there's lots of time, we will not panic. Give my dull roots rain. We will read poetry and many books, I will read again, each day slowly, no panic. That way lies madness. They walked and grew calm. One foot after the other. Just walk. And the warmth went out of the sky and then the light went. They went into their home and found that Vivan had put on the lights and called saying, 'What's for dinner, Ma? I'm very hungry.'

That's it, you see, thought Mukta. One thing at a time. The child is hungry. I will cook supper. We will break bread together. Outside the darkness will gather. But here we are, warm and together.

Only once did Ashok ask Mukta about her fear of hospitals.

'But why, just tell me why you don't believe in hospitals, it's surely fair that I should know. I'm part of this, remember?'

'Of course you are, and I'll tell you. You remember Zebun?'

'Of course I do—remember I told you of all your friends I liked her the best.'

'Well, it was the year you were away and Zebun got ill. From being well, suddenly she was ill. Well, I visited her every day for three months from the time she became ill. She went in so trusting— "Just some tests," they told her, "and you'll be as right as rain." Gradually even Ram stopped visiting—he couldn't bear to see what was happening to her, what she had become. Oh, I do believe in hospitals for almost everything, but not for this. Well, anyway, I being a real muggins, kept going every day, most days with flowers from Ram and a note, but he just stopped going. "God will forgive me—I love her more than my life but I cannot face her—" There was a barred window rather high up in her room, and you could see a small patch of sky—her bed was so high and she got smaller and smaller in that tall high bed, and her wonderful white hair, that was like a kind of nimbus round her face, died first—soon it wasn't there any more, and she wore a gay pink, cotton square round her head, and all the bones of her temples showed so prominent, like someone from Buchenwald. And that last time, I remember, I had taken gladioli, dark, dried-blood-red gladioli from Ram and when I held up the kidney tray for Zebun she vomited that same colour dark, dried-blood-red, almost black stuff, and she said, "I'm done for, I think, it's never been this colour before, and I'm sorry, I'm sorry, Mukta, for making you see me like this, but it won't happen again, because it won't be much longer now."

'She said sorry to me, I, who need never go there again, and she was never going anywhere from that room again with its high bed and tiny barred window, with its patch of sky. She was saying sorry—sorry, and I could leave when visiting hours were over and go home and eat and sleep and listen to music and open all my windows wide if I wanted to—and her Ram was afraid to look at her withered little face in its pink cotton square! Well, that's the reason, Ashok, since you asked me. Try to understand—do you?'

'Yes, I do, and I'll never ask you again I promise.'

The nights and the very early hours of each day were the times when Mukta battled with her fears and terror. Ashok had thought that caring about her so much he could share some of it, at least. Sad and filled with anguish, Mukta would creep to the bathroom trying hard not to wake Ashok. In the bathroom she would sob and rage against this thing that had happened. 'Why me, why me?' Sometimes Ashok would wake up and make her open the door and they would go to the kitchen and talk.

'I want my life, I want years and years—there's so much left unfinished—so much I have to do—so much I have put off till the right time. You and I, and Vivan growing up, and the girls and what is happening in their lives. I need time, I just need a bit of time.'

And once, only once when Ashok reminded her about what she had been told at the ashram, 'No self-pity—anything else and everything else—but no self-pity.' 'Easier said than done,' she said. 'It's my life. I want time and I do feel it's unfair. I do feel—Why me?'

There was nothing to say and so Ashok did not say anything. He felt that when the girls came things would be better—there'd be so much to do and the girls would bring their music, and there would be laughter and voices shouting and calling out, 'Ma, will you oil my hair, and, Ma, would you make that super masala cha, and, Ma, do I look nicer in blue or mauve?' Yes, it was certain to be better when they came. She'd have very little time on her own. Except the nights, except the very early mornings. 'Let's go up to bed.'

'I'm sorry,' she would say, 'I'm sorry for disturbing all your nights like this. I'll try to sleep and not think the things I think. Perhaps tomorrow will be better.'

A few nights later she said, 'You know, I should count my blessings, I really should. I have everyone I love near me, and I am in the place I want to be. Do you know about how my mother died? I have never told you, I have never trusted myself to speak of it before—never aloud. Now I can. My father was away on work and he was to return that morning. And that morning, very early, when it was still dark, my mother had a terrible pain, pain enough to make my youngest sister realize she was having a heart attack. She couldn't get hold of a doctor so she drove my mother to the nearest hospital, which was very far away. And when they reached the railway crossing it was closed. My father was in that train, yes, like a bad Hindi movie! He could not know who was in that little Fiat and my mother was certainly unaware of anything so bizarre. And when they got to the hospital the oxygen cylinder was not working and my mother died. We were all everywhere but with her, except my little sister. She need not have died, no one ever dies of a first heart attack. For years and years I would see the dark and the cold and that railway crossing and I could not bear it. I am so lucky. You are with me and Vivan and the girls next week and the sun shines, Dog is listening and cocks his ears because he heard his name, Dog. My mother had a daft dog, a dog called Joey. Oh, how he loved her. She had diabetes and loved sweet things so she would ask for them and then feed all of it to Joey. He wandered away when my mother died—he loved only my mother. So, that's why I have always been afraid of rain. Sad and heavy and burdened when it rains. In the rain I always see a railway crossing, the gates closed, and a small Fiat car. And it is very early morning and with that special kind of dark and I am trying to get to a hospital where my mother is and I will never get there in time. I will never get there in time to tell her everything she means to me. And I feel she is waiting. That's the terrible part. That she is waiting and I can't reach her, in time.'

He held her to him to give comfort as much to her as to himself. I shall love her through all eternity. But what did these things mean? Just seven words. Words to try and forget what the reality would mean. The real truth. There is no forever. No eternity. All is dust, disease, skin decaying, hair, teeth, bones brittle, breaking, torn bits and pieces. No such thing as eternity—ever. We have short, inconsolable lives. Lives that intertwine for a while, seeming to last because we waste so much of them. And those foolish girls, his three daughters, living so far away and missing her each day, alive with her.

Perhaps not so foolish. Maybe wiser than he. Perhaps they would miss her less—and live with guilt. Whereas he, foolish he, living here always with her—how would he do without her. Having failed her, failed to protect her and him. Failed. Finally. 'Dear heart,' he said aloud, for her to hear, 'I meant to call you that for years because you are that. But I felt shy—we have been so austere, so abstemious, somehow, in our use of endearments. But dear heart,' he said.

'You too,' she said.

Arrival

On receiving the letters and notes the three sisters met, talked over the phone and decided something was up. They consulted and then to try and travel together and arrive—safety in numbers. Valsa said, 'The one problem patient is a Labrador dying of cancer and the owners won't put him to sleep.' Mirai said, she hoped Jai wouldn't come or couldn't. And Suzy said, buffing her nails, it might be a load of fun—and what a lark, and would they lend her the money for the train ticket, she was that low on funds.

As they travelled up, Valsa said, 'I don't know why we go up so seldom—we love the hills, we like our parents, why?' The others said, 'We're always doing other things, or think next year we'll do it or something. Just smell the air—I'm glad, glad, glad that I've come and ashamed I left it so long that Ma has to ask.'

They climbed higher and higher and the air smelled so cool, so green and now they passed forests and small tucked-away wooden huts, now a woodman, now an old bent woman. Here being poor didn't seem so bad, didn't look so bad. They all thought of the stench of poverty in the cities where they lived, thought of the garbage high-piled, of sewers and high-rise and hardly any green except the self-consciously created little green gardens at the fiercer intersections of the city. 'We all have a choice and we live there.' They wondered why.

Then Mirai said, 'I read a reason why the old Irani cafes had those fantasy-land sort of paintings on their glass panels—because, the article said, in Bombay people living in one-room chawls with their entire families seeing only tenements on three sides and out of their one small window the neighbour's sari hanging to dry, needed after work, sitting over his cup of tea, needed to see and feel that somewhere there were castles amid lakes, or strange beautiful birds, mountains and flashing streams and beautiful women and so on, you know?'

And Suzy said, 'Ya, and we live in that place, and we needn't— we do. We're daft.'

'To say the least,' said Mirai. They all gazed out of the train windows and wondered why. At the station they spotted their parents immediately because they saw a little boy tugging at the hand that held him saying excitedly, 'There they are, they've come, there, just look there.'

As they walked towards each other Ashok and Mukta thought, how they have all grown, and they are ours. And the girls thought, they are so much older, and how thin Ma looks. After much hugging and excitement the girls said, 'Where's Dog? It's the first time he hasn't come,' and Ashok immediately thought of the future. Stop it, he said to himself. And aloud, 'He's not quite up to it, growing old like the rest of us—anyway he's in charge of the welcome home.'

'Ma, it's trendy to be thin, it's beautiful—but how did you do it? I tried lemon and honey for four days and thought I would die, then I tried a calorie diet, one kg a week it promised, but you have to keep counting and trying to make yourself happy on a starvation-type regimen—oh, Ma, you are lucky, you look super.'

'I didn't do anything, really. I think there are just two types—them that bloats and them that withers,' Mukta said.

'Ma climbs down to the valley, and then up again, she's the best climber I know,' said Vivan. They all looked at him realizing how small he was. He never left Mukta's side. Clutched her hand very tight.

'Well, that's what we'll do while we are here, down the valley and then up and down—' By now they had reached the house joking and talking at the same time, laughing at nothing, teasing.

Dog, guarding the house, pricked up his ears and then slowly unwound himself and came to greet them, heavy and wagging and wagging his tail. He circled round and round them, licked all their faces and still wagging his tail settled down in his favourite patch of sunlight. Ashok said, 'That was his welcome home.'

In their bedroom, unpacking and washing, brushing their hair, the three girls spoke of their shock at their mother's appearance—

Mirai said, 'It's not her age, Ma's young still—'

Valsa said, 'Ma looks so thin—'

Suzy said, 'Ma looks so tired and thin—'

Mirai said, 'Ma looks ill—'

They thought, Ma looks so thin, so tired so—yes, ill—do you think? Do you think that's why? Oh, stop it. It's impossible. Pa would have told us if Ma was ill. We aren't children. Anyway, let's go down. I'm so glad we came. It's heaven to be home.

Lunch in the kitchen with the soft sunlight streaming in. Familiar plates and glasses. Food so familiar, tastes, smells, Vivan on a pile of cushions. Dog half in, half out, under the table. And talk the kind you could never remember later what you talked about. The feel of the first hours home on a holiday. No place like.

Some Days

The first day home, they each thought, always so familiar, so known, so warm.

The Quiet of the Birds

Old photographs of each of them at different ages, familiar clothes, familiar hairstyles, calling up old fights, silly squabbles, everything coming alive—'Oh, Ma, it's so unfair, why does Mirai have to be the pretty one, why not all of us, we could all have been a bit pretty—now she's spectacular—everything will happen to her, not us. We look awful. Nobody would guess we were sisters.' Wail upon wail. And Ma, sensible and down to earth—'Rubbish, it's all rubbish, all of you have something nice, look at Valsa's legs, look at your hair, Suzy, anyway prettiness is all a lot of bosh, it simply ought not to matter, and that's that.'

But all these years later Mukta knew that it did. Mirai was a beauty, she really was. Her skin like old honey and her eyes that colour, nobody else seemed to have! Anyway, Valsa did have super legs and she looked good in anything she wore, except she never wore anything but jeans—and there you were. And Suzy, her hair long, very long and thick and black almost to her knees.

Old photographs on the wall, over the mantelpiece—recording birthdays, anniversaries, prizes won at games at college, picnics— their dogs. The new baby—crawling, walking, playing with Dog.

The girls roamed the rooms, old worn counterpanes, old rugs on the floor, an icon their parents had brought back from Paros, familiar cups and plates, the old fridge, they'd always called it the 'oldest fridge in the world', taste of food, taste of coffee. That first day back so filled with nostalgia—books with torn old covers faded and greatly loved, *What Katy Did*, *Little Women*, *Ballet Shoes*, *Hans Brinker and the Silver Skates*, The Twin Books, the William books—a much-read copy of *Gone with the Wind*, how they had all been loved by Rhett Butler, what aching days and years ago! Today they were all twelve and sixteen and eighteen again.

They went to look for Vivan. They found him in the garden with Dog. 'Why don't you come and talk to us? There's so much we want to ask you.'

'I thought you'd need a little time by yourselves the first day. You'd be so excited the first day—I thought I'd leave you alone. I'll come if you like—shall I come in or are you coming out? Dog likes to be outside in the sun. He feels the cold a lot now. He's getting so old. It's sad, isn't it? Because, really, he's like a puppy.

It's only his age. Like Ma.'

They walked about with their brother, charmed by the way he spoke. Where they lived now, when they heard children play, they all seemed to shout and use the most ghastly slang. Their brother seemed rather different. It must be because he lives only with grown-ups. Didn't he have any young friends then, they asked. 'Don't need them. I have Ma and Papa.'

'But apart from Ma and Papa, someone more your own age, to play games?'

'No, I don't have any at the moment because we are the same age and Ma and I do most things together—later of course, I'll go to school so I'll make other friends.'

They asked if Ma and Papa had any friends they visited or who visited them. Vivan thought for a while and then said, 'Yes—there is a cottage in the next valley—George paints and his wife writes poetry. We sometimes visit them—I like them very much. We should go and see them because it's our turn. You will like them.'

And who else, they persisted. Vivan said, 'Well, every year we go in the bus to a place where there are some people who live in cottages on a hill and there is a temple. When we go we stay the night, sometimes even two nights. It's super there. Everyone has a garden and there are cows and they make their own butter and ghee and they bake their own bread, and they make yummy jams and marmalade. We have a lot of friends there. It's an ashram. Do you know what an ashram is? They have a large dog. But he's on a chain.'

They said they did know a little about ashrams and they hoped they could go there.

'But,' said Vivan, 'first we are going to do lots of things together, Ma said, I mean just the family. All of us together, picnics and walks—you know. And if you like I'll take you to my secret cave— I've only taken Ma there.'

They thanked him very much and went into the house because Ma called out to them.

One evening's walk ended visiting a couple who lived in a collapsed-looking cottage with a beautiful garden; as they called out, a thin lady came flying down the steps and seemed to hug them all at the same time, crying, 'Darlings, oh darlings, how lovely to see you, I have been waiting and waiting—so these are the girls, such beautiful girls and here's my Vivan boy, every day I baked a different cake so now you have a real choice, there's lemon and chocolate and coffee and butter-scotch.'

This never happened in the cities where the girls lived.

They sat in the sun and ate and ate cake and drank tea, the girls were enchanted with her. Ashok and the old servant helped to bring out what looked like a bundle of blankets but which, when unravelled, proved to be a man who looked like somebody you might meet in a pub called the 'Worm in the Cabbage', except he looked pale and fragile under his rather bluff exterior. He followed his wife about with his eyes and said, 'She's just written a lovely poem about dragonflies—she's rather like one herself, isn't she? Always flitting about, hardly ever sits down, sometimes she wears me out flitting and watching—but she makes the most marvellous apple crumble.'

Mukta managed to make her friend sit down and said in a lowish voice, 'How is he? And how are you?'

'Oh, darling Mukta, I get so tired and you're the only one who ever asks me, really wanting to know. I'm so tired of his illness and I know it's going to go on for ever and ever. But I really am tired of looking out for the least little change in him, I'm tired of having to be alert all the time. I just want to run away—'

From a distance they heard her husband's voice call out, 'Did I hear you say something about running away? I hope nobody is thinking about running away?—' His wife soothed him immediately, and Mukta and she went on talking. 'He seems to hear everything—even things I'm writing or thinking, it's uncanny. I can never rest, never sleep. Let's walk about a bit, pretend you want to see the garden.' As they walked they heard his voice saying, 'She will never sit down for a while, she's so restless, she makes me so tired—when I painted I could never get her to sit for me—and she has an interesting face—have you seen the black Madonna of Montserrat? She reminds me of her, except there is no stillness about her. I do long for stillness.'

'He's quite impossible, he invades my thoughts, Mukta, he never leaves me alone. Always his needs—watch his face till it's a blur—at night I can't sleep because I keep thinking he's stopped breathing. Sometimes I wish, really, God help me, but I really mean it. Then I could sleep and wash my hair and have a long bath without thinking he'll die on me. Oh, terrible of me to say these things, terrible to have thought these things so often. Oh, Mukta! I complain and complain but in my heart I know that if anything happened to him I would just give up doing anything. That's dying. I know. If I died, I know he'd start painting again just to spite me, and he'd potter about and garden and even cook; but if he died I know I'd just stop doing everything. Oh, yes, I would. Mukta, you just don't know the dark side of me—you only see the person who copes with everything—manages when the roof leaks or a tap needs fixing or when a friend of his turns up to spend the night and stays for three weeks! That's the side you see. But that's not me. Oh, Mukta, girl, you have such a beautiful family you can't believe half the things I'm saying but they are true. And I can't write any more. I haven't written a poem about a dragonfly—it's what I have thought about and he has already taken it away from me.'

As they walked home the family was rather quiet and happy when they realized their cottage would be round the next bend in the road. Home. 'I'm glad we are we, and that they are they,' said Vivan.

Ashok Writes to His Daughters

Ashok wrote to his daughters—though there was very little he could write because of the enormity of the happening. After much pondering he wrote three identical letters.

My dear, your mother died very late last night. Because of the great pain she had been suffering I was glad that she died—she chose the manner of her dying. You will perhaps be angry with me for not telling you, but she had made me promise not to when she knew the worst. This was just before you came up for the holiday. She was the most remarkable person anyone could hope to meet and we were so lucky to have had her in our lives. You have lost your mother and I have lost my best friend and my wife. Don't hold it against her that she never told you, she didn't want to spoil that month we were all together. Try not to be bitter. Think how much worse it was for her to have known throughout that time. Try to understand. Try to understand her and love her forever. And come—

This is what he wrote.

What he thought was—'I cannot bear to live, I cannot bear to think, I cannot bear a life without Mukta, my life, my heart, my companion, my best friend. There is nothing at all that I need or want and the day means nothing, it is a day without her, the night is even worse because I cannot sleep and when I do I see her dying. Food is irrelevant, there are trees that I cannot see, there is sky, there is hot and there is cold and there is colour. And I curse it all for being able to carry on as if she did not matter. I cannot bear to be alive. I can hear a long scream. And it is me. And though he had all these thoughts, he was a good father because he did not say any of this aloud, nor write it to his daughters. He cooked for Vivan and comforted him and kept him by his side and did not tell him what he felt but only listened to him and wiped his weeping and hugged him and held him because he was only five and had lost his mother. He was a good father because no matter what his black, sad thoughts were—he was trying. With what was left.

When Ashok's daughters got his letter there was a terrible feeling of blank disbelief. Mirai thought, 'Oh God, it's impossible, it's not true, it cannot be. How could she, how could she?' And Valsa thought, 'It can't be true, only a month ago she was alive. Just a month.' And Suzy in her room in college, which she shared with two other girls wept and wept saying, 'Shit, oh shit, shit—oh Ma.'

'We'll travel up together,' they said, though that felt so raw, so near the last time, of just a month ago. 'We'll travel up together,' they said. And did. In all its unreality. When they arrived their telegram hadn't reached their father.

As Ashok and Vivan stood looking across and down the valley they saw, quite suddenly, three small figures and the figures got larger and larger, and it was them.

Ashok and Vivan waved—and the three waved back. And Ashok and Vivan started off downhill to meet them coming up.

Afterwards

Afterwards the girls thought, but for that month in the summer so much would never have happened. Mirai thought, Ma and I would never have talked about Jai. All that locked-up stuff. And Valsa and Suzy thought how that summer cleared up years of built up resentment, about being unpretty and boarding-schools. Without that summer. Oh, Ma. Ma was wise, how wise she was and what fun she was. If only. But that's it. All the guilt and now all the remorse, but, but what fun days we had, what happy things we did that summer. But for Ma, we would never have had those walks and those talks and laughter under the sun. And eating in the open, looking down into that valley, and sleeping under the same roof. Getting to know Vivan. Yes, that happened that summer. Ma must have planned it all. She must have known by instinct, if we were ever to be a real family it would have to happen that summer. We were all younger together that long-ago summer that seemed to stretch and stretch. We would never have met again as children—or as adults. But for that summer. But for Ma. As a family. Bottled up rubbish that had cumbered us all. Spilling out. And she never let us guess. That she was so ill. And none of it possible without Papa. We got to know him so much better only after Ma left. She let us say such dreadful things: 'You loved Mirai the best. When Vivan came you stopped loving us, he was the best. You sent me to boarding-school, not the others. You loved me the least. You didn't love me enough—you loved the others more.' Once we drove her to the only private place left. Her bathroom. We heard her sobbing and crying, 'What kind of mother have I been after all, that my children should say these things, think these things, oh, I'm a failure, failed at everything I have ever tried to do—stupid, stupid.'

Oh, she was wrong, she was the best. The best Ma in the world. Thank God for her. Thank God they had had that summer together. Often, when they now got together, they would think, but why, why was it so magical? After all, nothing spectacular happened. In fact, it was so ordinary. Family quarrels, family jokes. One day they remembered Vivan had asked them solemnly, 'Why did the Malayalee cross the road?' When they gave up—he said, 'Simbly.' And that had become a family joke. Vivan's first joke, Vivan rolling about on the grass shouting and laughing, 'Simbly, simbly.' So silly—so nice. That summer.

That summer entirely nostalgic, never to be forgotten. The sun through the leaves and through the pine needles, picnics with sun-warmed sandwiches and fruit. Ma's garden with its peculiar beauty, little packets of dried seeds stuck on twigs like little crosses in a graveyard, labelled—'pink poinsettias', 'yellow pansies', 'purple zinnias', and the date—neat. Ma's handwriting. In the pantry, jars and bottles of strawberry jam and orange marmalade. All labelled and dated. Ma sitting at the kitchen table marking neatly jam she'd never eat herself.

Photographs of that summer that hadn't been put into the family album yet. Mirai as beautiful as a gazelle, Valsa rolling on the grass with Dog, Suzy's long, black hair, drawing her cheeks in as the camera clicked, 'Suzy longing for cheekbones,' Ma had scribbled at the back of the snapshot. Vivan, solemn with his rucksack, ready to leave on one of his expeditions—and of Papa and Ma together and apart and group ones on picnics not self-conscious at all, and all as if the summer would, or could, last forever.

And Ma's straw hat—do you remember that, they would ask each other. How could they forget. 'Oh, Ma,' they would wail, 'not that old thing.' And she had said, 'Yes, this old thing, because I love it and it goes back a long time. Your father and I were in Venice and all the days it rained and even the pigeons were wet and sad and it was cold, so cold, but we went out every day just in case the sun came out. One day we saw this old woman huddled in a lot of old wet-looking shawls and she was selling sun hats— lovely, unlikely-looking straw hats in different colours—and she said, "You buy and tomorrow the sun comes out for you."

'And your father made me choose one and it looked wonderful—this hat in its prime, a kind of jaunty bluey-green, ever so smart. The next day the sun came out and shone and shone but we couldn't find the old woman to thank her. And we saw a different Venice in the sun in my straw hat. So my dear girls—now you know why I will never desert Mr Micawber.'

'Oh, Ma, you are so sentimental, you really are,' they had said in chorus, though they'd loved the story.

'Yes, I am, the last of that dying breed, and what's wrong with that? The past is what we were and are. Because of this hat the sun came out, and because the sun came out, we went to Murano. I have worn it every summer and up here in the hills, every day, so that's some thirty years. We need more sentimentality, not less, we need it every bit, especially regarding battered old sun hats!'

A Nest of Old Feathers

Here I am an old man in a dry month,
Being read to by a boy, waiting for rain.

'That's like you and I.' The old man said—'except of course
you're not a boy—but still it's youth and age and,
metaphorically, I am waiting for rain—anyway read on, it is balm
to my soul.'

This was one of the last good days the old man and she had.
After that day the ordered flow of their mornings changed a great
deal. For one thing he had the first of a series of falls, and then one
thing after another happened. Downhill. But before he died in a
faraway town—before he became an obituary, before the memorial
service for him, before all that—he and she had three quite unique
years. He had become her closest friend. There were more than
thirty-odd years' difference in their ages. Often because of their
loves and hates they were the same age. In chronological time he
was very old and she was, as he once told her, 'entering the prime
of life'. Perhaps in another age, another clime, they might have
been something quite other to each other—but that is idle thinking.
'You are a foolish, romantic girl and today I feel a young man in
my twenties,' he had said. But that is to start at the very end. She
had to find the beginning. It actually started when she lost her job
of twenty-five years . . .

The Beginning

She was between jobs. She looked at the Wanted ads every morning
and one morning there it was—the perfect job. 'Wanted—a lady
reader for two hours every morning. Sundays excepted. Handsome

remuneration, terms open to discussion. Must be educated. Should be prepared to read all kinds of material in English.' And the address.

It was perfect because it was the only language she could read in. She was educated. The address showed she could walk there every morning. And only two hours. About the pay—well, anything would be better paid than teaching. So. And no take home material. Luck. Lady luck was on her side. For once.

She set off next morning after phoning up for an appointment. The voice on the telephone pleased her. Clear, male, very well-spoken. Could be any age at all. She rang the bell. A man came to the door. He could have been seventy, or eighty, very bent, dressed in white with a very white beard and hair. A marvellous tree seemed to come right into the room. Two collapsed-looking cane chairs and a table keeling over to the left. Books everywhere. The sound of pigeons moaning and making love. A cat wandered in, looked and wandered out. 'That is Lima-lima. I am an old man and you are the young lady who rang yesterday. Do sit down—would you make us some coffee. Come and sit down till the kettle boils—it has a whistle so you needn't watch it. Marvellous invention—the whistling kettle, you should get one if you haven't one already. Now what do you normally read? Are you fond of reading? I have a lady who comes in at nine, she reads the newspapers to me. She reads very badly, mispronounces every second word but I can't get anyone else to come in early. There, that's the kettle whistling. Coffee and sugar on the lower shelf, biscuits on the to shelf and the milk is in the fridge. No sugar for me.'

She came back with the cups with blue roses and she did her reading—a test! A bit of Montaigne from 'On Repentance':

What metamorphoses do I see old age working every day in many of my acquaintances! It is a powerful disease, which makes natural and imperceptible advances. It requires a great store of study and great precautions, if we are to avoid the infirmities that it lays upon us, or at least to retard their progress. Despite all my entrenchments, I feel it gaining on me foot by foot. I resist for as long as I can, but I do not myself know to what it will reduce me at last. But come what may, I am glad that the world will know the height from which I shall have fallen.

Then, he said, some poetry, his favourite 'Go lovely rose':

Tell her that wastes her time and me,
That now she knows,
When I resemble her to thee,
How sweet and fair she seems to be.
How small a part of time they share,
That are so wondrous sweet and fair.

She was so pleased with what he had asked her to read. Good things to read. She had been afraid it would be law briefs or figures or something and here was the sun slanting in touching the branch of the tree. Bird sounds. And then he said, 'Good, well then tomorrow I think—ten sharp. Will you let yourself out.' She ran down the steps and rushed out elated: I have a job, being paid for what I love to do—oh, I shall do it well and he's a lovely man and just two hours every morning.

Next day, when she climbed the wooden stairs, a little old lady was leaving. Like a bird—she was so small. Twittered like a bird. 'Bad mood, old man had a bad night so we have to suffer—don't worry though, it will pass. I got the worst of it. After he was sharp once, I started mispronouncing everything. Never mind, you make his coffee and don't let him see you are upset, and don't cry in front of him.' She was by now severely frightened and felt like turning back but his voice from the inner room called out, 'Stop all that whispering—has that girl arrived to do a spot of reading or hasn't she?'

She went in. The room that had looked so light—filled and full of the acacia branch—today looked dark with his rage.

'Well, go in, go in and make my coffee—and you are five minutes late.' She made it nervously and then took it in to him, telling herself, if it gets too bad, I'll leave, after all this is only my first day—who needs a bully? I don't and I won't put up with it, that's all. After that she felt considerably better. On the table before them there was the copy of Montaigne's essays and the *Faber Book of Poetry*. 'Well, there's nothing to stop you starting—is there? No need to waste more time—after all, you are being paid for two hours!'

'What would you like me to read,' she asked.

'Start with the Montaigne—I would like to remind myself that such things still exist—"On Friendship" please.'

She read what he asked her to and came at last to:

In the friendship I speak of they mix and blend one into the
other in so perfect a union that the seam which has joined
them is effaced and disappears. If I were pressed to say why
I loved him, I feel that my only reply could be; 'Because it
was he, because it was I.'

'That's true and that's beautiful,' she said.

'Yes it is, but I would rather you didn't stop to comment till we come to the end of what Montaigne has to say.'

She felt snubbed, and then went on to the end. By now the two hours were over and she was tired but he was ready for more—so now it was poetry and he wanted something by Tomlinson— 'Does any one read him now?' She found:

Flat dwellers came and went in the divided houses.
Mothers unwedded who couldn't pay their rent,
A race of gardeners died, and a generation
Hacked down the walls to park their cars
Where the flowers once were—

He stopped her and said, 'There is a very fine line there—something about, "No one has recorded the place. Perhaps we shall become Sociology". It's true of course. No one will record people like me. Someone should write a novel about me—I'm the last of a dying breed. Well, I'm tired now so off you go. Don't be late tomorrow.'

She asked him about his lunch, it being so near that time—'Oh, I'll find a bit of cheese or something and there's always a Maggi cube, excellent with a dash of lemon.'

So it hadn't been too bad after all. As she turned out of the gate she saw a great Alsatian—really big and wonderfully well looked after with a marvellous shining coat—turning in at the gate. A little wizened man with bandy legs tied him up in an old-fashioned kennel. She turned back to look at him, he was so finely beautiful. He growled and moved on his chain as she spoke to him. The little man told her quite sharply, 'He bites, don't come too near.'

She thought all the way home that she was going to like her job—very much, though she couldn't put the little bird-like woman out of her mind. Anyway, she couldn't spend nearly four hours again! Clearly she was required for two hours and then she must get back to her own writing. Help me to write, she prayed. She wanted that more than anything else in the world. She turned in at her own gate and sat down at her desk, she put a sheet of paper into the typewriter and said firmly—now write. She sat for over an hour and wrote nothing. She thought of the old man, who looked like an Old Testament prophet. She thought, he said someone should write about him. Perhaps he meant it. She would have to ask him again. She thought about the pigeons, about Lima-lima, about the Alsatian.

Next morning she was greeted with, 'Oh good you're on time—I left the door open for you—my coffee please—I think I have fired Miss Billimoria.' She felt glum, thinking of that little bird lady. How bad could she have been? And how dreadful she must be feeling. She went in with the coffee. He seemed so cheerful and looked scrubbed, clean in white, and very genial.

'How awful for Miss Billimoria. And she must need the job—how badly did she read—surely, she might have improved in time—' she said.

'It's my business entirely—I could not bear to hear the way she read. I am too old to have to hear the language abused like that at this stage of my life. And then I had to hear about her relations and illness and hospitals all the time. Anyway, you can read the newspapers to me for an hour and our other reading for the remaining hour. You're not married—why aren't you married?'

She wanted to tell him it was none of his business and that it was wasting the two hours that he was paying her for but she said,

'Well, I think like that essay by Montaigne, on friendship, I mean, till it is as perfect as that, till I meet the kind of person where the only reason would be "because it was he, because it was I".'

There was a pause. 'Tish and tosh!'

She said, 'I beg your pardon?'

He said, 'You're romantic, and you'll be waiting forever. It's never like that—marriage is all risk for a long time and then, it works or it doesn't.'

'Were you ever married, you seem so sure?'

'No, alas, I was foolish when I was young, and then I got older and older and then I suppose it was suddenly too late. If I might ask, how old are you?'

She told him. And then she began to read to him. Two short stories by Coppard and some Arthur Waley translations. Both were sad reading.

'Tomorrow we'll have something happier—do you like *Cider with Rosie*?'

'Yes, I like *Cider with Rosie*, very much. See you tomorrow then.'

And so it began in real earnest, her new job. But not before she caught a glimpse of another side of him. It was the next morning, the door was open so she had gone straight in and heard voices. His voice was not gentle but harsh and bullying, 'You say you will change your ways, you say you will come on time, but you really must make up your mind—because I wait for you, I sit here on this balcony waiting and I don't need a watch to tell me how late you are, I know because there is a shadow from the acacia, can you see it? I said can you see it, Miss B, or are you not listening to what I am saying—you certainly do not look as if you were listening. What is your excuse today? Or have you not got one today? Anyway, it's useless, it really is. Sometimes you ring me up and say you cannot come, or somebody else rings me up to say you cannot come, and always the reason is the same, or very nearly always. A relative is ill, a very close relative is very ill, and has been taken to the Parsi General Hospital. Now, I am a reasonable man, always have been, also I think I am a reasonably kind man, but one must draw the line somewhere. I think the line is just here. I have enough problems of my own and the purpose in being read to is to think about the world outside, and not problems about ordinary people. I feel sure that you agree about this with me—do you Miss B? Anyway, I think that you must make up your mind— well? Have you made up your mind?'

'About what, sir?'

'My good woman have you heard a word of what I have been saying? Well? Have you?'

'Yes, sir, of course, sir.'

'Of course, what?'

'I mean, of course I have heard every word that you have said, but what have I to make up my mind about, sir—I mean, I don't understand that bit—'

'Obviously you have to decide whether you are coming to read to me as decided or not. I mean every day except Sundays at nine o'clock. Not nine-fifteen or nine-thirty or even five-past-nine. One hour, that was the agreement, exactly nine to ten o'clock. You know that my next reader comes at ten? You know this, do you not, Miss B? When you are late everything is upset, my whole routine—if you are late the newspapers are left half unread, if you are late my ten o'clock reader is unable to read to me all that I wish her to read because she has to read what you have left unread. Some months ago when you first started you came on time every day and apart from reading with several mistakes I had no complaints. But now—I am not a hard man and I am quite often an understanding man, but a job is a job. It is a commitment. Now, suddenly, you have other priorities. And how many old relatives do you have, Miss B? And why are they all suddenly taking ill? And why, at the one time in the morning when I need you, do you have to be involved somewhere else? Why can you not go to all these ill relatives after you have read to me? Why not go to them from say ten-thirty to whenever? Miss B, this is a job for which, I might add, you are being paid—are you not? Is there anything you would like to say? I see that you are not going to say anything at all. But you will have to say something because we cannot go on like this. If you knew that all your old aunts and uncles and cousins were all likely to always be ill, why did you decide to do this job?'

At last little Miss B seemed to come back from drowning in this unrelenting sea—in her little bird twittering voice she said, 'I needed the money, sir, and I did not know beforehand that they would fall ill. Also, sir, they are nearly all of them aunts who are ill and they do not have anyone to visit them. And I try to see them before I come here because I take their clean clothes and their food and I take away their—'

'Yes, yes, I understand without your giving me all these details.'

'But, sir, the difficulty lies in all these details and I thought you wanted to know why I am a little late these days.'

'My good woman, you are not a little late, you are sometimes fifteen minutes late—today it was even more, was it not?'

'Oh, sir, today was an exception—I could not find Syloo Auntie, nobody could find her in the ward or in the bathroom or anywhere—so I was delayed.'

'Good God! What is happening in these hospitals? Where was she? I trust you found her in the end?'

'Yes, sir, God is great! In the end we found her on a different floor, hiding behind a statue.'

'Good God! Behind a statue—what statue? And how was she allowed to leave her ward and wander about—what is happening to the hospital?'

'Sir, the statue is on the staircase and Syloo Auntie was hiding near it because she thought it was her mother—we had a very difficult time trying to take her back to her own bed in her own ward.'

'But she must be very ill your Aunt Syloo, if she thinks a statue is her own mother—what is the matter with her?'

'Sir, they cannot discover anything wrong but she is very old and she misses her mother very much, she is always looking for her mother. And she is not always wandering around it is only that there are so many old ladies in that ward and there are too few nurses and ayahs so sometimes the patients get misplaced. But all's well that ends well, sir, we found her and put her in her own ward—of course I got late for you, sir, but Syloo Auntie is found and the nurses are laughing and saying that now if Syloo Auntie is lost again they will know where to find her. Sir, shall I go on reading the newspaper?'

'No—I don't want the newspaper—and I do not want to hear about your personal life, Miss B.'

'Sorry sir, I only mentioned it because you asked me why I was fifteen minutes late today.'

'Why can't your aunt stay at home?'

'Because she is too old now and no one wants to look after her—she is old that is all—she can't help that.'

'No,' the old man said, 'she cannot help that, no one can.'

As soon as little Miss B had left she went and made the coffee and took it in and he said, 'Today I have fired Miss B.' 'No, you haven't. You have begun to understand why Miss B is sometimes late, and perhaps you will give her another chance. What are we reading today, I mean after *Cider with Rosie*?'

After an hour the old man said, 'I ask for so little. What I want is surely possible. I want to spend the mornings walking along eager rushing streams, and the afternoons reading or writing, then as it starts getting to sunset, a welcome Scotch with ice tinkling in my glass, a Beethoven symphony on the gramophone, the sixth, I think, then dinner cooked and served by Dhanji, coffee, a small glass of Cherry Heering and then bed. That's all. That's not much, is it?'

'Who is Dhanji?' she said.

'Oh, Dhanji is a familiar household god—he was my cook, valet, gardener, houseboy, guide, friend for nearly forty years. In Sind, in Bombay, in Delhi. Dhanji is dead, alas. But as I was saying what I ask for is so simple. Do I ask to cavort on Kashoggi's yacht? No, because I am a simple reasonable man. Do I ask to sail in leisurely fashion down the Nile to Luxor or to climb to Machu Pichu? Of course not, because I know what is possible and what is not. What do you think? You are very quiet, are you thinking, or are you just not listening?'

'Of course I'm listening, tell me about Dhanji.'

'Well, a long, long time ago when I was a young man I was stationed in Sind and Dhanji came to me as my houseboy. He looked after me entirely and with the strictest rules of what was right and wrong in the running of a household—whether I was living in a large tent or in a small house or a large bungalow. From early in the morning when he woke me up with my tea and chota hazri to my hot water and cold and laying out my clothes, right through the day to late into the night, he helped in every aspect of my life. And everything done so systematically and quietly with never a raised voice. Never angry, never contradictory, helpful and thoughtful. That was Dhanji. After him I could not bear to have anyone else. I tried but they were all impossible. Dhanji had set a standard too high for anyone to match. So, the result is I have no one. I mean no one to live here with me. A man comes in to sweep and swab the place. Another cooks me a hot meal once a day. The dhobi comes in every Saturday and that's all I will allow. No dusting, though, I cannot bear not to know where everything is. I cannot see too well so I memorize a lot of things. And of course regular callers bring the things I need from the shops, the chemists, the bank, the post office. Of course earlier, when I could see and arthritis had not bent me quite double, one of my great joys was walking. But, well, one by one all the pleasures are denied. To grow old is a great affliction. I think it is the worst thing that happens. It's worse than dying. Watching and feeling the shame of different parts of the body becoming unreliable, and then just ceasing to function at all. A curse. And something we cannot plan for, it comes from all directions—sometimes creeping on, sometimes suddenly. But enough of that. I am making you late. Tomorrow then.'

Gradually she found the time she spent with the old man seemed to get longer and longer. The two hours ended and she found she hadn't the heart to tell him so. He of course had no sense of time. After reading for about three hours, she checked his letter box and helped him with his letters, then she began warming up his lunch and then waiting till he'd finished it and then finding some music for him and finally down the steps often meeting the Alsatian in his kennel talking to him for a moment—he no longer growled at her—and then finally home. Once home she would consider what they had read and what he had spoken about. It was always so civilized and she was learning a great deal. 'He was an education. He was sociology. He was a novel.' One day just as she was leaving, he said, 'I am very grateful—' She remembered going home feeling as if she had been given a hundred red roses.

But as it all moved into the second year things began to change. It had been happy, sensible, intelligent, silly and some mornings she had wondered how she had managed her life or her days without him. He made her life so happy. They laughed a lot together. They read so much together. But it began to stop being like that— she wondered if there had been any pointers. Not in that first year. No. None, or hadn't she picked them up? Had she not wanted to. The second year began all right but something was changing, was happening. Gradually. Sometimes very good days, then some indifferent ones, and then by the third year very bad. A nightmare. So how further define that first year or year-and-a-half? The beginning of that first fine complete year—the arrival, the easy informality, the warm close hug, the coffee, the special shortened version of her name. What's in a name, an endearment? Everything, she thought. Only he would have called her by such a pet name. Clearly she had been wrong. She wondered why the good times had ended. He seemed to snap at her more. Snub her enough to make her want to cry. And she could never quite work out what was so wrong—if it was her or him.

She began to think of poor little Miss B. To Miss B he must have been for a long time a kindly old gentleman she went to read to every morning at nine. How gradually, very gradually, he had started to be very irritable about the way she mispronounced words, when she read the same word twice over or left out a whole line. One day even a whole paragraph—Miss B had hoped he wouldn't notice, he looked half asleep and she was running late, but he had sat up in his chair opened his eyes and said very loud and very clear, 'No, no more, not one word more! I cannot bear the way you read, I cannot believe that it is the English language that has so deteriorated—it is you, you, Miss B, it is you who change every second word, and mispronounce every third word and put the emphasis in all the wrong places. I cannot bear it any more. I do not know some mornings what you are reading at all—I have been very polite, I have just tried to guess the content, guessed and hoped for the best but been none the wiser about the content of your reading. But I do not pay you, Miss B, for this, to sit here morning after morning guessing what the morning news is all about. It is a great strain.' And Miss B's voice, mortified, soft, almost a whisper, 'Sorry, sir, I will try to do better.'

'No, it's no good—you have had a long time to improve, and you have got steadily worse and now I cannot bear it any more. It puts me out of sorts, I feel unhappy and distressed and angry. I am not paying you so that I should feel all these emotions each morning. Your envelop is on the desk as you go out.'

Little Miss B said, 'So you planned it for today—you are a mean man—and it was not because I read badly today—'

'Will you leave—just go.'

Miss B left crying into her handkerchief—little bird in her flowered dress. She remembered running after her and telling her not to cry, and Miss B hugged her and warned her, 'Don't get fond of him, he will eat you up, he will devour your whole life and then get rid of you—'

She had gone back upstairs. Slowly. Shaken.

When she reached the top of the stairs she was so upset she didn't want to read to him, to talk to him, did not want to look at him. The old man said, 'You are angry with me, you do not want to read to me or look at me. But you must see it my way. I have so little time and you have no idea how it feels to be read to by that woman—though I can hardly see enough to read again, I have all the right sounds in my head and she was driving me mad each morning—it's true, I should never have kept her as long as I did, I suppose that made her think it was all right but I felt sorry for her. Really I did.'

'No, I think you just waited till you got somebody else and then got rid of her. I think it was a dreadful thing to do. And it's true, I don't feel like reading to you, but as you will no doubt remind me you are paying me and today is only Tuesday so it's a working day. What would you like me to read?' she said.

'You need not read feeling the way you do—I'll talk to you till you feel better disposed towards me.'

He said, 'You know my baby sister fell from the third floor balcony of our home in Sandhurst Road—my mother didn't speak for a year. I have a bit of her sari under my pillow—brown georgette. I keep it always—if ever I am taken to hospital or anywhere will you see that it comes with me? Promise me. That is why I sit near this balcony near this tree, that other balcony had a tree and my mother always stood near the edge waiting for my father to come home. You are the first person I have ever told about the death of my sister. I just tucked it away. Oh, and another thing, if things get too bad would you help me on my way, so to speak? Don't look so shocked. When Lima-lima's mother had a tumour and a cataract in her eyes I gave her a little arsenic in her milk. You can get arsenic quite easily. Homoeopathic medicines. Over the counter. It's humane. All the pain stops. It's best. You will, won't you?'

 She said she would not. Anyway, she would have to think about it. He liked a good many things, food and music and his friends—so? Also he loved literature, looked out on his tree with fondness, had a cat, so? Why should he be thinking of an easy way out?

He said. 'My good woman you know very little.'

'Yes, so tell me more, tell me why? After all you are asking me to provide you with an escape route? I could get into trouble—you are not terminally ill and even then it's a grave offence.'

'I am terminally ill. What do you think this last stage is? What is extreme old age if not a mortal illness with no cure? For an intelligent woman you are stupid. Anyway, bear it in mind. At least bear it in mind. I wish my sister were alive. She would have understood. She would have known why I needed an escape route as you call it. She never argued, she just understood, she was the one most perfect person in my life. Anyway, are you reading or is it time for you to leave? If you would not mind too much, there is an ointment in a slim blue tube on my dressing table. I have a pain between my shoulder blades like a knife.'

She went into his bedroom for the very first time. A great four-poster bed, a great window with the rest of that marvellous acacia tree visible from it, a calendar with dates circled for X-ray, for a blood test, for an eye test, for the dentist. And the dressing table. A chaotic mountain of stuff. She started looking for the blue tube. From the next room his voice called out, 'What is taking you so long? It's next to the old cream in a brown paper bag—don't throw away the bag, you never know when that might come in use. Put it into the left-hand drawer—one for paper bags, one for plastic bags and the last for string, rubber bands and pins—have you found it?'

What was keeping her was dust and white hair and old bottles of 4711. Pantene. There was dust on the mirror and cobwebs and powder, and old bills, and a lovely bit of blue and white pottery, somebody must have brought back for the old man, lovingly wrapped in soft underwear, against jolts and knocks and the myriad horrors of travel, and now she thought here is that bit of ceramic which has travelled over land and sea and time for a young man who must have held it warmly and now an old man who can hardly see it any more lets it lie, if he remembers it at all, wrapped in a thick cobweb of dust on a dressing table between gooey, oozy cough drops and pink Cremaffin also oozing out of a rusty top, oh, time is awful, time is sad and we don't learn anything. If Dhanji had still been around all this would never have happened, if people never grew old, all this would be so different: 'Sahib, your chota hazri,' and a fresh flower on his morning tray.

'What's keeping you? Can't you find it?'

'Yes, I'm coming, may I tidy and dust your dressing table, I'll only be a few minutes.'

'No, no,' dreadful shout from the other room, 'leave it alone. I know where everything is, everything, and I don't want it touched because then I can't find anything, don't touch anything, just bring the blasted tube and leave me alone.'

'When?' she said.

'What do you mean, when?'

'Just that, when do you want me to leave you alone?'

'Oh, you young people, you are such a nuisance, you—'

'I am not young people, and you do not have to shout, and I have rather better things to do than be called a nuisance, so make up your mind.'

'About what? Confound you.'

'About your filthy, dirty, unhygienic dressing table, are you going to let me clean it up or not, if you could just see it—'

'Well, that's the point, I can't see it, so leave it alone, and if it offends you, you needn't go near it again, that's all.'

'But I will have to go near it again—and your comb and brush

The Quiet of the Birds

and tubes of medicine and old pills and wet capsules running their colours all over and old bills and letters and hair and fly and rat droppings and powder—oh, why can't you let me do it—I'll be careful, really I will. You'll see. And I promise to put everything back, just as you want. I'll just clear it up.'

'Oh, go away, go home and don't touch my things—I told you I can't see the things you're talking about and you needn't see them either. Just leave me alone—just go.'

'I am going and, thank God, I don't have to come back here again—ever. You are an impossible, selfish old man and each day you get worse and worse, bad-tempered bullying and shouting. Crude and ungrateful as well. You are not the only person growing old, and hating it, you are not the only person who can't see any more. You have good friends who keep on coming no matter how you treat them, so you are a lot luckier than lots and lots and lots of people who have no one. And you are not so special, except to yourself. All the literature you have read and still read hasn't taught you anything. If you could just hear yourself on one of your bad days, on one of your rotten, beastly, self-pitying days, which, I might add, are almost every other day, I wonder what you would feel. You think you have a special dispensation, don't you? To be as rude as you like, as boorish as you like, as cruel as you like, just because you are old? Well, you don't, because you are not unique, you are not special and you are, besides, changing my whole character, trying to put up with you day after day. All your delicate Persian couplets and your ability to quote them when it suits you mean nothing because you have learnt nothing from them but emptiness and selfishness—and it's a shame, a real shame because you are a cold, indifferent man, a small man and you don't know it yet, and you will never know, ever.'

'Go away,' he shouted, 'and don't you dare to ever come back again—don't stand there, just go—get out, how dare you—'

'I will go and you just think, if you can, about what I have said, don't close your mind to it. Think on it, don't be just angry, please— for peace of mind, for good times we have had in spite of you, in spite of me—'

'Go, just go away, and kindly close the door after you.'

She left and closed the door as he had said, after her, and ran down the stairs.

Freedom. Freedom. She would never go back. Never. Not even if he begged her. Which, of course, he won't, beastly old man, beastly, old, selfish, strong man. He was very strong. He managed to make her feel odd. Twinges. Surely not guilt? Rubbish. He would have to apologize. Catch him apologizing to anyone. God! When she thought of all those hours and hours, whole mornings through the rain and the sun, rushing, always rushing, to be on time for him, and reading and reading—after all that to meet bad temper and beastly selfishness. When she thought of the things she could have done, the things she could have got on with doing. Horrid man, pretending to be a fine, noble and just man, when all he was under that veneer was a tough, despicable, ruthless man who got rid of little Miss B, and now me, she thought. Only thinking of himself, all the time, never anyone else, except when it suited him—so nice to strangers, to friends, who only came now and again if they happened to be in the vicinity. My God, she thought. She had been an ass and a gullible fool for months and months, bullied hour after hour. She would never go back, never, wild horses would never drag her back even if, even if? No, never. She thought of him. How he would get up from his chair and painfully drag himself to the dining room and open the fridge and—stop it, stop it at once! He had managed before and he would manage again. He was tough. Tougher than people like Miss B, and herself. She turned the corner. Her feet began to drag. Her shoulder sagged with the weight of her shoulder-bag, so heavy with all kinds of things for him. Truly, her whole life had revolved around him. Books she read and planned to read to him, bibs and bobs from magazines and newspapers, lists she had made of things he would like, poetry, and social things and gossip and ideas for stories of her own, if he approved of the ideas. All the stuff in her bag was stuff to read to him, share with him, laugh over with him. All of it going home again with her, because he was so beastly about her wanting only to tidy and clear up his dressing table. From such small beginnings—well if that was the way he felt—all right. I am free. She would not go back even if he begged her, or sent messages or phoned her.

She'd not be fooled again or persuaded again. Now her time was her own. She would not neglect all the things she had stopped doing, she would start again. She found she was crying—must be tears of anger and frustration. What hours and bloody hours she had wasted being disappointed with what she had thought he was, and what he had become. And he didn't know what he had become. How he had bullied and harassed her. One day he had said, 'But I want so little—so little, I wonder why it cannot be given to me as a kind of gift, a bonus, after all it is not so much. Do you think it is much, do you think I am asking for anything unreasonable? Why do you not say anything?'

'Because I did not know you had finished speaking or thinking. But now since you are asking me I will say something. I think you are asking for the moon and more—no, please don't be angry, just let me finish, after all you did ask me. Shall I go on or will you suddenly shout or snub me?'

'You make me sound like a bully—if I am one it's only with you, no one has ever complained before.'

'Who would complain? Nobody else ever hears you. Miss B was too frightened and too gentle, so who would tell you? And you used to be gentle and so patient—always allowing one time to think and speak—long ago it was you I could share my fears with, I mean, you had time to understand hesitation, you waited, you did not make me feel a fool because I was inarticulate, you helped to unravel a thought, I was never afraid of you. But now you bring back all that, all that inability, insecurity. All my bumbling, fumbling, faltering, feeling—'

'Yes, yes, all right, I have changed, is there anything else? If not, would you please rub my aching back and then warm something up for my lunch and then I shall rest.'

'That's it, there you go, it's all I, I and I with never a thought for anyone, that's what has happened to you. You were not like that all the time, perhaps you realize that it has happened and you are appalled at what you have become and that makes you bully even more.'

'I don't really need all this analysis and lay psychology. Life was much more simple and peaceful before you came. So if you would go now, after all I did not ask you to stay. If it is so unpalatable why do you keep coming? Maybe you come because you need to come. Have you thought about that? Why not analyse your own motives a little?'

'Oh, yes, I have thought about it and I have thought how you get worse because now you have a victim—you didn't before. And yes, true enough, I have allowed myself to become that because I liked you very much, and then I became sorry for you and so now I am stuck.'

'Well, as I said, you needn't come any more, I'll get someone else, it's really quite simple. An ad in the papers. Look how you came. That's all it takes. Anyway, let me know what you decide. Have you left anything of yours behind? There's a hot-water bottle of yours you might like to remove, and some books. Close the door after you.'

'Bastard,' she thought, 'he's a right bastard.' She was furious. Not just sad or angry. She didn't feel remotely like crying though she was hurting enough. She would not let anything come in the way, not the good times, not his extreme old age, not his near blindness, not friendship, not laughter, not pity. She would think only of that imagined sharing of goodness, she would think of all the travelling back and forth through rain and filthy puddles, through rain and heat and the rudeness of strangers, it was after all easier to bear than the rudeness of friends. Trying to make it by ten o'clock, never be late for him, always him, worried for him, worrying something had happened, him, him, him. The dark side of the moon.

In all the mess she realized that she had forgotten to say goodbye to the Alsatian. He would miss that ritual—as would she. So she trailed back again and went to his kennel. Standing at a little distance she said, 'Well, old pal of many many mornings I shan't be seeing you so it's goodbye for now, don't frighten anyone and don't bite anyone and if I come this way I'll look you up.' She wished she could touch him but knew that it was against the rules. He stared at her with such soft and beautiful eyes. She turned away.

She realized that she hated the old man. For giving her so much. For taking it all away again, and in such a manner. Anyway she

The Quiet of the Birds

would not go back to be insulted or slighted by him any more. And she would not have to worry about whether he was in a good mood or rotten. She was free. But of course she wasn't, because she loved him as well. She knew that she loved him for certain specific things also for those she could not define. Somewhere among the coffee cups and the biscuit crumbs lay a fine friendship. The sudden loud burst of laughter, the soft quiet appreciation of so much reading, hours sharing with her old fine friends, long-ago friends, riding in the districts, to camp and back, being thrown by his horse and his wrist badly set, his love of Beethoven but not gloomy Mahler, his love of shortbread and burnt sugar caramel custard. His love of the Elizabethans, his dislike of T.S. Eliot, his fear of Yeats. She would never meet his like again. But he was a survivor. He'd outlive everyone. With his great bulk clad in white, in snowy white, how arrogant he had been. But how afraid of all the things that were happening to him. Things he had no control over any more. His rage against the sudden new pains that would come to plague him at knees or back. He was afraid of incontinence. 'I wish I could die with dignity, one night in my sleep, it's all taking too long, oh, lord how long—and the salt has lost its savour,' he would say.

After a whole week of doing other things, but thinking of him she began to worry and fret. Perhaps he can't find his medicines, perhaps he's not eating properly, perhaps the pain in his back is very bad. Perhaps he needs someone to read to him. Once he had hurt her by saying, 'There's nothing to stop you coming just to visit, that's it, just come as a casual visitor, not every day, just when you felt like it.' Perhaps she would do that today. She would ring him up first, just in case. She rang and waited, he had told her that when she rang she must wait by counting to fifteen because it took him a while to get to the phone. She waited to twice fifteen and decided he must be in his bath. She left for his house armed with some of his favourite reading and a new book by Anita Brookner.

As she turned in at the gates she saw a group of people near the kennel. There was blood everywhere. Blood on the paving stones and the leaves and the white pillars and the kennel. The great Alsatian lay spread-eagled on the ground, his wonderful fur covered in great splotches of blood. He was such a big dog. The bandy-legged little man who always looked after him sat near his head crying. In his hand there was an ordinary kitchen knife. The dog had bitten his little daughter, so—poor dog, poor dog, poor beautiful dog. After a bit she went up the stairs shocked and sad. The old man's door was open—maybe for me, perhaps he hoped I would come today, she thought. Lima-lima otherwise taking her for granted, came and rubbed himself against her legs and she called out excited, 'I've come, I've come to see you—' No one sat at the slightly tilting chair, the books on the cane table were the ones they had been reading when last she was here. The branch of the acacia seemed to lean further into the room and there were pigeon feathers everywhere. She called out to him again and this time she heard him calling to her cheerfully, calling her by the pet name he had given her—oh it's going to be all right, it's going to be a lovely morning. She was glad she had come back. She had come as a visitor but if he asked her to read she would. Only if he asked her. It was good to be back where she belonged. She waited a bit and then called to him again. But this time no one answered and a chill breeze caused a few pale acacia flowers to fall on the table and a sudden pigeon flew across the room and bits of white fluff and feathers fell on the book in her hand and she heard his voice saying, 'Yes, yes, go on, don't stop now, I want to know what happens next.'

Encounter—1

Well, I worked as a secretary to a group of fellahs (my Mum's terminology) in an off-shore oil rig set-up. I typed and filed and did the accounting, ordered flowers and weekend rooms or a shack, that sort of thing. 'Rosy is worth her weight in gold—literally,' they'd say. 'Ha ha,' I'd say. I may as well tell you right from the start that I am a bit on the heavy side. Always have been, and there is nothing I can do about it—and I did a lot I can tell you. 'Oh, Rosy, you'll starve,' my Mum would say, 'don't bother about it, it suits you, really it does.' In the meantime I could hardly remember what rice or potatoes tasted like and I never drank any beer, the fellahs put away quite a lot of those, it would get that hot. But I was plump at my best and running to fat at my worst. But I was good at my work and I worked hard. I never asked for leave and I never fell sick. I was lucky, straight after school my Dad sent me to a good secretarial college in Bombay. Then I came to live here with Mum and Dad. Of course, I am forgetting, there's my brother too. He'd been told by the priests in his school that he really could do something 'better', with his life. Perhaps they meant better than my Dad who was a first class mechanic till the arthritis came. Anyway, we were all waiting to see what that 'better' of the priests meant, because so far he just lazed about in bed all day, reading or listening to pop music. All the family good-looks had gone to him—such a waste, I thought. I could have done with some of them. Anyway, life was never exciting, just very routine and the same routine year after year. Getting to work on time, I'd bus it to the rig office or take a motorcycle rickshaw if I was feeling particularly flush. It was a long day at work with just an hour off for lunch. I never had to take any work home so you could say it was a good job. Oh, on the whole I liked the fellahs, except the time the Japs came. They were rather a dour lot but very polite.

Sometimes the teams came for as long as two years or a year and sometimes just for the six months. Sometimes they came from America, sometimes from Japan, once from France and at the moment, from Scotland. I was lucky to get this job, mind, because the nuns always said it's the really hard-working that never seem to get their due in this imperfect world. But I got this job first shot and proved the nuns wrong and I kept this job.

Our home was neat and poor. Awful curtains with large green and pink cabbage roses and plastic knick-knacks everywhere and a used tomato ketchup bottle always on the dining table, and a scratch-proof tablecloth and last year's calendar stuck to our twenty-year-old fridge. The bathroom floor was always wet because of some permanent leak in the plumbing, but it was our own and so it felt safe. It was the only house I had ever known except for that stint in the big city—and that was in a hostel. Now my small office at the rig was really nice. A chair and a desk, a filing cabinet, and fresh flowers in a vase even if it was just a sprig of bougainvillea. I had a lovely foreign calendar on the wall and the large window had a shutter blind and I had a pretty rug on the floor. The bathroom was freshly painted, it was always dry, with fresh towels and a new soap each week. I hoped one day to have a home of my own like this. Of course, a slightly bigger version of this. My latest fellah had been here about a month—he was a good-looking young man, gentle and thoughtful in his ways, didn't joke as much as some of the others, but always pleasant and smiling. He was trying to learn Hindi and had a Hindi tutor during his lunch break. One Friday evening he came to my room and said, 'Rosa, would you be free to have dinner with me—we could go to the place where I stay, it's rather nice. I'd run you back after, of course.' I was surprised but said I'd like it very much. I was glad it was him. He was nice and it was nice of him. I was glad I had my good blouse on, with a bit of lace at the neck. He was the only one in my whole life who called me Rosa. It sounded very special. To everyone else I had always been Rosy. I had thought he lived with the others a convenient distance from the oil rig in a regular hotel. But after work we drove out to this place where he lived. After following the main road for a while we suddenly branched off at a place

The Quiet of the Birds

where there was a small water tank. Girls with their water pots chattered and giggled and the air smelled of champak and wood burning. It was a narrow dirt lane with fields on either side and sudden immense banyan trees. Little huts and wells and even a delicate blue temple and old women carrying wood and dry branches on their heads. I fell in love with the place and its quiet, and I think I fell in love with Michael for living in a place like this, by choice. The air began to smell of the sea and suddenly we had arrived. A marvellous stretch of tall casuarinas and coconut palms and little shacks close to the sea. 'This is my home,' he said, 'come and meet my host and friend.' His host, Arjun, the owner of this marvellous place, was a tall, rangy, friendly man who brought out chairs and beer and ice and laughed and talked and as he spoke about his place, his two huge dogs nudged his knee and couldn't have enough of him.

We had dinner under a tall casuarina with a lighted dargah lamp hanging from it. As we ate prawns in green chutney the lamp swung in the breeze creating marvellous patterns of diamonds and triangles in the sand. We went for a walk on the beach afterwards. Bombay so far, so close, with lights as in a glorious necklace, and in the opposite direction two tall funnels from which immense flares of fire raged upwards. It was peace, it was quiet, only the soft sound of the sea pulling out and then in. There were three tall shrouded hills in the distance and Michael said they reminded him of the hills of Scotland. 'Do you like it here, Rosa?' I said I loved it, to think it had been here all my life, so near, and I had never imagined it. It took a young Scots boy to bring me here, I liked him so much, I had never liked anyone before as much as I did him. When it was time, Michael took me home. Fortunately it was late, only my brother's light was still on so there was no need for me to ask Michael in. I was ashamed to realize I didn't want him to see my home. I was embarrassed at the thought of our dreadful curtains and the half-empty tomato ketchup bottle on the tablecloth, the fridge in the dining-cum-drawing-room. Of everything.

After that first time Michael asked me very often to his temporary home near the sea. I was always free Friday evenings.

There was nowhere else I wanted to be. I used to think about it all week. By Thursday I was nervous, even planning to say I had another engagement. But I always went. I was so much in love with him. Fathoms deep. He never touched me. I wish he had. Except very lightly by the elbow when helping me down the steep path to the sea. Stupidly I wished and wished I were slim and pretty—but then, I would think, there were so many slim and pretty women and Michael chose me. In all those months he never had another girlfriend. I haven't told you what Michael looked like. He was like the hero in a film. He was a shock to me every morning when I reported for work. I never got over that feeling of shock— he was very slim and tall, his hair was a dark gold and his eyes were the colour of Paul Newman's and Robert Redford all in one, and when he looked at me I could barely stand the way I felt, and could not believe he did not guess. I thought, 'What do eyes that are so blue see? They surely don't see the world as we do. They must see everything differently from us with our brown or black eyes. Surely the light must filter through differently, surely colours were different—surely in the dark they could see like cats.' Soon he began to ask if I wanted to stay the night and all of Saturday, whenever there was a shack free. I did stay often.

Getting up in the morning, cold and fresh on the veranda, the sea very far, the rocks a black ring, and often tall white birds. One morning I found a small skull. Perhaps a sheep or a dog. I kept it with my small hoard of shells. I loved the early mornings the best because the evening seemed so far away. We read or walked and talked or slept. Everyone thought of me as Michael's girl. I thought of myself as Michael's girl. And my Mum would say as I packed for the weekend, 'Taking off with her young fellah, you deserve to have a bit of fun. But be careful. You can't be too careful.' I tried not to think about what she meant.

Though I wanted it very much, Michael never came to my shack. Of course I would never have known how to go to his. And then it was time for him to go back to his real home. And he went.

For months and months every morning I would expect to see him come through the door with something for me to type or just to say hello. I suppose I had just needed to be unhappy to grow slim. I got very thin. It seemed a pity now. Nothing happens when you really need it to. Or want it.

One morning, long after Michael had gone, I was in the market getting something for my Mum when I heard a voice call out, 'Rosa.' I felt so ill just hearing his name for me that I couldn't turn round. It was Arjun, and he asked if I'd been ill I looked so thin. We chatted for a while and he said I ought to come some time, they missed me, didn't I miss them? I asked about the dogs and I wanted to ask if he had heard from Michael. But I didn't ask. I said I'd come some time though I knew I never would. I never wanted to go back there where everything had begun for me, and ended. On the few occasions I felt angry I would think, well he can't see me slim and pretty. So there.

Encounter—2

There he was standing against a pillar watching people coming out of the concert hall. He looked the same; he looked different. A little heavier, greyer. Otherwise the same stocky figure and very blue eyes. I wonder if he will know me, as I know him. Impossible, she was thirty-seven years older and that's a lot in a woman. Alas, she was fatter, very grey short hair and hardly ever wore a sari. If he did see her he wouldn't recognize her at any rate—she had looked at pictures of herself then, punting or sitting in the garden at Whitstead and she had long hair, she always wore a sari, she was slim and she looked nice—or sometimes even pretty. Now she hoped he didn't remember how she had looked. But this time she was going to speak to him, not leave it like those countless other times. She waited and remembered the very last time. Scotland, the Edinburgh Festival. Usher Hall. Mahler. Fischer Diskau—the Songs of a Wayfarer. He had been there. And after the concert she had felt lonely in that strange city and had hoped he might walk her home, take her for a cup of coffee. Of course, none of these things had happened. And now she walked up to him and said, 'I think we have met many times, you don't know me but I know you.' And he said, 'Of course, thirty-seven years ago, at university, at concerts, I was just going to come over to you. I didn't think you would mind—any more.' And she said, 'I wouldn't have minded then, I wish you had then, so many meetings, sometimes I even wondered if I went to those concerts to see you.' Of course she had said too much, but he said, 'That's extraordinary, because I did, I used to work out which concerts you were most likely to go to. I know the music you like best, Scarlatti, and Bach and—'

'Shall we go somewhere for some coffee or something, it seems a shame to just be standing here, there is so much.' And he said, 'Yes, there is so much, I can't believe this has happened. During the Mahler I thought of you and wished very much that you might be here—somehow.' They left the hall together. As they walked she thought, how familiar it feels. All those times I thought how it would feel walking with him, in the snow or the rain and of course in the sun and this is how it had to feel. She went back about a thousand years because that was the first time she had seen him; six Sunday morning concerts in the Guild Hall, Sylvia Marlowe on the harpsichord and Julius Baker on the flute, trudging through the snow, but what a flute, what a harpsichord; and back in Whitstead the others washing their hair, some in curlers, all in Sunday sloppy dressing gowns groaning at the thought of what she was letting herself in for, snow and perhaps the cancellation of the concert—'Oh they wouldn't, would they.' 'No, of course not, darling, don't worry but you might be the only one there.' All of them at a long Sunday breakfast, chatting, sharing letters and photographs.

And she had seen him. Attendance was very thin. And there he was and she had noticed him immediately. During the short interval. Sitting and observing people. She had been all of twenty, he with a purple and black muffler and heavy duffle coat and she wearing a sari the hem of which was sopping wet and cold. But the music had been marvellous. 'I shall work and work in the hols and buy this Bach if it kills me,' she had vowed, 'one day I'll be far away from all this and I shall want to remember, this Sunday morning, this music and this man sitting here and outside the snow and the cold. I shall need to keep it with me. I shall keep this music, and she and he.'

The next Sunday she had left Whitstead with the fire burning and the extension wire for toast dangling from the overhead light, and Mrs Milne had left little bags of nuts and extra cheese, 'For the rabbits,' she would say meaning us vegetarians and all the bright morning faces and Pippa's long legs and fluffy red dressing gown, keeping her boiled eggs warm against her stomach saying between mouthfuls of toast, 'Sarah's as big as a house and wouldn't it be lovely to be married—' And she had said she wasn't sure, being behind in her Strindberg tutorial and marriage didn't seem to work out too well according to him, more like hell, really. To which

Pippa had said, 'Those morbid Northern buggers, it's something to do with not having enough sun, I shall see to plenty of sun and make jolly sure my marriage is happy, if only someone had the sense to see that I'd make a good wife, unfortunately here all anybody thought of was a quick snuggle on the sofa before Hall. And Eve said, very soft and thoughtful, 'I'd rather go on a dig, at least you know where you are in terms of hazards, but with marriage it would always be a shock all the time, I mean the good times as well as the bad.' And tall, slender Lizabet said, 'Well, is anyone likely to be ready in twenty minutes,' because she was walking into town, her bike was all messed up.

So she and Lizabet had left, Lizabet so sensibly dressed for this awful weather and she again inappropriately, in a sari and a coat. And because she liked Lizabet so much she said, 'Can one love a stranger, do you think?' And Lizabet said, 'I take it you mean an actual person that you don't know at all.' And she had said, 'Yes, well, someone that I have just seen.' And Lizabet said, 'Well, it is and is not unusual, but I would hesitate before I called it love. I think it's a kind of physical attraction for a person, that of course can happen—but not love. You really do need to know a person before you can call it love.'

'Yes, well, I suppose that's what I feel, a strong physical attraction.' 'And don't worry, it happens to all of us so don't feel too terrible,' Lizabet added.

And he was there of course. She would have felt terrible if he had not been. And she looked at him and then looked away when she found he was watching her. There's still next Sunday, she thought as she left, I'm so glad Bach wrote six of these.

And later that Sunday, listening to Ferrier singing Kindertotenlieder, and mending a warm vest she thought of him and wished and wished. What? And crossing the cold wet lawns to Hall to eat grey wet cabbage and watching the lost-looking, pink-cheeked girls from Sweden who served coffee she thought of him and wondered if she crossed his mind. Hoped. And now as they walked he said, 'And have you been back, to Cambridge—since—' And she said, 'Yes, once, disastrously. I should never have done it, one shouldn't when it's all over. One really shouldn't try

The Quiet of the Birds

and recreate things that have been truly important.'

And he said, 'Like us, now you mean.'

'Yes, I suppose so. Its time is over. It's done. You can't get it back again.'

And he said, 'No second chances?'

And she said, 'No second chances.'

And he said, 'What happened when you went back—that second time?'

And she said, 'Oh, in the train up from London all the names were the same, all the green sounding names, Kings Lynn and Cherry Hinton, and Barton and Coton and beloved Grantchester, and then, of course, Cambridge. It was raining. Perhaps that's what started it all. Remember how Cambridge changed in the rain, more than most places, like Venice? And then I went to Whitstead and my old room and the garden looked the same—only different. Other voices, other people's things lying around, bikes and books. In the dining room the wire for the toaster didn't hang from the ceiling light. They'd worked it out. And Mrs Milne was very ill. So I went to Addenbrookes to see her. There weren't any flowers to take her, but I had some Darjeeling tea for her—so often working late on some tutorial she'd come in saying, "How's my wee girl, would she like a cuppa?" Dear Mrs Milne, she was ready for the high jump—but she had remembered me, "And how's my wee girl," she said, I would have wept if she hadn't said that. And we chatted of this and that and when I left she cried and so did I. I should have left then. It was a warning not to try to do anything about the past. But I'm a sucker for punishment. I walked down the lovely King's College avenue, no sun, no green lawns, no daffodils.

'But the great vault was there and I could hear in my mind's ear the voices for Evensong. But you were not there. I walked down Kings Parade and to the Copper Kettle and to Heffers and then to old David's, but it wasn't a Saturday and it was raining, and then to the Soup Kitchen. And then I went to the station. I realized that that was one of the big points about Cambridge, that while you are up, it belongs to you entirely, everything in it belongs to you personally—the fens and the Backs and the old Malting House and Mill Pond and sun-warmed grass and cider, the punts all lined up and waiting, and oh just about everything is the same, yet different, because other people are now young and ride hired cycles in hired gowns, torn and rush to lectures; you see, now they own Cambridge—and you don't any more. All the things that made it so precious now are theirs. We are outsiders. All the books in all the libraries, all the music in the chapels and all the teachers and the foxgloves in Knapwell Wood and every richness is now theirs. Even falling in love for the first time is theirs. One does not belong any more. So Cambridge was very sad, it belonged to all the others who were not even born yet—they were hardly born when we were up, when we heard the summer sound of a cricket ball hitting willow sweetly, or felt the joy of a Saturday bargain at David's, a seventeenth-century copy of the *Book of Job*, very old, very dusty, crumbly dark-brown leather, heard for the first time the trumpet bit of *St. John's Passion* in King's College chapel that Easter. Other People Were Young Now, and you would have to be a Saint not to mind being thirty. And I go babbling on—you say something— don't you wish, wish that you and I had shared that. All that?'

'Yes, and no. Perhaps we would not have been happy. Perhaps we would have been sad a lot of the time and then have had to separate anyway, in the end. We lived a lot in the imagination, you and I, and we made things happen. But the truth was so different. I went up to university as a much older student. I was married. I had a small daughter. My wife worked. And I was in love with someone I had never met. You. That's why I never did anything about us. Now you know. We had nothing, but also we had everything. It's better like that, isn't it?'

She didn't say anything. Not about what he had said. There was nothing to say. They kept walking. Sometimes they talked.

Sometimes they didn't. They walked. Together. That's all. And that was a great deal. After so long. And the sea became dark. And the streetlights came on.

Teacher's Day

Early Days—the expense of spirit—

And taste of orange juice still in the mouth. Climb to the top of the bus. Sit. Another day. Hours of it left. It would be a good day if the conductor smiled. He does not smile. But somehow she would muddle through the day in spite of that. And if she were going nowhere, travelling on top of a bus it would be nice. People far below, a lame dog, an orange cat, a rubbish dump, nothing looked bad from up here. Past the picture framer, past the cemetery, past the children's park, past the dairy, past the ruined mosque. Nearly there. Routine kills the spirit. Bells ring because the hands of clocks move. Everything should be soul-time not clock time. And now rain. Lurch down from the top of the bus, clutching books and bag and sari. She hoped it would be a good day in spite of—oh, forget the conductor. First lecture, sonnet 64—last lecture, *Antony and Cleopatra*. Listed like that how glorious it sounded— the reality was so different. It needed the glory of a great day, a day of heat and splendour, and colour. Trumpets. A farewell of trumpets. Not this grey, rainy day with damp floors, the hem of her sari sopping wet and dragging on the floor. Wet black, electric lights shine dimly. Panic. Reaching-in-time panic. The other panic would come later on. Don't think just yet. It will come, just say what you planned to say—all the things you worked on the night before, just talk for forty-five minutes. That's all. About time and decay, and how different poets have said the same thing over and over but differently: 'Ruin hath taught me thus to ruminate—That Time will come and take my love away.' But not now. Now it's a lot different. Sloppy wet leather chappals, wet sari clinging. Up the stairs quickly, the key will open the tiger lock, the locker door sticks, kick it, books and papers and dry chappals and peppermints fall out. Three minutes. Time for a quick puff at a cigarette. Smile at a face that does not smile back. No time for smiling, we are all in this together.

Clangs the bell. More panic. Books, hurry down the corridor. So many young people, so early. Hurry, but don't run. Now up the stairs. What would she say about Time and Decay, so that they'd understand? Being eighteen. She had been eighteen and understood. She would tell them about Mr W.H., about the Dark Lady of the Sonnets. Quick up the dais—and there suddenly exposed like a lie found out. Look fierce. Wish one were tall. Plan. Know how you'll begin. Know how you'll end.

No time. Plunge.

Outside the rain dripping steadily on stone, dripping on grey, turning the grey black. Time dripping steadily on stone, on hearts, on beauty changing it utterly. Time defacing. 'When some time lofty towers I see down razed.' Rain and time and ruin. Wet pigeons flap.

Clangs the bell.

Down the stairs round the corridor, back to the staffroom. Forty minutes of quiet. Forty minutes to plan what to say also what not to say. *Antony and Cleopatra*. Talk of the glory, talk of Egypt and colour. Talk of Rome and discipline. Talk about love. Middle-aged love. Yes. Men in chairs pretending. Cups of tea. Men gazing vacantly at portraits on the wall. One day they would gaze from the wall at other men. In the meantime, minutes pass. Cups of tea to keep the spirits up, the cup that cheers—teacups rattle. The clock continues. The spirit flags. The swing door swings. Heads turn. Something new—perhaps a new face. Perhaps a death and so a holiday. No. Nothing. Tea and the clock still prominent. A gay voice, 'But, really, what do you think of this compulsory military training?' The voice waits, eager, enthusiastic waits mid-air. No one says anything because nobody cares at the moment. Rain drips outside. Minutes pass. Rain and ruin. And what will one say? Think about Cleopatra, think about Antony. Tell them how they loved each other, they weren't too young but enough in love to hop forty paces down the road. Yes, but the pillars of Rome sagged. Egypt and dissipation. Their hours ticked away slowly, minute by minute. Middle-aged both of them. Perhaps there was no glory. Perhaps there was no pageantry. Perhaps there was no love. Nothing. Only the burnt-out ends of other days. They were both married. No trumpets. But you can't tell them that, even if it was the truth. But you can't do that to them. Being eighteen, you can't make them feel the sense of middle-aged people being in love as intensely as young people. And both of them did think other things important, as important as love. Time had taken that away. Ruin. Rain. Nearly time. Another voice fresh from study leave, 'But, really, there's no question about it, the Germans are superior, I mean, look at their culture and scholarship, and—and—and well, their capacity for work and take a professor in Germany he is respected I mean really respected.'

Everyone waited, thinking of the Jews and concentration camps and Hitler youth. The swing doors swing, five girls and two young men swing in and deposit themselves around the room. Skirts swing. Neat ankles. Hair in quite the newest way. 'Sir, give us an off today, come on, sir, be a sport.' Light cigarettes. Talk extra loud. The talk is not about German culture or the German capacity for work and anyway who could possibly expect respect for a chap who earns two hundred a month basic with eighty thrown in for ballast and seven deducted at source. You gotta be kidding, baby? Voices fill the room. Laughter fills the room. Talk. And no RA or TA or DA.

'Oh, could we cut your lecture today, it's Anu's birthday today and we want to go to Excelsior for hot dogs.' And, 'Yes,' says Sir feeling sheepish looking silly, 'do go,' and like a gay blade feeling popular, 'Am I invited too?' And very coy, 'Oh, sir, of course.' Being eighteen. But what about Cleopatra and what of Antony? Think. Giggling they leave. All of them leave. Except one. One, quiet, tall boy stays and says, 'About that point you made last week,' yes, very quiet. Had she really made a point, that he had not only heard but remembered? Suddenly the bell. Fly. Down the corridor. Up the stairs turn in at the second door. Oh, let it be all right. Noise, stamping of feet. Noise, banging of desks. Noise, dropping of books. Noise, loud laughter, rude laughter. 'Poor Shakespeare, poor me.' Not to worry, just the coarse groundlings. Orange pips flying, orange peel flung. Up to the dais, just ignore them. Noise much worse. Get to the desk so she could lean on something solid. On the desk a picture. A large picture in colour. Grotesque in embrace. Cleopatra of Hollywood and Antony of Hollywood, sprawling, ugly. Breasts and lips. The noise terrible, look up quick, don't let them think it matters, or that you care and that you feel awful. Look as usual. Five huge boys—lounging, sprawling, insolent, bending, pretending, pouring over a book. Looking up and leering. Looking down again, leering. Speak up now or you'll drown. Tell them to stand up. They do, slow and insolent. Ask them. Ask them what they were reading. One of the louts answers, 'A guide, miss, to our textbook, notes to help us understand and appreciate our Shakespeare.' Ask him to bring it to you. He does. Tell them to get out. Tell them not to come back next week or any week. Tell them. The book lies, hang-dog, on the desk. Sheepish like its title *Sex and Love Explained . . . With Pictures*. Don't feel horrid, don't feel sick. Don't scream, and above all, don't cry. A thousand railway station book-stalls, a thousand pavement-sellers. Being eighteen.

Quiet please. Open to page thirty, Act 1, scene IV, line 54. Don't think, just read. There must be a reason why one does these things. Does anything at all. Think about it tomorrow, think about everything tomorrow, not now, not today.

The bell so welcome. Down the corridor, down the stairs, find the key, fit it into the lock, open the locker. Books, check tomorrow's timetable, umbrella. Out at the door. Through the gates. Fresh air. And two birds wheeling in a clear sky.

Staff Meeting

Staff meeting at 3 p.m. sharp on—.

    AGENDA
1. *Integrated teaching*
2. *Autonomy*
3. *Planning cell*
4. *Staff Seminar, K.5*

5. *Canteen*
6. *Problems, Queries*
7. *Tea*

Everyone had received these a week in advance. Groans in the staffroom, groans wherever the principal's special peon found them to make them sign and not forget. 'Damn,' some of them had said. Others had said, 'Oh God, not again,' and some others were already working out at fifteen minutes per item on the agenda that item no. 7—Tea—would probably occur about 5.30, so it wasn't so bad—they could play carom or correct papers or something till then: 'Why attend at all?' Shouts of, 'Sit down, Bishnoi,' because the poor man was trying to enthuse the groaning group into some kind of patriotic feeling for the college. Some said, 'Good egg, we have a BUTU meeting at 6.00 so we can leave after a quick tea'— a very quick tea, seeing that it will come from the canteen, one sandwich each, one piece of Mongini's slice, and, if they were really lucky, a samosa, and of course tea.

Bishnoi said, 'No, this is different—it is a farewell tea party at the same time, so there is going to be a special pink icing cake made by Professor Coutto's wife, and a speech, a farewell speech by the principal.' 'Hurray!' went up a general kind of shout, not because they disliked the principal, but, generally, for change and of course the new kind of cake. Bishnoi who always knew said, 'It was not for the principal, the cake, I mean, but for four of the staff who had reached retirement age.'

Another kind of betting game started up quickly, money passed hands, everyone was speculating about the staff who had reached that dreaded, long-awaited golden sixty. 'But I thought she was fifty-nine. Not nearly sixty, and he must be dyeing his hair, he doesn't look a day over fifty-eight—' and so on. It died out gradually as each tried to remember what age they had put down when they joined, some felt more vulnerable than others but in the end everyone more or less decided they better attend the meeting. Of course, the muttering continued, 'Cheapskates, fancy passing off a staff meeting along with a farewell for four staff members—there should have been four farewell parties with special cake considering the poor devils had sweated it out for over thirty years, and one staff meeting with ordinary cake.' Bishnoi brought in two bits of 'late news'—there was to be an acting-principal-for-six-months and he'd heard from a reliable member of the canteen that Professor Coutto's wife was being paid an advance from the staff pension fund for the cake. The staff council immediately got into an important huddle in a secluded part of the staffroom, the bit where the fan didn't reach and seats were piled with ten years of uncorrected term papers (only ATKT papers), and worked out a scheme by which the staff would have the option to go on a hunger strike starting tomorrow, or they would start making banners and leaflets. Bishnoi had fled the scene by this time because he always did when things got too serious. To be fair to him he had perhaps gone to check his facts. The unmarried male members of the staff felt that, anyway, things were looking up. They felt that if four whole members of staff were retiring then four new young people must be joining. Also by the law of averages the four new ones would be female. Would be young, might be very young, considering that nowadays the brighter female went to school by the age of two, left by the age of eleven, then add three more years for the BA degree and two more for MA that made her just sixteen. Also sixteen made them see visions of prettiness as well. So, gradually, by the time it was time to leave by trains that would take them to Virar, Karjat, Pune and places further—they were a mellow lot. Almost a happy lot. They forgot that on the morrow they would be taking about thirty lectures, give or bunk a couple, and saw hazy, rosy, visions of farewell parties with cake, a new acting principal, and four chicks barely out of school uniforms. Who could ask for anything more? Life was looking up.

The actual day dawned. Each staff member had got a reminder about the meeting and the revised agenda. It read quite like poetry:

Agenda for a meeting of the staff in the skylight room (top floor) 3 p.m. sharp.

1. *Farewell to the old*
2. *Welcome to the new*

It had been a trying day, more trying than most days. For one thing the weather forecast had promised a pleasant sunny day with showers late at night. It had rained all morning and noon. Clearly, there would be sunny spells at night. Not being geared for this unseasonable, quite unreasonable, reversal, the college was at its worst. No class bells rang for one thing. Professors were exhausted—having taken lectures each the length of three—some had had no lectures at all since no lectures had seemed to end at all. Lights had not worked, fans naturally had not worked, the priest-in-charge of maintenance was greatly in demand but was locked in the lift between floor six and seven for the last four hours. Little groups were seen grumbling about 'these priests', or the more knowledgeable 'these Jesuits'. Finally, on this day, the flush in the ladies' toilet (Staff Only) had given up. The Brother-in-charge felt more truculent than usual because he thought the Maintenance-Father was playing hooky, so said he could only follow up trouble in the flush, if it was true, and a typed letter was sent in triplicate on college-letter-paper. Anyway, there were no funds, he said darkly, why not form a fund-raising committee? Since there were thirty-four fund-raising committees, no one took this seriously, and left saying, 'All these Brothers are the same, because they are not full-fledged priests they take it out on the lay person.'

So things were not well by the time it was time for the meeting. 'A trying day,' someone said. 'Shut-up,' someone said and our wiseman-bore-of-the-staffroom said, stirring his very own thirteenth tea-bag of the day, 'The stars standing where they do, it is going to get a lot worse before it gets any better.' Devout Catholics crossed themselves quickly, reapplied lipstick rather daringly under Bishnoi's admiring eyes, started the steep climb up to the skylight room at two fifty-eight—'Mustn't arrive too early, it will look greedy.' The room, when they finally reached it, had some staff members having their afternoon naps, snoring in upright chairs. The stairs filled with the sounds of feet rushing in, somebody had put up a few balloons, there was a coloured paper hat on each chair and Terry, with the muster, looking mysterious, knowledgeable, and faintly amused, accompanied the old principal as well as the temporary-acting-principal-for-six-months. The Spanish priests looked exhausted—not having taken any lectures and been denied their daily pleasures—with the lift but brightened as a filthy-looking waiter and his assistant brought in a huge empty tea urn; 'For later, that's for later,' the whisper went around. The doors at the back of the room were firmly closed as that was a famous manner of escape from meetings after signing the muster. Some peered anxiously out of windows but realized that the skylight room was really too high to escape from and settled down. One or two of the lady teachers had festive clothes on and one had rushed home to don her wedding dress, daringly cut very short now—she raised a clap among the more sentimental ones and she blushed becomingly. Her husband, a surly staff member himself, groaned affectedly and gazed at the ceiling.

The meeting started with the old principal quoting, 'Ring in the new. Ring out the old,' delighting the Eng. Lit. lot but he also said we will leave that for later, business first. The Prof-in-charge-of-timing-everything, jotting down little figures and looking pleased, clearly believing that if things went so swimmingly tea and cake might yet appear before 5.30.

By 3.15 we were off to a good start except for Prof. Desai. The principal had made a quick resumé and stated his beliefs. He was for integrated teaching. Cheers went up. Warming to his topic his approach remained delicate, understated, and idealized. He would never have to teach the barbarian hordes anyway. The principal always played fair. He too was an academic. He took a Foundation course once a week in 'Catholicism for beginners', but when word of this reached the local mafia he had changed the subject heading of the course to Great Religions of the World—but stayed with the original material, planning to bring in younger priests if trouble loomed again. Some staff members had begun to look like early Christian martyrs before the worst of the massacres—others angry beyond belief. Prof. Desai who had been napping till the first burst of applause stood up and delivered a speech he had written out on a piece of paper. People swore it was the same piece of paper he brought to every staff meeting since the founding of the college. He usually found that if he changed a word here or there his speech applied to almost every crisis that had ever struck the college. Since his delivery was bad some respectfully felt the whole speech was written out in Sanskrit but others, more cynical, said it was in English, only the quotes were in some other language. After seven-and-a-half minutes' preamble, he launched into the main thrust of his argument. It is clear to most that he has the wrong topic this time. He is speaking in an impassioned manner about the integration of India—borrowing heavily from somebody's speeches at the time of the integration of the princely states. Even allowing for his loneliness the fact that he taught eight lectures a week to two students in a little cubicle, this was always his big chance to interact with a large group. He knew that his dept. would be closed quite soon, the college could not justify one student to a single professor, she had to bring a cousin or an aunt each lecture because it did not look right to have a student locked up in a cubicle for forty-five minutes, and anyway, the college couldn't spare a peon to act as chaperone. So Prof. D. prepared for the worst by polishing up his act which was to be the finest cheerleader the priests had ever had. Always cheerful when he wasn't napping, always able to bring little titbits of information to the priests, he had become invaluable to them. Even they would have stopped any other staff member but they never had the heart to stop him. But the others did and forthwith a series of 'Shut-ups and go to sleep', etc. filled the room and some really irreverent began to sing, 'Onward Christian Soldiers', and 'We Shall Overcome', and 'India Expects Every Man' etc. and even 'Chamcha' etc. till he did sit down. After this no attempt was made to revive this topic on the agenda. To this day no one knows whether this college follows integrated teaching or not. On to topic no. 2.

Canteen matters went swiftly. A strike of the canteen staff averted by concessions. Knitting warm vests for the wives of the waiters and cooks, and tea to cost fifteen paisa more. Groans. The knitters gave in their names feeling proud that they were at last acknowledged as ones whose special skills would now be recognized, and that they had entered a larger arena—nay even perhaps the magic words 'Welfare for the downtrodden' would be attached to their names. Already they started to think about bits and pieces of wool left over from larger pieces of knitting they had done. This staff meeting was beginning to go rather well. Salvi, the canteen representative, after saying 'Jai Maharashtra, and Jai Shivaji Maharaj', left to report the meeting to his fellow malingerers in the canteen. The meeting treated this in a sombre way, feeling that now those 'damned SS' had taken over the canteen, some others said not to worry it was just that Salvi's son and daughter went to a new municipal school where this was said on arrival and at the end of each day, and before and after each class. 'What are things coming to?' said still others, and then they came to topic no. 5—Autonomy. A young, much-disliked priest stood up and said the college should now protect itself—they should free themselves from various strangleholds. Free themselves from the university—that den of iniquity and mediocrity, free themselves from the UGC and be run entirely by the 'good Fathers'. He sat down. Thunderous applause from the Fathers. The lay staff now demoralized, very quiet, but some firebrand asking boldly, 'Which good Fathers was the young priest meaning?' Receiving no support, they moved on to topic 6. Topics 6 and 7 went very fast because both were handled by a new hotshot returnee from a refresher course in Mizoram. He was a scientist, very boyish and handsome. His brain was like a computer and half the female staff was in love with him, the other half languishingly remaining in love with a handsome Spanish priest who remained oblivious of the havoc he had caused among the married and unmarried staff for half a century. The hotshot said he would head the planning cell for the next ten years with just one assistant. About the question bank, he said he had bought a new postal letter box of the newest design at a huge discount, since the city might never take to it, and it had a lock. All professors should put in the questions. This was the new idea he had picked up at the refresher course in Mizoram and it should prove effective. Theirs would be the first college in Bombay that would try it out. Topic 8 was a popular one. K.5 staff seminar meant a holiday in the old monastery belonging to the order since the early fifteenth century. The staff loved going, because it meant a free Saturday and Sunday, it was in a hill station, it was paid for by the establishment and though a lot of work was done it felt like play. Immediately fifty staff members started putting their signatures down and were told to work on the subject for the two-day workshop and the menu. At last, topic Tea. Everyone woke up and crowded round the long tea table. The cake was very pretty. The cake was very small. Everyone formed a queue as for rations or boarding a bus. Some wags had put on their paper party hats and looked silly. The tea was over very quickly, and before people could escape, the meeting was called to order. The principal introduced the acting-principal-for-six-months and then said his goodbyes to each of the four sixty-year-olds and welcomed the new staff members. Everyone craned their necks for this. It was a major disappointment. Two of the new members had been on the temporary teaching staff list for the last twelve years. Being almost 'rendered surplus' they had literally hung on for dear life teaching rock climbing and rappelling from the highest church steeple. The other two were young priests brought back to the teaching fold, a form of punishment for having dared to work among the slum-dwellers in a famous slum outside the city. They had been forced to climb out of their jeans and T-shirts and been lent rather short cassocks for this meeting. One would be helping the new acting-principal, the other would be told what subject he would have to teach by the weekend. After this anti-climax it was felt that topic 10a might not produce any 'grouches'. But the old trooper, Prof. Kini, said that his brother worked in an airline and after twenty-five years of service was presented with a briefcase, with his name embossed in metal, and after thirty years of service he would be given the latest HMT watch. He felt that the good Fathers should start something like this, even though they had never done so before. The good Fathers said theirs was a selfless job, their only reward would come in heaven. Some other staff members said they did not believe in heaven and would like an earthly reward, however humble. Cheers greeted this bold and clever thought. The principal declared the meeting ended. Everyone trooped out. The good Fathers from Spain waiting in a queue for the lift which was now working. Those who had retired looked chaste and lost and sad. They cleared out their lockers and said goodbye to the staffroom peons and left. The four new staff members proudly claimed the empty lockers and felt a new day dawning.

K.5

The air crackled with heat and excitement as they gathered at the station. They were to leave by the 2.23 Fast Up train to Khandala. Some had come with plans of hard work, some because they always went to staff seminars—it helped when teachers got their increments, it showed willingness, it showed helpfulness, it showed a 'spirit of cooperation which the college had always expected of its staff members'. Some had come in the spirit of 'we'll try anything once', some had come because they had never gone before and there was a black mark against their names, and some rebellious ones because as they said, 'Let the buggers pay for a whole weekend, yaar.'

Some of us who went regularly had sensibly brought blankets, pillows, lotas, biscuits, candles, odomos, mosquito coils and one had even brought a kerosene lamp—'It gets pitch dark there, yaar, you never know what's in those dark corners.'

The priests were wearing their smart casual wear. La Costa shirts and neat trousers or jeans, the rest of them in everything their teenage sons and daughters longed to and did wear from trips to Fashion Street: this year it was all flowered, loose Bermudas and this year's colours were purple and electric green. Everyone had sports shoes and day-glo laces. Some 'hero' types wished the students could see them.

The train came in and people started flinging themselves in thinking it was their normal morning and evening mode of travel, but this journey was luxurious—a whole compartment and a seat for each one. Some started their weekend pleasures in earnest not meaning to miss a moment. Lap carom boards were placed in position, cards, those in love immediately in position for palmistry and fortune-telling. The priests counted heads and then settled down to their rosaries, Hosie counted and then recounted luggage, Furtado and his young assistant started peeling potatoes as there were no lights in the old kitchen in Khandala and the floor of the compartment was strewn with sweet papers and potato peelings and bits of batata vadas, and then the singing began. No journey was complete without this and they set to with vigour. Only two songs were known to the entire group so these were sung several times over. The first was '*Hum dono kamre me bandh ho jaye or chabi*' etc. and the other 'Doe a deer, a female . . .' A new staff member tried to interest the others in 'She'll be coming down the mountains when she comes', but some felt the priests might not approve because of the pink pyjamas. Considering what the priests had to put up with in the way of weekend sartorial elegance this was not taken at all seriously. Some looked out of the windows and then in again at the walls of the train which read, 'Pearl Clinic Rs 75 for first abortion. Come one come all, help your nation achieve its target.' Other walls said, 'Romeo for firm hold, stick-free kitchenware', and 'Juliet for skin-tite grip-tight panty ware all at half price—with no regrets.'

Khan Sahib, realizing the sun was about to set, was beginning to lay out his prayer rug, the priests said their evening prayers with renewed vigour and Furtado continued to peel potatoes. And then they reached the station. The air smelled cool and fresh as they piled out. The priests counted heads again, and Hosie counted luggage. And then they set off. They walked and walked, being edged off the road by motorcycle-rickshaws and cycles and cars. When they finally reached the old monastery they took over like a film crew. Furtado rushed to the old kitchen and peeled further potatoes, his assistant flung himself at a very lean and bony but swift old chicken, a hurrah went up at the thought of a chicken curry with pullao. Khan Sahib barely made it to a fair bit of unbroken four-hundred-year-old flooring and continued with his prayer, the priests went about their priestly duties and the rest cast lots for the only beds with a few springs still left and then cast lots for the mattresses with something in them besides birds-nests built since the last seminar, K.4, last year. Hosie was writing out the evening's programme on the blackboard. So far it read: Arrival 6.10. Free time—settling in 7.30—Dinner 8.00. Sing-song 9–10 p.m. Bed. Item: mosquito coils and candles available from Brother Mathew at Rs 2 and Rs 3. Item—no alcohol to be consumed in the rooms, verandas, bathrooms or in the garden.

7.15 found most of the group huddled in the old swimming pool. They were drinking country and feni and somebody had brought some Cinzano for the women. This was being drunk out of tooth mugs and plastic glasses and even straight out of the bottles. Someone had brought wafers and peanuts and life was beginning to look up but then the mosquitoes found them and somebody saw or felt a snake and then the gong for dinner. Avoiding scratchy nettles and burrs they made their way to the dining room. Long tables and benches and Furtado's special laid out. He had done them proud. A huge cauldron of potato curry and another cauldron of many bones and even more potatoes for the non-vegetarians, dal and rice for everyone, and even dessert—a banana and an amusing Cadbury eclair each. The sing-song was not a success. They had sung too recently and the serious classical singers said they were feeling too tired. They would sing the next night at the campfire. And so to bed.

The next morning found long queues at the icy-cold doors of the three medieval bathrooms. Some very brave ones had managed a bath in a begged-from-Furtado mug of hot water. But spirits were high. The blackboard now said—Day 1: Breakfast; Hike to Duke's Nose, Lunch, Short rest, Workshop 1; Chalk Talk, Dinner; Charades and other games, Campfire. Bed. Day 2: Free expression, optional mini hike; Lunch, pack, leave for station. Furtado's special fried eggs—which meant all fifty eggs tipped into hot oil and deep fried and then allowed to freeze— along with some excellent bread and, wonder of wonders, a whole pot of Mala's mixed fruit jam.

Things had really improved since the last seminar. Food-wise. Only three names had been put down for the hike to Duke's Nose so it was cancelled, but Hosie insisted that they all go for the mini hike. This hike was all around the property and up to the gates and back. Some were in bad shape, had not walked so far in the last ten years. Later we gathered for the first serious workshop entitled Chalk Talk. It was very lively and we all thought very seriously about using the techniques we learnt; they would greatly enhance a dull lecture and might be just what would enrapture the students who were still reading Bronte and Hardy in abridged versions, some even as comics. All you had to do was use coloured chalk and illustrate things you were saying with little stick figures, or arrows in different colours and stars and boxes and circles and squares. Since we had not gone on the hike we had our second workshop as soon as we found Chalk Talk getting too rowdy. This was called Free Expression and involved those of us who had been chosen from various disciplines. We had to meditate, and then get up and do whatever we felt like doing. This had such extraordinary results that the professor in charge put a stop to it at once. Furtado's assistant was sent off to buy some rum and a bottle of lemon squash and we made a heavily disguised but immensely potent fruit punch. The whole bottle of rum, all the lemon squash and a few bits and pieces of fruit thrown in for ballast. After dinner we played Charades and guessing games and some who had had extra shares of the punch dressed up and danced that old favourite, the sexy Bangra dance. Then we collected an enormous amount of dried wood and sticks and dry leaves and started our campfire. It was beautiful and people sang and told frightening stories and became good friends and no one wanted to go to bed with bats flying around and those dark corners. On our last morning we were taken on a nature walk and the professor in charge pointed out a wild daisy, a mogra, a champak, a tree lizard, a spider, some crab-grass, a bit of ivy, a clump of bamboo, a wild pink rose and even a ground orchid. We felt knowledgeable and refreshed. After lunch we left for the station and did everything we had done on the way up—in reverse.

The next day in college hardly anyone spoke to anyone else.

Morcha

We tramped, trudged, slouched, walked out of the college gates
stared at by some late students. We carried banners which read
clearly what we began chanting at regular intervals something that
sounded like, 'Fuck two three four,' 'Fuck two three four,' and
startled passers-by certainly thought that was what we were saying.
We were in fact shouting out the initials of our unions. Because we
were also known as the 'backbone of the nation'—the President of
the nation called us that once a year when he gave sad-looking
teachers, all around seventy years old, shawls and citations, though
they always came from places like Dhulia and Akola and
Sabarkantha—we felt proud. Once a year on Teachers' Day. Not
today, though. Today people were muttering, 'These are not
teachers, they are obscene scoundrels, our poor children being
taught by these types, they look like domestic servants, they look
like fisherwomen. And all these shameless women, in sleeveless
blouses, so shameless marching with men, they should be dandling
their babies, rolling out rotis, touching their husbands' feet, hai
hai, what is our country coming to, what would Macaulay think,'
and so on. We walked on, pretending not to care. At about the
time we reached Handloom House it started to rain and when we
reached Jehangir Art Gallery it became really hard, dirty stuff and
some of us said, 'Let's nip into the Samovar and have a cup of tea
and join this lot later, no one will notice.' Feeling we had done
more than our bit we disappeared. The way we were feeling, beer
would have been our natural desire but we settled for tea. By the
time we rejoined the others they had crossed the Oval, and we
made for Mantralaya. Our cheerleader, Hosie, called out even more
vigorously, 'M. Fucto zindabad,' and she was glad she was wearing
brown so that she merged with the filthy streets and looked like a
brown Indian in a brown overcoat, lurking in Earls Court. From
the tops of buses people stared and called out rudely, 'Shame on
our teachers behaving like dirty union types—they have no
vocation.' We trudged on like a defeated army and the gates of
power were closed, 'Cowards!'—we shouted and 'Cowards!'—we

shouted again, then with a few last, 'Education Minister hai, hais,' we dispersed. It was still raining—we were all drenched, all depressed.

The next day the front page had a large picture of us. Triumph. Undreamed. We looked like bedraggled domestic servants marching for free Saturdays, or fisherwomen fighting against bad hooch for their husbands. We hadn't stopped the traffic, crowds had not collected in admiring groups, no journalists had asked for interviews, the minister had not received our union leader or his deputy, but at least it was over for another year and though a great number of us had bad colds and hoarse voices, at college that day some students did ask what we were demanding this time. Those who hadn't marched with us looked sheepish and we looked quite triumphant. After all, the newspapers had bothered to take a photograph, just near Handloom House and our banners read upside down 'M.F.U.C.T.O, zindabad.'

But of course we realized that we had failed again and we wished the Education Minister had looked at our memorandum because all it asked was to look into our terms of service and revise or implement:

1. *Salary: which was still 350 plus*
2. *Pension (None)*
3. *Security of Service (None)*
4. *Medical allowance (None)*
5. *Rent allowance (None)*
6. *Travel allowance (None)*
7. *Gratuity (None)*
8. *Not more than twenty-four lectures a week*
9. *Not more than a hundred students per lecture.*

That's all.

P.S. After all, the Minister's driver and peon took these things for granted—and were we not the backbone of the nation?

Ink-Stained, with Love

She had never told him of the affection of eighteen years. Not once. Not once. Because it was always panic time—exam time. But eighteen years is a long time and she must pay her dues, now that he was dead. She was twenty-six years old when she met him. He must have been, well, no age that she could work out, and he stayed the same age all those years, though the rest of them had babies, got older, got greyer, fatter. He stayed the same. Very thin and tall, always in black trousers and a white shirt and always keeling slightly to the left as he walked and a cheerful wave of his thin hand and his greeting, 'Still alive.'

'After a long illness, patiently borne our dear Cyriaco Ferns died. He worked long and selflessly as a member of our clerical staff. The funeral will be at 3 p.m. today in the college chapel.' That's what the blackboard at the college entrance said. 'Whoever that is, it would be more to the point declaring a holiday,' some said. Others said, 'Poor chap, we didn't think he would ever fall ill. We didn't know his name was Cyriaco did you? Quaint.'

She thought of the first time she had met him. It was about a query he had about an exam question paper which incensed her so much—later she realized from the twinkle in his eye that he was only teasing: 'I just wanted you to come and see me—I didn't know what you looked like.' The question he had sent her a note about was asking whether in her English paper for First Year Arts (Poetry and Prose) if he could type out the poetry like prose—that way the whole paper would fit on one sheet of paper and think how much paper it would save the college! So often his teasing and his silly idea of a joke got on our nerves and we would think or we would say, 'Oh for God's sake, of course not,' or, 'for Heaven's sake, not now Ferns, later, much later.' She hoped now that he had known that their irritation was really at bottom, affection—because we took him for granted, thought he would always be there to iron out their problems. They never asked if he had any. Never asked about his family or whether he was married, if he had children. Where he lived. Nothing. We thought he belonged to the college, knew that he loved his cycle, wore an old-fashioned bicycle clip for his trousers and was never absent, year after year. We could never have managed without him. His office was tiny and crowded with a mezzanine floor for all the files and registers going back at least fifty years. He had a slow revolving fan perched on a precarious mound of account-books and a money plant in the window sill. So often he would be up in the stacks—he would peer down looking through his steel-rimmed glasses, smile and say, 'Still alive? Don't touch anything, I'm just coming down.' Fan revolving slowly, dust flying everywhere, smell of ink, smell of glue. He came to college right through the holidays, he hated change. He hated 10 + 2 + 3. He hated Junior College, he hated change in the syllabus, he hated the Emergency. During the long monsoons he looked so wet, but he always smiled—no matter what. To the students he was Uncle or Uncle Ferns. He cycled sideways—he was so tall—he walked sideways, so that he wouldn't crash into doors and walls and pillars.

The nuns who looked after him in the nursing home said that even when he was a very sick man with a raging fever they found him wandering down the corridors of the hospital looking for his bicycle. On the very last night he left his bed and the white walls of the ward and the nuns found him near the gates trying to get to college in time, before time, up the stairs and down the corridors and into his mad, yet ordered, room—with its huge bottles of red and blue ink and its pens and fine-nibbed stencilling equipment and the money plant that we had told him would do so much better on ink rather than water since it always looked dusty and half-dead—and he'd smile and say, 'Why, it's still alive.' This was his watchword, it was true of his plant, of himself and what he expected of all of us. He and his room were like characters out of Dickens, dust and high stools and ledger-books, glue and ink and paper. Never dusted, because he couldn't find anything if it was dusted or moved an inch. And through the heat of so many Octobers of exams and tiredness, we would take it out on Ferns. 'The marks aren't ready, no they won't be ready not yet, not yet.' Marks and totalling marks and meeting impossible deadlines and little notes from him in his spidery handwriting—'Please come at your convenience between 2 and 4 to read your proofs. This is a third reminder.'

Year after bloody year. Still alive. And so today at a quarter-to-three we trooped up to his funeral mass in the chapel and the stained glass windows glowed gently down on his long coffin. He looked so kind, lying there, and she could have sworn there were ink-stains on his fingers.

Mama's Boy

Lusito sat at the window and looked down at the now-familiar Sunday quiet street—he wondered if the bag lady would come up the underground steps. It had become very important to him to see her every day. Important as well as fearful. After a while he wrote a letter to his mother.

> Dearest Mama, I miss you very much—I wish we had talked more, but we understood each other very well. Did we not? Maria Amelia is not home yet—today's tour is a long one, even when she is firm with the tourists somehow it does not work so well when she takes them to Fatima. They are overwhelmed in a very emotional way. They will walk on their knees, some of them on their bare knees for great distances, helped by sons or daughters or husbands praying the while. I wonder what they are asking for, or giving thanks for or perhaps guilt-ridden. I bleed upright for you. Standing upright for you. Also for me and you as we were. I bleed for my lost life.

Fortunately his mother would never read this letter. Only a month earlier Lusito had heard the parish priest intone solemnly, 'Man that is born of woman hath but a short life to live, and is full of misery. He cometh up and is cut down like a flower, he fleeth as it were a shadow, and never continueth in one stay.' So he knew for certain that she was dead—and though he longed for the impossible he also knew that no matter what he did the dead did not rise.

So. Now he was here. Something he had ached for for three years, and he missed her dreadfully. Powerfully. He could smell her faint perfume—she had always dried rose-petals and carnations and little bags of these hung in her cupboards. As a child he had often hidden there when she went out. And felt she was with him.

Three years ago, on his only trip abroad, Mama had said, 'Only come back, I'll take care of you. Promise. You go, it's good for you to go, you have never been to Lisbon, you have never been anywhere. Travel is good, it makes you strong in yourself, it teaches many things. You go. Only, come back.'

And he had gone. Mama had insisted. Three years ago he had been thirty-seven. Now he was older. He was no longer a boy. He was a man. Also, he was no longer a young man. Mama had always called him her boy. And that is what he had always felt like, 'her boy'. Widowed very young, she had turned him into her husband and her son. He fulfilled—almost—both needs in her. What it did to him, of course, was difficult to assess. But gradually what emerged to the observer was a man of beautiful manners of the last century, towards all women, especially slightly older ones. He had delicate wrists—like a girl's. He had fair and delicate skin and dark hair. His eyes were like his mother's, the colour of honey, or brandy with light shining through. Throughout the year when he left the house he wore white suits wonderfully cleaned and pressed. A straw hat—'Protect your head and neck, my boy,' his Mama would call out as he left, 'Be careful of the sun.' And this after living in the tropics all their lives. His Mama was still the most beautiful woman he had ever seen. Tall and slender and elegant in anything she wore. Of course she knew exactly what to wear. She embroidered delicate little pieces, she played bits of larger pieces on the piano—'nothing too violent'. Distress caused headaches. They lived almost entirely on what her husband had left behind so thoughtfully. Neither of them really worked. Of course she cut the flowers and arranged them in all the rooms they actually lived in. For this she wore gloves. She was a perfectionist. Sometimes she took the greater part of an hour over the centrepiece for the dining table—the length of the stems, the colour—she must be able to see her boy even as they ate and conversed over the meal.

He worked very part-time in a bank. Their neighbourhood had changed over the years—as whose had not?—and sometimes Lusito was caused some distress by small boys calling out as he passed, 'Mama's boy! Here he comes; there he goes, our Mama's boy!' Of course he had not.

Once a friend of his Mama's had brought a visiting niece and Lusito enjoyed the young woman's company. His Mama observed this and said after they had left, 'Lusito, did you notice what vulgar feet that girl had?' And Lusito was ashamed at having enjoyed the visit so much. Now, over three years later, he wondered what his Mama would have made of Maria Amelia's feet—most of the year they were in open sandals and in the house she always padded around barefoot. He loved her feet. He hoped he would not mind if his Mama found her feet vulgar. He reminded himself that his Mama was dead. He still thought of everything in terms of his Mama. He wished he could stop. Surely, it was time. He had a mind of his own—it was just that he felt insecure, he had no real confidence. He remembered exactly what she had said, regarding feet: 'You can always tell from a person's feet and hands'—and he had asked, 'Tell what?' And she had said, 'Who a person is, of course, his background. We have always been the best for hundreds of years and you can tell from our feet and hands—try and remember that.' His own feet and hands were like his Mama's, pale and slender without a blemish—delicate. In his own country his work had never involved anything that might rub off on his hands—he was not really trained for any kind of work. His Mama had said, 'We are intelligent, and of a very good family, and where we need to work people will always realize this. It is their gain to employ people like us—you must never do a job that in any way makes you feel ashamed or embarrassed while you are doing it and when you are talking about it.'

Well, they had never talked about it, each evening when he came home. There was never anything to say—about his bank—and she greeted him as if he had just come home from a stroll through the park or along the promenade near the sea.

Here, of course, it was different. People rushed to the metro, or to catch buses or trams, carried briefcases (even Maria Amelia carried one for her translator's pamphlets, her tour maps, her lists of hotels and vouchers for coffee and lunch). Some of her tourists came from the strangest places. Each day's lists carefully typed by her, her own guidebooks marked with little strips of paper as she studied them each night for the next morning's tour. When she left each morning, so early, she would call out, 'I'm going to be late—don't forget we need bread, vegetables, don't wait for me, it's a late tour. I have my key.' And he would turn over and dream. Late in the evening he would go out and buy the things they needed and hurry back home. He called it home now and yet it was so different from his real home with Mama. That had been the house he was born in and lived all his life—large and set in a garden and so familiar. Of course, for many years most of the rooms were closed, everything covered in dust-sheets, but the rooms they had lived in were large, with carved and beautiful furniture, lovely things everywhere and, of course, Mama's flowers, arranged with her own hands.

Maria Amelia's apartment was one of many and there was a lift. He only knew the other occupants when he shared the lift with them or met them at their front doors putting their cats out. No dogs, no children. It was very quiet. The rooms were very small. The furniture too large for it. Sometimes they walked sideways to avoid bumping into things. No flowers. Once when Lusito had bought some Maria Amelia had said, 'We can't afford flowers, anyway, I don't like cut flowers—they have no life.' Seeing his face she had added, 'Perhaps on very exceptional occasions,' and when Lusito said, 'When, which exceptional occasions?' she said, 'The night you make love to me and do not think of your Mama, only me.' He had hated her for saying that. It had lain like a great heavy sword between them ever since. He had thought he was good at hiding things. After all, his Mama had never guessed about Maria Amelia. Not for three years. He really loved Maria Amelia so it troubled him. But the other love had been nearly all his life. Rather like the matter of his white suits.

When he had first come he had worn them till Maria Amelia had said, 'They are too expensive to look after and I don't have the time to do them myself. Perhaps you could dress like other people—?' So the white suits hung in the closet like pale ghosts of his past life. That is why he hurried to the shops in the dusk: he could not bear to be seen not wearing his white suit. He was afraid someone would see him and recognize him and he would lose his identity, something that he had brought with him when he came to this country. 'But,' he said, 'when I came here three years ago I wore those suits and you liked them, didn't you?'

'Yes,' she said, 'I liked them, but then you were a tourist, so it was charming, it was different, unusual. Tourists wear all kinds of clothes—but now it is different. You live here. Also it is not practical. Surely you realize it. They are not for ordinary days— maybe for special days like weddings or christenings or funerals.'

His Mama had always worn very feminine, very pretty flowered dresses in the summer, but then it was almost always summer in that country, always hot or very warm, and she had worn pretty hats, and carried a silk parasol, pale mauve and faded. Her husband, that is his father, had brought it for her from Venice. Maria Amelia wore jeans and large faded T-shirts at home and on holidays scuffed, many-times-mended open sandals, and for the tours an elegant appropriate uniform with a perky little cap. She never bothered much and she always looked nice.

That long-ago holiday when he had been a tourist seemed now set in a magical land, a time set-out of time. Not all of it, of course. The early part—when he first got there he had visited relatives and close friends of his Mama's youth—and then he had come to Lisbon. He had had just a week left. At his small hotel there had been a friendly man called Miguel who had said he must go north, there were wonderful things to be seen—Coimbra and Alcobaca and Batalya. There were good guided tours leaving every day. He must, otherwise he would miss much. So the very next morning he left for the first of these guided tours. He waited in a park with a tall equestrian figure and soon a bus with deep picture windows arrived and a young woman with a clipboard checked all their names and they set off . . . She and he had been delighted to speak in Portuguese. She pointed out many things as they left the city and made for the highway, she was pretty and she seemed to smile only at him. All day she remained fresh and pretty, never tired of pointing out places of interest, as they drove, little incidents about the landscape the pine forests or the vineyards, or a tower, a ruined monument. The first stop had been a charming small town, walled with cobblestones, and a castle called Obidos. Over coffee she asked him where he came from as he spoke Portuguese and he told her he was from Goa. At lunch he had hoped she might be at his table but she sat with her assistant and the driver of the bus. The place he liked very much was the cathedral at Alcobaca, twelfth-century gothic, pure soaring pillars white and unadorned, Batalya also, with marvellous Moorish cloisters and the beginnings of stained glass windows were a wonder to him—he had only known the great cathedral in old Goa the altars covered in gilt and much carving. He spoke to her of this and she was much interested and said she would love to visit Goa. He had not liked Fatima at all.

Two days later he went on another tour after he had checked very carefully that she would be the tour guide. Her name was Maria Amelia. They drove all along the River Tagus, they saw Santarem and Tomar. Again, he did not much care for what was supposed to be the high point of the day, the university town of Coimbra, the senate house chapel and Bibliotica—very ornate and crowded with tourists. He and Maria Amelia spoke at every opportunity but the day had to end. They exchanged addresses and telephone numbers and that was almost all. It was the last time he saw her but just before he left for home he managed to telephone her and tell her that he would come back. Soon.

When he got back he spent hours telling his Mama about the visits to all her relatives and friends and told it as if that had been the meat of his first holiday ever. He never told her about Maria Amelia. He knew instinctively that she would pretend no interest and become cold and distant. He could not mention how much he loved her. So he never spoke of her. Of course he spoke of Obidos and Batalya, of Alcobaca, and she loved the lace and the fan from Nazare and the statue and candles from Fatima. His secret he kept from her—it was the first and the only secret of his life. He filled his accounts with the wine and the food and the vineyards and the churches and the River Tagus and the Museum of Old Carriages, but he never mentioned Maria Amelia. He was afraid to do that. He felt that she would laugh about it or belittle the most important thing in his life. He went dangerously close—talking about the Moorish courtyard and cloisters of Alcobaca, but he never once mentioned Maria Amelia, his new love. At the end of his recitals his Mama would say, 'You seem to have managed very well to enjoy yourself without me.' And he felt ashamed and guilty but all he said was, 'But if you had been with me it would all have been so different so much more, much much more,' which was of course true and untrue.

'I have had a pain,' she said, 'an unusual, nagging pain in my side. It has troubled me, especially at night. I might have it seen to, though perhaps it will go away, just as it has come—now that you are back. After all, it came when you went away.'

But the pain did not go away but became much worse. Immediately, Lusito's holiday receded with all its joys, and he became troubled wondering, thinking only the worst. He had terrible forebodings. Something evil was growing inside her, causing her pain. Perhaps she was going to die. He could not imagine his life without her. The month away had been a dream—perhaps it had not really happened. Perhaps, he was being punished for having gone, punished for having met Maria Amelia. Punished for having forgotten his Mama. Punished for thinking only of his new love. He thought this even more strongly several months later when he sat with his Mama, hour after hour in the hospital, overlooking the water. The room was white and the bed was white and they kept his Mama so drugged against the pain that they could hardly talk to each other. He wanted to tell her he loved her so much and was so sorry he had gone away and enjoyed himself and made her so mortally ill. She wanted to tell him to take her home, not to let them operate on her, take her home, and let her rest in her own bed and arrange the flowers—carefully, taking an hour over each vase. Her eyes remained closed. He gazed out of the window at the barges moving from the river to the sea, and in the distance, the island of Dewar and lights from Piedade. Waiting.

When it was over he was so numb with the shock—dead almost of her pain—he was hardly able to understand what happened. But he performed all the rites for the dead correctly, and all the mourners murmured how brave he was, what a stoic he was. They did not know that it was easy for him because he had become a stone, a bit of ice inside. He wanted it to happen those last six months. He never wept for her—he had wept too often in that white room overlooking the waters. He performed all the tasks mechanically and with great correctness, often quite surprised that his Mama had not praised him for this or that. If she did, he could not hear her any more. When the forty days of mourning were over, he packed and he locked all the windows and doors and watered the flowers and closed the gate and left. He left for that other land, thinking, 'I can recapture that, after all it has only been three years, no more.' He would recapture all the joy and happiness of that other time and place because she was there.

It was not summer any more. It was raining when he arrived. For the first time he became a little afraid. He should have written, warned her. She would not know anything about what had been happening to him. Through the rain he saw that the evening was turning dark. He rang her number from the air terminal. He hoped she was not on a tour. After a while her voice answered, breathless, as if she had been running up the stairs. 'Who speaks, who speaks?' she said again. 'Sorry, I just came in, who is that?' He said, 'It's me,' and then a long, long pause. She was so calm and accepted him and told him how to get to her apartment. It was quicker than making him wait till she picked him up. Could he manage? He marvelled at her voice, and the fact that her life was the same—she had waited for him, she had not disappeared. He loved her all over again—for her constancy. He loved her for being in the same apartment, for not having a different telephone number. He loved her for not saying, 'It's late, we'll meet in the morning.' She had run up the stairs and answered the phone and not asked any questions. She had accepted the fact that he would come back. She had waited. He had not changed his pocket diary for three years, it contained only her address, her telephone number, the things they had seen and done together. Three years ago.

The street where she lived was very quiet and the streetlights were lit. Shaded lamps glimmered through curtains. His heart thumped hard, he knew he was alive again. And why. He was nervous even though he had heard her unchanged voice. She had met and talked and smiled and helped hundreds of people in three years but she had remembered him. He climbed the stairs. He rang her door bell. When it opened, it was her. It was her, in jeans and a T-shirt and nothing on her feet. She was smiling and welcoming.

The Quiet of the Birds

He wanted to cry. But he did not.

'So you did come back,' she said.

'I told you I would. Only it took so long. I had to wait—' he said.

'And now you have come—'

'Yes, you see I could not leave her—she would have been alone.'

'But now—you have left her—she will be alone.'

'No, she left me—she died, you see.'

'I'm sorry, that you waited so long—too long—I think.'

His heart like lead, he said, 'Will it not be the same—?'

'The same?' she said. 'Time does not stand still for three years— not for anyone. You did not write, not once, did you not think I too could not bear to be left so long?'

'No, I could not, she would have spoilt everything.'

'And now she cannot any more—is that what you mean?'

'Yes, that's it. Now I can start again—we can start again.'

'Perhaps. Have you eaten anything? Where are you going to stay?'

She gave him food and he said, 'Still, I wish you could have known Mama.'

'She is more real than I am, how could I fail to know her,' she said, looking at him as she handed him a glass of wine. As she made up a bed for him on the couch he looked out of the window and saw an old bag lady shuffling along and disappearing down some steps. Maria Amelia joined him at the window and said, 'She sleeps down in the metro. She has lived there all the years that I have lived here. She never moves to another street. I would miss her. Sometimes she is the only thing that moves on this street.'

It was very quiet. He wondered what it would be like in the morning. Feel like. He was very tired. He hoped he had not made a terrible mistake. What he had done might seem impulsive. He had not thought of anything else through all that had happened to him for three years. But there were affairs of the heart—one-sided. He would think about it in the morning. In the night he dreamed of the bag lady and then she became Mama and when it became unbearable he woke. It was morning. Maria Amelia had a tour. He watched her from the window, hurrying and then disappearing down the steps of the metro. He was filled with resolve. He would find a place to live—he would wait for Maria Amelia. He would wait till he was glad he had come back. It was just a matter of time. He had waited so long. In his mind. He had not shared that with her. For three long years—she had not known. But now he was here and she was here. It was the same bit of earth. With nothing in between. No shadows. No ghost. No Mama.

As he turned away from the window he saw the bag lady come up the steps of the metro to start her long day on the street. She was munching something and talking to herself. As he watched her she looked up suddenly and saw him at the window—her hand went up in a greeting, in recognition, and he saw that it was his Mama.

There Are No Brownies at
St. Anthony's

Of course a great many things had happened that year. Rather quickly, and yet the year couldn't really be said to have got into its stride. One afternoon, while she was watering her trees in pots on the terrace, she was told that her husband had died, and because she loved him very much and had spoken to him just that morning, of this and that as he left for work, she didn't believe it was true. She knew, but she didn't believe it had happened. She thought of it as something that happened to other people. She and her husband had spoken of it quite often but in the way that totally disbelieves such an occurrence could mar the even temper of their days and ways. Because she didn't really accept it she consequently did not grieve. Or rather, did not grieve enough in the way that might have helped her in the long run. She merely switched off one area, just blanked it out, and got on with bits and pieces of her life.

She walked the dog, she read, she wrote, she listened to music, she watched television. She dreaded the nights but managed with pills.

It was now that she realized she talked aloud to her husband, to herself and to the dog.

Then, the house—their home for twenty-five years, a sort of cottage-cum-bungalow with the nicer aspects of both, because it had been converted very creatively from a stable-cum-carriage house—she was told would be pulled down to build a nasty high-rise.

Then, just a week ago, with the first rather mild rains a magnificent gulmohur tree was uprooted, taking down a part of the roof and terrace. The crash was terrifying—in the very early hours of the morning still dark with a thin rain falling and falling as she rushed out in dressing gown and slippers to see what had happened. There it lay, its great height and its great spread torn out of the earth, spread-eagled with great splotches of red and orange everywhere. Its red flowers lay on the driveway, and in the flower-beds and on the parked cars and drifted down to her rubber slippers. Blood everywhere. Because of erosion and white ants there seemed no way to save the dying tree but she had wept and stormed saying over and over, 'But we could try, at least we could try to save it, they could get a crane and hold it upright—hold it with ropes, at least try.' But four men had come that very afternoon and started chopping it up. They stripped down to their shorts. They laughed and joked as they straddled the tree and ate paan and hacked and hacked at the branches, and flung them down to the ground, spitting red paan juice on to the red carpet below. By late evening they began to sharpen their chain-saw and ruthlessly carried on with the massacre. She hated them all. Even if it was just a job of work, even if they were being paid to do it as quickly as possible, there was no need to be so clearly enjoying themselves. The man supervising the operation was a lout who smoked constantly and cheekily hung his umbrella on one of the branches from where it swung. When furiously she had snatched it down he merely looked at her as though she was a foolish old woman, and casually spat and lit another cigarette. She had rushed out of her house so often to watch and somehow protect the tree from further assault and indignity that her house was strewn with crushed red and orange blossoms from the tree. Crushed into the carpet and the doorway and her rubber chappals spread the blood everywhere.

The next morning she had rushed to the window because she couldn't see the great tree of red from where she lay—and realized it was true. Yesterday, had, in fact, happened. The tree was just not there any more. No tree, no great spread of green, no canopy of flaming red. A gap. An ugly bit of a high-rise. Just the stripped carcass, a yellowish-white underbelly showing. They had done their job well. No one seemed to care. The newspaper boy did not glance that way, merely chucked the furled paper as usual. The old bread man did glance but turned away. The postman delivered the letters as usual. No one living in the lane even mentioned it—the fact that the tree was dead. That the tree was not there any more. They must have seen it every day for much longer than she had. Every day as she walked the dog. Every day when she had left for work and come back every day for twenty-five years. The first thing she saw as she turned in at the gates—different in different light, morning, noon and late evening. Different in the summer, different in the rain. Years and years ago she had left the pram under that tree so that the child would look up and feel the tree, see the sky through the leaves, see the leaves and the branches, learn all about it long before she could speak or walk. Like all the music you play to a baby so that it enters the senses, and remains.

And then there was the dog.

So there really were reasons enough for distress, for not sleeping, for wandering about the house in the semi-dark, checking from time to time that the dog was still breathing. Pleased and sad when he padded after her to the kitchen as she made a mug of coffee and cheated with the first cigarette of the day. He was thirteen years old this year, he had been ill and now was well again but different. His face looked older—thin around his most beautiful eyes, and grey. Where he had looked golden and white he was grey. Also he had trouble with the stairs—seemed to grope, hesitate and fumble and sometimes even miss his step altogether. In a certain light she could see a milky greeny bluey inside-a-well sort of look in one of his eyes but she refused to think about it. Her husband would have helped her to face all these changes. He had a way of calming fear. A way of dealing with anxiety and sadness. He would have helped her to face the great emptiness, now he was gone. But she was alone.

She felt sometimes a great anger towards him for going the way he had. He might have waited for her—or allowed her to go first.

One day her visiting daughter said, 'You are to come with us—just a short holiday, Ma, it will be good for you, just a fortnight and you'll feel better. We'll go to your favourite place and after that you can make up your mind about coming to live with us. We want you with us.' She had protested, of course, saying she was all right—why should she need a holiday, why were they fussing, they hadn't fussed before, she would be all right. Anyway it was just that she hadn't been 'sleeping too well—it happens, it's happened before—really'. But her daughter and son-in-law hadn't listened to her, had helped her to pack and just swept her off for a 'see Goa in the rains' holiday. Looked at in a certain way, of course, it was so sweet and dear of them to have worried about her enough to plan this holiday with them. But she hoped they weren't thinking that 'old Mom is getting odd again, like she sometimes does—it's been a long time since the last time but it always starts with not being able to sleep.' She would prove them wrong. That's all. She was feeling a kind of *tristeza de corazon*, a kind of heart-breaking. Everyone felt it, knew it, some time or the other. It's just that some people disguised it better. Or pretended better.

Arriving in Goa was always so immediate. Its assault complete even before she had unpacked. She had never come before in this season. Everything was being readied for the rains. Her small cottage faced the sea and from her balcao it was all sea or seemed to be except for the green hill. The air smelled different. The sea was a different colour. Angry coloured. The waves were high, and a yacht bobbed about at a short distance. Why have they not taken it in yet, she thought. Maybe the monsoons had not really come yet, though everything was being got ready for it. But they should take in the yacht, it's madness to leave it there with the sea looking like that. But they know best, after all they have dealt with their boats season after season. Maybe they will take it in tomorrow.

All the other boats were in, even the wooden platforms had been put on high ground and nearly all the sun umbrellas made of coconut palm thatch all stacked and safe under tarpaulin. She heard the clean sound of cutting shears close by. They were pruning the hedge of yellow flowers in front of all the cottages. Real pruning. Almost down to the mother roots. All around in neat high piles the already cut, sheared-away alamanda flowers, their leaves still such a healthy shiny green. Terrible business, pruning, and such drastic pruning as this. But then the soil was so rich in two months it would all be back, lush and thick and green with the ploppy, clear-yellow trumpet flowers. Some of the cottages were spared she noticed—her own, her daughter's and some others. 'Maybe they will prune when we have gone.' Good. She would not think about it till later. In a strange sort of way it was exciting. All the preparing as if for the day of battle. Barricades to be set up against the enemy. Soon the storm would break. But now hundreds of dragonflies flew up disturbed, flying in different directions. She hoped it wouldn't happen while they were here. Rain, gloom and doom, she thought. Don't let it rain and rain. Or if it must, let it rain all through the night. And give me clear days. That's fair, she decided.

People who had observed the woman with white hair said later, 'Well, yes, we did notice her, she was unusual in some ways. Quiet and yet animated, read a lot lying in the sun, seemed to scribble a lot too, smoked a lot, rather outspoken—pulling up other people's children, that sort of thing. Told one of the guests to pick up a coconut he'd just chucked out on the front lawn (mind you he was so shocked he did pick it up).'

The staff, particularly room service, liked her very much, wanting her early morning coffee really early and in her balcao she always talked to them about their villages and where they had gone to school and how long it took them to get to work and so on. Others observed that she collected shells like a girl and swam every day at the same time, not in the pool but always in the sea, though it was rather rough, often tumbling her down with its strength.

Some noticed that she talked to herself. Others still, that on the nights when a rather good group played and sang during dinner she applauded with enjoyment and went to talk to the group and thank them, even telling them that had her husband been with her they would have danced to nearly everything they played. She never left the table with her daughter and her son-in-law, but left when the band packed up, then walked a while on the beach before turning in.

During the second week of the holiday she followed the same pattern, unvarying. The very-early morning coffee on the balcao, then the lying or sitting in the sun, then the collecting of shells, then the swimming in the rough sea and gazing at the yacht still left out at sea, then the reading and writing till the sun changed and evening began to come, then a long walk on the beach often joined by her daughter and then dinner in the open dining area near the pool.

One late evening a terrible storm came up. Sudden deafening thunder and great flashes of lightning and the woman with white hair became very agitated. The boat, she said, should be taken in, they had left it till so late but even now they must take the boat in.

The next evening again there was an even more dramatic and very beautiful storm and the waves were very high and the lightning lit up the green hill. This time the woman with white hair went to the reception and said they must take that poor boat in, they must, it could not withstand such a fierce storm. But the boat club was closed and there really was no one to deal with this now. Truth to tell, they didn't take her too seriously—another woman kept ringing room service about a frog in her room. A girl of four screamed right through the storm.

It poured with rain nearly all night. The next morning was calm and peaceful again. But when she went out on to her balcao she noticed immediately that the boat was gone. It just wasn't there any more.

She set off to look for it. She found it at the very end of the beach where the high rocks began. Its keel was smashed, its sides all battered, aground on the rocks. Its mast tilted bravely and its name intact: FIRSTBORN. She sat down next to it. She stayed there till the others came. Men with useless ropes. Later, nobody could remember anything else upsetting happening. She seemed the same for the rest of the day, and even the next day.

The day after she walked into the sea.

Just like that. There were quite a lot of people, as it happens, playing, and splashing about in the sea. It was far too rough to actually swim. And that's when this happened.

At first she was there, walking in the sandy shallow bit, and then just kept straight on. She was wearing a sari. She just walked into the sea. And that was it. Nobody panicked really, at first. Some hadn't noticed. With those who had, it was a case of delayed action. They were too shocked to begin to move. They just could not believe they had seen what they had. And by the time they did it was too late. It was too late for anything at all.

Of course after that it was pandemonium. Knots of people. Children crying. The manager, a doctor. The daughter and the son-in-law could not be found, and then were.

Surely nothing could be so bad, nothing could be so terrible, people were saying. Could be heard to be saying. How could she? How could anyone just walk into the sea? Deliberately?

That morning her daughter had walked over from her cottage saying, 'Ma, we are crossing over in the ferry to the other side. It will make a change—we could eat at St. Anthony's—you will come?'

And her mother had said, 'Thank you for asking, but I'll stay here—I'd much rather—have a good time.'

And her daughter had said, 'Are you sure, Ma? Is there anything you need, or want? Will you be all right?'

And her mother had said, 'Of course I'll be all right. And, yes, there is something I'd like from the other side of the water—do you remember those lovely brownies from St. Anthony's. Will you bring me some?'

'Of course, Ma, is that all? See you then.'

And that is why they couldn't find the woman's daughter and son-in-law when the dreadful thing happened. And when they did come back from the other side of the water, the distraught girl kept repeating over and over, 'St. Anthony's was closed, Ma, so we couldn't get you your brownies, it was closed for the rains so we couldn't get the brownies you asked for, I'm so sorry, Ma, it's the only thing you asked for and we couldn't get them.' This went on for a long while till a doctor managed to give her some sedation. It took a long time to work and she kept muttering over and over, 'I wish we could have got Ma the brownies, if only St. Anthony's had been open—'

'Poor girl, poor girl,' people began to say, and in their Indian sort of way, curious, 'But where is the lady's husband?' They began to ask the quiet young man. Though he did not want to talk to them and wished they would all go away, he said, 'He died, he's dead, he died quite recently—perhaps, that's the reason, that may be the reason—you know—I mean, was this an accident or what?

What is being thought, what, we were not here?' Then he stopped talking for a long while.

After a while he said, 'She could not have planned to do this— why would she have asked us to bring her back those brownies, she loved those particular brownies, she asked her daughter to bring back some, just this morning before we left. It must have been an accident. Maybe she went out too far, maybe she got knocked down by a wave, swallowed a lot of sea water, something like that. She can't possibly have just walked into the sea, nobody does a thing like that. I mean, they may feel terrible but they would never, never do that—' He had said a great deal for such a quiet man.

And he started again, saying, 'Perhaps we left her alone too long, too often, didn't ask her enough about how she was feeling. Perhaps we should have talked to her more, but then she was a private person, she wanted to be alone.'

The doctor realized by now that the young man needed some sedation too.

'Is there anyone to inform, we would like to help in any way we can,' the manager said. At last, after some thought, the quiet son-in-law said, 'No, I don't think so. No, there is no one else to inform in that sense, but there is her dog, he will be waiting and that's going to be difficult—'

People started wandering off, they had seen and heard enough, more was not to be borne.

The manager, kind, but really upset with all this happening, and at the end of the season, wondering how this would affect the monsoon package—'See Goa in the rains'—said, 'We will, of course, make all the arrangements, perhaps you should try and sleep or at least rest. Our doctor could help you—' Saying which he left.

The young man, not wanting any help from the doctor, was left alone at last with his wife who slept fitfully, turning from time to time muttering something that sounded like 'brownies and saints'. He walked about the room and then let himself out quietly on to the balcao. He sat down and listened to the sea and thought about his mother-in-law. His thoughts were terrifying. He kept thinking about her, alone and small, walking out into the sea. This sea, he

The Quiet of the Birds

thought, that I can sense and hear, that has been close to us from the moment we arrived. For close on a fortnight she had seen it and heard it from early in the morning to late at night and she had thought her thoughts all by herself. He began to feel quite angry with her after a while. After all, he thought, she liked being by herself, she liked reading and scribbling stuff, and lying in the sun for hours. We couldn't have spoilt that part of her holiday for her. Only perhaps, that was it, that beastly, perhaps. Perhaps we should have been with her more—somehow. Talked to her more when we were with her. Anyway, it must have been an accident. It was an accident. She had been calm and poised, loving the music of the hotel band, they had played each night so many of her old favourite songs. She had walked every day, collected shells.

But it had been her first time here alone, without her husband. They should have remembered that more often—kept it more in mind, been more thoughtful of it no matter how she had seemed. They should not have brought her here at all. That was the real point. They had not thought it through. It must have all been too much for her—she hadn't grieved enough when it happened—so now here, where she and he had come so often, all their lives.

It had been her first time alone and in this season. Restless, knowing he would not sleep, he thought, 'I shall pack her things so that her daughter won't have to think about it tomorrow'— Thinking this, he walked across to her cottage. Except for the very first evening when they had foregathered here for a sort of start-of-a-holiday drink he had not come here. The room was very tidy. Very quiet. He went straight to the cupboard and found her small suitcase. He had always been a good packer. He packed swiftly— her clothes, her toilet things and then moved to her bedside table to pack her books. Here he paused and sat on her bed, reading the titles, feeling the awful unreality of it all. She had brought with her a small leather bound *Sonnets of Shakespeare*, an old worn copy of *Voss* and the very new Nadine Gordimer. He felt some familiar things were missing: her spectacles, her cigarette case, her pens, her journal—of course, they must be on her balcao.

He went out. Here he stopped short and sat down. Here he seemed able to relive her morning, some part of it at least. He saw her rubber chappals with sand on them, shells laid out in neat rows. On the table her spectacles, her silver cigarette case, her journal, a couple of biros. Everything lay as if she had sat where he was sitting now and then decided to go for her swim. As he picked up her journal her old blue leather bookmark fell to the ground, he bent to pick it up and replace it. Instead, he read in her untidy scrawl:

Woke so early again, the sound of the sea very loud, went out into the balcao very quietly as if he were fast asleep and I must let him sleep because this was our holiday. It must have rained hard during the night, everything washed so clean. Two old women and a young boy gathering clams in the rocks—and the yacht is not in its usual place, it is nowhere, it is not where it was last evening. It must have broken free finally from its anchor. How could they let it happen? Perhaps, though, they have taken it into safety.

There is no one to tell. I would have told him and we could both have gone to look for it. Everything has lost its savour, it's not just that I don't think I can manage much longer alone, but that I don't want to any more. Perhaps long relationships are a frightening thing—they make one so dependent, the habit of sharing so much without realizing it. I think I have tried for a time, but there really does not seem much point—day after day without our life together. I don't really make all that much difference to anyone's life except the dog and I know he'll be loved and learn to forget. Before I really get old and become a burden, or sick and become a worry—God, there goes Mom again—she's behaving odd—I think, and yet again I think if I get over this great hill, this difficult hill of missing him and not managing anything properly—maybe I'll be all right. Maybe, if I could live each day carefully, just one day at a time, then maybe—but I cannot. The months loom ahead, the years and years ahead are too terrible to contemplate.

The Quiet of the Birds

I must find the yacht. Today the gardeners will prune my bit of alamanda. Also I really can hear his voice saying, 'Let's cross over in the ferry to the other side of the waters today, I'll have sarpotel at St. Anthony's and you can get your brownies—'

That's where the journal stopped, she had stopped writing it.

He closed the journal and collected her shells and her rubber chappals, and her cigarette case, her spectacles and her pens and went into the cottage as it began to rain.

Wedding

Well I'd been staring a while out of the window of my kitchen which looks out on a most peaceful back garden of a church. It has a naked white lady who gleams in the moonlight and glistens when it rains. The naked lady is a real silver birch of a beautiful shape. Tall white lady with long white legs. First cigarette and first cup of coffee. When I heard a letter plop through the letterbox. It was an invitation to a wedding. My son marrying someone and would I come to the wedding. Also a little note from my son's stepmother. So I thought I have nothing to lose. I have nothing to wear. And I thought why not? He's the last of my five. And I thought after all he's my firstborn. And I thought well all that was a long time ago. And I thought after all why not? And it was so cold here. There it would be warm again. Warm all day.

Just then it started raining again. Outside the naked lady gleamed in the morning light. And she thought, that's it. Well that decides it. I'll go. I'll diet a bit. Get into some shape. I'll walk every day in Hyde Park. And no more Mrs Crimbles chocolate muffins. Not one. Till after the wedding. No more beer. No more chips with everything. When everything started feeling bleak and impossibly abstemious she locked up the flat and went to see Anna. Anna was her good friend. Anna was Spanish and beautiful and wise and a good listener. Anna missed her children back in Spain. Of course you have to go. No one stays away from a wedding, a son's wedding. Are you mad. Even if you didn't, couldn't, go to the wedding of your other four children you will go to this one. You've been invited. They want you. And you are his mother. His real mother. You'll always regret it. You have to go. She left Anna really convinced. She resolved to shape up. She had almost a month. She replied to the invitation. Said, of course, she would be there. She'd be honoured. And thanks for asking me.

Next day she started her strict regimented life. No more comfort foods. No chocolates, no sweets, no beer, no white bread, butter. No chips with everything. Lots of water. First walking for half an hour and then for an hour Sundays included. No munching anything from the fridge while watching TV. Just sugar-free chewing gum was okay.

She started growing out her hair. One night not so long ago she had chopped it off in a rage of self-pity. It looked as if it had been chopped off with a knife and fork. She'd have it shaped properly just before she left.

The days passed slowly. The days were very hard. She felt cold and hungry all the time. The days were very long. She felt she had bitten off far more than she could manage. She felt stupid. She didn't know why she had agreed to go. The invitation was just a formality. And she'd fallen for it. What did that make her?

Other days she felt triumphant that she'd made it through the day. Often towards evening without her many beers or G&Ts she felt lonely and bleak, her whole life gone. She'd stand looking out of her kitchen window at the stone and the stained glass window and the naked lady and she'd think I'm the scarlet lady. I'm the tramp. I'm the worst. I ran away. I abandoned five children. I never went back. Often she was cheerful with the new day and thought, 'After all I'm the first, after all, I was exhausted. All the time. I'd had five babies. I was so young. I had no time for myself. All day and night feeding them and bathing them and rocking them and staying up half the night. And all this over and over. Five times over. And I was only twenty-three. My whole life was over. I could see no future.

My young days were over. The days of my youth was changing diapers and sterilizing bottles and losing my figure and my hair. Twenty-three. No adults to talk to. Her life felt over. Was over.

So she ran away. She just upped and left. And then she was afraid to go back. She knew why she'd left. But it wasn't something she'd be able to explain.

It would always come down to 'But how could you leave all your children. Five children. Unheard of. Unnatural.' She never went back. And the years passed. She never explained. Her side. And so the stories grew. And grew. Monster.

But now she'd walk and jog and starve and go back. It was time. She'd raise a toast to the young couple. They'd allow her that. It was her right. She was after all the birth mother. That should count for something. She'd borne him and looked after him for nearly six years and a bit. Apart from the other four younger ones. That should count for a great deal. She'd work on her speech. She didn't want to sound like the wife of Bath. She didn't want to sound defiant. She didn't want to sound too abject. She wanted to hit just the right note. She wanted. In the meantime she walked, she jogged, she starved, she stayed beerless. Also she planned what she would wear. She dreamt of how she would look. She planned to look good. Better. She planned to look stunning. So that even if they didn't listen to her they'd have to look at her. She hoped there'd be a mike. Her voice was rather soft. And she'd be nervous so it might break or something she'd always wanted to use a mike. Like a crooner. It always looked so sexy. She didn't want to sound like a girl, reading out a school composition on 'My Son's Wedding'—or 'Thoughts of a Mother' or the 'Musings of an Errant Woman'. She would say, 'Ladies and Gentlemen. I'd like to say a few words.' Yes that was best. 'I'd like to say a few words. I live in a house called Marina Dourade, a Portuguese singer lived there for many years. Now I have lived there for many years. I live alone— now this was just for starters. Now for the main meal—'

Somehow, the waiting month was over. She had lost weight. Her hair did look less chopped up and she got on the plane but that's when the jitters started. Anna at the airport had said, 'Now have something to drink to calm your nerves and then take off your shoes and go to sleep. Promise?' 'Promise,' she had said. Easier said than done. She was cold with fright. She really was afraid. What had she let herself in for. She wished herself back at her kitchen window looking out at the naked lady. She wished she was safe with Anna. She didn't know any of her children. It was all alien territory. She was the bad guy. She was the outsider. She asked for a G&T and then another and another. She ate some nuts and then another G&T. Soon she'd had a month of G&Ts and it was landing time.

She came out after all the formalities blinded by the glare, the heat, the guilt, the fear. Through a crowd of faces and placards, she saw the dear, familiar face of old Ram Singh. He greeted her warmly. He was the same. The car was different. When he greeted her she nearly wept. She put on her dark glasses. Thank God for something to hide behind. If old Ram Singh the driver makes you feel like weeping, what will you do later when you meet the children, you old booby? She'd keep her dark glasses on. She'd pretend to be Garbo. I want to be alone. She could be anything she wanted to be in that darkness. She would scatter her enemies, she would be a mystery to her friends.

And now I will sleep till the evening. And then I will dress. Most carefully. And please, please, she wished crossing her fingers— Let me look really nice. Let me not shame my children. Let me be the envy of their stepmother. Let my husband of so long ago say, 'My word and who could that gorgeous creature be?' She had a long bath and got into bed in a darkened room. And she woke to real darkness. She thought she was back in Marina Dourade. She wished she was there at her kitchen window looking out at the naked lady. She couldn't. She couldn't bear to be where she now was. She couldn't see the night unfold. And then she began to transform herself and after a while she was ready. She turned this way and that. Having grown unaccustomed to wearing a sari she took a while to adjust to this new image in the mirror.

It was the best she could do. And she was done. She wished she could hear a voice saying, 'Take her anywhere.' But now she was late. She broke into her Duty Free and had two drinks quickly and felt better. And then she couldn't find her carefully written out 'toast' to the bride and groom. She grew frantic and it was now really late. I can remember it anyway. Most of it. Who needs a scrap of paper. I'll be all right.

She knew that she'd arrived when she saw bright coloured lights and heard music and the singer was belting out, 'Pleasure with you was always a treasure, do it to me, baby, oh do it to me.' She was very late. All the guests were seated having their dinner. She couldn't see anyone she knew. Maybe she wasn't really looking. She saw people bent over their plates—their food, their wine. There was someone at the mike on the small raised platform. That someone was her husband. He looked almost the same. He looked so different. He was saying, 'and now if anyone would like to say a few words on this occasion do come and speak'—For a while or two no one went. So she went. The moment was right. She adjusted the mike and said, 'I would like to say a few words, at the wedding of my eldest son.' She heard or thought she heard a flutter of little gasps and whispers and she repeated, 'My eldest son and his bride. I wish them well, I wish them happiness. No matter how many marriages turn out unhappy people still risk it so there must be a way to be happy and married. Perhaps the answer is to work at it. Not to take anything for granted, always to care and not to care too much. I have no answers. But I would like my son to know that I tried at mine and failed. And because of that failure on my part and all the heartbreak that followed I have thought a lot in all these years about how difficult it is to be a good woman, a good wife, a good mother. I have asked myself, how should a good woman live, how should a good wife and mother live? Try. We try. That's all I can say. We try. But I would urge my eldest son to always be aware of the difficulties. It is very difficult to be a good woman and fulfil all the so-called conditions. He should always be aware of the difficulties and never ignore the day-to-day problems. Because that's what marriages are about. Small problems. Big problems. Don't let them mount, take all the time, never bottle up anything and never go to sleep having quarrelled. Having said a harsh word. Understand. Talk about everything. Talk everything through. I failed. But I also tried. That's the main thing. And remember most deaths at least the death of marriages are from heartbreak. Most of us die of heartbreak and a lot of the time this does not show. But it's a killer. But my life has done one good thing. No child of mine will ever try to be like me, and that's a blessing. But still, I have a place. And for a short while or long, I had my place. Now I have another. That's all. I wish you well in your happiness and joy and in your unhappiness and sadness because your days will contain a good measure of both. I'm sorry I've said too much, put it down to the power of having a mike in your hand. Anyway, not to worry. I'll not be singing "Feelings" or "The lady is a tramp". I know when to stop milking the moment.'

The Quiet of the Birds

She stumbled off the platform and left the room.

Afterwards, that is, after the shock, the children were in tears even the sons-in-law and daughters-in-law. After a few guests tried to sing Christmas carols, it being close to that season, but failing miserably everyone went home.

Getting ready for bed the erstwhile husband said to his second wife, 'You are very quiet. I thought everything went off rather well—didn't you?'

'Oh yes,' said his second wife and stepmother of his five children, 'even the Tiramisu was really good. I'm rather tired as it happens and I'm rather sad. I was happy for a long time. But now I'm sad.'

'You're not thinking about that woman—surely she is not the reason you are sad.'

'That woman, as you call her, was your wife. She has a name. She is also the mother of all your children. What she said made me sad.'

'Why think about what she said, she always did analyse everything to death. I'm not thinking about her or what she said. It's all in the past. In fact it was rather cheek, her turning up like that—'

'I wanted her—I invited her and I think it was very courageous of her to come. And as for your remark, "It's all in the past," what's that supposed to mean? The past is what we are. Surely you must have learnt that by now. We are nothing without the past. We are the past.'

'Try not to be too thinking, there's a dear. Sleep on it. It will all feel different in the morning. You'll see. Sleep now.'

He turned over and away from her. He switched off the light. For a long while she lay awake in fact till the light of a new day crept up and all she could think was 'How should a good woman live? How?' And then she thought, don't give anybody grief. It lasts a lifetime.

The first wife arrived at the airport and found her eldest son waiting for her and he hugged her and asked her why she had left all that time ago. 'Tell me now, I have to know. I need to know. I was too young before. Now I need to know.'

And she said, 'Well I left really because your father was a mean man. He never could praise me for anything I did. The food I cooked, the new flower that I helped to grow, the new child born to us. The way I looked. Never a word of praise, only blame all the time. And I was young. Far too young. He never encouraged me in anything I tried to do and at eighteen and nineteen and twenty-one one is so vulnerable, and sensitive and he never never had a good word for me. I got more and more miserable and disheartened I began to be afraid as evening came knowing he'd be back from work with a disparaging word. I think it was those ways of his that gradually made me lose my sense of being able to accomplish anything. I felt useless and increasingly hopeless, and then he criticized the way I looked. I kept getting fatter with each pregnancy, never able to lose the weight I gained. He'd praise other women and their lovely bodies, slim women. I felt lumpen and ugly. He really was a mean man your father. His cruelty was like this. He never was cruel except in this way, but it worked in breaking me and I began to wonder why I put up with it day after day, year after year and no one to share it with. I was so ashamed. He had managed to make me feel ashamed of myself. I had to get out, I was ashamed of myself for taking it. Maybe that's why he dished it out so relentlessly day after day. So one day I left. It was the hardest thing I ever did. But I did it. I could never forget what I did. Ever. The guilt pursued me all the days I have lived away from you. My children would never understand, they would never forgive me. Still you asked me, my son, and so I have told you what I never told anyone before. One life to live. I had to start. And I did. Perhaps you will understand. Perhaps not. But I would want you to think of things I have said in terms of your new young wife. Think of her. Think of her all the time.' She embraced her son. And then it was time to leave. She went through the door that said 'Security'.

End Cottage

And one evening on one of their walks they found it. The cottage. They had walked for a long time. They were tired but they persisted, wanting to find the perfect place to watch the sunset from. The notice board said, 'Nursery plants and flowers for sale. Cottage for hire (rent).' It was so charming—like an afterthought so they went in through the gate. The owner/gardener showed us the cottage. The view took our breath away. Time stood still. All the clichés in the world could not describe the perfection of the cottage. Two rooms, a neat bathroom and living room and a deep veranda and a private garden with a bench and a swing under a great tree. And the view. The view and sweet peas, wild roses and of all things wonderful, even gardenia. We had tea sitting on the bench and watched our first of hundreds of sunsets. We sat till the colours changed and darkness came. Of course we took the cottage for the night and most of the next day. 'Just for starters, just to test its ghosts, just to feel that it approves of us as much as we do.' And so that's how it happened. How it began.

That year we stayed in the cottage a whole week in the dead of summer. And then two weeks when the rains broke. And then a whole month in the winter. The cottage adapted to every season. 'The view' kept changing with the light and the garden flourished except in the dead centre of the rainy season. Soon the owner/gardener realized they only wanted to stay in Cottage No. 1 so he never gave it out to anyone without first checking with them. It became theirs virtually. So they began to bring books and favourite cushions and bedspreads, music and pictures.

The place became their own. One day the owner asked if they were in a position to buy Cottage No. 1. Strangely it all worked out. They sold their home of thirty-three years, the trucks and lorries were filled with their lives, their books and their paintings and some of their favourite furniture and all their potted plants and trees. They left the big city forever.

They renamed their cottage 'End Cottage' and really moved in. For a long while it was perfect. Their life was so simple. They walked. They read. They wrote. They sat in their garden and looked at their view. They sat in their veranda and looked at their view. They found a new walk nearly every evening and found a new place to watch the sunset from. Yet every day was quite different. New. When the rains came it was exciting and the earth good enough to eat. The rain beat on their roof. It drummed on their roof. The thunder felt far and suddenly very near. The lightning was brilliant and lit up the sky and then sliced it into jagged ribbons.

The winter skies were very dark, very quiet and full of wonderful bright stars.

They noticed everything as if for the first time. It was as if they had looked but never really seen things before, not properly anyway. Bird songs in morning. The hum of insects in the lazy afternoons. Frogs croaking in the lily ponds. The nose of the Duke, arrogant but familiar.

Every night she prayed that all this might last forever. Well if not forever then for a very long time. Of course it didn't.

One quite ordinary evening, RK said he had a lump. He had thought that it was an insect bite. It had persisted though and was now quite large and hard. He thought he might get it checked. She merely said, 'Good we'll both go down. I'm due for my check-up and also need to do some bibs and bobs.'

But the day turned into a nightmare. Days really. They went from one doctor to another. And from one check-up to another. And then one test to many tests. And then the waiting. Not just the waiting in waiting rooms, but waiting for the results of tests. By the last day of many a kind of writing appeared on the wall of their lives. 'I'm sorry,' said RK. 'I am so sorry for spoiling everything. I'm sorry. Really sorry.' And she said, 'How could you know, there was not anything you could have done. I'm sorry for all this, I don't want you to have to suffer. I couldn't bear that. I wish it had happened to me. It's so unfair. Why? Why? How will you bear this grief?'

One doctor said, 'We can't operate because of the position of the lump.' Another doctor said, 'Chemotherapy and then radiation is the way to go. After a course we decide what to do. We must see how you respond to the treatment.'

RK said he'd need to think about this, about a lot of things. They took the results and the findings and the doctor's recommendations. They went back to the cottage. They sat on the veranda as the sun was setting. A complete different world. It felt so safe. They felt less fraught. No white coats and stethoscopes and smell of disinfectant. No large yellow envelopes with the X-rays and the results of X-rays.

This side up. Handle with care.

Here it was peaceful—the air so clean and fragrant. The view was theirs. It was reliable, it was unchanging.

But as the sunset pink turned purple and then grey and then dark they knew that decisions had to be made. Things to discuss. Things to decide. It was a world they knew nothing about. An alien world. A shocking world—they felt as if someone they knew had been murdered. It would be with them now for a long while.

RK said, 'I have made my decision and I hope you can bring yourself to agree with me.' She waited. A late bird swooped down out of the sky. The sky was now really black. She waited.

RK said, 'I cannot go the chemotherapy way. It will spoil everything for a long while and then if it is not successful it will be so useless and such a waste of precious time. I will not be able to work or be here with you. And I will lose all my hair,' he smiled. 'But I met a most unusual doctor. And I would like to go the way of Dr Anand. He understood what I was saying. I told him about my writing, about our cottage. He said there was one other option. One other way. The way of doing nothing at all. Nothing.'

She said, 'So it's inoperable?'

RK said, 'Yes.'

She said, 'And when the pain starts and becomes difficult to bear?'

RK said, 'He will give me medication for the pain. As much as I need.'

She said, 'And what else?'

RK said, 'Nothing else, just painkillers of strength.'

She said, 'So you and this doctor have decided to do nothing, nothing at all?'

RK said, 'Yes that's about it.'

She said, 'And how long have they given you, if you do nothing at all?'

RK said, 'Well, they feel a year or more, or less.'

She said, 'So you don't want to fight this thing, this awful thing. You want to give up before it's really started?'

RK said, 'Well, that's the other finding. This awful thing hasn't just started. The lump is just the outward manifestation—according to him it's been with me a long time. It's been silent but there, spreading for quite a while. Dr Anand told me everything. He was very frank. He helped me in my choice of the more "dignified end". His words. I really don't want to be a mess and not know what is happening at the end. I want to be here with you in this cottage.' He wept then. There really was nothing more to say. For now.

She wept for a long while thinking of their lives together. She wept for when she would be without him. She wept for the long time alone. She wept for the unfairness. She wept for everything. She wept for all the suffering for him. She wept because she had thought the big C happened to other people. RK let her cry but he hugged her and they sat on their swing till it really was night and the moon came out. RK said, 'Don't worry about things too much, it really is for the best. I'm glad I met Dr Anand. He has promised to help us in every way. And we can stay here, we don't have to ever leave this place. Think of that. And the pain may not come for a long while yet. So.'

They went inside and drew the curtains. She thought that night of how they had named their cottage 'End Cottage' without dreaming what it might signify.

She thought everything will change from now on. From this day. This night. Everything. And she cried again thinking RK was asleep.

RK was not asleep. And he knew she was crying. There was nothing he could say to her. There seemed no comfort anywhere.

But the next morning brought hope. Morning always seems to do that. It was fresh and new. The air smelt clean and a few birds and then many wheeling about in the sky and the garden smelt and looked like heaven. It was impossible to believe last night. Impossible to believe that their good times were over. They couldn't believe that the reality was different. And that all this was just a beautiful picture frame.

RK said, 'Today we will talk about things. It's not going to be so terrible. There is this place for a start. How amazing that we found it. Almost as if it was needed, was necessary. Which of course it is. Greatly so. I'm sure we couldn't have borne things in the big city. Things somehow don't feel so dire here, don't you think? No sounds of cars and impatient horns honking and streets and streets of parked cars and pavements dug up like First World War trenches. No angry shouting voices, no garbage. This heavenly view, this garden. It's a miracle and we just stumbled across it. We'll have good times for a long while yet. And when the bad times start I'll face them. I'll have you with me. But we'll not think of it for ages and ages yet. What do you think? Shall we walk or do you first want to swing and read.'

She felt so much better after that, the unnaturalness seemed gradually to slip away and she was sucked into the peaceful feel of the place.

Day followed day and became weeks and then months. The doctor had been right about RK. He was in no pain. Of course he became very thin and began to look as he had looked as a very young man. Of course she worried but only privately. Often she had little weeps in the bathroom.

The good doctor managed to come up every so often and so they never had to go down to the grim city hospital and then when it was nearly a year the bad times began. The bad times. She began to keep a journal for the good doctor and for herself. She wrote about when RK pretended to eat. The food pushed round and round his plate. When RK pretended he wanted to go for a walk. When RK pretended to be working but wrote not one single word all morning. When RK sat on the swing or on the bench all day. Not doing anything. When the pain began. For a long while the tablets helped. Then gradually the tablets just were not enough. The good doctor gave him other painkillers, she knew they were getting stronger and stronger.

But soon he was in a daze of pain and surfaced only every now and again. When he did surface he was RK again, asking her questions, wanting to hear music, sit in the garden. Smiling the old smile. Asking why she didn't go for a walk he'd be fine here, as the sun was warm and soon they could watch a glorious sunset. She walked every day and realized gradually that now she would always have to walk by herself. No more talking and laughing and remembering and dying for the first drink of the evening. Walking had been among their favourite things and had been with them for as long as she could remember. They had walked in Bombay and in Ranikhet and in Wellington and in Panchgani and in Nepal and in Goa and in Greece and in Italy and in London's parks and in the Cotswolds. The familiar 'Let's go for a walk' became 'When are you going for your walk and where will you walk today?' Soon it was, 'Are you leaving for your walk, hurry back, I want you with me.'

They read to each other. They played Scrabble, they played Monopoly, they played snakes and ladders, RK propped up in bed with lots of pillows. It was companionable. They drew the curtains on the outside world. And then it was all pain. All suffering. And RK was not RK any more. The good doctor kept his word. The morphine dealt with everything. And RK was gone.

Friends and family came up of course and helped and she stayed in a daze not really knowing that this terrible thing had really happened. Had finally happened.

When she began to feel again, she was able to cry and she cried all the time. She missed him all the time. She didn't think she could bear it and she hated the good doctor and she hated RK. 'Where are the tablets to fix my pain?' she cried and cried.

But because she had to bear it, in time she did. And time did not stop. As always time went on. The season was changing again. And she found, unbelievably, that she was alive.

She began to eat again and sleep a whole night through.

She walked again. She went for long walks again every evening.

She began to see the colours in the sky and in the earth again. She stopped talking to herself. She stopped talking to RK. She still heard his footsteps but she could not find him anywhere. But she began to watch dragonflies in the morning.

She began to smell the flowers in the garden.

She could see stars in the night sky. 'Maybe this is what it is all about,' she thought. Relationships you rely on lasting forever or what's the use. Investing everything in relationships and then suddenly there's nothing.

No, not nothing. Not really. She was not left with nothing. With emptiness. In a strange way RK was part of everything she was and thought and did. Even in snatches of song. 'Hey there— you with the stars in your eyes—'

And he was in the cottage and in the veranda and in the garden and on the swing.

And he was with her when she walked. He was everywhere. Soon she heard the voices of children. Soon she heard bird song in the morning.

A Grief Ago

And she said, 'Sweetheart we've checked the gas and everything, you know those old beautiful flats in Lisbon, you know old and quiet sometimes, just the sound of a cat brushing past, but beautiful,' and I said but before you actually move in, check the gas—you'll be wonderfully happy here but sweetheart check the gas, I'm worried about old flats and gas and gas in old flats, and my pretty baby, 'Mama and ovens and heads in ovens, you worry too much Mama.' So I said, 'Okay, but check the gas,' and she said, 'Yes, Mama, I am so happy, and there's so much to do but I will, I promise I will do as you ask. I will do as you ask, I will check the gas, I'll have it checked properly before we move in.' We had a house-warming party for her and then we came back to Bombay—but at the airport she said, 'Don't worry Mama, you worry too much and a lot of the time it's the right kind of sad worrying but sometimes it's not, I'll see you Christmas and we'll have a party.' And she waved and she walked away independent-like, because always first I'm her friend and second I'm her Mama and that's the way it's always been share everything, well almost everything and that's quite a lot to share, oh, yes and something she said, 'Don't drink so much, drink okay but not a lot, promise,' and I said, 'Promise,' and I said, 'You'll look after yourself,' and she said, 'Yes, I'll look after myself and see you Christmas'—and that was November and we came and whenever I watered the plants I said to her Daddy, 'Do you think my pretty baby is watering her plants back there in Lisbon?' and he said, 'Yes bound to be doing just that,' not looking up, just reading in his way because he listens—it's sort of automatic, he reads, never looks up but answers when he hears and he hears right, and every time I looked at our floors and at a chipped tile I'd think of the beautiful old worn tiles in my pretty baby's flat out there and that was all of November with everything turning cooler and the pretending smells of winter and on the 12th of December she called me, I had it circled the 12th not for the curse on my calendar in the loo but because a daft Easter lily bloomed in one of the pots and I thought it's daft to appear in December and not in Easter but nice because if it's going to do that then I can perhaps expect an Easter lily miracle just any season at all and so as I say I circled 12 for lily and later I double circled it because my baby called, phoned all the way, she there and me here, and what she must have spent, what it must have cost her that call and what she said was, 'Mama this is me,' and I said, 'Sure baby, I hear you, I know it's you I hear you as if you were here.' And she said, 'Mama only three minutes,' and I said, 'Do we only have three minutes? But why are you ringing from so far, is everything all right, I mean, is anything wrong, aren't you coming for Christmas, tell me first,' and she said, 'Mama can't I just ring and say I'm coming, I'm excited and we're having a party, and Mama please ask just about everyone I love, and you love and Papa loves and it's so good to hear your voice Mama,' and I said, 'Then you haven't called to say that you're not coming,' and she said, 'No, no Mama, no and stop crying Mama or I'll start, of course I'm coming I just wanted to hear your voice.' I said, 'But baby are you happy,' and she said, 'Mama, happy of course, I'm happy, are you?' and I said, 'Me, I'm happy,' so she said, 'Kiss kiss'—and I said, 'See you then,' and she said, 'Say promise Mama'—and I said, 'Promise,' and we got cut off but not before I heard her say, 'Twentieth airport yes?' and then, 'Yes,' and sweetheart couldn't we get the chap to freshen our glasses, well freshen mine anyway, what I say is damn it, let's have another drink, I like booze it's safe, it gives a great deal. I mean it helps and it gives a great deal. It sort of gives a great deal and it does not ask for anything—it does not ask to be friends, it does not ask to talk, it does not ask to make contact, I like it, I like booze it gives what you need, and no strings. So will you sweetheart ask the chap and I'll have the same only to hurry with it and yes as I was saying me and my baby got cut off.

Anyway about the middle of December we had a wedding out of town, a niece, but I was so happy about Christmas so close that

I can't remember the wedding or the girl's name or who the groom was, there was nobody there who looked like a groom but then nowadays there is hardly any way to tell is there? But anyway in this strange hotel room you always had to have the lights on and her Daddy was reading and I was slopping around not getting dressed to go to the church though I should have been ready and her Daddy looked up from the book and said would I hurry and I said yes but there is no real hurry our baby is not coming till the 20th and her Daddy put down his book and said sharpish, 'The wedding is in half an hour and we've got to find the church before we get to it,' and I said, 'All right, all right I'm getting ready,' and went to the bathroom and he said, 'Are you all right?' and I said, 'Yes,' and then I heard the phone ring and I shouted, 'What is it?' and he said nothing and after a bit I shouted, 'What is it why is somebody phoning just now?' and he said nothing and then I came out of the bathroom and there was nobody in the room just the phone and nobody and I was in this towel and a knock at the door and I shouted, 'Wait a minute,' and again a knock and I said where is that goddamn Daddy of hers and then I opened the door and there was her Daddy and another man and the man said, 'Please will you sit down?' and I said, 'No, I'd rather stand,' and her Daddy said, 'Please sit down and do as he says,' and I looked at him and he was not looking at me and I said, 'No, I will not sit down and what's happening why should I sit down?' and the man said, 'Please, please sit down it will be better for you,' and I said, 'No,' and then shouted, 'No something is wrong isn't it and I'm standing and I will not sit down and what is it, what has happened?' but I knew what it was, what else could it be, if you think of something day and night and if you long for it day and night and if that thing is there always in everything you're doing that's the surest sign it will go away, the only thing you want will be the only thing you will not be allowed to have, and I knew my pretty baby was not coming for Christmas or for Easter or for Carnival or for anything, she'd gone and why can't we all have another drink it's a comfort that's what it is, not a crutch at all, just a comfort and I did not cry then not once did I cry, I did not cry at the airport and I did not cry when I saw her in a coffin coming down the steps of the plane and

The Quiet of the Birds

they said, 'She must cry it's bad not to cry, make her cry or she'll break.' And they kept saying this in voices sometimes far, and sometimes quite near and I heard them but I did not cry. And the voices said around me sometimes near and sometimes far, 'Yes, it was the gas—you can't trust the gas in old flats they are beautiful some of them, those old flats in Lisbon but you can't trust the gas,' and the voices said but I thought she must have lain there till the Monday, yes she fell on the Saturday night and lay there because there was no sound, I thought it's a killer but it does not make a sound and she must have made no sound and no one to hear or see till the Monday when the cleaning woman came but by then there wasn't any sound anyway, so many hours and no one to hear the minutes and the hours even the plants had no water and the voices said, 'Why can't you make her cry?' and I shouted at them, 'No,' and again, 'No,' and I did not cry and her coffin was beautiful and they said she would stay beautiful in that coffin for many days so I counted the days and watched her in the coffin and remembered a Sunday in Goa in Bom Jesu standing in a queue waiting to see the saint in his silver coffin when suddenly out of the gloom and reverence a little voice shocking us all saying, 'I want to see, I want to see, I want to see,' and another voice, 'Leo, Leo, pick him up so he can see—now pray so that you become a good boy'—and the little boy said, 'I won't pray I won't I only want to see his toe, the place where it got bit off,' and 'SHSH and SHSH gosh, isn't he naughty, isn't he a trial—so who would have thought he'd remember—' but this was not a silver casket, and would you freshen my glass please, yes now I want a drink now, nothing to shout for now nothing to wait for she was and now is not and I still have not cried for her and now it's another year and I don't answer the phone ever, or water the plants, because the phone might ring and it might be her and I might listen to her and believe her voice all over again and I won't answer the phone or water the plants and I hope she didn't call out for me or anyone when she tripped against the gas and just lay there. I hope she didn't think or call out or say, 'Mama.'

Not Drowning: Just Waving

There is this cottage it overlooks the huge pipeline that runs through the whole town but the pipeline is almost covered with shrubs and all kinds of wild grasses. If you sit in the small veranda at the back of the cottage the land slopes downwards and there are trees and bamboo and even a great pond with pinkish water lilies and a frog. Bird songs all day but also ominous sounds of axe on wood in the distance and the middle distance and stone-breaking sounds. But no human sounds. No car horn sounds. No loud noises or loudspeakers. And at sunset a huge rock for the sun to set behind and spread the sky in pink before rock and sky are a sudden black. And there is one bent tree. An ancient tree. This tree is the only tree on that huge rock. It is always there. Always. Always bent. Almost leafless but standing.

The pond was deep, the stones and stone wall that encased it were dark black and grey stones. Jagged. But the water held its secret like a jewel and the jewel was the water lily pink and its flat leaves like plates. And its one frog. He was a Prince. There seem to be hundreds of stone breakers. And the thing is you never see the stone makers. You hear the axe-against-wood sounds but you never see the axe wielder. The arm raised, the arm coming down. All of them are disembodied sounds coming from the undergrowth. Before you there are trees, there is the concrete pipe, there is the huge rock. There is the bent tree on that rock. And there is the dark pond with its jewel and the frog Prince. But there are no faces, no bodies. Nothing but the regular beat of the sounds to tell you that there are people somewhere.

And as she said all this to him. He did not hear. But:

What matters it, oh breeze
If now has come the spring

When I have lost them both
The garden and my nest.

'Could we live there when we get back?' she thought, and then said aloud.

He said, 'We will see,' meaning, 'no, of course not.'

This is my life.

And she thought, 'I am sick of many griefs—always I think of things said in books, in plays, in poems. I have nothing of my own. But I do have something of my own. I chose this. So I must see it through. Or stop. Give it up. With him I am as nothing. Alone I might do something even now. Even heartsick as I am.' And how had it started. Now it was water all around. Wherever she looked. The tindal hardly ever spoke. Smiled only when she smiled at him. He of course never smiled. She should have thought of that a long time ago. But then she was smitten. She hadn't really noticed that about him. He was attractive without ever smiling. How long ago was all that. How could she have been so young. So foolish.

She did a lot of climbing when she was in college. She continued to do a lot of climbing when she was teaching and that's where she met him. He was also a walker, a climber. He was very good. He became the leader, the organizer, the teacher. All the women had a 'thing' for him. The first time she realized that he was very firm, she also realized he was gentle and understanding. It was the day of the ladder. A very steep rock face to the temple. The final bit. You could take the long way round by a path. That would take about an hour. This ladder would take only ten minutes. She baulked of course. She could not bear its steep grey austerity. 'I shall go by the path'—'No,' he had said, 'everybody is to go by the ladder. The sun's going down. It's the best way.' She was really frightened—he urged her on. His voice saying, 'Go on one foot, now the other, now the first, and now the other,' steady voice while she was perspiring, she was dangling, clinging, afraid, very afraid but she got to the top and just lay there unable to move or open her eyes. And then she heard his voice saying, 'You see you did it—you did it the very first time. I knew you could, good girl.'

And she opened her eyes and knew that she might follow him to the ends of the earth if he urged her on. Every weekend nearly all the hot summer holidays she trekked and climbed and there came a time when she stopped being afraid of terrible, steep rock faces. She became a good climber.

He disappeared then for a very long time. So long that she thought he had gone forever. But then he had not said goodbye. He owed her that at least, after all, nearly everything she had tried to learn and do was because of him. Once she got a postcard from him saying, 'I hope you are still climbing and walking. I have a proposal. See you anon.' Anon proved to be another two years. That meant she hadn't seen him for over four years since the climbing days together. But she put her life on hold. She taught. Six days a week, and walked and climbed on the seventh day. And waited.

One day he returned. After classes she met him in the canteen. Because everyone liked him even the tea was not its usual filthy beige brew. It was something you could drink. He asked her if she got seasick. She said no. He asked her if she had ever sailed. She said she'd often sailed to Mandva and Manori and once to Aksa. He said he would like to teach her to sail a yacht. He was going to sail around the world and he would like her to be his sailing partner. She swallowed hard, wondered if he was joking—knowing he never joked. And she said she would like to learn to sail and if she was good enough—he interrupted saying he was going to teach her so of course she would be good enough. She joked a little about thinking they were going to climb Everest after all that climbing. He didn't joke. 'It will be very useful—what you have learnt,' is all he said.

She began to learn all about yachting. About the sea. About winds about tides. She learnt well and quickly. She asked him when they were going. He said when the time was ripe. She said she had to ask for leave. He said, 'Ask for a sabbatical, a year.' She could hardly breathe. Her whole life up to now. What was she doing? There was nobody she could ask about the wisdom of all this. Well I deserve a year. After all the years I've given. It's just twelve months in a life. A lifetime. Anyway he chose me. There must have been hundreds of people he could have chosen. He chose me.

And now there were just endless days of sailing. On being becalmed. Water, every day all around, just the sea.

Hot Goa in May at a building site mounds of red laterite stone and mounds of cement and grey stone and the grinder going round and round 3 sand 3 stone 1 cement and 1 water. Dark, glistening skin bathed in sunset, the workers from Andhra and Kerala working ceaselessly. And suddenly a child in a filthy white vest eating an ice cream very white dripping down his chin ecstatic, wreathed in smiles. She had waved, sharing his pleasure, and the child had waved back. She remembered this one hot afternoon in the doldrums, the yacht becalmed not even a zephyr a hot day, hot deck, a hot sea, and she thought of that child and his white ice cream. 'I wish,' she thought. Surely green fields are better than stretches and stretches of sea—sea. He never listens to anything I am saying. No sharing, he stares out at the sea, at the sea and the sea. Not me. Not what I am saying.

During the four years she had waited he had never written to her. Just that one postcard. She still had it. She saw very little of him, he was always going off to Delhi about the sponsors and equipment. So much paperwork to finish. She was told to get her things together. A list she must follow very strictly. No, absolutely no extra weight. They met once to choose the tindal. There were six hardy men from a village near Ratnagiri where the best men came from. They were all hardy of limb with curling hair and fine smiling eyes. She liked them all. He told her not to be silly. To think of questions she wanted to ask. Think carefully, he said, you can't suddenly begin to be irritated or dislike things about him, remember you can't just pitch him overboard! So ask him questions and think about him, look at him. See if you can depend on him, we each have to depend on each other. We are only three people. It was a solemn interview. I realized I had not been interviewed. I had been put through my paces. I suppose I had been chosen. I realized I could not be pitched overboard if I proved irritating to anyone. I had not been irritating to him. He must have liked the fact that I hardly said very much. Never complained. We chose Vithal. He was our tindal.

Often he'd be angry and I'd think of the country song—'But don't be angry darling—I'm still a work-in-progress'.

She had never called him darling. And then one day they left. To sail around the world.

Day after day she looked at the sea and thought of that cottage. The cottage she had spoken about to him. She needed land under her feet. She wanted trees and leaves and earth to walk on. Rocks.

She sat on the bleached deck and stared out at the waters. She hated this endless sea. Endless sky. He would not talk. He would not listen. It was not days any more. It was months. She did not sleep in the small cabin any more. She slept on deck. The cabin was a coffin. She dreaded it. It was his.

But there was Vithal. He also slept on deck. She thought of the little boy eating ice cream. He had waved to her. He had seen her. She was not invisible.

One evening about sunset she saw what looked like land. It was some distance away. It was very far. But she thought she saw a rock and a tree on that huge rock. It was always there. It's just that she hadn't seen it for a long while. It was leafless she knew—but standing. And as she slipped quietly over the side of the deck into the water she thought:

What matters it,
Oh breeze
If now has come the spring
When I have lost them both
The garden and nest.

The water was cold. She was going home.
At first light Vithal saw the empty deck.
He went down the steps to the cabin/coffin.

The Quiet of the Birds

Chasing Edens: One July

Dusk. Almost dark. It had rained hard all day. Late evening now and it had stopped raining. July. He walked to the end of his garden. He felt that there was another person. Close by. He stood very still. There was. It was a woman. She was standing under a chikoo tree. Absolutely still.

For the last four years when he had walked to the end of his garden at dusk he had been quite alone so he was startled and called out, 'Hello there.' When she turned he walked a little closer and stood still. She came closer too and stood quietly.

Then he said, 'I live here.'

'I'm going to live here soon,' she said.

'You mean really live here?' he said.

'Close by is my land now,' she said. 'And I shall live here for always.'

He liked the sound of that 'for always'. It had a sense of permanence that he hadn't started feeling yet. Even after four years. Permanence was something he laid great store by. Never having known it himself. All he said though was, 'I'm glad, if you like you might join me for a drink.'

She said, 'I'd love to. I had not expected such civility in this place so soon.' He wondered why but said nothing.

There being no wall or hedge or barrier of any kind they walked back to his house.

'And what do you do?' she asked.

'I live here and paint.'

The leaves of the chikoo trees glistened and little drops of cool wet fell on him. He had been struggling in his mind with a painting that wasn't happening. It needed something. All day today while it rained he thought about what it needed. He did not know how to fix it. Fix it. What a term. He stopped dead. She was wearing

Wellington boots and an anorak. Her hair was grey. Her anorak was grey. Cudi did not bark but wagged his tail.

'This is Cudi,' he said.

She said, 'All the time I was standing there trying to realize that a bit of land was mine. A primitive need I suppose. To own just a bit of land.'

He said, 'Four years ago I felt the same. I'm glad you are going to live here and not some awful, dreadful people.'

'You don't know whether I'm awful, dreadful people or not,' she said. 'How can you know?'

'Well, they look different somehow and come in red cars with a great deal of noise. There's the house now, and now here comes the rain again.'

They had walked down his long gravel walk to his four-year-old home. He felt so proud showing it to her.

She took off her welly and her wet anorak. He gave her some slippers and a towel for her hair.

'This is nice, this is very nice,' she said. Looking at the room.

There seemed to be trees and green in the room and it was because all the doors were half doors as in stables and barns.

'This is very nice,' she repeated and he gave her a drink.

Cudi was sitting very near her. She patted her lap and Cudi jumped into it.

He said, slightly shocked and a bit jealous, 'Well she likes you. She never jumps on anybody's lap and never at a first meeting.'

'I should think not. She probably smells all my dogs past and present on me. Not to worry.'

'I'm not worried,' he said.

They sat quite companionably and in quiet, till he realized she'd dropped off. Her glass in her hand. Cudi on her lap. She had a gold wedding band on her finger. He noticed. He made up the sofa bed. He woke her and told her to go back to sleep.

She said, 'I'm sorry. I must be tired. I'm sorry,' and went back to sleep.

He went up the stairs to his studio and switched on all the lights. 'Yes,' he thought, 'I might finish this tonight. It needed a kind of silvery grey. Like her hair. I've used too much dark red.

Yes, silvery grey—at the very farthest end of the avenue.'

Next morning when he went down, she had gone. A note said, 'Thank you, sorry about falling asleep.'

He felt a great impatience.

'Why did she leave like that, I wanted to show her the finished painting. When will she come back?' Will she? When?

She had been standing under the tree for a long while.

It felt damp. As she breathed in the air. Sweet peas, she thought. Yes, that is what she could smell. Quite suddenly. The sent of sweet peas and her mother. The gentle pastel colours, the way they grew, the curling tender green tendrils. Her mother grew them most carefully in her garden and she cut them herself for the Gwalior pottery vases of those long-ago days. Smooth and usually also pastel colours—pale green and mauves and pinks. They never intruded in the experience of sweet peas. Just merged. Not like pottery nowadays, all designer pots—spiky, sandy blacks and browns bristling and asserting themselves.

You daren't put a flower into them. Spoils the line. The potter would say. Doesn't need a flower. Whatever happened to that pottery, its vases were largely two shapes flat like this or tall

like this flowers were so easy to arrange. Whatever happened to their lovely uncomplicated tea sets in mauve and green till the sudden exciting explosion of black with green insides and fat tea pots—the days of tea cosys? Whatever happened to tea cosys? I suppose the vulgar, convenient stainless steel dripping tea sets to go with tea bags. All that was childhood and growing up years. And then it all stopped. But of course everything associated with a mother like that. All that was part of what a good mother was, wonderful quilts and pillows made of old soft silk and satin saris taken out reverentially of great steel trunks and blankets with bits of dry brown neem leaves and smell of moth balls. Taken out and into the sun in the garden to become fresh again for the long, cold winters. Actually to think of it, whatever happened to winters or all those wonderful distinct changes of seasons? Not just hot and then wet. Then it was very cold, becoming warm then very hot and flaming gulmohurs and jacaranda and laburnums and rusty shield bearers and then wet wet and all the blossoms on the red gravel paths.

Her mother was also Chanel No. 5 and there were other things in our mother's garden but sweet peas personified her. Her sweetness, her givingness, her simplicity and sense of fun. Her cotton saris.

But strangely nowhere had she lived with sweet peas again—so, may be that was what kept her moving and living to find it again somewhere chasing Edens, trying to find our mother's garden. Wearing her mother's wedding band on her finger.

Whatever happened to Gwalior pottery? Now it was Hitkari, all the same, sand coloured and heavy.

But now standing under this chikoo tree she knew. Suddenly. She knew exactly what her house would be, what it would look like and how she would feel living in it. She would get the Warlis to build her house. She was going to live in a house built by the Warlis and live like them adjusting to the rain and to the sun and not disturbing the landscape. She would merge into it. The karvi plant spliced and sliced and forming the walls and then covered with mud, burning red mud mixed with gobar and spread on the karvi plants and it would form a pattern of karvi leaves coming through the adobe-like stuff and drying like old tracing of fossils found in places with an old old civilization. Of course she would have proper windows and an angan to sit in at evening to watch and smell the woodsmoke rising out of the distance. And the moon would come out and hundreds of stars and a white owl would fly across like a shadow remembered but hardly seen. Then she would go in and tomorrow would be another day. And she would have dogs like all the dogs she had ever known and loved from long ago—Susie and Taffy and Jany and Judas and Pelinore, Morgan and Ginger and Ginger and Ginger. That's what she was thinking when the quiet man came up to the boundary with his dog and called out, 'Hello there.'

Many days later she thought, I shall go and visit that nice quiet artist and see what he thinks about my plans. About my house, my home. She turned off the lamp and went to sleep. She did not have to repeat her mantra of the last fifteen years, 'Give me a piece of land, let me find a piece of land I can live and live the rest of my life in. Just give me that. Please.'

He was there in his cool, green home with the trees coming into the half doors and she said, 'Would you like to see my bit of land before the workmen start work?'

He got into her old, battered Gypsy and they drove off.

She drove rather fast but well and they arrived in about twenty minutes. I asked her how she came to be so close to my land that late evening in the rain. She said she'd had a hard, tiring day and then on the way back to her room she had seen lights through the trees and thought she'd stop and walk. And that's where I had found her.

Cudi sat between us, comfortable, alert. A desolate creek with a few women banging clothes about, a broken bridge and then a very clean village with a school and a large playground and then her land. A beautiful-shaped piece of land facing a hill. A real hill that you could touch. A hill you could walk up of an evening to see the sun set behind it and whatever was on the other side. A hill of your own. Largesse. Her land with many mango trees, two neem trees and a large jamun tree, the boundary of tall cacti. Water. Yes. At the far end of a kind of natural avenue the land rose gently upward to an opening with huge black boulders and rocks. And the hill. The hill. The sun began to go down. The hill was quiet and you could hear a small wind through the leaves of a bamboo grove. It was beautiful. 'I think it's beautiful,' I said.

'Yes,' she said. 'It really is. And I shall grow things, herbs, vegetables, perhaps even sweet peas.'

All around them long, yellowing grass. Birds going home. Far away a dog barked. Waited. An answering bark. The hill began to darken.

'Your hill is like a great elephant protecting her young, your land,' he said.

After a bit he said, 'Will you not be lonely—mean at evening ?'

'I shall read of evenings and listen to my music. Perhaps I will manage to meditate. I'm so glad you are my neighbour. Shall we go?'

Driving back he asked, 'So did you find this place quite soon or after much looking?'

She said, 'No, after much journeying, much heartache. I was much younger when I started looking. I only knew two things I wanted. No cities and noise and I wanted the hills.'

'So where did your journeys take you?'

'Oh to the south to the Nilgiris and to the north as far as Binsar and even near Pune and Goa. Oh yes, I travelled years and years.'

'And were you sorely tempted? I mean by a piece of land before this?'

'Yes, I was. In fact just before this I was looking for over a year in Goa.'

'At the tail-end I went to a very lovely village called Aldona. Sitting in a little bar called Manoel's. Just stone floors and cotton curtains flapping in the breeze, two calendars on the walls and a slow fan turning and turning and about four tables. At one of them there was a tired, oldish but young man with a glass of feni at his elbow. I thought greatly of Spain in the fifties when I was young. Here they spoke of Mario, the man alone with his memories, his feni. He was a legendary football player and in Spain at that taverna sitting and dreaming of being young it had been a bull fighter put out to graze with the old bulls. I liked that village, its river and its ferries, its hills and its winding road up the hill and its green fields—but I had no luck. Everything was very expensive. But that time at Manoel's bar in Aldona, watching Mario that old–young man with his feni dreaming gave me a real fright. I had to hurry. I had to find my land soon. But now I have my land. I have quiet. I have a hill like an elephant. And I have a friend. You. Journey's end.'

He said, 'Did you find your land here quickly?'

And she said, 'Well it was my fifth trip to this coast and I had nearly given up hope.'

'Are you the one that Surya calls the agricultural lady?'

'Perhaps that is me—'

'And are you?'

'Am I what? Oh, an agricultural lady? I suppose I was once, a long time ago. I have some degrees and I had a farm for a long time, a long ago. Do you remember how wearily Meryl Streep says that in *Out of Africa*—I once had a farm in Afarica.'

'Yes, I remember. And laughed. Though it was a sad film.'

'Well, this bit that is now mine, the young man wouldn't show me because there was somebody rather keen but he lived in New York. Also the "painter man" did not want his area invaded. Well I have invaded your area, so watch out, painter man.'

'Yes,' he said, 'and I'm, glad it's you.'

'You don't know yet,' she said.

'Oh I do, you won't build anything ugly or cut down trees and build high walls and play loud music and have loud parties.'

'No I won't, but there are bound to be other things but we can draw up some friendly ground rules, I should think.'

He said, 'Instead of driving miles out every day to your room in Bordi why don't you stay, live in my strange-looking zigarat in the garden? You passed it that first evening in the rain. It's small but it's quite comfortable and private. Then when your "Tribal" hut is ready you can move.' They got out of the Gypsy and he pulled her back quietly—a thin, slender snake slithered past. She had almost stepped on it.

'That must be good luck,' she said. 'First your kind, kind offer and then the snake. I thank you kindly. I really do. Oh and sometime when you know me better would you let me see your paintings? How it happens? How do you know when it's finished? Or is it always unfinished?'